Two Hearts One Piano

A Novel

Catherine Richmond

For everyone who's suffered trauma, including church hurt—your journey won't look like Maren's, but I hope it's just as healing.

Chapter One

"The last of it." Neil dropped two canvas mailbags beside his outdoor fireplace, raising a cloud of dust. "Ten years late, but it's not like *you* ever stayed on schedule."

His nieces and nephews didn't need to see this side of their father. He glanced past his own house toward the family home. The path remained empty. School had started, keeping them busy.

Neil scraped a kitchen match on the fieldstones and caught the tinder. Sitting on a lawn chair, he reached into the bag, pulled out an envelope, and slid open the flap. The yellow light of the fire showed the usual *love you, love your songs*. The letter flared as he tossed it into the flames. Their nature-loving fans would call this air pollution. His sister-in-law said it was a waste of time—toss it in the garbage and move on. It was his long shot. He glanced at the sack, the seventh he'd gone through. No guarantee. *If her letter wasn't here, if she hadn't written...*

Next? A picture of a teenage girl in a bikini draped over the hood of a red Pontiac. "None of these wherever you are, Alan." He dropped it into the fire.

The third one held a photo of a girl wearing nothing but a smile. "Now that your daughter's sixteen, this isn't funny. I talked to her.

Catherine Richmond

Told her how we used to pass these around the bus, how crude guys are. Without mentioning your name, of course."

Another letter, another picture. Polaroid this time. "No negative for Daddy to find, smart girl. If only she'd known you were as old as her pop and had a house full of kids."

Three requests for autographs, another photo. "Where's she now, Alan? Probably teaching second grade in," he glanced at the postmark, "Des Moines." The flames shot higher.

"And this one? Maybe raising twins in Cedar Rapids. Fine looking women in Iowa."

Night settled over the hill, washing yellow and red leaves with gray. The sun ran down the straight tracks of the tulip poplars, heading for the Blue Ridge Mountains. Damp air off the Potomac brushed his back as the fire heated his front.

Purple ink. Wrinkled ovals of frosted pink lipstick. School pictures. Request for a concert in a village in Alaska.

Three more letters, no pictures, then, "Another verse for 'Midnight Fireworks,' written by this year's Country Music Association Male Vocalist of the Year. Didn't think the kid was even born back when we were touring. This could be his first songwriting attempt." Neil's baritone tried the lyrics, stumbling on the awkward fit of words to music. "Good thing I didn't answer this letter. I'd have told him to join the army, go to dental school, anything but write songs." Flames curled over the lyrics. "There goes my chance for blackmail."

The next envelope held a curl of bleached-blond hair. Neil held it up, letting the wind take it.

"If this is what I think it is..." He crumbled a brittle leaf into the fire. The musky smoke of *cannabis sativa* twisted from the ash. "No pot parties where you are, Alan. The ultimate dry-out."

The smell took him back. He could hear the audience chanting, "Al-an, Al-an!" louder and louder, erupting in a high-pitched roar when the spotlight captured him. The singer leaped across cables to center stage, shoulder-length blond hair blowing, adoring fans screaming. Sweat slicked Neil's fingers on the keyboard.

In the ten years since, Neil had left the madness of his brother's

6

world for flight training and the regulated life of an airline pilot. And he'd learned to live without his brother.

Alan had raced through Neil's life, eight years ahead. While Neil was taking his first steps, Alan zoomed through the neighborhood on a two-wheeler. When Neil inherited the Schwinn, Alan had moved on to a Mustang GT. Big brother charmed every teacher, sang every solo, played the lead in every musical. Leaving a trail of broken hearts, he sped off to Nashville. His albums went platinum. His concerts sold out. His wife had babies. Then, in 1979, Alan bent down from his lofty perch, offering Neil the keyboard job, and an up close and personal view of the fans' adulation. The glory hadn't shone far from the throne. Neil had been the butt of every joke and only Alan got the punch line. And got the girls, including the one who'd been interested in Neil.

Lacy pink stationery crackled in his fist, bringing him back to the present. "Whew. Lost it there a minute."

Find the rhythm. Rip, scan, toss. The place where you don't have to think. Rip, scan, toss. The numb place where you get over it, accept it, move on. Rip, scan, toss.

Firelight caught on the postmark, "Kalamazoo, MI". The same unusual first name, and now, finally, a last name. Neil braced his elbows on his knees, trying to hold his hands steady. For ten years all he'd had was her given name and the memory of sky-blue eyes. Not enough to find her. But now—*Maren Tollefson*.

The address listed was Smith Burnham Hall, Western Michigan University. Yes, she'd mentioned college. She wouldn't still be there, of course, but the school might have some record of where she'd gone.

He flopped back in the lawn chair, overtaken by memories. They'd met at the after-party, the night *Banned in Nashville* went Gold. Maren had sought Neil out, pulling him into a corner where the smoke wasn't so thick. Her clothes had been practical for attending a winter concert in a hockey stadium—a white turtleneck sweater, jeans, boots. When she leaned close to hear him, her light brown hair brushed his wrist. The talk flowed from synthesizers to airplanes. She never took her eyes off Neil, never mentioned Alan, even when squealing groupies heralded his arrival. For one shining moment, love-at-first-sight moved from myth to possibility. Then she'd disappeared.

Neil turned the envelope over, the paper sticking to his sweating fingers. All along, the answer to his prayers was in his brother's fan mail. A last name. Finding her might be as easy as a call to the phone company.

Pulse accelerating, Neil opened the rainbow-covered flap and pulled out the single sheet of paper. One word jumped out at him: *pregnant.*

Neil's guts turned to ice and he pitched forward. *This is my fault. All my fault.*

The whole tour, Alan had razzed Neil as a washout with women. High on the album's success and whatever chemicals he'd taken, Alan targeted the only woman who'd shown any interest in Neil. The next morning on the tour bus, Alan trash-talked her. Neil hadn't been exactly sure what Alan had done, but he knew it was bad. He'd gotten in a gut punch and two kicks before the roadies pulled him off. He should have told their bus driver to go to the nearest police station. He should have called the hotel to check on her. He should have...done something.

He wanted to kill his brother., but Alan was already dead.

He reread her letter, slower this time. No demands, only notification. He closed his eyes, trying to imagine the vivacious young woman he'd met. She'd seemed delicate, with long fingers and smooth skin. But something in the way she carried herself, standing straight, holding her head high, spoke of strength and confidence. What had she done? Abortion, adoption, kept the baby? She must not have told anyone it was Alan's—the scandal would have been all over the tabloids.

Wait a minute. What if she'd written again? He stowed the letter in the back pocket of his jeans, then plunged into the half-empty mailbag, raising ten years' worth of dust. The concert had been in winter, after Valentine's Day. February plus nine months. He rooted through the next bag. November! He started to dump it, then caught himself. Slow and careful. Don't miss anything. He pulled an envelope from the stack. Wrong handwriting, wrong return address. But opening it, and every other piece in the bag, was his job as the surviving brother. He scanned the postmarks—Lafayette, Cincinnati, Louisville.

What if she changed her last name? He could search the newspapers, hire a detective, check courthouse records...

Breathe. Focus. He needed a song. He discarded all of his brother's raucous tunes, then settled on The Moody Blues' "I Know You're Out There Somewhere."

Statesboro, Macon, Myrtle Beach. The band had toured the Southeast that fall, working their way home for Christmas.

Somewhere, somewhere...

A half-dozen letters from NC State, Duke, Wake Forest. C'mon, now, just one more from Western Michigan.

Somehow, somehow...

Norfolk, Chesapeake, Blacksburg. Maybe she'd written earlier... if she'd had a miscarriage...

His fingers stilled on another rainbow-covered flap, another postmark spelling out "Kalamazoo, MI". Different address, but the handwriting matched. She'd moved out of the dorm, her college days interrupted, into an apartment. The timing was right. His shaking fingers peeled it open and unfolded a sheet of copier paper. Firelight yellowed the page, as if it were older than ten years. *Certified Copy of Record of Birth.* The space for the father's name had been left blank.

Ten years ago she'd had the baby in Kalamazoo. She could have married, moved away, left the country, even. Neil hunted between the trees for a star. "I will find you...and make this right."

Chapter Two

"Hey, Fidel." Maren hefted the sack of canned goods onto the Kalamazoo Metro Transit bus, handed a cruller to the driver, then took a seat behind him. "How's the game going?"

"Not so good." The driver twisted the dial of his transistor radio, leaving the struggling Detroit Tigers for a news brief on President Bush's response to Hurricane Hugo, then an ad for *The Jeffersons* TV show. Fidel nodded toward Maren. "You moved on up outta Northside, eh?"

"For a not-so-deluxe apartment in a basement. The elementary school has the best music program in the city."

He pulled out of the A&P parking lot onto the highway. "You're a good mom, doing right by your little girl. You far from the bus stop?"

Was he fishing for her address or wondering if she could carry this week's dented cans? Erring on the side of caution, Maren named the cross street. "Only few houses in."

"How'd your interview go?"

"Thanks for putting in a good word for me, but they want people with experience and a Commercial Driver's License."

Fidel patted the steering wheel. "Aw, you can drive this thing, no problem."

They left the retail district for her new neighborhood. The driver swung the bus to the curb and opened the door. "Thanks for the doughnut, Maren."

"See you tomorrow." She hurried off before the other passengers could complain. Good to be on a first name basis with the drivers. Never know when you might have a heavy load and need to be let out between the official stops. She shifted the bag, her no-cost version of Lady Shapely Health Club, and walked into the warm September day.

A golden retriever bounded out from the corner house, tail wagging, and rested her front paws on the brick wall for a dog biscuit. "You're as welcoming as the house where you live."

The arched doorway, stained glass window between floors, and slate roof said cozy and safe. The yard needed flowers—vintage cultivars to go with its age—but instead the landscaping service pruned the shrubs to severe neatness. If it were hers, she'd plant white blossoms—alyssum, phlox, mums—to stand out against the dark red brick. She hummed a few bars of Graham Nash's "Our House." Life would be so easy. Her daughter could practice to her heart's content and no one would complain. She could have friends over without embarrassment, and they could have a dog, a car.

But none of that would happen on what A&P pays.

Please, Lord. I've filled out so many applications.

Consequences.

A Buick Regal with "I LIST" license plates wheeled around the corner, spraying Maren with gravel, reminding her not everyone approved of Mrs. Vanderhoef's arrangement. Let in one tenant, pretty soon the whole neighborhood went rental, property values dropped, riffraff moved in. End of the world according to real estate agents.

Maren blew her nose, then continued down the sidewalk. Allergies. She had skipped this morning's dose, trying to stretch her medicine until the next paycheck.

A new car sat in front of Mrs. V's house. A man climbed out, wearing khakis with a pager attached to his belt and a white polo shirt. He wasn't one of the Vanderhoef scions, but vaguely familiar.

Catherine Richmond

Well, working in a grocery meant everyone was vaguely familiar. Instead of heading to the front door, he walked toward the school bus as it turned the corner and stopped four houses down.

Maren opened what Mrs. V called the service entrance, dropped the bag of canned goods in the garage, and ran to meet the bus.

Fingers tapping his slacks, the man watched. The doors opened and two kindergarten boys shot off and across the street. A fifth grader swung his backpack at the kindergartners. The Chinese professor's twin daughters trudged home, bent under full backpacks. Then Rhi climbed out, carrying her cello and backpack. With a whoosh, the bus pulled away, sending her curls flying.

The man stepped forward and spoke to her. Rhi stared at him, eyes wide, mouth open.

So much for all the stranger danger education. And so much for Waldenbrook being a safer neighborhood. Maren broke into a run and slid her keys between her knuckles.

Rhi spotted her. "Mom, Mom! Guess who came to see me! It's my Uncle Neil!"

No. Can't be. Chills washed through her. Maren stopped in front of her daughter and looked into a face she hadn't seen for ten years. Time hiccuped with a snatch of rowdy music, writhing bodies, pot smoke. In the distance, keys jingled on pavement.

"Easy there. I didn't mean to startle you." He retrieved the keys and put them back in her shaking hand.

"Wolfe." The heat of his touch had her yanking her arm away. She struggled for the next breath. "Neil Wolfe." She'd worked so hard to forget and now this man brought back the worst night of her life. Hot fury shot through her, tightening her muscles, sharpening her voice. Throat strike, groin kick, head butt... deck him and stuff him in his trunk... No, not in front of her daughter. Maren would end up in jail and the state would take Rhiannon. She wanted him to disappear, not bleed on the driveway. "Leave. Now. Or I'll call the police." An empty threat since she couldn't risk Mrs. Vanderhoef evicting them. She grabbed Rhi's hand and pulled her toward Mrs. V's.

"Mom, no. I want to find out about my dad. Why are you being so mean?"

"Please, could we go in and talk?"

As if Maren would let him inside. "No time."

"It's Friday. I have a lesson," Rhi told Neil solemnly, then asked, "Could I skip this once?"

"Absolutely not." Maren took the cello and sent Rhi inside for her music, then rounded on Neil. *You loathsome toad.* Where do you get off telling my daughter anything? Can't you see, she's better off not knowing...all this sleazy stuff. You can't be sure—"

"She's the spitting image." His smile twitched.

"Which does not give you any right to be involved in her life." Questions about her father would lead to questions about how she was conceived. Maren hadn't figured out when to have *that* conversation, but she knew nine was too young. "She doesn't know and you have no right to tell her."

"Maren, please. I'm sorry I didn't stop him."

"I put the groceries inside." Rhiannon dashed out, carrying a Selmer music folder. "I don't even know my dad's name."

"It's Alan Wolfe," Neil said.

Maren locked the house, then dragged her daughter down the sidewalk. "Let's go."

"I could give you a ride," Neil said.

"We are not going anywhere with you."

Rhiannon looked over her shoulder. "Bye Uncle Neil!"

From the main drag came the whoosh of air brakes, then the roar of an accelerating engine. The city bus flashed between the houses. Maren checked her watch. Her shoulders slumped. They'd missed the bus.

"I'll be glad to take you," Neil called.

Consequences. Always Consequences.

MAREN'S DOING ALL RIGHT, Neil had thought as he waited in the rental car, admiring the quiet neighborhood of well-kept houses and

13

big trees. Kalamazoo seemed like a livable college town, decent airport, not much traffic.

A young woman out for a stroll paused. A look of raw longing crossed her face while she studied the small house on the corner, then she adjusted her grip on her grocery sack and continued down the sidewalk. Groceries? He hadn't seen a store nearby. She stepped from beneath the shade of an overhanging maple and Neil recognized her—Maren. The big hair and heavy makeup of ten years ago were gone, replaced by a long braid and clean face. If anything, she looked younger than twenty-nine.

Maren turned up the driveway and he broke out in a cold sweat. Ever since finding her letters, he'd been praying about what to say first. *I'm sorry* didn't come close. *Is it true?* No, she wouldn't lie. *I want...* What did he want? He'd seen enough to know she was okay; he should go.

Then Rhiannon got off the bus, looking ever-so-much like Alan, and he'd lost his mind.

"I'm your Uncle Neil."

Deep-set blue-green eyes, Alan's eyes, studied him. "You are..."

"I'm your dad's brother, Neil."

"Are you kidding?" Her smile showed Alan's dimples. "All my life I've been wanting to know about my dad. I have so many questions!"

Maren raced up. She turned pale, her eyes widened and mouth dropped open, as if she might faint. Saying his name ignited her rage. He tried to explain, but she wasn't having it. He was cool, calm, and collected in the cockpit, but with Maren, he tripped over his tongue, bungled his intro, botched his apology. Total wash-out.

Maren towed Rhi away, and his heart sank. Then the city bus left them behind.

"I'll be glad to take you."

Rhiannon hurried back to him. Maren stalked behind, her chin up and eyes narrowed.

Neil ushered them into the car. The girl perched on the seat next to him, pelting him with questions. Maren sat in the back with the cello.

"You'll stay for the lesson, won't you? Maestro will let you, I'm sure he will. I'll tell him you're my uncle I've never seen before from far away. Where *do* you live?"

"Virginia." He flashed her a look. "Buckle up. How long have you been playing cello?"

She fastened her seatbelt, then gave him directions and answered his questions. When she was five, she'd taken a month of Suzuki violin lessons before their car broke. Last June her mother talked the strings teacher into letting her bring a cello home. Neil recalled his other nieces' screeches and squawks four months into violin and viola; earplugs would be appropriate, but this girl might take it as an insult. Neil parked and Rhiannon bounded out, her father's energy all over again. "This is great. Hardly takes any time at all to get here in a car. Maestro will be surprised to see us so early."

Neil followed the girl into the elegant ranch house. The room across from the foyer contained a Steinway baby grand without a bench. Floor to ceiling windows draped in teal velvet formed a half-circle around the piano, giving a view of manicured flower beds.

"Arrive so soon! Wonderful!" An older man, his silver hair oiled into a pompadour, rolled down the tiled hall in a wheelchair.

Rhiannon unzipped her case. "Maestro, this is my Uncle Neil. Is it okay—"

"Uncle? But of course. Begin your scales while we talk." Maestro directed him to a velvet upholstered chair, the style of some French king, probably one who was beheaded. "Good of you to come, Uncle. I talk to Mother, but she won't listen."

"Maren?" Neil looked around. She hadn't followed them in. The familiar conversation of tuning sounded across the room.

"I tell her, must have a good cello. This one does not stay in tune, rattles, tone dull. Girl out-plays her instrument." Maestro clawed Neil's arm, keeping his attention and making him squirm. "I tell her, move out of basement, dampness ruins cello. I offered spare room, live with me. She refuses. Mother holds her back. A waste. Talk to Mother."

Talk to Maren? No chance he could convince her of anything...

unless he could provide a new cello. "What size is she playing? Is she ready to move up?"

Rhiannon began the C scale, each quarter note clear, in tune, but the rattle was audible from across the room.

"Half size. She is ready for three-quarter. You must tell Mother—"

Rhiannon syncopated the G scale.

"I'll get the metronome!" Maestro threatened.

The girl winked and played the D scale. A low hum outside added its accompaniment. Maren passed by the windows, pushing an electric lawn mower. *What was she doing?*

Instead of the "Twinkle, Twinkle, Little Star" or "Grandfather's Clock" of other first-year students, Rhiannon was working on "Greensleeves." They went through it measure by measure, practicing bowing and changing strings. The teacher had her play the entire piece, then rolled back to Neil. His bony fist pounded the chair's arm in time to the music, but the lecture clashed with the music. "You see what we have? Talent! It must not be wasted."

Neil leaned forward, trying not to upset the spindly-legged chair. It made no sense—it had to be an illusion—that those small hands, smooth with a layer of baby fat, could produce beautiful sounds with incredible skill. Little girl fingers danced on the strings, hitting each note with precision, adding vibrato for expression. She had perfect pitch, a great sense of rhythm, and emotion to bring the music life. Letting the music flow, Rhiannon belted out "What child is this?"

"Stop," Maestro commanded. "This is cello class, not voice. New music." He set an étude on the music stand.

Finally breaking a sweat, Rhiannon stumbled through with frequent stops for correction. Maestro called for his cello. She arranged his motionless legs around the instrument, telling Neil her teacher had played with the Kalamazoo Symphony. The melody poured out. Demonstration complete, Rhiannon took back her cello with a "why didn't you say so" flounce, and played a recognizable rendition of the piece.

Maestro shook his finger. "Sight-read! Not by ear all the time. Suzuki made you lazy."

Neil checked his watch. They'd been working hot and heavy for forty minutes. Alan would have thrown his guitar across the room. Rhiannon must have inherited patience from her mom. Where was she? As Rhiannon attempted the étude with Maestro accompanying on piano, Neil excused himself and stepped outside. First he'd explain, then he'd apologize, and then he'd tell her he'd been thinking about her for the last ten years. He turned the corner of the house, and found Maren singing and weeding the flower bed with fierce energy. She spotted him and glared.

He recognized the melody. "Billy Joel's 'My Life'?"

She threw a handful of wilted plants into a bucket. "This is *my* life." Her voice was low, but full of venom. "Go away."

"But...you *are* a victim of circumstance. You're working off the cost of the lessons. Let me help so you can see how your daughter's doing."

She shook her head. "Tell me."

"Amazing. Alan's talent all over again."

Her eyes twitched.

He trailed her as she cleaned up the flower bed. "You didn't tell Rhiannon about him. You must have been pretty angry."

"Understatement of the year. And now I'm angry at you, for butting in, for not respecting my right as her mother to decide when and what to tell." She slammed a dandelion into the bucket. "Why now?"

"I found these last week." Neil pulled the two envelopes with rainbow flaps from his pocket.

Maren's shoulders slumped. "He didn't get my letter or the birth certificate."

"They were buried in fan mail. We tried to wade through it, but by the time *Banned in Nashville* went gold, we were getting a bag a day. His secretary left for a commune in Tennessee. So we put the mail in storage." Nerves had Neil rambling. "When I saw Rhiannon, looking so much like Alan—"

"Appearance does *not* make her your family." She held the grass clippers at arm's length and closed them with a snap, dangerously close to his family jewels.

He backpedaled out of range. "Has anyone else noticed the resemblance?"

"No."

He trailed her into the garage where she emptied the weeds into the garbage. "Someone will when she starts performing. Maybe her first Christmas concert. It's better for her to know than find out from Geraldo Rivera."

Quick scrapes of the broom cleared grass clippings. "Your brother's been dead for nine years—he's not newsworthy. Not worth the trip to Kalamazoo."

That sounded like denial.

Maren hung up the broom and dustpan. "There's no evidence, no DNA test, no police report."

"Why not? You could have filed a paternity suit."

"And further shame my family? No." Clasping her elbows, she faced the wall of yard tools. "There were no witnesses. My last memory was taking a sip of champagne. Then it was morning and two hotel housekeepers were hauling me into the shower. In between, a complete blank."

Neil slumped against the garden bench. He should have protected her, should have gotten her out of there. "Someone spiked your drink."

"Which explains why I want nothing to do with you, why I must protect my daughter from the likes of you." Maren slapped her hands together, dismissing him. Her voice dripped with disgust. "You've done your damage, let the cat out of the bag, opened Pandora's box, wreaked havoc on my life. Just beat it."

He pressed his palm to his heart, considering the contradictory legacy of Alan Wolfe. The cello and piano duet continued inside. He lowered his voice. "Maren, I know the horror of realizing I share genes with a brute. The song I wrote for his funeral..." He sang the chorus, his voice breaking again as new pain piled onto old. "*You're my brother, tormentor, mentor, monster. I adored you, hated you, followed you. And I pray I can forgive and remember the good...* I don't want Rhiannon to think less of herself because of her father's terrible choices."

Maren made eye contact, fury melted into agony. Then she curled in on herself and pressed her hands to her mouth.

Neil continued, "I can help you. I know music. I'll rent a better cello, buy you a car, pay for lessons…if you'll let me."

She straightened. "We are not for sale."

"May I take you out to dinner?"

Rhiannon burst into the garage. "Yes, let's go to dinner!"

"It's up to your mother." He'd barged into their lives like an elephant trampling a piano. Time to back off and show respect. "She's had a rough day."

NEIL PARKED at Bill Knapp's Restaurant, a white building with green shutters, then held the door open for them. "Order anything you want. It's on me."

His generosity was ten years too late, Maren wanted to say, but her stomach voted for food.

The waitress seated them, then took their orders.

Maren had been up late mending Rhi's backpack, no time for a shower. This morning she'd thrown on her garage sale finds—polyester high-water slacks with baggy knees and a white tee shirt, both stained from work. Wait a minute. What difference did it make? He wasn't here to see her.

Rhi said grace. Neil leaned toward her, chin in palm, enraptured, and asked about school.

Don't tell him anything, Rhi. He doesn't deserve to know.

Rhiannon told him about life in Mrs. Stoney's Fourth Grade. Glowing in the warmth of male attention, she described her classmates with wit, detail, charm. The story about a classmate's shoes hit Neil's funny bone. He grinned and winked at Maren. She looked away. Nightmares should be set in dungeons with spider webs, not a restaurant decorated in mauve, teal, and ivory, and filled with families celebrating birthdays.

"So... tell me about...the family." Rhi's usual curiosity had muted into caution. "Are you the older or younger brother?"

"Younger by eight years. I've known Alan all my life."

"Where are you from?" She circled around asking about Alan.

"We grew up in northern Virginia, near Washington, D.C."

The waitress delivered the food. The aroma of ham and au gratin potatoes had Maren salivating, but the mention of Alan Wolfe made her gut churn. She stabbed her meat, dicing, shredding, pulverizing. Her first restaurant meal in years and she couldn't choke down a bite. She dug in her purse for an aspirin.

"You okay?" Neil's focus wavered for a moment.

"Peachy." Maren downed the pill with a gulp of water.

"Sometimes Mom gets headaches from her allergies.."

To her list of dust, mold, trees, and ragweed, add Neil Wolfe.

"Bill Knapp's is a cheerful restaurant." Rhiannon's sneakers tap-danced on the tile. "Their background music is all in major keys."

"Major keys?" Neil pretended an interest in the child's musical knowledge, asking questions about her favorite genres, composers, singers. Out of the corner of her eye, Maren studied him. His complexion had cleared up, pimples giving way to a scattering of laugh-line wrinkles. His jaw had grown over his Adam's apple. He'd filled out, shoulders broadening in proportion with his long legs. And he'd found someone to cut his sandy brown hair so it wouldn't curl into ringlets down his neck. His voice still hinted of Virginia, yet it had dropped half an octave.

The waitress arrived for dessert orders. Maren declined, but Neil ordered hot fudge ice cream cakes for three and a doggie bag for Maren's dinner.

"Are you married?"

"Rhi!" Maren jumped to hear her question verbalized.

"Normal curiosity," Neil smiled. "No, I'm not. What do you think of these names—Andy and Cody."

Maren recognized them from the *People* magazine article about Alan's death. Neil ignored her frantic head shaking.

Rhi swallowed a spoonful of ice cream. "Four letters, like Alan and Neil."

"Their real names are musical. Andy and Cody are nicknames they use to keep from getting teased at school."

"Coda?"

"Very good. Andante's the other one."

"Who would name their kids Andante and Coda?"

"Your father."

"He was a musician? What instrument?"

"Guitar—acoustic, electric, six string, twelve string. He had a rock band called Predator. Ever heard of them?"

"We don't listen to rock much." The tap dancing stopped. "Oh wow. I have brothers."

"And sisters. Melody and Harmony."

"Are you kidding?" Rhiannon grabbed Neil's arm. "Brothers and sisters! Oh, wow, oh, wow! This is great! How old are they? Do you have a picture? Do they know about me?"

Neil shook his head. "I wasn't sure if I'd find you. But I will tell them all about you when I get back, how smart and funny and talented you are."

"Patti will be thrilled," Maren warned. If there was any justice in this world—and Maren knew better than to expect that—Patti would murder Neil. The family would be livid, devastated, heartbroken. And Neil had no clue.

"Who's Patti?"

The waitress's arrival saved Neil from answering. He handed over his credit card, then unfolded a plastic sleeve of school pictures. "Melody is sixteen. Andy turned fifteen last week. Harmony's twelve and Cody turned nine in May."

"He's younger than me. Still the Coda." Rhiannon studied the faces, ice cream forgotten. "They don't look like me. Are they Chinese?"

"Their mom is Korean."

"Do you have a picture of..." She flipped to a photo of the family sprawled on the porch swing of an old house, the same photo *People* had printed.

"Your dad? He's in the shadows, but this is the last one taken before he died." Neil pointed to a man on the end, his chin resting on the head of his pregnant wife. "You keep these. I'll bring more next time."

"Thanks. Wow. I've always wanted a big family. Where do they live?"

"Next door to me. Let me give you my phone number and address. Call any time. My schedule is irregular, but I check my messages every day." Neil wrote on the back of a business card and added it to the stack of photos. "I'd like to come to your concerts, if you let me know in advance."

Maren pushed her untouched dessert away. This guy's as much trouble as his brother, she thought, rubbing her temples. Waltzes in here, getting Rhi's hopes up, promising the moon. He lives a thousand miles away; he'll never come here again. Not a chance he'll tell his sister-in-law about Rhiannon. Doesn't have the guts. Even if he does, Patti won't let him ruin their dearly-departed father's sainted image.

Neil looked at Maren. "Your mom's not feeling well. I'll run you home."

Rhiannon peppered Neil with questions on the drive back to the house. When she paused for a breath, he heard Maren humming "Get Back" by the Beatles. How could he convince her he meant no harm?

"Can you come in, Uncle Neil? We can talk some more."

"Sorry, I've got to catch a flight. I'm on call after midnight." He parked. "Say, could I have a picture of you to take with me?"

"Sure. Just a sec." She raced inside.

"She's wonderful." Neil watched her go. "Mature, bright, well-adjusted. And a remarkable talent."

Maren braced the cello on her hip. "Do *not* tell his wife and kids. They don't deserve this."

"Who's out there?" The front porch light went on and an elderly lady yelled from the front door. Her voice set dogs barking around the block.

"It's Maren, Mrs. V."

"Maren, you didn't rake today!"

"It's dark now. I'll do it tomorrow."

"They're predicting rain. Those heavy leaves will smother the lawn. Who's with you? That car better not be blocking me in. I have a ten o'clock hair appointment tomorrow."

Neil stepped into the light and extended his hand. "Good evening, ma'am. I'm Neil, Rhiannon's uncle. You must be her grandmother."

The old lady fluttered. "Heavens, no, we're not related."

"He'll move his car right away," Maren volunteered.

"Oh, no need." Mrs. V retreated to the house.

Rhiannon returned with a handful of photos. "I couldn't find kindergarten, but here's first grade."

Neil examined it. "Where's your teeth?"

She giggled. "Here's second grade, third, and this year's."

"You look so much like your dad in second." In his peripheral vision, he saw Maren turn away.

"I didn't even smile that year."

"He never smiled for school pictures. Kids teased him about his dimples." He slid the photos into his wallet.

"Dimples are cute."

"Yours are." Neil gently tugged her hair, finer and not as curly as Alan's. "Rhiannon, I wish I'd found out you sooner. I would have loved to know you as a baby, and now here you are, all grown up. So now I have a grown-up request—keep this," he pointed from her to himself then to Maren, "secret between us for now."

Rhiannon made a zipping-the-lips motion. "Okay."

Maren cleared her throat. "It's late, Rhi. Go on to bed."

She dragged her feet back inside, glancing frequently over her shoulder.

The door closed behind her daughter. Maren lifted an eyebrow at him. "Nice speech. What do you want?"

He put his hands up. "Nothing. I'm an old bachelor uncle who enjoys spending time with his nieces and nephews."

"Then Patti's four ought to be enough for you." Maren entered the garage, then slammed and locked the door behind her.

. . .

MAREN GOT READY FOR BED, then tucked her daughter in. "Lights out."

Rhi bounced on the mattress, photos of the Wolfe family clutched in her hands. "This is even better than Christmas!" Tugging on her mother's hand, Rhi pulled her close. "How can you be sad?"

Maren pulled the comforter up to the child's round chin. "Can we talk about this tomorrow?"

"Oh, yeah, your headache. Sorry." Rhi burst out of the covers to give her a hug. "Dear Jesus, thank you for Uncle Neil, and for a ride to my lesson, eating out, and getting into Honors Orchestra."

Honors Orchestra! Where was it? Who might give her a ride?

Rhiannon asked God's blessings on her family, including the Wolfes, finished her prayer, kissed her cheeks. "You're my one-and-only Mom. I'm always going to love you best."

Maren buried her face in the wild mess of sunlight curls, breathing in the scent of sweat and toothpaste with a hint of rosin. Oh this child. Her throat tight with tears, she whispered, "And I'll always love *you* best." No matter the Consequences.

Chapter Three

"*Slut! Disgrace to the family! No one wants to marry worthless trash like you!*"

The nightmare thundered through Maren's head. Shaking and nauseous, she sat up and braced her head in her hands. It'd been months since this terror had disturbed her sleep. Months of peace interrupted by Neil Wolfe. He'd invaded their lives, and now she'd have to tell Rhi how she was conceived.

Maren got ready for work, then checked on her daughter. Rhi slept soundly, clutching the bunny that Mrs. Coffey had made for her when she was a baby and hanging her feet off the end of the bed. The scent of lemon shampoo hung in the air. Maren closed her eyes. *Thank you, Jesus, for the temporary reprieve from questions. If you'd use this time to give me answers, I'd appreciate it.* She hurried to catch the bus to work.

As the morning rush eased, Mr. Coffey strolled into the bakery department. "You running the show by yourself?"

"Sandra's on break." Maren dumped a handful of flour on the pastry table, hiding behind its cloud.

The store manager coughed and waved his hand. "Hey, watch it! Trying to turn me white?"

She slammed a mound of dough the size of a basketball onto the table, sending hot pain through her neck and back.

"Lay it on me," he said. "What's making you look like week-old roadkill?"

"Rhi's uncle showed up. Unannounced."

"Not your brother."

"No." She landed a hard left in the glob.

"Her father's people."

"Yes." She slammed the dough, folded it.

"Kinda slow answering their mail. He didn't call or send you a letter?"

"I would have lied. I was ready to murder him yesterday."

"You're protecting your little girl." The phone rang. He took an order for a birthday cake.

"I have worked..." She spoke slowly, in rhythm with her kneading. "...so hard... to raise her right...not think of herself as a mistake... then this guy waltzes in."

"Don't know why he'd want to tell her different. Besides, I thought the dead brother was the bad guy." Mr. Coffey bagged three jelly donuts for a customer.

She rolled out the dough, scanning to make sure no one else heard. "He thinks...knowing about her family, might help Rhi... when she finds out...half her genes are from a thug."

Mr. Coffey made a low uh-huh in the back of his throat.

"He stared at her like, like..." Her fingers mangled the dough and she had to start over, rolling and twisting.

"He's looking for family resemblance, is all."

"He knows where we live, where I work." After months of looking for a rental in Waldenbrook, they couldn't move again. Maren pelted the raw shapes with cinnamon sugar.

"Nothing wrong with where you live."

She moved the tray to the oven and set the timer. "I'm sure *he* doesn't live in a basement. Probably has a mansion on a hill, pony in the backyard, color TV in every room."

"You're worried Rhiannon's gonna think he's more cool than Mama. Rest easy—you're raising a blessedly unspoiled child."

"She hung on his every word. And the way she looked at him..." Maren pressed the back of her wrist to the headache spot between her eyebrows. "If I could take Rhiannon somewhere, somewhere wonderful enough to make her forget these half-siblings... Bottom line—even if Disney World, Sea World, and Six Flags were all rolled together, Rhi would still want to know about her father."

Stealing a glance at the clock, Sandra rushed into the bakery. "Hey, Mr. Coffey. You got flour on your face. Oh, Maren, I was going to do those doughnuts."

"I need you to decorate the cakes and cookies." Maren's hands were shaking too much.

"Morning, Sandra." Mr. Coffey dusted himself off, then told Maren, "As always, you got my prayers. If there's anything I can do—"

She grabbed another batch of dough. "Enroll us in the Witness Protection Program?"

Mr. Coffey paused, his gaze on the ceiling. "I'll do better than that. Jesus and I will bring that man to his knees."

Where he belongs.

WHEN MAREN LEFT A&P at the end of her shift, Mrs. Coffey was at the curb, leaning on her minivan. She opened the passenger door and motioned Maren inside.

Maren sank onto the seat. "Mr. Coffey called you."

"Uh-huh," she hummed, then got behind the wheel with a whiff of her cocoa butter lotion. Her wise eyes assessed Maren with a glance. "I don't get much chance to love on you, now you've moved."

"I could do with some love."

"Thought so." She started the van and sang along to a cassette of the Five Stairsteps' "O-o-h Child" as she drove.

"You had to testify today?" Maren nodded at Mrs. Coffey's power suit with its shoulder pads. A silk blouse with a tie and high heels completed the outfit.

"Yes. The judge agreed Yvette can have her baby back."

Maren pulled in a deep breath, trying to relieve her queasiness. "Nothing would be worse than losing my child."

"That's your main worry?"

"Not just that he could get a lawyer and try to take her away, but that she'll abandon the faith we've taught her and adopt whatever wacko thoughts he has. That she'll start wanting the stuff his money can buy. That she'll disrespect me. And the big one—how she'll feel about herself when she finds out what that man did."

They turned into Waldenbrook and Maren remembered, "Mrs. V wants her leaves raked today,"

"Does she now." Mrs. Coffey parked in the driveway.

Maren got out. No leaves on the front lawn. She walked around the house. None on the sides or in the backyard. She couldn't see Mrs. Coffey doing lawn care, especially while wearing a suit, but then again, her friend did a lot that no one knew about or expected. Maren returned to the car. "What happened?"

"Jesus still commands the wind." Her gaze met Maren's. "He has a plan for you today, which does not involve raking."

Someday, Maren thought, she'd be good enough for the Consequences to lift and God would bless her. Someday.

The school bus squealed to a stop. Rhi raced out and bounced onto the back seat. "Hey, Mrs. Coffey, you'll never guess who I met yesterday."

Maren gasped. "You were supposed to keep it a secret. How many people did you tell?"

Blue-green eyes blinked at her. "No one. But Mrs. Coffey is special. I figured you told her and Mr. Coffey."

"You figured right." Mrs. Coffey drove to her house as Rhi bubbled on and on about her uncle Neil. When they arrived, Mrs. Coffey sent Rhi and her cello inside, then nodded at the buff-brick church across the street. "Nobody there but you and God. I'll come get you in a bit."

Maren walked to the church. No cars in the parking lot, no lights on inside, but she still called, "Hello?" when she let herself in. The building was silent. Scents of the old hymn books and Pine-Sol tinted the air. Soft light through the stained-glass windows showed the pews were empty. Maren locked the door behind her.

In the months after Rhi's birth, when she'd lived in a house packed with three other mothers and their babies, Maren had found a refuge here. Whether filled with the welcoming congregation or empty like today, these walls, in soothing cream with light wood trim, had become her oasis of peace. How many times had she come here, when money had run out, when the car had broken down, when earaches and teething had Rhi inconsolable for days....

Sometimes she poured out her prayers on the piano, but tonight Maren barely choked out "Help," before her tears flowed. She sank onto the last pew, beside a tissue box. "Please, Lord," she sobbed. "I've tried so hard...." Her words ended, but the worries and tears kept coming, spasming up from her aching heart. The weight pushed her onto the pew. "Help me Jesus, please...."

As the tears tapered off, a scent of cocoa butter reached Maren's nose, then Mrs. Coffey's strong arms wrapped around her. "'Cast your cares on Him, for He cares for you,'" she quoted from 1 Peter. "Good thing Sister Lucille keeps extra tissue boxes in the coat closet. That one's done for."

Maren had emptied the box. "I'll buy her another."

"You need to be in our young mothers group. I'll pick you up Tuesday evening."

"I'll be an outlier in the mothers group, like I was the odd one out in the rape survivors group." Maren shook her head. "No one else gets a surprise visit from the rapist's brother."

"Half the women in that survivor's group are related to their attacker, see him at every family gathering. You got plenty of company on the messy life bus." Mrs. Coffey squeezed her hand. "Our guest speaker Tuesday is a lawyer who specializes in cases involving children."

Free legal advice? "What time should we be ready?"

"Six."

Maren found the driest tissue in her pile and wiped her eyes again. "I haven't told Rhi... she's a product of rape."

"Your daughter is a child of God, made in his image."

"But she's going to have questions. You know how she is."

"Do I ever." Mrs. Coffey chuckled, then closed her eyes and raised her free arm. "Dear Lord, who made heaven, earth, and a force of nature we call Rhiannon, please give her mother Your wisdom and Your answers to her questions. We know Rhiannon is no accident. She is no mistake. She is fearfully and wonderfully made by You. Comfort and guide Maren with Your presence, and relieve her headache. Thank you, Lord. Amen."

"Thank you." The pressure between Maren's eyebrows eased.

"Now we best get you fed, watered, and home for your talk." Mrs. Coffey pulled her out of the pew and threw away her wet tissues.

As they left the church, Rhiannon, Nicole and a half-dozen other kids shot hoops in the parking lot. Reverend Gibson encouraged, "Almost. Nice try. You got this."

"I tell you, that man is a child-magnet." Mrs. Coffey turned to Maren. "Your dad ever play games with you?"

"He's not that kind of dad."

Warm hands cupped Maren's cheeks. "Just because your dad's an earthly grouch, don't think God our Father is a cosmic grouch. He's more like Reverend Gibson."

The minister passed the ball to his daughter. "You can do it, Nicole." When her throw went wild, he gave her a hug. "Just like Isiah Thomas when he started out. Keep trying."

Mrs. Coffey eyebrows raised. "Loving and forgiving."

Maren nodded. But missing a basket was easier to forgive than having a child out of wedlock.

WHEN THEY RETURNED FROM THE COFFEYS', Maren sat on the loveseat and pulled Rhi onto her lap. "I couldn't talk last night, but I'm ready now. You can ask anything you want to know."

Warm arms slipped around Maren's shoulders. "You didn't choose me..."

"Yes, I did. I chose you." Maren turned and hugged her daughter. "Every day of your life. The first time I held you, all wrapped

30

like a *krumkake*, I knew you were the best baby in the whole world. I am so thankful you're my daughter."

Rhi put her hands on Maren's cheeks. Her eyes filled with tears. "But you didn't choose to get pregnant."

How had she figured *that* out? Maren held her close, tucking her daughter's head into the curve of her shoulder. "True. But I've never, *ever* regretted keeping you." Although she did regret not providing a better life for her daughter. "You're my joy and sunshine. God turned a sad time into my best blessing." She planted a kiss on her forehead, breathing in the scent of rosin, sweat, and cut grass.

Rhi picked the skin around her thumbnail. "Yvette told someone on the phone when she thought I was asleep."

Yvette and her big mouth. Maren's jaw tightened. They'd shared an apartment until her housemate's boyfriend spent the night, forcing Maren to explain sex. "I'd planned to tell you when you were older. It's...tough... to understand."

Rhi's voice quieted to a whisper. "I thought rape was someone making you take your clothes off, but the dictionary said it's forcing someone to have sex. Was..." She swallowed and shifted on Maren's lap. "Was my father a bad man?"

Please don't let her carry his shame... or mine..

"I didn't know him, but I do know he made a bad choice that night." Maren couldn't do anything about Alan's genes or Rhi's resemblance to the man, but she did her best to teach her daughter to follow Jesus and know right from wrong. "The Bible says we all sin. And it says we should forgive."

"What about Uncle Neil?"

"We trust God and we're careful with everyone else."

Rhi shrugged and sniffled. "Let's sing."

They went through their favorite Mahalia Jackson songs, "Precious Lord, Take My Hand," "Trouble of the World," and "Just a Closer Walk." They finished with Carole King's "Child of Mine," with Rhi singing "Mom of mine."

"Thank you, Jesus, for being with us all the time," Rhi prayed.

"Amen." They hugged and said "I love you's" and "sleep well's."

Catherine Richmond

Maren watched her daughter walk to her bedroom. If her shrinking baby fat didn't announce Rhi's maturation, her mind would. Her amazing, wonderful, brilliant daughter.

Carole's line about looking behind echoed in Maren's head. It wasn't fair to blame Neil for bringing that night back; Maren had never let go of it.

Chapter Four

"Well, Tango, good thing you're an imaginary dog. If Patti kills me, you won't starve to death." As the last of Alan's fan mail had turned to ash, Neil had stopped talking to his brother and started talking to Tango. Much as he'd enjoy a wagging tail and furry welcome home, imaginary dogs tolerated erratic flight schedules better than real ones. "Let's go." Neil grabbed the wine bottle, went out the patio door, and followed the path.

The woods opened to Wolfe's Den, the two-story colonial their folks had built on the foundation of an inn for river travelers. Alan and Patti had added on a family room and a garage with an apartment above, and turned a barn into a practice studio. They'd swapped furnace and air conditioner for geothermal and solar systems. Spacious lawns had been turned into wildlife habitat. As he climbed the porch steps, he hoped his ancestors couldn't see him now, shaking in his Nikes.

Neil entered the combination, their childhood collie's birthdate, into the keypad, then called, "It's me." He let himself into his sister-in-law's kitchen and set the wine on the counter. Only the murmur of Patti talking into the phone disturbed the quiet. The children were at school, and Jim and Sun-hwa, the Korean couple Patti employed, must have the day off.

Neil rummaged through the cabinets and drawers until he found a corkscrew and a plastic sippy cup without a lid.

Outside her office door, he paused for a final briefing: *there's a mission to accomplish, delay will only add to the damage, so get in there and—* The wine bottle slipped an inch in his sweaty hand. He tightened his grip and marched in. Patti shot him a glance, then resumed her conversation. The chorus from Freddie Mercury's "Killer Queen" rocked through his head. Enough already. No dynamite or laser beams here. Although Patti did own one exceptionally well-honed letter opener.

Look what you got me into now, Alan, you royal pain in the butt.

Patti's office looked like a museum whose curator died of overwork. Books and magazines crammed the built-in shelves. Newspapers and catalogs formed a maze on the floor. Bulging manila folders, binders, and loose paperwork competed for space on every horizontal surface and spilled from file cabinets. *I should buy her a fire extinguisher for her birthday—if I live.* Neil consolidated several piles of mail to open a spot on the desk and used a Kennedy Center program as a coaster. He pulled the cork, filled the cup, and set it near Patti.

His sister-in-law finished brushing TWA-red polish on her nails. Every baby had added extra pounds to Patty's short frame, prompting Alan to make the usual jokes about having more of her to love. His sister-in-law carried it well, coming off stylish instead of sloppy. Like today, when most moms who worked at home would opt for a sweatshirt and jeans, Patti wore a tunic and slacks in dark red silk. To some, her weight made her look soft, but Neil knew better.

She hung up the phone and glanced at her watch. "Wine? I haven't had lunch yet."

"Good. Drink up." *This is going to hurt.*

She took a sip. "This isn't your usual Boone's Farm."

"I've got some good news and bad news."

"*National Enquirer* spotted Alan in Burger King."

Neil shook his head. "Back to the night *Banned in Nashville* made number one."

Patti turned away from him, staring out the window at the woods, the trees motionless in late-summer's heat. "Whatever happened, I forgave him years ago and I don't want to hear about it now." She drained her glass and, in response to Neil's questioning look, added, "Two dozen long-stemmed red roses from a man who wouldn't pick a dandelion for his mother."

"There's a child." He held out the bottle and she grabbed it from him.

"A paternity suit? Sic Parton on 'em." She flung out the name of the lawyer she kept on retainer, then filled and drained the cup. "I'm surprised we haven't been hit with this before."

"This was the only time, the entire tour, anyone female talked to me."

One eyebrow raised. "You're saying there's some basis for this claim."

Neil removed the photos from his wallet and set them in front of her. The blood drained from her face and she froze in place. He'd seen her like this when he had to tell her about Alan's accident. "They're still living in Kalamazoo. The mom works at A&P—"

The wine bottle slammed on the desk. Her face turned as red as her nail polish and she yelled, "One more word about this, this *other woman*, and I'll smash you upside the head. I don't want to hear it! Any of it! How dare you dig up—"

Neil rushed through the explanation of the after-party, finding Maren's letters, his trip to Michigan, and Rhiannon's talent, concluding with, "The good news—no paternity suit."

"A musical prodigy? What instrument?"

"Cello."

"We might have time. But not much." Patti sank into the desk chair, assuming the counterfeit calm of one who can't afford to break down. Her color returned to normal. The muscles in her jaw tightened as as she returned the photos. After a long moment, her cold voice ordered, "Tell the children. They'll all be home for dinner. And lock the door when you leave."

"Tell them what?"

"It's your circus." She dismissed him with a curt gesture.

Neil tiptoed out, snapping the lock in the knob and pulling the door shut after him. He'd gotten off easy, with all his essential body parts. Patti probably couldn't find her letter opener. Now if he could keep the kids from bothering her, she might forgive him before the end of the next ice age.

The junk drawer held everything except writing instruments and tape. In the silverware drawer, Neil found a stick of Double Bubble and a broken purple crayon. He wrote "Do Not Disturb" in block letters on the back of last month's PTA flyer. Chewing the gum into a wad, he wandered back to the six paneled walnut door. Something crashed on the other side, too light to be the wine bottle. Best guess—the framed photo of Alan. Neil posted the sign, then started dinner.

As he packed the ingredients into the loaf pan, a nine-year-old stomped into the kitchen. "Meatloaf? I want pizza."

"Hello to you too, Cody. We'll have pizza when you learn to make it."

"I know how to make it." The boy grabbed the phone and punched in the number for the local pizzeria. Neil reached over his head and hung up the receiver. "Aw, Uncle Neil!"

"Put your backpack away."

He complied with the classic whine, "Why do I have to do all the work around here?"

Avoiding the well-worn argument, Neil turned to the one thing he had control over: food. He slathered Korean gochujang over the loaf and slid it into the oven.

Wearing his dad's Washington Senators ball cap, Cody dragged back into the kitchen. He made a raid on the refrigerator for Coke. Most nights, Neil would remind him to drink nutritious stuff like milk and juice, but tonight he let it slide. He had bigger battles to fight.

The boy belched an echoey two-parter, then asked, "What's the deal with the note on the office door?"

"That's what I want to talk to you about. Where's the rest of the gang?"

"The girls are supposed to be cleaning the stables, but they're riding in Turner's field. Andy's at soccer."

"Should I go get him?"

"Naw. He's got the hots for Jeff's sister. He'll ride home with them. Should be back around four."

Neil checked his watch. "It's almost six."

"Probably went home with Jeff, since it's warm enough for his sister to sunbathe."

Neil frowned. When did Andy get interested in girls? "Go get your sisters," he told Cody.

With more burping and complaining, the boy shuffled out. Neil called Jeff Riggs' house and talked to their answering machine. Darn it all. He wanted all four kids home so he could get this over with. He rinsed the romaine and started ripping it apart with his bare hands, shredding, tearing... *I need counseling.*

Gravel crunched in the driveway. He glanced out. Andy vaulted out of a BMW convertible, then waved to the blonde driver. *Whoa. Jeff's sister* had *grown up.*

The lanky teen sauntered in, dropping his duffel bag and trombone inside the door.

"How was your game?"

"Game?" His freckled face blanked for several seconds. He swiped through his hair, leaving a trail of spikes, then grinned. "Oh, yeah, game. We lost."

"Sorry to hear that. Put your stuff away."

"Later."

"Now," Neil growled.

"Touchy, touchy." Andy bumped a cabinet and two kitchen chairs on the way out.

Melody clumped in, smelling of horse. "Hey, Uncle Neil, give me a hand with these boots. I'm not eating tonight."

She plopped in a chair. Neil grabbed the ankle of the leather riding boot and yanked. "You were supposed to muck the stables."

"Far be it from me to deprive Jerry of a job. I've got to change. I'm getting picked up at seven."

"Make it eight. We've got to have a family talk." Neil tightened his grip on the other boot. "This better not be a percussionist—"

"Oooh, you are so cute when you're serious." Melody fluttered her lashes. "Okay, eight, but tell Mom I won't be home until one."

He shook his head. "You turn into a pumpkin at midnight."

Harmony kicked off her manure-caked sneakers in the doorway and added a French horn and viola to the pile. He should make a tape loop: Pick up your shoes, do not leave your backpack on the kitchen floor, put away all musical instruments, set the table.

Andy, wearing an MTV cap, grabbed the garlic bread.

"Hats off, hands washed," he reminded them. "And don't you say grace anymore?" Rhiannon said grace when they ate at Bill Knapp's. His heart twinged at the thought of his newfound niece.

"Grace," Cody volunteered, serving himself a hefty portion of meatloaf.

"Bless the meat and let's eat," Andy added, a little muffled around his full mouth.

Neil closed his eyes. "Thank you for this food and these kids. Help me tell them... this news, and help them receive it in, with, uh, receive it. Help their mother feel better about it. Amen." He looked up at four worried faces. Neil had loved these children from birth, and looked after from the day of their dad's death, hoping to nurture their talent and guide them to a better path. Andy rubbed one eyebrow with the heel of his hand. Melody's long fingers paused over the salad tongs. Cody's dimpled jaw worked up and down. Harmony's freckled face wrinkled into a frown. Pieces of Alan.

"Is Mom sick?" Harmony had turned pale.

Neil squeezed her hand. "No. She needed time to herself."

"Out with it, man." Andy used his father's favorite phrase.

"Some people when they're away from home and partying... do things they normally wouldn't do, um, like drugs and alcohol. When your dad and I were on tour—"

An empty wine bottle thumped onto the counter behind Neil. "Family only." Patti stepped to the table. If she was drunk, she hid it well. "You have a half-sister in Michigan."

Patti snapped her fingers in front of Neil's face. She snatched the photos from him and tossed one to each child. "I'm going to Dal-Rae's." She grabbed her purse, went out, and climbed into a waiting cab. *Dal-Rae's? Her counselor takes appointments in the evening?*

Silence held for a long moment.

"It *can't* be true," Melody whispered.

Andy muttered a Korean cuss word, then, "She looks more like Dad than we do."

"Another sister," Cody moaned.

"No. She's not our sister." Melody slammed her fist on the table. "She is not."

"How old is she?" asked Harmony.

"She'll be ten in November."

"Cody's still the baby."

Neil nodded. "Still the Coda, Rhiannon said."

"Rhiannon? Dad didn't give her some goofy musical name?"

He shook his head. "Your dad didn't know."

The kids were quiet for a few seconds. Neil braced for the next round of questions.

"How did you find out?" Andy asked.

"Found her birth certificate in the fan mail."

"With Dad's name on it?" If music didn't work out, Harmony could become a lawyer.

"No."

"It might not be true." Harmony asked. "People lie about this all the time, to get money. Did you get a paternity test?"

Melody turned on him. "So we're not good enough for you. Look too Asian maybe. Slant eyes. You find this imposter—" Tipping over her chair, she stormed away from the table, up the stairs, and slammed her bedroom door.

"PMS," Andy diagnosed.

"Huh?" Cody asked.

"Perpetually Mad Sister."

"She hates being upstaged." *Like her father.* Harmony, on the other hand, tapped into her mother's legendary self-control, collected the photos, arranged them in order, and handed them back to Neil. "How much do they want? Are we going to be, like, broke? Will we have to sell the house?"

"We could sell you." Cody resorted to the familiar territory of sibling rivalry.

Harmony leaned on the table, dinner forgotten. "Are they going public with this? Tabloid or regular?"

"No. And we are keeping it quiet," Neil reminded them, then held up the fourth grade photo. "For as long as we can."

Harmony frowned at the picture. "If her hair wasn't in braids—"

Neil nodded. "She looks like the *Predator* album cover."

"Got to be bogus." Andy thumped his Coke can on the table. "Dad cheated on Mom?"

SATURDAY MORNING, as soon as the ceiling creaked with Mrs. V's footsteps, Maren went upstairs to earn their rent. She scoured the bathrooms and kitchen, then started laundry. Rhi's note said she'd eaten breakfast and gone out to play with the neighbor girls. Maren vacuumed with a vengeance, the racket sending Mrs. Vanderhoef out in her Cadillac. She swabbed the floors until the Pine Sol fumes made her dizzy, then battled the lawn as if it were the *Terminator*. Stomping downstairs, she dumped the wet clothes into the dryer and started another load, then scrubbed their bathroom.

This anger is ruining a lovely September day.

It's easier than being afraid.

What are you afraid of? Neil seems like a nice man. He's interested in Rhiannon.

Entirely too interested in Rhiannon.

What does that mean?

She's all I've got.

Maren mopped her way into Rhiannon's room, finding the photos on her nightstand. She hadn't wanted to look at them in front of Neil, but now she couldn't hold back. She flipped through the pictures, finding no resemblance, no surge of memory at the one of Alan. Neil had printed his phone number and address on the back of a business card. The front had the navy and maroon airline logo, his name, and the title First Officer.

Her chest tightened and she strained for a breath. *She* should be flying, except...Consequences.

Neil Wolfe. Ten years ago at the after-party, he'd been gentle, attentive. They'd shared ideas and plans. Her starry-eyed self had entertained the notion of love at first sight.

Then his brother hijacked her life, crashing and burning her dreams to ashes.

Curling up on the bed and crying would result in another headache, so she got back to work. Maren hung Mrs. V's clothes, made her bed, and started a load of their clothes. She mixed lentils, spaghetti, and zucchini for dinner.

Rhi came in from playing, showing her how to count to ten in Chinese with her hands and words. The Chinese twins had taught her a different way to jump rope and a song to accompany it. A neighbor boy had let her ride his old bicycle. It sounded like a good day, but Rhi's lack of eye contract told her more questions were coming.

"So which musical should we do tonight?" Maren asked as they finished dinner. "*The Wiz, Grease, Godspell?*"

"I know!" Rhi put her empty bowl in the sink and raced to her room. She returned with the cardboard set they'd made of an orphanage. It had a backdrop of New York City, a wall of windows and a door, and six cots. She set it up on the steamer trunk with cutouts of the characters. "Let's do *Annie,* only her mom finds her, then she and Annie go live with Daddy Warbucks."

Maren sat on the couch and pulled her daughter onto her lap. Much as she tried, their financial struggles couldn't be hidden. Rhi had eaten down-to-their-last dime beans, witnessed negotiations with unscrupulous landlords and mechanics, and heard too many broken promises about the next paycheck. "Worrying about money is my job, not yours."

"Aren't you tired of the hard-knock life?" Rhi pumped her fisted arms.

"Neil Wolfe is not a billionaire."

"He has more than we do."

Who doesn't? "We may never hear from him again—"

"He said he'd come back."

"Sometimes, when people spend money on you, they expect something in return."

"Like what?"

"I don't know Neil well enough to say." The answer curled on her lap, right in front of her eyes.

"How come people in musicals don't have mothers?" Rhi wiggled, her sneakers tapping the trunk, toppling over a half-dozen cut-outs. "The little mermaid's mom died. The girls in *Annie* are orphans. Dorothy in *The Wiz* is an orphan."

"*Fiddler on the Roof* has Golde, and *I Remember Mama* has Mama. Maybe it's because cleaning and cooking makes for boring theater."

"Yeah, but raising children isn't." Rhi flashed a grin, then looked up, thinking. "Maybe it's because stories are about problems and if you have a mom, you have someone to help. Like if Grandma was still alive."

"She would have loved you so much." And she would have taken care of Rhi, so Maren could finish college. So then...Consequences weren't the result of attending the after-party, but from her father?

Chapter Five

A handwritten sign in the Sunday School wing pointed children upstairs, moms downstairs. Mrs. Coffey and Rhi headed up to the nursery.

"I'll find you afterwards," Maren told them. *Don't barge in during sticky legal discussions.*

Five women chatted the meeting room. Three were from the neighborhood, but Maren couldn't remember their names. The other two were former housemates, from back when their babies were little.

"Heard you moved out of Northside." Royetta gave her a hug.

"Near a school with the music program Rhi wants. And how's Darius?" He had a few months on Rhi.

"Preparing for a career with the Pistons. Nobody's told him, with a daddy as short as his, ain't happening."

"Never know. There might be a tall gene in your family tree." What was in the Wolfe half of Rhi's genealogy? Besides Neil. "How's life in the paper mill?"

"Money's good, but the hours about to kill me." Royetta rolled her shoulders. "Sometimes nights, sometimes days, most times twelve hours. Good thing my husband's job is flexible."

"Twelve hour shifts? Rhi can't be alone that long."

"Get a husband."

"Haven't found a man I'd trust with my daughter."

"Hey." Sandra doused her coffee with creamer. Her coworker's presence would keep her from speaking; anything she said would be spread all over the store tomorrow. "Why are you passing up a Sister Lucille cookie?"

"Sister Lucille's? Thanks for telling me." After baking all week, sweets held no appeal—except Sister Lucille's. Maren grabbed a cookie, sat in one of the folding chairs, and sank her teeth into the soft and moist delicacy. An out-of-this-world mix of spices hit her taste buds.

Sandra sat beside her, then took a bite. "Oh baby. We should totally go into business selling these."

"You get the recipe out of Sister Lucille, and we'll send our kids to college on the profits."

A woman with a Toni Braxton hairstyle entered and closed the door behind her. She wore a sleeveless mock turtleneck, tailored slacks, and heels, all in black. "Welcome. I'm Bernice, kin to Sister Dorothy. I work as a lawyer in Detroit. Hope you've brought your questions. But before we start, let me deploy *Get Smart's* Cone of Silence." She curved her arms to include everyone in the group. "What you say won't leave this room. Raise your right hand to show you agree."

The women quieted and raised their hands, even Sandra.

"All right. Who has a legal question?" The lawyer grabbed an empty chair.

Sandra started. "I've been living with Mama since I got pregnant. Now I'm wanting my own place, but she's threatening to take my girl away."

Bernice raised her index finger. "I'm saying this because we're in a church, and it goes for all of you—'as far as possible, be at peace with everyone.' Romans 12:18. Your mama will always be your mama. She'll always be your daughter's grandma. Work things out with her...if possible."

Maren rubbed her forehead. Be at peace with Neil? Only if he stayed away.

44

"As to the legal issue," Bernice continued, "Be the best parent you can be. Don't give anyone a reason to side with your mama. Stay clean, stay out of trouble, don't date trouble. Provide a safe home for your daughter. Consider living nearby, so your daughter and mama can continue to spend time together."

Did Neil think Maren was a good enough parent and Mrs. V's basement was safe?

The rest of the group dropped all pretense of shyness and shouted complaints about visitation, custody, and child support.

Maren realized she was picking at her cuticles. She squeezed her hands between her knees. If Alan had found her letters and showed up in Kalamazoo ten years ago, the tabloids would have been on it like white on rice. Would he have wanted custody or visitation? Probably not. Touring, recording, and raising the other kids would have kept him busy. Bottom line: Maren and Rhiannon's privacy would have disappeared faster than her weekly pay. The Consequences would have been worse than ever.

Bernice stomped her foot for silence. "Remember, we're in a church, working for peace, trying to do what's best for our children." The lawyer waded through the legal requirements, documentation, when to go back to court, and how much it might cost. When the furor let up, she turned to Maren. "All right, quiet one, what brought you here?"

"My child's uncle showed up last week, no warning. Is there any way to keep him from coming back?"

"The father's brother?"

Maren nodded.

"Did this uncle threaten, harass, or assault either of you?"

"No."

"Will he tell the father where you are?"

"The father's dead."

Royetta snorted. "Wish that Old Beelzebub who raped me was dead, then he wouldn't be showing up at Thanksgiving, Christmas, funerals."

Maren shivered. "That's awful."

"Is he stalking you?" Bernice asked.

"No. He's kin. Can't get rid of him." She pointed to her heart. "He ain't gonna steal my joy."

Ain't gonna steal my joy. Seemed like...Consequences had stolen Maren's joy.

"Understood." The lawyer nodded for Maren to continue.

"What if he thinks our basement apartment is inadequate?"

"Does your daughter have a bed, her own bedroom?"

"Yes. There's a smoke detector, fire extinguisher, and locks on the exterior doors, but otherwise it's basic."

"Courts aren't asking for fancy." Bernice leaned forward. "You're here for free legal advice, so you're not independently wealthy. Did the dead man have any assets you could tap into for child support?"

"Yes, but he has four other children. The publicity would harm them and my daughter."

"So...he's famous." Bernice braced her chin on her fist for a moment. "As long as neither you nor your daughter is in danger from the uncle, your best option is to make peace with him. Is that possible?"

Inside Maren's head, Mrs. Coffey's voice quoted Jesus, "With God all things are possible." Maren swallowed hard. "Guess I'd better try."

"For your daughter's sake, ask for the father's medical history. And that brings us to our last topic—writing a will." Bernice passed around a fill-in-the-blank form. "If anything happened to you, who do you want to be guardian of your underage child? Before you name someone, ask them. Your child deserves someone who is willing. You can fill it out in your own handwriting or type up a new copy. Have two witnesses sign when you do."

Maren made a note on the form to ask for medical records. Guardianship? Who could she ask?

NEIL PARKED in the rain-drenched A&P parking lot. Since his news about Rhiannon last week, Patti had been as turbulent as today's late-season thunderstorm. Expecting no less from Maren, he dashed into the grocery and scanned the line of cash registers. No Maren. Maybe she has the day off.

Two people staffed the service desk: a skinny woman with bowl-cut beige hair pounding on an adding machine and a Black man who looked up with a smile as Neil approached.

"Good afternoon. I'm looking for Maren Tollefson. Is she working today?"

The man, whose name tag read Mr. Coffey, Store Manager, gave him the once-over, not hostile, but cautious. "Depends on who's asking."

"Her daughter's Uncle Neil."

The handshake was firm and the twice-over more than thorough. He flashed a grin. "Yeah. Little girl's got your chin."

Neil's hand touched his round chin and smiled. He'd been looking for glimpses of Alan, so a resemblance to himself was a pleasant surprise.

Mr. Coffey stepped around the end of the counter and motioned for Neil to follow him to the front windows of the store, an alcove between the shopping carts and the wall of the service desk. "First, let me tell you how I met Maren and Rhiannon." He nodded at the empty field on the west side of the parking lot. "Every Thanksgiving, some old fellow from up north sets up a tin-can trailer and sells Christmas trees out there." Even today, ten degrees above freezing, and wind blowing fast-food trash through the weeds, heavy traffic in both directions, it was a grim site. Mr. Coffey shook his head. "Every year except one. In 1979, the Christmas tree seller was a young woman with a newborn tucked inside her coat."

Maren. Neil slumped against the window, eyes closed against a wave of dizziness. "But...the winters here."

"Every day a toss-up between burned in a space-heater fire or freezing to death." The man waited until Neil opened his eyes again. "The security system was a wire hook into a scrap of pine, so danger of robbery, murder, and another rape. Toilet a paint bucket. Water hauled in jugs."

For Alan's last Christmas, his brother had given Patty a diamond bracelet. The kids were up to their eyebrows in gifts. The table groaned under an eighteen pound turkey. Yet, Maren... "And Christmas Eve, she'd be out of a job again."

"Neither of them would have lasted the week." Mr. Coffey shook his head. "I called my wife. Mrs. Coffey hauled them out of there...forty-five minutes before Child Protective Services showed up to put Rhiannon in foster care. They lived in our house as Maren recovered from the birth, then we connected her with other single mothers to help each other with baby-care while they worked."

Neil broke out in a sweat and his lunch threatened to make a reappearance. Worse than he'd ever imagined. He had to make it up to her. "She didn't have family? Anyone?"

"That's her story to tell." Mr. Coffey shook his head, then faced Neil, arms crossed over his ample chest. "Which is to say, Mrs. Coffey and I take a *parental* interest in those two."

Neil met his gaze and swallowed. "Thank you, sir, for saving their lives. You and your wife."

Mr. Coffey nodded. "The second thing you need to know— Maren is an excellent mother. She'd do anything for her girl, even taking night shifts so she could be home with her during the day."

"When did she sleep?"

"She didn't. They lived in a house with three other mothers and their babies. Too noisy. Mrs. Coffey gave her a talking-to about staying healthy for her daughter and I put her back on day shift."

Neil fought off another wave of nausea. It had been a nightmare, more miserable than he'd ever imagined. "I'm here to help...if Maren will let me."

"You're on our prayer list." One side of his mouth tipped in a half-smile, then he strolled back to the service desk. "She's supposed to be in Bakery, but she might be in Deli. If she's trying to fix a meat slicer, tell her repair guy's on his way."

"Against the rules," the other worker said without pausing her assault on the adding machine.

Mr. Coffey consulted the grid taped to the booth's wall, then pointed to the back corner of the store. "Maren hasn't taken her lunch, so she can leave. Tell her I'll clock out for her."

"Against the rules. If you let Maren leave, all the employees will want to clock out early."

"If everyone worked as hard as Maren..."

Neil left them to argue. He took the aisle of seaweed chips and sugarless cookies marked "Healthy Food"—prompting him to wonder if the rest of the store sold "Unhealthy Food"—and headed to the Bakery.

MAREN REMOVED the motor housing and peered into a large machine. "Okay, Hobart, what's your problem? I treat you good, clean you, let you rest between orders, polish you every night."

Her coworker put a piece of gum into her mouth. "Sweet talking junk won't get you nowhere."

"Watch what you say, Sandra. This slicer and I go way back. It's lasted longer than most of your boyfriends."

Her coworker blew a bubble and popped it. "Time to trade it in on a new model."

A spark jumped to Maren's screwdriver. "Ow!" She flinched and dropped the tool. "Hey, who plugged it back in?"

Sandra stepped back. "Well, it don't work unless you plug it in." She propped her hand on her hip. "Girl, Mr. Coffey said to leave it be. I heard him. What're you messing with it for?"

Common sense wasn't required to work here. Maren yanked the power cord. "Taking apart these gizmos is interesting."

"As much as the fruitcakes."

"Don't speak ill of the customers." Maren stood up straight in imitation of the Troll at the Desk. "Against the rules. There's one. Go wait on him." The screwdriver pointed, then a shock worse than Hobart's shot through her. Neil. Her face heated and she set down the tool.

He strolled to the counter. "How about a ride home?"

"You weren't coming until tomorrow."

"I got released early. You, too, according to Mr. Coffey up front."

"Is that the uncle?" Sandra stared. "He's *fine.*"

In God we trust... Maren went to the phone and confirmed

Neil's claim. She grabbed her coat and backpack, and followed him out. The cashiers gawked. Mr. Coffey gave her a thumbs up. The Troll glared.

Neil opened the car door for her. When was the last time anyone had done that? Prom, maybe? She climbed in and buckled up.

"We should talk before Rhiannon gets home." He started the car.

There was so much she couldn't say in front of Rhi.

Neil motioned toward the empty field. "Mr. Coffey told me how he met you and Rhiannon."

"He shouldn't have said anything. We're good now." What's the least she could say?

"You were in college."

"I had to drop out."

"Your family didn't help you?"

"My father uses Consequences as discipline."

"Withholding support isn't a consequence, it's punishment...for something that wasn't your fault." He glanced at her, but she stared straight ahead. "What about church, friends?"

"Church said I was a bad example to the younger girls."

"You had no help, yet you didn't choose abortion."

"Don't make me out to be a saint. If I'd known my father would...how my father would react, I might have made a different choice." No baby should have to grow up in squalor.

He turned to face her. "Did you consider adoption?"

"Requires strength and planning. I had none."

"Wish I could beat up my brother again." Neil growled, then his voice softened. "Maren, I'm so sorry. How can I make this up to you? Could we go look at cellos before the store closes?"

Taking a car would be easier, but... "Today we go see my father."

He scowled. "Yeah, I'd like to have a talk with him."

Maren groaned. How many more ways could she be embarrassed in front of this man? Her father had made up his mind; anything Neil told him would only increase his ill temper. Was this another Consequence? "Don't even try. It won't help. Drop us off at his house—it's near the airport—then leave. Don't go inside."

"Can I take you out to dinner on the way?"

"No."

"Well, Rhiannon did all the talking last week. What have you been up to these years?"

Why would he even ask? His only interest was Rhi. "You've seen it. While you went to flight school, I worked at A&P. While you flight-instructed, I worked at A&P. You flew night freight, checks, or blood, got a commuter job, then went with a major, I worked at A&P. And raised Rhi."

He winced, then gave her a curious look. "You remembered all my plans?

Enough of his digging into her life. "Speaking of family, did you tell yours?"

He nodded. "As expected, Patti yelled and threw things. Cody's bummed that he's still the youngest. Harmony's worried about the legal angles. Andy's weirded out. Melody's turned it into a racial thing." He shrugged. "Normal for that bunch. They're dramatic. Overreact to everything. They'll come around."

"Don't count on it. You kicked over their father's pedestal."

"How did it go when you told Rhi?"

"She'd figured out most of it."

"These kids...too smart for their own good."

He parked in the driveway, then leaned toward her. Maren shot out of the car. At the service entrance, she glanced back. But Neil had only grabbed a box, the size of a pie box, from the back seat. He gave her a wary look as he got out of the car, as if questioning her emotional stability. Hurrying through the rain to join her under the eave, he handed it to her. "It's an answering machine, so I can warn you of my visits. I recorded the outgoing message, you know, male voice for safety. If you want someone else on there, like Mr. Coffey, I understand."

Maren had been looking for an answering machine, so her lawn customers could leave messages, but thrift stores and garage sales only sold broken ones. A male voice might deter creeps. She set the box inside the garage on the workbench. Could she trust Neil...a little? "Thank you."

He held up two fingers in a V, making a peace sign.

"Out of date."

"Since when is peace out of date?"

"Ever since you showed up."

The bus rounded the corner and stopped.

Rhi managed to be the first off this time. She ran up the driveway, yelling, "Uncle Neil! I knew you'd come back!" She handed off her cello with a "hi, Mom," tackled Neil with a full-force hug, then dove into a recitation of the wonders and woes of fourth grade.

Maren's jaw tightened. "He's driving us to Grandpa's on his way to the airport. Let's get out of the rain."

"Do you drive?" Neil asked Maren as they headed south.

"Yes." Maren sat with her arms crossed and didn't look at him.

"Uncle Neil," Rhiannon said, "car exhaust pollutes the air, cars use nonrenewable energy sources, and they take up space in landfills when they're thrown away."

"So you're holding out for an electric car?"

"Their batteries have toxic stuff like acid, lead, and cadmium."

"Cadmium?" Neil glanced at Maren. How did her daughter know about chemicals? "Don't they make chocolate Easter eggs?"

"No, silly, that's Cadbury."

Rhiannon navigated him into a neighborhood of older ranch houses with single-car garages, showing remarkable sense of direction. She jumped out of the car as soon as he parked. "C'mon, I want them to meet my new uncle!"

"Neil." Maren said his name for the first time in ten years. She leaned over the seat back. "You do not want to do this."

"Yes I do." Her father had to understand this wasn't her fault. He was to blame. He followed his niece to the front door.

"You'll be sorry," Maren muttered, trailing behind them.

Opening the door without knocking, Rhiannon pulled him in, then waved to a dark corner of the living room. "This is my uncle,

Neil. This is my grandpa, Arne Tollefson, and his friend, Helga Hoofer."

As his eyes adjusted to the room lit only by a television, two people in recliners emerged from the gloom. The man had Maren's firm jaw and lean build. The woman's eyes bulged and her mouth drooped. The outline of her head extended to her shoulders without an indentation for a neck, as if the Wicked Witch had a child with a pug. Her short arm raised the remote and muted the game show.

"Your only uncle is Karl." The man scowled. "Who are you?"

"Neil Wolfe." He reached out. The grandfather's grip was strong, but his hand was cold.

Rhiannon chatted with her grandpa until Helga waved the remote. "Hush. I can't hear my show." The sound resumed.

Neil sat in a side chair. The glow of the TV showed walls covered with framed studio portraits of a family of towheads with two boys.

Maren propped the cello in the entry, nodded to her father, then went to the back of the house. A moment later, he heard footsteps on the basement stairs and water running.

Rhiannon got out her cello, perched on a stool beside her grandpa, and waited. As the program went to commercial, Helga muted the TV, and his niece played and sang "Greensleeves" from memory. She'd corrected the few issues the maestro had pointed out, her rendition perfect. Midway through the second verse, the sound resumed.

"It's not Christmas," Helga said, "but it is time for my show."

Neil applauded. "Well done, Rhiannon." She bowed to him, but the others didn't react. His niece showed no sign of pain from the disrespect as she stowed the instrument. When she carried it to the car, Neil moved to the stool. He got right to the point. "I was there, the night my brother drugged your daughter and raped her. It wasn't Maren's fault. She's not to blame."

The man scowled and lowered the footrest. He turned toward Neil, eyes blazing. "She made her bed. She has to lie in it." He pushed out of the recliner and headed down the hall.

"But she didn't—"

Rhiannon returned, spotted Neil, and tipped her head. He followed her to the kitchen.

"All right, I've met your family," he murmured to Maren. "Let me take you out to dinner."

"I warned you. Go catch a plane." Maren handed her daughter the makings for salad.

Rhiannon pointed to a notepad on the refrigerator. "Mom has chores."

Neil scanned the list, finding a dinner menu, laundry, bathroom cleaning, kitchen floor. He had questions, none of which he could ask in front of Rhiannon. "No lawn mowing?"

"Done for the year." Maren hurried downstairs. "We had a hard frost last week."

Neil followed Maren into the unfinished basement."Why do they treat you like this? Why do you put up with it?"

With quick, jerky movements, she moved wet laundry into the dryer. "The Bible says to honor your father and mother."

"I'm no expert, but God didn't make you to be a doormat, a whipping boy. If you're trying to earn forgiveness, I told your father it wasn't your fault."

"Waste of breath. I shouldn't have been there. I should have been home, studying, so I didn't lose my scholarship."

"Studying on a Saturday night? Get real. Your father should have let you stay here, helped with his granddaughter, been a supportive parent." Although his gloom might have infected both Maren and Rhiannon. "You could've finished school."

"You're not a parent. What do you know about Consequences?"

"I know about love, taking care of each other, sharing each other's burdens. This is the opposite." He tossed in a stray sock. "It's disrespect, abuse, exploitation."

"I've heard it all before." The oven buzzed. She slammed the dryer door, punched the knob, and raced up the stairs.

Rhiannon finished the salad and set the table. The dining room walls had been decorated with school pictures of those same two boys. No photos of Maren and Rhiannon. Maren took a tray of food to the living room for Helga.

"Sit next to me," Rhiannon said as the family took their places around the table. The chairs looked like ones he'd seen in a steakhouse.

The father bowed his head. "Bless this food to our use and us to your service. Amen."

Neil blinked. Mr. Tollefson had skipped the phrase about being mindful of the needs of others. He looked at Maren to see if she noticed, but she didn't make eye contact or change expression.

"Jen at school has unicorns on her shoes," Rhiannon said between bites of chicken.

Maren said, "You could paint unicorns on your shoes."

Before Rhiannon could respond, the pug-witch howled over the noise of the TV. "You put garlic in this. I told you not to use garlic."

Maren hurried to the living room. In a calm voice, she said, "There is no garlic."

"I know what I tasted, you liar. Make one without garlic."

Maren brought the plate back into the kitchen, scraped the breading off the meat, rinsed it, then returned it.

"Where'd the breading go? I said to get rid of the garlic, not the breading."

Maren returned to her meal, now cold, as the bellyaching continued from the other room. Why Arne let the pug-witch attack his daughter? Neil scanned the room for a suitable murder weapon. The light fixture's chain looked like a good possibility.

Arne paused in shoveling food into his mouth. "There are no unicorns."

His granddaughter shrank in her seat.

"What if you bedazzled a unicorn?" Neil asked. "Melody and Harmony like to bedazzle."

Rhiannon straightened. "I'll bedazzle my cello case when I get my own."

Neil decided to buy her a Bedazzler.

Mr. Tollefson finished eating and set down his utensils. "I have cancer."

Maren looked up from her plate, her expression still neutral. "I'm sorry."

"I'm not changing my will. Your brother will inherit everything."

Again, no reaction. "What kind of cancer is it?"

He shrugged. "The kind that kills. Doctor wants me to see someone in Chicago. I'm not fighting big-city traffic to be told they can't do anything."

"I'll drive you," Maren said. "Or you can take Amtrak or fly Northwest."

"No." He dug into his stubbornness.

"Grandpa, please," Rhiannon whimpered. "You don't have any hair anyway, so why not take your cancer medicine?"

Arne slapped the table. "Don't waste your tears."

Finally, a way he could help. Neil passed his paper napkin to his niece and rested his hand on her shoulder. He said to Arne, "I can fly you into Meigs." The small airport near downtown Chicago.

"Who do you fly for?"

"Legacy. DC-9 copilot. Thirty-five hundred hours total time."

The man stared at him. "Well, since I can't show my face at the Upjohn hangar since..." He made a jabbed a thumb in Maren's direction. "I'll think about it."

"I'll let Maren know my days off."

Maren cleared the table. Rhiannon and Neil joined her. Arne returned to the living room.

"Let's get out of here," Neil whispered.

"Uncle Neil, the dishes. Mom, bathroom. Me, laundry." Rhiannon pointed, then headed to the basement.

They hurried through chores, got in the car and drove away. At the first stoplight, Neil let out his breath. "I'm exhausted. How do you do this every week?"

"Thanks for driving us, Uncle Neil. It helps a lot."

In the rearview he saw Maren shake her head. "You could have bailed out. But instead you offered to fly him to Chicago. Glutton for punishment."

"I'm here to help." If she'd let him.

Chapter Six

"No begging," Neil told Tango as he took his sandwich to the couch. He propped his feet on the coffee table and opened the Cessna Cardinal owner's manual as the dog settled beside him.

Three bites and five pages in, something heavy thumped against the floor-to-ceiling window. Neil jumped, dropping the manual. His oldest nephew slid down the plate glass, face distorted by the impact, fingers squealing on the slick surface.

Pressing a fist to his pounding heart, Neil stomped across the living room to slide open the door. "Stick your tongue out, Andy. Clean the bird poop off."

"Gross." The kid sauntered in. "Scared you, didn't I? Should have seen the look on your face."

"Better than the look on yours. Window doesn't do anything for your complexion."

The dog hadn't eaten Neil's sandwich, but it vanished as soon as Andy sat down. Neil grabbed a couple New York Seltzers in black cherry flavor, a bag of Doritos, and a package of Oreos. After Alan's death, Andy had made regular appearances at Neil's, appetite in hand. The visits dwindled as grief eased. Neil couldn't remember their last "chew and stew."

"What? No beer?"

Catherine Richmond

"The FAA says eight hours bottle to throttle. Too much math on a day off." Neil returned to the couch. He'd been called out on a trip right after he'd told the family about Rhiannon, so the aftershocks would hit today. "What brings you to my neck of the woods?"

Sneakers jiggling the coffee table, his nephew snarfed a handful of chips and the whole bottle of soda. "Dad."

Buckle up and off we go. "If you promise to keep this between us, I'll answer your questions."

"Yeah. Promise. Creeps me out, so, for sure."

"Me, too."

They stared at the woods for a long time.

"Dad cheated on Mom." Andy swallowed. "I don't get it. Weren't they, like, totally in love? Is *her* mom a supermodel or something?"

"What happened had nothing to do with your mom and how much your dad loved her. It had nothing to do with what Rhiannon's mom looked like." What was the best way to explain this? Neil concentrated on twisting the Oreo apart. "Remember on Cody's birthday, when he got a remote-control car? You watched him run it around the driveway for a couple minutes, then grabbed the controls—"

"He was about to wreck it!"

"Exactly. Throughout the tour, my brother had been giving me a hard time about my lack of experience with girls. Then he saw me talking to Maren." The cookie broke into three pieces. "It was about power, being macho, showing me who gets the girls. It was about being high from the concert, the album going gold, booze, and illegal substances."

Andy's eyes narrowed. "Did she come onto him?"

"No. Absolutely not." Guilt crawled up his gut, turning the ham and cheese to acid. "Bottom line—when people get high, they do things they'd never do when they're in their right mind. He did a bad thing, but it doesn't mean he's a bad person."

Andy groaned and pressed his fists into his face. His breath quickened, then he whispered. "Dad raped her."

"Yes."

The boy exploded off the couch. Long legs propelled him up and over the coffee table. Dorito crumbs sprayed everywhere. He slammed the sliding glass door open, arms flinging. "Why?" He crossed the backyard, turning at the edge of the woods, his face distorted, and shouted. "I didn't want to know. Nobody wants to know. I hate you."

Neil followed the boy out to the patio, but realized he'd never catch him. "I love you," he yelled, his voice cracking on unshed tears.

Andy disappeared into the woods.

Neil went inside, closed the door, and called Patti's office. "You still have a counselor for the kids?"

"Dal-rae? Yeah, they've been seeing her since your rude awakening. Who are you worried about?"

"Andy." Neil gulped. "He asked about the after-party."

"He has an appointment in two hours. He's been seeing one of her partners."

"I'll drive him." If he could find him.

"Neil, where are you going with this?" Patti used his first name; she was furious.

"I don't know." *I didn't mean to hurt the kids.*

"When you figure it out, tell us, because we never asked for this." She hung up.

In the silence of his house, Andy's words echoed, *Nobody wants to know.*

Then Maren's voice, *He's been dead for years. No one cares.*

He plopped onto the couch with a crunch of crumbs. A real dog would have eaten the mess. A real dog would have wagged his tail and loved on him.

Neil leaned forward, head in hands. He'd prayed to find Maren, so God was on board with this...right?

Then he saw Rhiannon, her glow when he introduced himself, her boundless energy, the way she got a two-bit cello to sing.

Neil wasn't sure how to go forward, but he knew he couldn't go back.

. . .

MAREN SET her sewing machine on the kitchen table and started in on her mending pile: reattaching the pocket to her uniform smock, adding extra denim to the bottom of Rhi's jeans to compensate for her growth spurt, and closing a rip in her daughter's favorite sweater.

The phone rang. The clock said 6:50, so Mrs. Vanderhoef might need her TV adjusted or Mrs. Yang would tell her the girls had finished their homework. Instead it was Neil.

Maren updated him. "The strings teacher found a three-quarter cello and Maestro deems it acceptable. Rhi's working on a social studies project with the girls down the street. You can call back in forty-five minutes."

"It's good she has friends nearby." Another jab at her lack of a car. "Anyway. I'm calling to give you next month's schedule. Hope your dad can get an appointment."

Maren wrote down the dates and circled the one most convenient for Neil.

"Do you need anything from me? Logbook, references from coworkers, copies of drug tests?"

Except for barging into her life, he'd been well behaved. He drove safely. "No, I'll take the airline's word for it."

"I wanted to ask..." his words slowed, "Your dad mentioned Upjohn. Didn't you tell me you worked for them? One Uniform Papa."

Neil remembered their conversation at the after-party. Maren said, "Upjohn's flight department hires students from the university's aviation program for internships. Always male, of course. But Arne went to bat for me, telling them I had strong morals, and wouldn't lead the pilots and mechanics into temptation."

"It's hard for women to get hired in aviation, especially in corporate aviation."

"He took my pregnancy as a personal affront, as if I'd deliberately done it to shame him. He won't change his mind." Her family was beyond hope, but his... "How are things at home?"

"The fifteen-year-old is mad at me. I don't know about the rest. They're going to counseling."

Counseling? Should she be taking her daughter? "Rhi seems all right."

"If you want her to see a counselor, I'll pay for it. You don't have to find one who needs his lawn mowed."

He knew too much about her life.

Into her silence, he said, "Maren...did you get help...ten years ago?"

"Yes." The rape support group had been useless, since she didn't have flashbacks or a trial. When she quit school, that group had closed to her. Realizing she was pregnant eliminated the option of suicide and had given her a reason to live.

He cut into her thoughts again. "I'll pay if you need more counseling or anything."

"I'm fine."

"I wondered if her name is from the Fleetwood Mac song, after that remark Alan made about their rivalry during the concert."

"She's named after a Welsh queen."

"Good. The rivalry was a publicity stunt. They were friends."

Enough about Rhi's father. "I'm running up your phone bill."

"It's worth it."

No, it's stressful. "I'll see when Arne can get an appointment and call you back."

"If I'm not home, leave a message on the machine. Please."

They said goodbye and hung up. Maren glanced at the clock, grabbed her coat, and headed for the Yangs to pick up Rhi. Talking to Neil was like a minefield, never sure when he'd bring up his brother. He promised to help, but these past ten years had taught her how few people she could depend on.

"Hɪ, Tᴀɴɢᴏ," Neil said to his imaginary dog as he returned home from a trip. He dropped the mail on the entry table and the laundry into the washer. After changing into a sweatshirt and jeans, he popped open a can of Sprite and settled into his favorite reading chair. His schedule kept him from attending church and knowing the minister well enough to call, but the way Maren's father treated

61

her had to be wrong. He opened his study Bible and turned to the concordance.

This verse in 2 Corinthians seemed to apply—parents should save for their children. Maren's finances could use a boost. Disinheriting her seemed over-the-top harsh. And here in Ephesians—don't exasperate your children. Arne's behavior had to hurt. And 1 Thessalonians told fathers to encourage and comfort their children. Neil couldn't find anything close to "she made her bed and had to sleep in it." He closed the Bible with a groan. Beating Arne over the head with it might be fun, but not helpful to Maren. And not Christian.

The phone rang and Neil answered. Background noise of the children dropped as a door closed. "Cody's not feeling well. The rest have rehearsal. Sun-hwa and Jim went to English class." Patti sounded out of breath.

"How sick?"

"No fever, breathing normal, but didn't eat dinner. You're staying. I need to talk to the choir director about Melody's solo. It's out of her range and she's straining. He needs to change the key."

"Do I have time to tell you about Pavarotti serenading my passengers?"

"He has his own jet, *babo*." Patty called him *fool* in Korean, the first time he'd heard her affectionate nickname since Neil had told her about Maren and Rhiannon. "Cody's waiting for you." She hung up.

Neil pulled on a coat against November's chill. "C'mon, Tango," he called. He followed the path through the dark woods, his feet knowing which roots and rocks to avoid, as Tango rummaged through the underbrush. The path ended at the driveway of Wolfe's Den. As usual, the children had left all the lights on.

"Guard the house," Neil told Tango, then let himself in. "Cody?"

"Hey."

Neil found him in the TV room. He lay on the couch, watching video of one of his dad's concerts. No matter how hard Neil tried, the kids always felt Alan's loss. Cody wore the pajamas with airplanes Neil had given him last Christmas, ankles and wrists sticking out. A package of saltines and a glass of ginger ale sat untouched on the coffee table.

Neil joined him. The boy wiggled onto his lap. The hand-to-forehead felt normal, but Neil pulled an afghan over him anyway.

The video sputtered to an end and Cody shut it off. "I miss Dad, but I know a lot about him. Do you think Rhiannon misses him more or less, since she doesn't know anything about him? Maybe she'd like to see these videos. Do you know how to make a copy for her?"

Neil's heart hit a downdraft. He'd figured the kids had questions about their half-sister, but he hadn't guessed what Cody would ask. And with such understanding. Easy question first. "She doesn't have a VCR. Or a television."

"What?" After a pause, he rolled over to look at Neil. "Are they poor? We could send them the TV in the basement, nobody watches it, and buy them a VCR."

"Her mom won't let me rent her a cello or buy them a car."

Cody sat up, his curls taking on a life of their own. "No car? How do they get places? If you want to give me a car, I'll take a red Corvette."

"Not an option for a guy who plays string bass and euphonium." Neil finger-combed the mane. "I think her mom is worried there might be conditions. Like when you want to borrow Andy's bike and he makes you clean the bathroom for the rest of the month."

Dark brown eyes peered up. "Well, Mom never checks our bathroom."

"Gross and double gross. Speaking of which, did you barf?"

He shook his head. "Andy said the taco meat at lunch was roadkill."

"I warned you about things older brothers say." If Alan hadn't been a musician, he could have been a con man. "Are you hungry? Can I make you something?"

His mouth twitched. Probably calculating the odds of getting ice cream for dinner. "Let's call Rhiannon!"

Neil returned his smile. He wanted to talk to her too, and see how she would take to running with the Wolfe pack. "As long as you don't mention being poor. It might embarrass her."

Cody grabbed his ginger ale and gulped it down. "A good burp always impresses the girls!"

"Brotherly thing to do." The phone on the end table had a speaker. Patty had used it for the kids' calls to their dad when he was on the road. Neil punched in the number. What would he say if Maren answered?

"Hello." Rhiannon's voice echoed, telling him she'd figured out how to use the answering machine's speaker.

"Hi, Rhiannon, it's Uncle Neil—"

"And Cody! Hey it's me!"

"Wow." She paused. "It's great to hear your voice."

"You think my voice is great, try..." He let a big one rip.

"Oh yeah?" She played a *forte* dissonant chord on her C and G strings. "Take that!"

"Hang on, let me get my euphonium."

Neil caught Cody before he could get his instrument. "Not on long distance." Uh-oh. Patti would find this on her bill.

"You have a euphonium? Kids here don't start band until fifth grade."

"Got it this year. Dueling farts!"

This conversation had deteriorated rapidly. "Where's your mom, Rhiannon?"

"Upstairs, working on Mrs. Vanderhoef's snowblower."

"Is it snowing?" Cody bounced on the couch. "I love snow days!"

"No snow yet. They hardly ever cancel school here. We slog through it." Hearing Rhiannon's voice made Neil smile. She asked, "What are you doing, Cody? Where's your brother and sisters?"

"I have a belly ache, so I'm hanging with Uncle Neil. Everyone else has rehearsal."

"You're missing rehearsal?"

"It's okay. I have choir tomorrow, unless I eat cafeteria food again."

"Don't trust anything but the tater tots. What are you singing?"

"'Jingle Bell Rock,' 'Rockin' Around the Christmas Tree,' 'Rudolph.'"

"Sing it, Cody!" Rhiannon plucked the cello and the kids belted it out. With each song, they became more adventurous with their arrangements and giggled through their mistakes. Neil sang bass and added a jingle with his house keys.

"This is so fun!" Cody said when they finished. "I can't wait until we sing together!"

Rhiannon hesitated. "My mom is weirded out...about this whole thing."

"Yeah. Mine freaked at first, but she hasn't thrown anything this week."

"But she might throw the phone bill at me," Neil said.

Rhiannon played a phrase, then sang, "Goodnight, Cody, It's Time to Go," to the familiar tune. Neil sang the "do, do, do, do, dooo" bass line. How'd she pick up a 1950s rhythm-and-blues tune? Maybe Mr. Coffey had sung it to her. He guessed no one had taught her the verses.

They said their goodbyes and hung up. Neil made the parental suggestion of homework and practice, which Cody fended off with sudden onset of starvation. They headed to the kitchen to heat soup.

"You know, Uncle Neil," Cody said. "I think Rhiannon might be my favorite sister."

Neil gave his nephew a kiss on the head, but couldn't say anything over the lump in his throat.

THE PHONE RANG as Maren got ready for bed.

"Hey, girl, what's happening," Royetta said. "How's it going with Lucifer's brother?"

Early on, Maren and Royetta had created aliases for their attackers, a small way of taking back their power. "He's now known as Rhi's Uncle Neil." Maren stepped into the stairwell, in case Rhi was pretending to sleep. "He's visited a couple times. Offered to help take my dad to a doctor's appointment in Chicago."

"Cool. Sounds like you're making peace."

"Trying. How do you do it? The holidays are coming..."

"And Old Beelzebub always shows up. I stayed away a few

years, hid from him and everyone. Then Darius was born. I want my son to play with his cousins, to know his kin. So I wrote down what Beelzebub did, how it wrecked my life, what I thought of him. Called him every name in the book. Got it out of my head and onto paper."

"Sounds like journaling." Where could she stash a journal that Rhi wouldn't find it?

"More like spewing. I'm not gonna give Old Beelzebub space in my head, let him keep me down or put me in a victim box. Gotta live my life, not let him steal my joy."

"I'm no longer angry with Lucifer, but I'm furious with my dad."

"Oh girl. This is where Mrs. Coffey would have a good Bible verse for you. Here's what I say, and 'cause we lived together, I know you'll get this. Bad thoughts are like bugs. Set out traps, spray, clean up, swat 'em, step on 'em. Keep after 'em. Maybe you never get rid of all, sometimes one will surprise you, but you'll get rid of enough." She paused. "Uh-oh. Darius popped out of bed. Gotta go. Call me."

"Will do. Thanks, Royetta."

Maren stepped back into the apartment and put the phone away. So... instead of a "Neil repellent," she needed a bad-thought spray?

Chapter Seven

"Good morning, Uncle Neil!" Rhiannon climbed into the front seat of the rental. "Mom said it's a great day to fly. Clear and visibility unlimited."

Maren sat in back, holding a worn Marshall Field's tote on her lap. "What do you have for hearing protection?"

"Good morning to you, too." He turned with a smile, earning a twitch of her left eyebrow. "David Clark headsets all around."

She nodded. "What plane?"

"Cardinal RG. One of my captains hangars it here. Fifty hours out of annual."

"Good."

Rhiannon gave him a recap of her week on the way to Arne's, then moved to the back seat and quieted when they picked up her grandpa. They drove to the airport and parked at Kal-Aero. As Maren and Rhiannon used the restroom, Neil went to the counter to file a flight plan, and pay for the overnight and fuel.

Arne looked over his shoulder at the receipt. "You airline jocks have money to fling around."

That little girl on TV would say 'how rude,' but Neil didn't want to make life worse for Maren and Rhiannon, so he stifled. No wonder Maren didn't react to her father's insults.

Catherine Richmond

"You forgot my x-rays?" Arne said as they walked to the plane.

"No." Maren showed him the tote.

"You sit up front. Keep an eye on him." Arne climbed into the back, rolled up in a blanket and leaned against the window.

Maren narrated the preflight for Rhiannon. "Checking the oil, to make sure it's topped off and light brown. Engine looks good. Cowling fastened."

When he finished the walk around, Maren helped Rhiannon into the back and adjusted her earmuffs. By the time Neil buckled his seatbelt, Maren had her headset on and the Chicago sectional folded to their route. They completed the checklist, fired up, then taxied to the end of the runway.

"You've got the airplane." Neil took the map.

With a glance, then a smile, Maren completed the run-up as Neil worked the radios. With confident, effortless motions, she steered to the runway centerline, brought the power up, and eased the plane into the sky. She hit each heading and altitude on the nose, and kept them there. Better than some of the captains he flew with.

"Like riding a bicycle," Neil said. "How much Cardinal time do you have?"

"None. Mostly Cessna 150 and Piper Colt, some taildragger time. You'll have to land. I've heard these crow-hop."

He nodded. "It's touchy about ground effect."

Lake Michigan slid under their wings. To the south, the yellow-brown smoke of Gary, Indiana spewed into the clear blue morning. Chicago's skyline spiked the horizon. Jets lined up for O'Hare and Midway. Meigs information system reported crosswind gusts.

"I've got the aircraft," he said and Maren released the controls. "Let's hope I don't embarrass myself." He managed to fly it onto the runway, taxi, and park without ground looping.

Maren gave him a thumbs up.

Neil glanced back to see if Arne was still alive. The man pried his eyes open and gave Chicago a surprised look. He'd slept through the flight.

"Great job, Mom and Uncle Neil!" Rhiannon applauded.

68

Maren helped her father climb out, then Rhiannon walked him into the terminal.

"Thanks for doing this." Maren tied down and chocked the starboard side. "Wish I could cover the gas."

"You're welcome." Neil secured the port. "You're a good stick. If you want to fly again, I'll fund it."

She heaved a sigh. "If you had a child and no backup, would you have a flying job?"

Neil shook his head. "Best I can do is an imaginary dog."

Her face, which had been hard since he'd dropped in two months ago, softened with a trace of a smile. They walked into the terminal together.

Rhiannon stared at the city. "I always wanted to visit Chicago."

Her grandpa roused enough to complain. "Don't get too excited, kid. It's a dump."

Neil squeezed her hand. "It's the third largest city in the US, with three million people."

"Did Mrs. Leary's cow really burn it down?" Rhiannon asked, then burst into the song. She continued singing in the taxi and the driver joined her, then he belted out Frank Sinatra's "Chicago."

"Can't anyone be quiet?" Arne muttered, but the others ignored him.

The waiting room's blank walls and industrial carpet proclaimed "no money was spent here." They settled on plastic chairs, then after a few minutes, a woman in a white uniform called for Mr. Tollefson.

"I don't think this will take long," Maren told them, then followed her father.

Now what? What could he do to amuse Rhiannon? He should have brought Mad Libs, or at least a pad of paper to doodle on. The only magazines were ancient issues of *Field and Stream.* Thumb war? No, nothing that might damage her hands.

Before he could come up with a plan, Rhiannon grabbed a box of tissues from the receptionist's desk and sat beside a teary woman curled in the corner. They exchanged a few words, then a hug. Starting softly, Rhiannon launched into "Lean On Me," with all of

Bill Withers' expression and cadence, but an octave higher. The woman joined in on the chorus, and the man across from her sang backup and provided percussion with palms on his knees. Others sat up and joined in. By the time the song finished, everyone in the waiting room had relaxed and found a smile.

The medical assistant called for the woman. She thanked Rhiannon and hugged her again, then left. Neil expected his niece to return to the seat beside him, but the backup singer asked for "You've Got a Friend." Rhiannon harmonized on the chorus, then segued into "Precious Lord, Take My Hand." Then a woman in the other corner asked for "What a Friend We Have in Jesus." People raised hands and closed eyes. The receptionist rocked in her chair, hands over her heart.

Another patient entered, scanned the room, and her shoulders relaxed. "Lord knew I needed this." She sat and added her voice.

"Lord Almighty." The man beside Neil shook his head. "Never thought I'd see a girl that little sing like Aretha."

"Is that your daughter?" whispered the young woman on Neil's other side. "She looks familiar."

Neil shook his head, unable to speak over the lump in his throat. Rhiannon may have gotten Alan's looks, talent, and entertainment gene, but instead of using her skills to show off, she sang to comfort and encourage.

The door opened, and Arne and Maren emerged. Rhiannon stopped singing, then waved goodbye and they hurried out. A chorus of "bless you" and "thank you, dear girl" arose from the patients and families in the waiting room.

They rode the elevator in silence. Neil raised his eyebrows at Maren and she shook her head. Whatever happened wasn't good.

When they reached the street, Neil asked Arne, "Where would you like to eat lunch?"

Arne muttered about overpriced food poisoning, so Neil turned to Rhiannon. "Chicago is famous for hot dogs and pizza."

"Even I can make a hot dog, so I vote for pizza."

Fortunately there was a Giordano's around the corner.

While they waited for their order, Arne headed to the restroom.

Rhiannon grabbed her mother's hand. "What happened?"

"He refused treatment. He doesn't want to spend his remaining days feeling lousy, as if cancer doesn't do that. And, even though he has Medicare, he's sure medical bills will drain his bank account."

"He can't take money with him." Rhiannon propped her chin on her hand. "And Uncle Karl doesn't need it."

"So...hospice?" Neil asked.

Maren shook her head. "According to him, hospice is where they shove you in the corner and wait for you to die."

"When my grandma died, they kept her comfortable—"

Maren tapped her foot against his and nodded toward Arne shuffling from the Men's. "Sorry to waste your day."

"Good to know you've tried everything." Neil turned to Maren. "And it was worth it to get you flying."

"Go, Mom!"

Maren looked at her daughter and her mouth curved. She didn't smile at Neil, but he had a part in it, so he'd count it a win. Maren's smile was even bigger when she greased the landing in Kalamazoo.

They returned Arne to his house. He went inside, plodding as if heading to the electric chair. Neil glanced in the rearview mirror. "Rhiannon, want to sit up front?"

"She's asleep," her mother answered.

"Is she okay?"

"Tired. It was a short night."

"Excited about her first flight." Neil headed to Maren's. The neon lights along Westnedge Avenue reminded him of the hours since lunch. He joined a line of cars in a fast food drive-through lane. "What would you like?"

"I'm not hungry." Maren stared out the side window. She hunkered down in the corner, out of his reach, Rhi's head in her lap.

Who will take care of your dad and Rhi if you get sick? "I'd rather take you out for steak, but I don't want to wake Rhi."

"Hamburger."

He placed the order. A few dollars floated over the seat. When the food came, he stuffed her money into the bag.

Neil tried to fill the silence on the drive to Mrs. V's. "While you were with the doctor, Rhiannon sang to the waiting room. Not just entertaining them, but blessing them. She's got a great voice. How'd she learn so many songs?"

"Church."

"Does she sing to her grandpa?"

"When he lets her."

Neil heard the weariness in Maren's voice and quieted until they pulled into the driveway.

"Rhi, wake up. We're home."

"I'll carry her, if you bring in the food." Neil lifted his niece. She stirred and put an arm around his neck. So trusting.

Maren led them to a bedroom and turned down the comforter so Neil could set Rhi in bed. The girl sighed and curled away from the hall light. He bent to untie her sneakers, bumping into her doll-house. A family of paper dolls spilled onto the floor. Neil gathered up a mostly-white dog, a girl with dark curly hair, and a round headed boy, and set them in the box with large alphabet blocks. Strange furniture. Wait a minute. He'd seen this before. It's the set for *You're a Good Man, Charlie Brown*. The next box was the Captain's house from *The Sound of Music*. Then the tea party scene from *Alice in Wonderland*. "Amazing. Where did you get these?"

"Shh." Maren tucked the covers around her daughter and brushed a kiss onto her forehead. She left the door open an inch. "We made them."

Neil circled the main room, past a Pullman kitchen with metal cabinets, a board and brick bookcase topped with a stereo and classical records, a worn loveseat, and a steamer trunk. It reminded him of his student apartment, except Maren's was clean. He picked up the only photo on display. Maren held a bundle in a pink blanket. A Black couple stood behind her, each with a hand on Maren's shoulder. He recognized the man from A&P, store manager Mr. Coffey. The woman next to him, must be his wife Mrs. Coffey, who'd saved Maren and Rhiannon from the Christmas tree lot. He put the photo back. "They're good people."

"Yes."

The nippy air had followed them inside. "It's chilly in here. Where's your thermostat?"

"Upstairs." Maren shrugged. "The furnace doesn't run much on sunny days."

"You don't have any control over the temperature?"

"Rhi's used to it—she's warm-blooded." Shoulders hunched and hands stuffed in her pockets, Maren left the room. "I'll set up the portable heater."

Wishing he'd bought hot chocolates instead of shakes, Neil unpacked their food. He slipped her money under the microwave, where she'd find it soon, but not before he left.

Now, which one of these chairs howls? He eased into the seat, its blood-curdling screech telling him he'd chosen the wrong one. "Hollywood could use this to make soundtracks for horror movies."

"It's safe." Maren plugged in the heater.

Okay, Maren wasn't in the mood for his jokes. He opened his hamburger. The fast food joint had skimped on mustard. He should give up on condiments, as many shirts and ties as he'd ruined. Leaning, he opened the refrigerator and pulled out the mustard. Store brand. Good. That brown stuff, honey mixtures, and deli brands with chunks of onions seemed un-American. Mustard ought to be glow-in-the-dark yellow and smooth. Maren watched him with one eyebrow raised. Oh. This wasn't his house. It wasn't his sister-in-law's house, either. He should have asked. "Sorry. Uh, mustard?"

"Pardon me for being out of Grey Poupon." Maren took the bottle and added a neat circle to the underside of her bun, keeping it from dripping. Smart.

"Maren, I am sorry. Technically, legally, we're not family, but my heart says otherwise. I don't mean to be disrespectful." Their history meant they weren't strangers, but she wouldn't call him a friend. Where did that leave them?

She dipped her French fry in catsup. "I'd like to send the Cardinal owner a thank you note for use of his plane today."

Neil pulled his notebook from his coat pocket and wrote out the name and address.

She looked at the paper. "Frizzell? Any relation to Lefty?"

"Distant cousin. Country music reached this far north?"

"Some nights we can tune in the Grand Ole Opry."

He put his hand over hers. Even without touching the milkshake, she'd turned to ice. "I'm sorry about your dad. Is there anything I can—"

"No!" She jerked away and took a shaky breath. Looking at the floor, she said, "You got him his second opinion. It's more than enough."

"If there's anything else..."

Elegant fingers pressed her forehead. Maren swayed in her seat and her bottom lip trembled "For you to go."

Neil crumpled the wrappers into the wastebasket, and left.

Chapter Eight

"Aha! Here's where all the pens and paper are hiding!"

"Not *all*, Uncle Neil." Harmony sat cross-legged on her bedroom floor, surrounded by markers and poster board. The air smelled like fake fruit. "Melody has most of the art supplies in her room."

He hurdled mounds of clothes and books to sit on her bed. "School project?"

She pushed her fluffy black bangs off her face. "Carly's birthday."

The sock monkey her father had given her for her second birthday still had a place of honor on her bed. "Can you find your homework?"

"Homework? Who cares?" She cared enough to make honor roll, but didn't want her diligence to be common knowledge. "So what brings you to my humble abode, dear uncle?"

"Rhiannon has a birthday coming up. I got her a Bedazzler, but it didn't seem like enough. I want this birthday to be really special. Any ideas?"

"Your alleged long-lost niece. A paternity test." She snapped the cap on the marker.

Neil rested his hand on her shoulder. "Hey, we're trying to keep it friendly."

"And avoid legal bills. I get it." She looked up at him, leaning her cheek on his fingers. "Birthday for a ten year old. What does she like? What does she have?"

"Not much." Especially compared with these kids. Sweaters and shirts spilled from Harmony's drawers, dresses slithered out of the closet, a box of hairspray and lotions teetered on the desk chair.

"Michigan is probably behind in fashion. Hey! What size does she wear?" Harmony rushed to the closet, tromping on a Monopoly board and a set of rubber stamps. If she stepped on a stamp pad and tracked ink on the carpet... What color was the carpet in here anyway?

"She's smaller than you. A little taller than Cody." Neil held his hand a few inches above his waist.

"Good thing Mom hasn't taken these to Salvation Army yet." Harmony emptied a Giant Foods sack onto the floor. Whoa, messier every minute. "Her hair is blonde. What color are her eyes?"

"Blue-green, like your dad's." Did she remember him? She'd only been two when he died.

"So, she's probably a Spring. This'll work." A turquoise sweater returned to the bag.

"Spring? She was born in November."

Harmony gave him her "poor old uncle" face. "I'm talking about her coloring, what colors she looks best in. I'm a Winter, so dark, muted shades for me, but they won't work for her."

"You're too young to wear black."

"Uncle Neil." Drawing out each syllable of his name, she folded a pair of striped and riveted jeans into the bag.

"Maybe Kalamazoo isn't ready for all this style."

"Get real. Does she have any collections?" Harmony waved at the dolls lined up on her hutch. "Sports or hobbies?"

Neil frowned, remembering Rhiannon's neat, almost bare room. "She plays cello."

"Sheet music? Not much of a gift. What did I get on my tenth?

A Walkman! And you could get her some tapes? Who does she like —Hanson, Celine Dion, Backstreet Boys?"

"I don't think her mom lets her listen to rock."

"Wow. If she's strict, she probably wouldn't like you buying her a TV either." Purple glitter nails tapped the portable set on her dresser. "Hey, speaking of TV, did you know they're having a blizzard in Michigan? I saw it on the Weather Channel. Bet Rhiannon gets a snow day, lucky dog." She handed him the bag.

"Thanks for everything." There was only so long a man can be knee-deep in twelve-year-old girl dross. Neil took the bag of clothes and began the journey back into the hall. If he left now, he could catch the national news and call Rhiannon. Hope they're okay. Neil was used to having his family where he could keep an eye on them. This long-distance uncle-ing cramped his style.

As he bounded down the stairs, Harmony yelled, "When you call to see if they're all right, ask her what's on her birthday list."

"Good idea!" Neil hurried home and turned on the TV. Pictures of snow-choked interstates and closed airports flashed on the screen. He reached for the phone.

Rhi answered on the first ring. "Hello?"

"How's my favorite cellist?"

"Uncle Neil! We got out of school early today and don't have to go tomorrow!"

"How much snow do you have?" Oops. She couldn't see out of the basement windows.

"Lots. It was almost over my boots when I got home."

"What are you and your mom doing tomorrow on your snow day?"

"Mom doesn't get a snow day, silly! Grocery stores are always open. Mr. Coffey will pick us up in his Jeep and I'll go to work with Mom."

"Don't they have child labor laws in Michigan?"

"The government has a snow day, too," she giggled. "We'll probably decorate the break room and play cards. Fun stuff."

"The boss lets your mom play cards at work?"

"Not Mom, my friend Janae. Her mom's a cashier."

"Sounds like you've done this before."

"Every snow day."

"I'd better let you get some sleep."

"I'm waiting for Mom." A note of worry crept into her voice. "She went out to shovel."

"Isn't it cold there?"

"Yeah, and she's been gone a long time. Mrs. V's snow blower is broken. Mom tried to fix it, got books from the library and took it apart twice, but it still won't run. So, she has to shovel. I tried to help, but the snow's really heavy and my toes started to hurt. They're okay now, but Mom said I couldn't go out again."

"How many driveways does she have to shovel?"

"Only Mrs. V's. Everything's canceled, so most people are waiting until it stops."

"Hey—almost forgot—you have a birthday coming up. What's on your birthday list?"

"A snow blower. Just kidding. Too expensive."

"Great idea. Get out your phone book. Who sells those in Kalamazoo? Do you have Sears?"

She read him the number.

"Now, how are we going to get this snow blower to your house?"

"The city buses are canceled, too." Phone book pages flipped. "How about a delivery service?"

"Rhiannon the Resourceful. Great idea." He took down the numbers. "Don't say anything to your mom until I know if this'll work."

"She'll be so surprised! Oh, don't forget gas. And oil if you get a two-stroke engine."

"Gas and oil," he noted, embarrassed to admit he knew nothing about snow blowers and their engines. "And Rhiannon, I will get you something for your birthday."

"Ugh," Maren grunted with each throw of the shovel. It wasn't a feminine noise, not a polite sound, but she was too tired to care. After a busy day at the grocery, a slog home from the bus stop through knee-deep drifts, and shoveling the world's longest drive-way, she was entitled to grunt. At the end of a row, she stopped to blow her nose. Cold-stiffened fingers fumbled the tissue. Gusts blew snow across the streetlight, painting the landscape with purple shadows and silver glitter. It would be beautiful if she weren't so tired.

"Maren? Maren, come here, please!" Mrs. V called from the front porch.

Pushing against exhaustion, Maren hurried up the driveway. Surely Mrs. V will tell her to stop. The radio said all activities were canceled; the old lady was sensible enough to stay in. "Yes, ma'am?"

"Myron's coming over, so the whole driveway needs to be cleared."

"The police are asking everyone to stay off the roads." Including the sainted Myron.

"Well, just the sidewalks then. Don't want anyone to fall." Mrs. V closed the door.

Maren trudged back to the end of the driveway and shoveled in time to the argument in her head. Anyone foolish enough to walk in this mess deserved to fall. It was snowing so hard, shoveling was futile.

The shovel weighed more than ever. Pain burned between her shoulder blades and spasmed down her arms. Each breath scraped raw. Push, lift, throw. Push, lift, throw. What was Rhiannon doing now? Maren hoped her daughter had gone to bed. Five a.m. came too early. No, make that 4:30; as hard as it was snowing, the driveway would have to be redone.

Most of the time Maren didn't mind being single, no one to answer to, no one to question her decisions. But it also meant no one to share the burden. The endless round of waiting on customers, housework, and raising a daughter weighed on her. A little TLC would be welcome...as welcome as a hot bath... impossible since their basement apartment had only a tiny metal shower stall.

An old pickup bounced around the corner and churned toward her. Who'd be out on a night like this? If he had any sense, he'd put a blade on the front and make some real money. The truck lurched to a stop at the end of the driveway. "Darrels Deliverys" read the hand-painted sign on its door.

"Hey, you Karen Tow-left-son?" The driver cranked down the window and yelled around the cigar stub cornered in his lips. He jumped out and pushed a clipboard at her. "Sign here. And write down the time. Your boyfriend said he'd throw in a bonus if I delivered before eight."

"I don't have a boyfriend." A stray snowflake melted on the paper, over the penciled block letters "Neal Woof."

The man lowered the truck's gate. "Honey, you got a driveway. So don't be telling him he ain't your boyfriend. Not 'til spring at least." He swung a shiny green snow blower to the ground. "Hey, this is more lovey-dovey than buncha roses that die in a week. Take her for a spin. It's topped off and ready to blow."

The engine roared with a single pull. The machine cut a clear path, pivoted with a twist of her wrist, and zoomed back across the driveway, snow arcing out the discharge chute. Maren cut the power. "It's great, but I can't accept it."

"Got to. Store don't take returns on used stuff." The delivery man grinned around his cigar. "Gotcha gas, oil, and paperwork—warnings for dum-wits with lawyers. Sign off, so I can get home. Wife's burning dinner."

Darrels Deliverys rumbled off into the snowy night. Maren restarted the machine to finish the job. Somehow she would pay Neil back. If she cleared driveways at, say $20 each, she ought to have the debt worked off about the time Rhi graduated from college.

The snow removal business would have to wait. Tired arms stowed the machine and its fuel in the garage. Heavy legs plodded down to the apartment.

Rhi looked up from the phone. "Here's Mom. Did you get your surprise?"

Maren pried off her boots. "You should be in bed."

"I'm keeping Uncle Neil company. Don't worry; it's his nickel." The girl stage whispered, "Gotta go. She's giving me the look. Love you, too."

With a kiss on Rhi's head, Maren took the phone. "Neil."

"Is the weather as bad as they say on the news?" he asked, his voice deep with concern.

"Thank you for the snow blower. I'll pay you back." Fatigue had her swaying on her feet.

"Get some soup or cocoa to warm you up. Wish you could stay home. I'll call tomorrow."

Maren hung up. Soup and cocoa would be wonderful. Coat still on, she flopped over on the loveseat and curled up. The Beatles got by with help from friends...could Neil be her friend?

RHIANNON STOMPED in and out of the circles cast by the parking lot lights, blazing a path through two-foot deep drifts. "I'm writing out 'A&P'," she yelled, "'cause the sign's covered over."

"Where's my man and his plow?" The store manager frowned at the unbroken expanse.

"Probably can't get out of his driveway." Maren followed her boss inside, stepping in his footprints. She shifted the backpack, books and crafts for Rhi, trying to find a comfortable position in the hot soreness of her shoulders, her reward for shoveling then falling asleep on the loveseat. "C'mon, Rhi. It's too cold to stay out."

Mr. Coffey paused inside. "Should've had you bring your new toy, clear the lot."

"I'm being bought."

"No, child." He unwound the gold and brown scarf she'd knitted him nine years ago. "You're finally getting your due."

Two BLOCKS from the turn for Maren's house, Neil spotted the birthday girl. Rhiannon balanced on a snow pile and swung from a Kalamazoo Metro Transit sign. Sunset lit her golden braids against her purple-and-pink snowmobile suit. Maren stood behind her, hunched against the cold. He honked and turned onto the side street.

"Uncle Neil!" Opening the car door, his niece bounced onto the front seat. "Good thing you got here now. If the bus had been early, you would have missed us."

"Did you tell us you were coming?" Maren climbed in back.

"Sorry, I didn't, no time between flights. It's not cello lesson day. Where are you ladies off to?"

"The hospital." Rhiannon's mittens flapped as she gave directions. "Grandpa's sick."

Neil looked over his shoulder, checking traffic and his backseat passenger. Maren stared out the window and shivered. He clicked the heater up a notch. "Wasn't Arne on a trip?" Although spending time with Helga wasn't what he'd call a vacation.

"They airlifted him off the cruise ship," Maren murmured. "The hospital in Miami patched him up and sent him home. But he took another turn for the worse late last night."

The truck ahead bumped through a pothole, coating the windshield with saltwater slush. Neil fumbled for the wiper switch.

"You can drop us in the next block, by the transfer station," Maren said.

As they approached, a fight erupted in the bus shelter. A skinny guy bolted, dashing across traffic. Neil slammed on the brakes and narrowly missed him. Two women who'd been walking to the shelter did a one-eighty and hurried away. The men on the curb yelled obscenities.

Between the weather and the gang war, no way would he let Maren and Rhiannon out here. "Too cold."

"We're polar bears, Uncle Neil. We're used to it." The girl's stories of snow castles, sled runs, and snowball fights took them across town.

"Forecast says you'll be down to zero Monday." He glanced in the back seat. Maren hadn't thawed. "Where's your other coat, Maren?"

"It got stolen from work," Rhiannon answered.

"You don't have a locker?'

"I keep my coat in the bakery, for when the back door is open for deliveries." As he turned into the crowded parking lot behind the hospital, she said. "Drop us off."

And leave them to change buses in the war zone? Not happening. "Won't get rid of me so easily." Neil parked.

"Hanging around a hospital can't be your idea of fun."

"No, but hanging around Rhiannon is." He glanced at his niece as he said the words he knew would perk her up. "I brought your birthday gifts."

"Radical!"

Neil grabbed a tote from the trunk, then Maren led them into the red brick building. No wonder she was cold. Wind flapped the thin tweed jacket. Patches showed on one shoulder seam and under the pockets. She needed something longer, bulkier. Maybe coveralls like her daughter's.

They rode the elevator to the third floor. Maren entered her father's room. To Neil's untrained eye, Arne looked worse. He struggled to inhale through blue lips. Helga stared at the television. The roommate frantically pushed the call button and yelled, "Need help in here!"

Neil steered his niece into the adjacent waiting room. "Let your mom go in first."

Helga's whine carried down the hall. "They called the doctor."

Maren ran to the nurses' station. "Mr. Tollefson in 342 can't breathe."

Braid swinging, Maren dashed back into her father's room.

"Put down that phone!" Helga screeched. "You're upsetting your father!"

The intercom paged Dr. Gibson to room 342, stat.

Rhiannon loaded a CD into the player, put the headphones on, and listened to music, blocking out the racket from Arne's room. She raved over the Bedazzler and, unlike Alan, read the instructions.

Neil looked through the *Kalamazoo Gazette* for car ads. None today. Maybe they run them on weekends.

A tall woman in a white coat raced into 342. Nurses hurried after her.

"But he sees Dr. Helwig!" Helga protested, only to receive her eviction notice. She shambled into the waiting room and oozed to the TV.

Rhiannon grabbed an issue of *National Wildlife* and blocked their view. "Look at these termites in Australia."

Neil hid behind the magazine. "Ah, yes, bugs as long as a man's hand. Pleasant sight. Thank you."

The doctor emerged from Arne's room, her arm around Maren's shoulders. Rhiannon pulled off her headphones and ran to them. "Dr. Gibson!"

The woman returned the girl's embrace. "Your grandpa wants to see you, but he's mighty sick. Give those hands a good scrubbing before you touch him."

"Yes, ma'am!" Rhiannon skipped into the room.

With a hug for Maren, the doctor left.

Neil caught Maren in the hall. "What's happening?"

"He was having trouble breathing and his doctor wasn't calling back. So I called my doctor and she put him on oxygen." Her trembling hand brushed perspiration from her brow. "He's better, but I probably made the nurse's list."

"You did the right thing."

She sighed and returned to her father.

From the hall, Arne's face had returned to its normal color, his shoulders relaxed. In the waiting room, Helga found a talk show about policemen who moonlight as strippers. Neil leaned on the wall outside 342 and prayed for Mr. Tollefson.

MAREN CLIMBED into Neil's rental after leaving the hospital. Automobiles have advantages. No icy waits for buses. No passengers who conversed only in curse words. No dragging Rhi back to Mrs. V's in the dark an hour after bedtime. But instead of heading straight home from the hospital, Neil turned south.

Maren leaned over the seat and interrupted Rhi's plans for the Bedazzler. "Where are you going?"

"Well, since car dealerships are closed this time of night, I'm taking you to Sears, to shop for a new coat. Unless you'd prefer a different store."

"No coat. I haven't paid you for the snow blower."

"Winter hasn't started and your jacket won't keep you from hypothermia or pneumonia."

"Cold weather doesn't cause illness."

"JCPenney's is on the way," Rhi gave directions and the golden boy snagged the closest parking spot. Sales clerks fell over each other to wait on him.

"I'd like to see the warmest women's coat you have," Neil said, "with snow pants, please."

"Which one is least expensive?" Maren asked, but they ignored her.

Recognizing a cash cow when she saw one, the clerk steered them to splashy jackets with matching bib overalls. As Rhi searched through the ski clothes, Maren found a cheap jacket on a nearby rack. "I don't need anything fancy. This is fine."

Neil shook his head. "Not black. Drivers can't see you at night."

"Look, Mom!" She held up a set in purple with colorblocks of magenta, and turquoise. "We'll go together and it's in your size!"

"Adorable," the clerk gushed. "How about boots, hat, ski gloves, scarf? Après-ski wear?"

"No, thank you."

"Need anything else, since you're here?" Neil asked.

Maren glared at him. "No, thank you."

The clerk rang up the sale and cut off the tags, then Maren slipped into the warmest coat she'd had since her freshman year of college. She gave herself a mental kick in the pants. Time to stop being resentful of the gifts he'd bought her daughter and embarrassed about her lack of money, and be grateful. She took a deep breath and faced Neil. "Thank you. It's a wonderful gift."

Neil took them to a nearby diner the clerk recommended.

After the waitress took their order, Rhi went to the bakery display to pick out a birthday cake.

"Thanks for the ride and the coat," Maren said.

Neil whispered, "You and Rhi could have been in the middle of that fight. You need a car."

"We've never had any trouble. Kalamazoo doesn't have a crime problem."

"Looked like gang colors to me."

"They fight with each other."

"What if they decided to rob you?"

"All they'd get is my bus pass."

Neil reached for her hand. Her narrowed gaze stopped him, so he patted the table. "Your very pretty little girl will soon be—"

"Enough." Maren jerked up her hand, palm out, barely keeping herself from slapping him. Rhi's safety had been her biggest worry and most constant prayer since the health center nurse had confirmed her pregnancy. "I know. *I know.*" Through clenched teeth, she said, "Okay. The least expensive clunker you can fit a cello into."

"Any preferences on brand, color, model..."

"None. I can drive stick shift."

Neil removed a wad of cash from his wallet and pushed it into her hand. "I don't know when I'll have time to car shop. Until then, promise you'll take a taxi for hospital trips."

"Only to keep you from freaking out." Maren glanced at Neil. "Although we do have a perfectly lovely asylum here in town. I'm sure they can find a padded cell for you."

He leaned back. "I saw it when I drove in. So, what diagnosis would you have me committed under?"

As Rhi spotted the waitress coming with their food and returned to the table, Maren pretended to consider the matter. "I'd say wackadoodle uncle with white-knight syndrome."

His grin had her foolish heart doing Snoopy's happy dance.

Chapter Nine

Neil emerged from the woods and scanned the driveway of Wolfe's Den. Grateful Dead Dancing Bears trucked across the back window of a Volvo, the Mercedes smelled like French fries because it ran on recycled cooking oil, and a new VW Vanagon sported a Greenpeace bumper sticker. The old hippies had returned for Thanksgiving. They'd been Alan's band members, roadies, managers. The activism from Earth Day had become a job with the Environmental Protection Agency, picking up litter on the Appalachian Trail, and buying low V.O.C. paint. In lieu of protest marches, they wrote letters to the editor, voted, and sometimes changed out of jeans to harangue the school board. The salt in the nation's wound had become the salt of the earth.

Unless...had one of their people drugged Maren? Neil shuddered. Better to think that criminal was long gone.

"Hey, little brother, get your keyboard," Alan's rhythm guitarist called from one end of the porch, where he was playing his part from Alan's "Night for the Wolf."

"Gotta eat first."

The other end of the porch held a cluster of people debating the impact of wearing rayon, none of whom had been on the *Banned in*

Nashville tour. Before they could remember Neil flew noisy, fossil-fuel-sucking jets, he escaped into the kitchen.

"Jim!" Neil greeted the male half of Patti's staff as he cleaned a turkey carcass. "Take a power saw to the bird and get back to the football game."

"Hey, you hack your meat. I do it right." He nodded toward a clean plate. "Grab some quick, before Andy gets it."

"Okay." Neil sniffed the spicy air. "Sun-hwa made my favorite tofu stew."

"Done soon." Sun-hwa stirred the pot on the stove. "I'll bring you a bowl."

Harmony emerged from the pantry with a pumpkin-walnut pie from Safeway, deftly separated it from its foil pan, and slid it into a ceramic one. "Snag some pie while you're at it."

"Happy Thanksgiving!" Neil hugged her. "Are you the only one helping?"

She tossed her dark-brown curls. "The boys are downstairs. Can't you hear the pool table? Melody went to her boyfriend's."

"Bet your mom's in a funk."

"Yeah, and when she thought you might not show. How was..." She caught herself before saying *Rhiannon* and lowered her voice. "...your friend's birthday?"

"Good. I was told to keep it low-key. She's crazy about the Bedazzler, jazzed up her headband. I gave her Pablo Casals and Jacqueline Du Pré CDs, then realized she doesn't have a CD player."

"So, instead of exchanging them for tapes, you bought her a CD player," Patti guessed as she sailed into the kitchen, elegant in a burnt-orange silk tunic and slacks, and set a platter with a picked-clean ham bone next to the sink.

"Got it in one." He hugged her. "I wouldn't miss Thanksgiving at your house."

Pain sparked behind her mask of dignity. "Everything ok?"

"Her grandfather's out of the hospital. For now, at least."

"Come on, then. Sol's been asking for you."

"Why?" Neil whispered. "What does he know?"

She shook her head.

Jim handed Neil the platter of sliced turkey and he carried it to the dining room. A sit-down dinner, family only, would be Neil's preference, but the buffet accommodated the schedules of Patti's guests. He set the platter next to the cornucopia centerpiece he'd ordered from the florist, then stocked his plate and carried it to the couch near Alan's publicist. "Hey."

Sol greeted him with a flash of his half-glasses. "Hey, little brother. Working on a new concept, sure-fire hit, *The Partridge Family* meets *Fame*." He nodded toward Harmony who sliced pies. "We'll follow the kids around school as they hone their chops, form a band, hit the big time. MTV is chomping at the bit. It'll be great."

It'll be a disaster. These kids would be picked on by jealous classmates. And reminders of young Alan would spotlight Rhiannon. "You're telling me because—"

"Because I said no." Patti sat beside him, her slice of pear pie tempting him with the aroma of ginger, cinnamon, and nutmeg.

Neil nodded, glad he and his sister-in-law agreed. "They don't need cameras shoved in their faces as they explore, try to find their instrument, refine their style."

His clawed hands circled in sync with his words. "People want to see Alan's kids growing up. They adore these kids. It's an opportunity—"

"No." Patti and Neil said in unison.

"School won't let you film. It's in the contract with the parents." Harmony handed Sol a piece of pumpkin pie. At the kitchen door, she paused, hand on her hip, and said over her shoulder, "Give me six years, then we'll talk."

Sol looked from her to his pie, one corner of his mouth lifted. "The sweetest 'don't call me, I'll call you' I've ever gotten."

MAREN FROWNED AT HER CHECKBOOK. Endless days of packing turkey-and-trimmings dinners had fried her brain. None of the numbers looked right. The bank statement wavered under the glare of the overhead light bulb. This wasn't her account. It wasn't even her bank. Couldn't be. Not with Christmas—

The apartment door banged open. Rhiannon scuttled to her room, head down, silent. Maren started after her, but a beefy hand grabbed her elbow. Her brother slammed the door.

"Cancer!" Karl shook her. "When were you going to tell me—when it was time to bury the old man?"

Maren checked her watch. 7:40. Mrs. V hadn't taken out her hearing aids yet. "Keep your voice down." She motioned for him to sit on the couch.

He scowled at her furniture. The closest Karl ever came to a thrift store was his wife's donations of last year's fashions. "I wouldn't touch that ugly thing with ten gallons of disinfectant. Probably full of lice, maggots."

"We have to eat something." She gave him her sweetest smile.

He waved her away. "You used to have class." He stomped around, dismissed her chairs as too rickety for his bulk, then stood like a gunfighter next to the dryer. "When did Dad tell you?"

Maren leaned against the kitchen sink. "October. He said he'd call you."

"October? I was in the middle of the Shinjuku-Quivera merger. I couldn't be disturbed." His lower lip drooped. "I'll get him into Cleveland Clinic Monday."

"He refused treatment and now it's too advanced. All they can do is keep him comfortable."

Karl's shock lasted only a second. "Doctors can't do anything, but you can bet they won't forget to send a bill." He slapped the dryer, his heavy fraternity ring clanging. "And why did you let that woman move in? What if Dad's written her into his will? I'm taking mother's silver back with me, keep that woman's greedy little claws off it."

As if Maren had any say in what their father did. "He decides who lives in his house and who to leave his money to. He can spend it all. He's an adult and *compos mentis*."

Karl flinched, still irritable about his failure to pass the bar. "Speaking of money, what's this about a rich uncle?"

"Rhiannon's uncle visited." Maren wished she could have kept that piece of information from him. Karl would make the worst of it. He always did.

"You're settling for a few puny gifts instead of child support? Your little braggart says he coughed up a CD player."

Maren wouldn't let that one pass. "As if your kids don't flaunt their color TVs, backyard pools, and trips to Disney World."

"I only want the best for my kids." He crossed his arms, pushing his belly further out.

"And I only want the best for mine, so you're leaving." She pointed to the door.

He had to have the last word. "There was nothing to eat in the house. Doreen was lucky to find an open grocery store. She didn't see you there. You told everyone you were working, but you're out trying to catch another sugar daddy."

"There's more than one grocery in town," Maren said to the slamming door. The exterior door banged hard enough to vibrate through the house. Mrs. V would feel it even if she had her aids out.

Maren pressed her fingertips to her forehead, silently calling her brother every name she could think of. Enough already. Rhiannon needed some mothering. Who knows what trash Karl had thrown at her. Maren peeked into the bedroom. "Rhi? Are you ok?"

Rhiannon pulled off her new headphones. Her eyes were dry, but her voice quavered. "Mom, I like Uncle Neil better."

She sank to the bed and wrapped her arms around her daughter. "Me too."

Chapter Ten

"Hurry, Mom! He'll be here any minute!" Rhi fidgeted on the toilet seat lid as Maren tried to put the girl's hair up in hot rollers. "What am I wearing?"

"Your red corduroy jumper and white turtleneck, and the headband you Bedazzled." Summer's tour of garage sales and thrift stores hadn't yielded a good holiday dress. Rhi would have to go in her Sunday best.

The door rattled with a shave-and-a-haircut knock.

"Oh, my gosh. He's here," Rhi squealed. "Quick, Mom, take these curlers out!"

This is what life would be like when her daughter hit her teens. "Chill." She hurried through the living room. Forcing a smile, she opened the door.

The living room light reflected on the gold braid of Neil's uniform. "Sorry I'm late. We had a mechanical."

She bent to move her daughter's snow boots out of the way, so he wouldn't see admiration and jealousy jockeying for expression. "It's ok. I'm still working on Rhi's hair."

"Don't come in the bathroom," the girl called.

"Why not?" Neil followed the voice. "Ack! A monster from the beauty shop lagoon! No, it's only my niece."

Rhi blushed and held her hands over the still-hot rollers.

He handed her a white bag with *Lord & Taylor* scrawled across it in red. "In honor of your first concert."

Rhi peeked into the shopping bag. "Thank you! Quick, Mom, help me get these curlers out!"

"I'd better change, so they don't think you brought a bus driver to school." He backed out of the room.

"No chance," Rhi told him. "We know a lot of bus drivers and you're much too snazzy."

He should stay in his uniform. An airline-pilot uncle outranked a grocery-clerk mom.

Rhi dressed, then Maren pulled her hair up with the matching scrunchie. Rhi oohed and aahed over the gorgeous ensemble, less young girl's section of the thrift store, more teen sophisticate. From the quality of the fabric, Maren guessed it cost more than her week's pay. No sense protesting; Neil had decided to help them and Rhi deserved a splurge.

"Where's your cello?" Neil asked as they suited up for winter and hurried into the snowy night.

"School," Rhi told him. "Temperature swings wreck the tuning."

"What's this?" Maren stopped in the driveway. Where Neil usually parked his rental sat a late-seventies Oldsmobile Cutlass, medium brown, pitted with small dents.

"Take it for a spin. Well, hopefully not much spinning." The driver's door squeaked when Neil opened it. He handed her the key and she climbed in. "Although we'll need to see if the cello fits."

"It will." Rhiannon climbed in back. "I like it. It looks like a leopard."

"Hail damage." Neil took the copilot's seat.

Maren backed the car into the street, then headed to school. It drove well, unfazed by the ice and snow coating the roads. "I thought you didn't have time to car shop."

"I called Captain Frizzell, who loaned us the Cardinal, about car dealers." Neil adjusted the windshield defroster. "His daughter had graduated, moved on to a newer car, and he hadn't gotten around to selling this one. Comes with the manual, snow brush, shovel, case of oil. Add a can with every fill-up." Maren joined the line of minivans entering the parking lot. "Maybe I should look for a minivan."

"Or maybe not." Maren maneuvered the Cutlass into a parking space several minivans had passed. In her heart, a dissonant chord resolved into harmony. A car opened up so many possibilities.

"Next time bring your plane." Rhi joked as she took an adult in each hand and led them in. She flitted around the classroom full of students and parents, slipping out of her snow suit to show off her outfit and introducing Neil, who had exchanged his uniform jacket for a forest green merino sweater, muting snazzy into handsome.

"Hey, aren't you Alan Wolfe's brother, the keyboard player for Predator?" The second chair violist's mom recognized him. "I saw you in concert at Wings Stadium. Must have been ten years ago."

On the night my life turned to ashes. Maren shrank against the wall. She'd told Neil no one cared about Alan, but any second now Kelly Huizinga would put two and two together, and Rhi's paternity would be all over Kalamazoo.

Kelly looked from him to Rhi. "I thought Rhiannon looked like—"

"Whose pick?" Neil leaned over Kelly.

She lifted the macramé necklace. "Clapton's. What a concert. We drove through the worst—"

The strings teacher flashed the classroom lights. "Parents, please take a seat in the cafeteria. Students, tune up."

Rhi introduced her uncle to the teacher.

"May I see you after the concert?" the teacher asked Maren and Neil.

"Sure." Neil pulled Maren off the wall. "Your hands are freezing."

"Michigan winters." She stuffed them into her coat pockets.

"My next Anchorage overnight, I'll pick you up mukluks with fur on the hood."

"Mukluks are boots." Was he trying to joke his way out of their close call? She shook off the funk, coming back to the present.

They followed the crowd to the cafeteria. Mr. and Mrs. Coffey waved from the third row of folding chairs.

"Thank you for coming." Maren hugged them both.

"Thanks for holding seats for us." Neil took Mrs. Coffey's hand in both of his. "Honored to meet the woman who saved Maren and Rhiannon."

Neil sat next to Maren, making her wish he was hers, that she could hold hands with someone this handsome and generous.

The students filed onto the stage. Head held high, Rhi strolled to the seat to the right of the conductor, first chair, and sat. She positioned her cello between the knees of her red velvet split skirt. Gold threads sparkled in her cummerbund and scrunchie. The emerald satin blouse draped without hindering her arms. She searched the audience, found Neil, Maren, and the Coffeys, and flashed them a grin.

"Now that's what I'm talking about," Mr. Coffey said.

"She's so poised," Neil whispered. "Focus without anxiety."

"Ready for the red carpet." Mrs. Coffey put her hand on Maren's, then leaned over to speak to Neil. "She participates in worship music at church. Audiences don't scare her."

The orchestra opened with "Good King Wenceslas." Not bad for fourth and fifth graders. Then they offered up the world's slowest version of "Deck the Halls." Neil's index finger started conducting, encouraging the kids to pick up the tempo.

The whole group played the chorus of "Jingle Bells," then the first violinist soloed on a verse. She performed competently, staying in tune, adding vibrato on longer notes. After another chorus, the first cello got her turn. Maren leaned forward, hands clenching her knees to keep from biting her nails. Which of her many renditions would Rhi choose?

Rhiannon schmaltzed the first line, then stopped. The audience held its breath: did she forget the rest? But no, with a wink to her uncle, she added a double-stopped "cha-cha-cha." She played the second line, hesitated a moment, then "cha-cha-cha-ed" again. Someone in the second row chuckled. Grinning, Rhi picked up the pace. Spicatto notes become hoofbeats. She ended the verse with an arpeggio up an octave, then led the orchestra into the final chorus.

The piece ended and the parents applauded. The conductor motioned for the soloists to bow, then the full orchestra.

Neil let out a breath. "Wow! What an entertainer!"

Maren reached for a tissue and elbowed Neil in the ribs.

When Rhi had transferred to this school, Maren had hoped her daughter would blend in. Instead she stood out as much as when she was the only white student. Maren wiped her eyes, thanked the Coffeys again, then led Neil down the hall.

The strings teacher motioned them into an empty classroom. "As you heard tonight, Rhiannon has left us all, including me, in the dust. She plays better than half the kids in Honors Orchestra. With your permission, I'd like to talk to the middle school, to see if she can join their orchestra."

"I work during the day, so I can't transport her."

The teacher bit her lip. "Another option, given her strong academics, is to skip fifth grade and go straight to middle school next year. Or she could join a quartet with some of the high school students."

"What about Interlochen?" Maren asked.

"She'd love summer music camp, but their arts academy doesn't start until high school." The teacher blinked. "I've never had a student with this passion, this creative genius. She astonishes me every day. Talk to Maestro. The next step might be Julliard."

Julliard? I can barely keep our heads above water in Kalamazoo. How can we survive in New York City?

As the world wobbled off its axis, Maren thanked the teacher, stepped into the hall, and wiped her eyes again. She hadn't thought this day would come so soon. How would she manage?

"Take a breath." Neil touched her elbow. "You've got several options. And a car to make it happen. I'll help. We can fly up to Interlochen to check it out."

Maren marched across the hall to collect her daughter.

Parents gathered music folders, stowed bows, and located snow boots as they negotiated a sleepover for their girls. Rhiannon stood alone in the corner, her instrument in its case, watching her class-mates make plans. Maren's heart hit the floor.

She glanced at Neil. "Okay, we'll talk about it...but not tonight."

"Hey, Tango." Neil dropped his flight bag and carry-on inside the front door and took a deep breath. "Good boy, as usual. No accidents, no dead mice, no tipped over trash cans." Nothing. No aroma of roast, no fake pine of air freshener, no lemon of the shampoo Rhiannon and Maren use. He should count it lucky he didn't detect the sulfur of a gas leak or the reek of a chicken package left in the garbage. But, still, home should smell like something. He tossed a bag of popcorn in the microwave.

While the timer counted down, he checked his answering machine. A message from a coworker about the next ALPA meeting merited a note on the calendar, then, "Neil, this is Sherilyn, wondering what you're up to these days. Fourth of July was fun. Let's do it again. Give me a call."

"Apparently the Redskins didn't make the playoffs," he muttered and hit the erase button. Was there such an animal as a football widower? He had no intention of becoming one.

The microwave dinged. Neil grabbed the bag, then he and Tango headed for the living room. He scanned the woods beyond the floor-to-ceiling windows, checking for wildlife. Something white flashed in the trees, but Tango didn't bark. Dressed in her cashmere coat, his sister-in-law stepped out of the trees and crossed his patio toward the house.

She startled when he opened the door. "Oh! I didn't think you'd be home."

"Planning to burglarize me?" He pulled her inside with a one-arm hug.

"Stealing some peace and quiet. Andy's listening to Weird Al Yankovic."

"Kids these days. Why can't they be like us, singing about noble causes, like drinking wine with Jeremiah the bullfrog."

"And profound issues like Daddy taking the T-bird away."

"Not to mention the popcorn song." He held up the bag. "Help me with this?"

"I'd be delighted." Patti set an Eddie Bauer sack on the sofa. An Air Safety Foundation box stuck out; Neil's Christmas card order. "We have a new mail carrier. I explained your work schedule, told him to leave it in your box—it's big enough. But he says he can't put mail in if you haven't taken out the previous day's. He wants you to pick it up at the post office. I told him you don't get home until after it closes."

"Thanks for bringing it." He divvied the popcorn into two bowls, then sat on the couch and propped his feet on the coffee table. "Anyone ever write a protest song about the post office?"

"Elvis. 'Return to Sender.'" Patti grabbed two cans of Diet Coke from the kitchen and joined him. "They put him on a stamp."

His sister-in-law filled him in on the latest drama at the Wolfe's Den as they crunched popcorn. The sun slipped between the bare branched trees.

Neil turned on the lamp. "So...you didn't hire a caterer for Thanksgiving this year."

"Parton said we need a war chest. I'm thinking of it as...a prodigy fund."

"Good luck getting her mom to take it."

Patti cleared her throat. "How was the concert?"

Neil moved the Coke out of range of her feet. "When Alan played trumpet in eighth grade jazz band, I must have been in kindergarten, Mr. Cronkite let him do a solo on 'When the Saints Go Marching In.' He took it and ran with it, set the audience on fire. He wasn't showing off, so much as sharing the joy. Not only tackling a difficult passage, but doing it up with all the bells and whistles."

She nodded. "That energy got him thrown out of the Grand Ol' Opry—the audience wouldn't stay in their seats."

"And that's the way it is with Rhiannon. Playing the crowd as much as playing the cello. She's amazing. Light years beyond her classmates. The elementary strings teacher's trying to work some-thing out so Rhiannon can skip a grade into middle school, or join a quartet of high school students, if she can find a ride."

"Does she sing, dance, act?"

"She has a good voice, but I don't think she's had much opportunity to explore." A memory flashed of the cardboard sets for in Rhiannon's room. Had she done musical theater?

Patti rolled a popcorn kernel between her fingertips. "There's a music camp in Michigan."

He nodded. "Interlochen. If she's admitted, I'll pay for it and get her up there. Only thing, it's two hundred miles north of her mom." What airport was closest? And what airline served it? He'd figure it out.

She shrugged. "I've sent mine away younger than that."

"Yeah, but your kids are well traveled and used to being away from home. You've got the rest keeping you company. And if you really got lonesome for them, you'd point your Volvo in their direction and go." He took a swallow of Coke. "Rhiannon needs more than summer camp."

"Couldn't they just move up there? There must be a grocery store..."

"Their arts academy doesn't start until high school." He finished his bowl. "And they're not leaving town with her grandpa this sick. He didn't make it to the concert. Their life is complicated."

"How complicated can it be with only one child?" Patti set down her empty popcorn bowl.

"Working off rent and cello lessons. Although no more bus—I found them a car." Neil paused, reminding himself to ask about the car next time he called. "If Interlochen's smart, they'll create a cafeteria job or something for Maren—" Patti's flinch shook the sofa. "Sorry."

"She has a name. Of course she has a name." She stood and headed for the door. "You miss your brother. I get that. But this Rhiannon, no matter how close the resemblance, can't bring him back."

"It's not about Alan," Neil said. "It's about making amends."

Patti paused, then slipped out the door. "Oh, *babo*."

Chapter Eleven

As Muzak droned an innocuous version of "We Three Kings," Maren found the fancy veggie tray for her customer. Onion fumes had her eyes watering. "Mrs. Jansen, did you request onions?"

The woman made a face and shook her head.

"You're requested red, green, and white. Let me replace them with cauliflower."

Behind her, something large and glass crashed to the floor. The sharp odor of vinegar filled the air. Maren spun around. An elderly man stared through the open space between his hands at the shattered pickle jar on the floor. "I'm so sorry. I'll pay for it."

"Don't worry about it. Those gallon jars can be slippery." And the floors slipperier. "Do I detect the aroma of kosher dills? Here you go. Merry Christmas." Maren loaded an unbroken jar into his cart and escorted the man to it.

She hurried behind the counter to pick up the intercom. "Clean up in Deli."

The phone rang a second later. The Troll at the Desk intoned, "We're too busy up front. You're responsible for your own cleanups."

"What if I'm busy back here?" she asked as the line went dead. If Mr. Coffey was here, he'd help.

Maren yelled into the Bakery for Sandra to keep an eye on the Deli, knowing her coworker was swamped, too. She raced to the back, grabbed a "caution, wet floor" sign and two dustpans. She positioned the signs, directed a customer to the Parmesan cheese, and scraped up most of the glass.

Muzak chirped "Have Yourself a Merry Little Christmas" as Maren dashed to the stockroom, prepared to do battle. The enemy was a five gallon yellow mop bucket with a wringer. Its contents looked like stew if you could imagine sauerkraut and cigarette butts as ingredients. Using the mop, she pushed the bucket toward the drain. It steered as well as your average shopping cart. Slime splashed over the rim, leaving a noxious trail across the concrete floor and Maren's sneakers. The drain, for some indeterminable reason, was fortified by a five-inch curb. Maren propped the mop on the wall. It promptly slid to the floor. The noise should have attracted attention, but no burly stock boy appeared. Holding her breath, she bent and lifted the bucket. Halfway over in its emptying arc, the wringer fell off and crashed into the drain, splashing her from the elbows down. Mrs. V better not be using any hot water tonight; Maren had shower plans. She upended the bucket, then hosed out the remaining inch of unidentifiable sludge.

"It's the Most Wonderful Time of the Year" was interrupted by the assistant manager ordering, "Deli, 255. Deli, dial 255."

She'd like to tell the Troll what she could do with her page, but couldn't risk a breath this close to the drain. Her arms shook from the weight, so she lowered the bucket. Letting the hose run, Maren stretched to the overhead shelf for the bottle of all-purpose cleaner. It tilted over her fingertips, tumbled off the shelf sideways, and hit her on the head. Liquid seeped through her shirt. Who left the cap off? The sting ran down the back of one shoulder and her calf into her shoe. Maren pulled her braid out of the way, grabbed the hose, and gave herself a quick rinse.

"Rockin' around the Christmas Tree" cut to "Deli, 255. Deli, dial 255."

"You *do not* want to hear from me," Maren growled. The paper towel dispenser held only an empty tube. She grabbed a box knife.

Holding it in front of her like a machete, she plunged sideways into the stockroom jungle. Where are all the people who work here? She headed for the nearest Kimberly-Clark logo, plunged the knife into the carton, and yanked out...Kleenex. Close enough. Clutching her prize in one hand, she sidestepped back to the cleaning area, where the water sloshed over the bucket.

"Arg!"

"Maren, 255. Maren Tollefson, dial 255."

She turned the faucet off and grabbed the phone. "Stop paging me and send help!" She slammed down the receiver.

Using half the box of tissues, she blotted her shoulder, leg, and foot to the tune of "Frosty the Snowman." Still no one came. Hoisting and tipping the yellow monster sent a tidal wave over the drain. She jammed the wringer back into place, found the bottle on the floor and emptied it into the bucket. No one else would get doused. A pass of the mop reduced the spilled cleaner and water to a harmless depth. Afraid to look at her watch, she returned to the spill.

"Thought you'd died, girl," Sandra shouted around the queue of Bakery and Deli customers, and "We Wish You a Merry Christmas."

A lady in blue jeans and waist-length silver curls approached Maren, "I need a quarter pound of Prosciutto." Mrs. Jensen informed her that she was first in line.

The pickle juice had dried to a dull spot shaped like Florida, with glass shards marking the tourist attractions. Maren wiped down the panhandle, cleaning off Pensacola. "I'll be with you as soon—"

"Excuse me. I believe I've been waiting longer. Two pounds of roast beef." The young mother shoved her cart back and forth, trying to soothe her squalling baby.

"Be right with you." Across to St. Augustine, down to Miami.

"Maren Tollefson!" The Troll stormed through the milling customers.

Through the Everglades, up to Tampa.

"Leaving the Deli unattended! Against the rules!"

Maren wrung the mop, trying not to imagine running an assistant manager through the rollers, and gave the floor a final rinse.

The helmet-haired coworker spit out her words, as red as the baby in the cart. "What are you doing back here?"

"Making whoopee with Mr. Clean."

"There's no spill."

"I cleaned it up." She pivoted toward the stock room and spotted a familiar face emerging from the next aisle. "Hello, Neil."

"Merry Christmas, Maren." Looking unbearably fresh, he joined the parade of customers trailing her and the Troll to the stockroom.

"You cannot leave the Deli unattended!"

"I cannot leave glass and slippery pickle brine on the floor."

"And you cannot yell over the intercom!"

Maren paused for a second. "You mean to tell me, the entire store heard me, but no one—" She stopped, remembering Neil's obsession with safety. She shoved the bucket into the stockroom. Helmet-head caught the swinging door before it hit her in the face and pushed through. Neil and the customers waited on the other side, peering through the portholes. Muzak advised "Christmas Time's a Coming."

Maren returned the bucket to its place and faced the Troll. "Let me tell you something about the grocery business. First of all, gallon jars of pickles do not belong on an end cap."

The desk Troll snapped to attention. "*I have a degree!*"

"I know. An associate of arts from the esteemed institution of higher learning known as Kalamazoo Valley Community College. When we're shorthanded, customers will wait for a cashier or bag it themselves. Once they've filled their buggies and paid, we don't lose them. If the line is long in Deli, they'll consider shopping at Meijer. But one slip and fall lawsuit and we're all out of a job." Maren raced to the deli. Her faithful followers trailed her, adding customers on the way. Behind the counter, Maren scrubbed her hands, crumpled a paper towel, bounced it off the assistant manager's hip into the trash bin. "I'm going on break in ten minutes, whether the Deli's covered or not."

"Against the rules!"

Maren finished Mrs. Jensen's veggie tray, then measured two pounds of roast beef and threw in an ice-cold carrot for the fussy baby. "Thank you for waiting. Merry Christmas!"

"Against the rules!" The Troll stomped off.

Each customer in line received a little something extra, another slice of meat, six packets of mayonnaise, whatever might keep them happy. Finally, the line dwindled down to Neil. Maren wrote "Back in 15 Minutes" on a white #8 bag and taped it to the front of the cold case.

"Sorry about the wait. My part-timer quit yesterday. My relief doesn't come in until three." Maren led Neil to the break room, hoping he didn't freak over the squalor of the table covered with wood-grained Contact paper, the chipped tile floor, and the fifties-style chrome chairs.

Neil took it in with a glance. "Decorated by the same people who do pilot lounges."

Maren returned his smile. "Buy you a Coke?"

"I should buy you one. I've never seen anyone work so hard."

She opened her locker. "You will on this mission, should you decide to accept it."

"Glad to help out." He sat across from her. "How's your dad?"

"At home on oxygen." She opened her sack. "Would you like half a peanut butter and jelly?"

He shook his head. "You need the fuel. How's the car?"

"Running fine. Thanks."

"So, what's on Rhiannon's wish list?"

She handed him an envelope bulging with cash. "Can you read my writing? Watercolors and paper. From the bookstore in Western's student union. Most of the students left last week, so you should be able to find a parking spot. There's quarters for the meter, unless you want a souvenir WMU ticket."

"Keep eating." He scanned the rest of the list. "This'll work."

"Have you ever used layaway? The money in the envelope will pay the balance."

"I'll figure it out."

"It's a lot to do in two hours."

"No goofing off. Got it." Standing, he checked his watch. "Meet you at Mrs. V's"

"Neil, thank you."

He gave her his best crooked smile. "Hey, what's family for?"

Her family? Consequences. So Neil thought helping was the kind of thing families did for each other? What a lovely world he lived in.

NEIL GLANCED at the rental car's clock as he navigated the snowy road. Maren choreographed her shopping scavenger hunt as well as she handled her critical assistant manager. In two hours, he'd found six gifts at five different stores. For bonus points, he'd kept track of the receipts and change. And he'd arrive at Mrs. V's on time. No problem. Anyone who can find Nantucket floating in Atlantic fog, spot Alpena on a snowy night, shoot an ILS down to mins, ought to — Oops, missed the turn.

He turned at the next block and got to Mrs. V's without further mishaps.

Maren had George Winston's *December* album playing, a fine selection. "How'd it go?"

"Great. Got everything on the list. The sweater and socks were on sale, so here's your change."

"Wow." Maren burrowed through the shopping bags. "You did get everything!"

Mission accomplished, victory at hand. The returning hero deserves a hug and kiss. He glanced at the woman sorting through receipts. Weathered in. Don't even try an approach.

Maren found the roll of wrapping paper he'd bought. "We usually recycle comics."

Oops. From hero to zero in one fell swoop of gold foil snowflakes. "I use High Altitude Charts for wrapping paper. But Christmas is special, especially this one." Here goes nothing. "If it's all right with you, I'll take Rhiannon out while you wrap. She wants to shop too."

"Okay." Maren nodded without looking up, focusing on sliding the roll back into the bag. "Rhi will appreciate it."

"Thanks for trusting me." Neil was allowed to take Rhi to the store by himself. He wanted to hug Maren. "What's on your Christmas list?"

"You already got me a coat and a car." As she flipped the record over, she sang, Aretha Franklin style, "All I'm asking, is for a little respect."

"LP, cassette, CD, concert tickets?" The gleam in his eye gave him away.

"Always a jokester." She made a sound halfway between a huff and a frustrated laugh. "Just remember I'm Rhi's mother. All decisions concerning her go through me." Her hand thumped her heart.

"I thought I was doing better."

"In the future—"

The service door upstairs opened, shooting a draft through the apartment. Maren hid the gifts behind the sofa.

"My favorite uncle!" Rhiannon declared as she hugged him, prompting Neil to wonder if the other uncle's sin involved omission or commission. Had he forgotten her birthday? Put a bow on a can of lima beans and called it a present?

Footsteps, heavier than he'd expect from Mrs. V, thudded on the inside staircase and the door opened an inch before the chain stopped it.

Maren signaled "quiet" with a finger to her lips. "Yes, Myron, how can I help you?"

"Mrs. V's son," Rhiannon whispered to Neil.

"Open up." The man rattled the door. "I need to check the furnace."

Maren crossed her arms. "Hendriks did the scheduled maintenance in September. I changed the filter the first of this month. It's fine."

"Mother thought she heard a man's voice."

Rhiannon rolled her eyes. "Mrs. V is hearing impaired."

"It's my daughter's uncle. It's family." Maren caught herself and slapped a hand over her mouth.

Finally Maren acknowledged him as family...if only some creep hadn't pushed her into it. Neil reached for the security chain, then remembered *respect*. He raised an eyebrow at Maren. "May I?"

"Don't let him in," she mouthed.

Neil nodded and released the chain, but blocked the doorway with his body. He shoved his hand toward the man, noting he was older and out of shape, and gave him an overly-firm handshake. "I'm Neil Wolfe, kin to the tenants of your mother. Appreciate her renting to my relatives, providing a safe living situation. My family's well-being is my utmost priority. You understand." *Dude, your mother's tenants are none of your business, but they are mine and I intend to protect them.*

Myron backed up a step, bring his head level with Neil's. "Oh, of course. Just making sure everything's okay down here. I gotta go."

"Good night." Neil closed the door and examined the chain, then checked the one on the other door. "Whoever put these in knew what he was doing."

"Mom." Rhiannon said. "She used extra-long screws into the frame."

"Good." He turned to Maren. "Will you be all right while we shop?"

She nodded. "He disapproves of his mother becoming a land-lady, so he tries to catch us in nefarious activities."

"My mom bakes better than his mom, so he's especially pesky when we make cookies." Rhiannon pulled on her coat. "Let's go, Uncle Neil."

On their way out, his niece pointed to a box in the garage. "Could we set up the tree first? Everyone in my class has theirs decorated, presents under it and everything. It won't take long."

"Sure, but...." He reached for the box then stopped. As Maren had just reminded him—Respect. "Better check with your mom."

Maren considered his request, then cautioned, "It won't give you much time at the mall."

"If she's as organized as you," Neil grabbed the carton, "we'll be in and out of the store before Elmo and Patsy get to the punch line of 'Grandma Got Run Over by a Reindeer.'"

"One can only hope." Maren led them down the stairwell. "I'll get the ornaments."

Neil pulled out three feet of plastic needles wired to a dowel trunk.

"Can you believe someone would throw it out? Some of the branches were loose, but Mom fixed it." Rhiannon set the tree on the steamer trunk. "Like she fixed the microwave."

"The microwave was a throwaway?"

"Garage sale. Mom replaced the cord, and now it works. Same with the stereo."

Neil would fry himself if he attempted an electrical repair.

Maren reappeared carrying a box from Three Rivers Egg Farm. "I could finish while you shop."

The girl showed him an elaborately woven paper crane. "Mom made this. Isn't it awesome?"

"Lights first." Maren reminded her.

Neil hung the single strand of lights—seven less than Patti's tree held—his niece showed him more ornaments: a clothespin reindeer, a mouse sleeping in a walnut shell, a pine cone dusted with glitter. The Sierra Club couldn't have done a better job recycling.

Maren stretched, reaching deep into the cabinet over the washing machine, and bringing out a stationery box covered with rainbows. Neil's heart skipped a beat—this box had held the envelopes and sheets she'd sent to Alan, telling him about her pregnancy and Rhiannon's birth.

His niece opened it and sorted through the scraps. "Here's last year's. I'm still growing." She measured the paper hand against her own, then hung it on the tree by its ribbon loop.

Neil took the pile, sorting back through cutouts labeled age eight, seven, six. With each year the paper yellowed and curled more. Five, four, three. Neil sank to the sofa. Two, one, 6 weeks. He tried to say something, but a big, heavy ornament stuck in his throat. He smoothed the smallest against his knees.

"Those little ones, I traced while she was asleep. She had such long fingers." Maren knelt beside him. "Whenever she heard music, her hands would open and flutter like she was conducting."

Neil laid the cut-outs in a row across the trunk. Long graceful fingers, curling around his heart. How much he'd missed.

"Uncle Neil? Is the dust bothering you? Do you need a Kleenex?"

"No." He shook his head and wiped the tears on the back of his wrist. "I brought you an ornament...it seemed special... but these hands are *priceless*."

"What did bring?" Rhi bounced on the couch.

His gesture took in the ten paper hands. "I could never, nothing I could buy—" He swallowed.

"What?" She gave him a combination hug-shake. "Don't make me wait until Christmas!"

He pulled the package from his suit coat's inner pocket. Rhiannon snatched it and unfolded the tissue. The facets of the crystal caught the light, sprinkling the room with sparks of color.

"It's not what it's usually for—"

"Oh, Uncle Neil, it's perfect!" She held it out for her mother.

Maren glanced at the inscription. Her jaw dropped, her mouth forming a circle, and she looked away.

Rhiannon read, "'*Our first Christmas Together*,'" then hugged her uncle.

BYPASSING the mall for a combination grocery-department store called Meijer's, Rhiannon made short work of her list, picking out a green turtleneck, lotion, and Sanders chocolate for her mom. As they got back in the car, she looked in her envelope. "Christmas shopping is done and, this year, Mom didn't have to sell her hair."

"Your mom... sold her hair?" Maren's gorgeous, thick, beautiful hair? Neil stared at his niece. She wasn't kidding. "Why?"

"So she could buy Christmas presents after I got sick."

"But you have medical insurance."

Rhiannon gave him a "you dummy" look. "In second grade, I got strep, chicken pox, and strep again, all before Christmas. Mom ran out of sick days."

"How does selling...it work?" His gut soured.

"The wig shop cuts off at least twelve inches. She keeps enough to make a ponytail. They pay $50."

"Never again. You've got me. Promise you'll call if she even thinks about it."

The crease between her eyebrows disappeared and she grinned. "You're on speed dial." Relieved of her worry about finances, she resumed her usual play-by-play of fourth grade as they returned to Mrs. V's.

"Don't look!" Rhiannon called as she and Neil clattered down the steps.

Maren covered her eyes, but Neil caught her exhale and the release of tension in her shoulders. Trust wasn't easily given.

"I found a new hot chocolate, with cinnamon, on my Omaha overnight." Neil put the canister on the table as Rhiannon snuck her shopping bags into her room. "And it's snowing again. Dry this time." This Virginia boy was learning how many varieties of snow there were.

Maren fixed the hot chocolate and served beef stew. "Good skiing weather."

"You ski?" Neil asked, surprised she'd volunteer a morsel of personal information.

"I took a cross-country class for PE credit."

Must have been her last semester at Western. Did she finish or have to drop it for morning sickness? Did she worry about the baby when she fell? Maybe she didn't fall.

Rhiannon sat at the table. "*I've* never been skiing. Samantha goes to Boyne Mountain every Christmas." She pointed to the last joint of her ring finger, locating the resort on Michigan's hand-shaped lower peninsula. "Hey, we could go too! We could stay in a cabin with a hot tub and rent skis. You could fly us—they have an airport. We could take the tree and presents; they don't weigh much. Please, Uncle Neil."

"Rhi..." Maren's voice held the weariness of having to say "no" too many times.

Neil bopped his niece on the nose with her stocking cap's tassel. "We'll put it on our wish list. Thanks to low seniority, I have to work

Christmas Eve, Christmas Day, and the day after, then celebrate with the other kids, then work through New Year's Day."

"But I *want* you *here* for Christmas," Rhi whined, then sobbed. "It's my turn."

"Rhi. Take a time out."

The girl stomped to her room.

Maren slumped. "Sorry."

"Between the holiday hype and her grandpa being sick, of course she's falling apart." Neil lowered his voice. "I wonder what's holding you together."

Rhiannon returned to the table, waving a wall calendar. "How about President's Day? Or Spring Break? They'll still have snow then."

"I don't know." Neil didn't know his January schedule, or what was going on with Patti's kids, and most of all, he didn't know how much longer her grandpa had. "I'm not so sure I want to try skiing again. I went once on a scout trip in Virginia. The wool long underwear itched. Mean old skis slipped out from under me and I hit the ice so hard I wanted to cry. But crying's not in the scout handbook. Then when I stood up, it looked like I'd wet my pants. Little kids zoomed down the mountain, laughing at me."

"How embarrassing." Rhiannon's mouth twitched with a smile.

"You might enjoy cross-country skiing better," Maren said. "It's like hiking."

"And we can go anywhere, right? Down the middle of the street?"

"Before it's plowed." Maren nodded. "Golf courses, high power line accesses, Asylum Lake."

Might be fun to give it a try.

Rhi thumped her mug on the table. "Gag. Tastes weird."

"Rhiannon. Apologize."

"Sorry."

"Sometimes new foods don't taste right," Neil said. "But it's good to try different things."

"Then you should try Christmas in Michigan." His niece burst into tears and pounded her fists on her legs. "I don't want you to go! The other kids have gotten you for all the other Christmases."

"I've had to work seven of their last ten Christmases." Neil pulled her to his side. The rigidity of her body told him she held onto her hurt. "But, thanks to my flight schedule dropping me in Chicago at the right time, I've gotten to see your cello lesson and your first concert."

"You took us out to eat and gave us rides." Maren's words were intended for her daughter, but Neil's heart warmed at her support.

"This fall, I've missed Harmony's birthday, Andy's jazz band recital, Cody's vocal concert, and Melody's fusion project. She sang and danced to Bizet's 'Farandole.'"

Rhiannon scowled. "Sang? It doesn't have words."

"She wrote lyrics for it." Neil sighed. How could he say this without mentioning Alan? "The downside of some jobs, like flying or musician on tour, is being away from family a lot."

"I get it." Rhiannon huffed. "But it's not fair. Stupid cancer."

Poor kiddo. Neil tried to hug her, but she squirmed away and ran to her room as Maren called, "Don't slam the door." It shut with a firm thud.

"Your honeymoon is over." Maren gave him a sidelong glance with a slight lift to the corner of her mouth.

"All the kids pitch fits," Neil said. "Let's blame it on their father."

"And then avoid mentioning him again." She took her dishes to the sink. "She'll talk about her father. No one can or should stop her. But if you would refrain, please, while I'm around."

Neil closed his eyes and bowed his head. Then he looked up. "Yes. I would gladly do that for you. After living in his shadow all my life, I'd be happy to never hear about him again."

This man would do anything for his family. He knew how to love well, even when it hurt.

"I'd appreciate it."

Neil reached around Maren to set his empty mug in the dishpan. She stiffened and inched toward the refrigerator. He'd worn out his welcome with her too. "So, I'll get going." He took his time putting on his coat, giving her a chance to deny it, to ask him to stay, to say she liked having him around. Reaching for his gloves, he found the cash he'd gotten from the ATM, and tucked it under the silverware organizer. "I'm leaving you an emergency stash. So you don't have to..." How could he say this respectfully? "So you don't have sell your hair, unless you want to."

Maren watched him close the drawer, then met his gaze. "Thank you." She washed his mug. "Although it gets heavy and causes headaches."

Much as he liked Maren's hair, he didn't want her in pain. "Good reason for a cut."

The bedroom door opened and Rhiannon hurried out, holding a wrapped present the size and shape of a Pringles can. A Bedazzled luggage tag in his airline's colors decorated the top. "I made cookies for you. Mom said you wouldn't have much room in your suitcase, so I couldn't send the whole batch."

"Thank you. If I can't fit them in my carry-on, I'll eat them." He opened his arms and she grabbed him in a hug.

"Sorry I'm so ornery."

"You might be coming down with something. Get a good night's sleep."

"You too." Rhiannon went back to her room.

Maren resumed washing dishes. Over the sound of water, her soft voice said, "Merry Christmas."

Neil quoted another guy who had to fly on the holiday, "Merry Christmas to all, and to all a good night."

Chapter Twelve

"Keep a lookout for a parking spot," Neil said as he wound through the hospital lot.

"All righty." Facing him on the front passenger seat, Dixie blinked her wide brown eyes. Loose grey curls sprung from under her crocheted pink hat.

Should have named her Bunny, he thought. Her bewildered look reminded him of his first-grade class's pet rabbit, the one who never learned to use the litter box. No dropping Dixie off at the door. She'd get lost in the maze of hospital corridors and Arne Tollefson wouldn't get his dying wish to see his favorite waitress. At Maren's request, Neil had picked up the woman from her trailer park on his way in from the airport, and he would see her safely delivered.

He found a spot and extricated Dixie from the rental car's low seat. Wind flapped at her royal blue coat, showing the Hawaiian print smock and hot pink slacks beneath. Neil eyeballed the distance to the entrance and mentally calculated the wind chill. "Uh, Miss Dixie, maybe you should fasten your coat."

"All righty." Her voice would have sounded young and high on Rhiannon. Coming from a senior citizen... Neil wasn't sure whether to laugh or find a doctor for her. Dixie stopped to secure the three large buttons. Then looked up at him with what seemed to be her permanent expression—a puzzled smile. Neil led her to the building, hoping she'd still recognize Arne. Inside, she stopped again, this time to unbutton, and bumped a half dozen ornaments off a Christmas tree. Corridor traffic ground to a halt as she chased after each plastic ball.

"Where do they go?" Wide bunny eyes pondered the tree.

"On the tree."

"I know. But which branch?"

Neil grabbed a shiny green globe from her hand. "Anywhere is fine. They'll be taking it down soon. Christmas is over."

She lowered her voice. "They'll keep it up a while. This is a *Catholic* hospital."

"Yes, ma'am, it is." *Go with the flow.* "The red ornament goes on this branch, and the gold one here, and the striped one down on the bottom."

"All righty!" Stepping back to admire her work, Dixie almost collided with a woman pushing a squeaking food cart. "Oh, hello and merry Christmas, dear."

"Miss Dixie, Arne's waiting." He tucked her hand under his elbow and they made it all the way to the oncology floor without further mishaps, greeting everyone in their path.

Neil peeked into the room and caught Maren's eye.

"The coast is clear," she said.

"Hi, Uncle Neil!"

Dixie tottered to the hospital bed greeted Arne with a kiss. "Hello, sugar pie."

The roommate pulled back the curtain and muttered, "What's with the baby talk?"

Maren and Rhiannon stepped into the hall. Neil hugged his niece and admired her Bedazzled denim vest, then started to tuck Maren under his other arm. No, she wasn't his sister-in-law. He settled for touching her elbow. "How's your dad?"

"Good." Her cheeks pinked and she turned away from him. "His new medications have decreased his pain and depression, but Dixie will really cheer him up."

"Hey, I haven't had lunch yet. Would you ladies accept my invitation to the hospital cafeteria? I'll let you pick the color of Jell-O."

They passed up the Jell-O for herbed chicken and mashed potatoes.

Rhiannon had another topic on her mind. "Uncle Neil, do people ask your other nieces and nephews about their dad?"

Maren gasped. "Did someone ask?"

Rhiannon shook her head. "I was wondering, just in case."

"Not often," Neil said. "Adults share memories of concerts and what his songs meant to them. If kids their age bring it up, they say he died. Stops further questions."

Maren leaned on the table, her lunch forgotten. "But what if it doesn't? What if someone mentions her resemblance to..."

"You could burst into tears. The other nieces tap into their drama vein. The nephews might crack a joke or say something outrageous. Once Andy told someone his father was Carlos Santana."

"Now that's funny." Rhiannon grinned. "I'll say Michael Jackson. I can moonwalk."

"It's a plan." Neil grinned back.

They finished lunch and returned to room 342.

Dixie sat on Arne's bed, spooning pudding into his mouth and telling him what a good boy he was. Arne's eyes sparkled and he looked decades younger. Neil decided he wasn't needed and stepped into the hall.

The elevator doors opened and Helga swooped out, eyes blazing. She shoved past Maren and Rhi into Arne's room. "What's going on here! You!" She pointed her talons at Maren, then Dixie. "How dare you bring her here! I'm taking care of your father, not her. She has no business—"

Dixie turned pale, scrambled into the corner furthest from Helga, and burst into tears. Neil tried to step around Helga, but she blocked the door. Over the pug-witch's head, Neil said, "Miss Dixie, how about I take you home?"

"She's no 'miss'. That hussy's been married more times than Liz Taylor."

Large bunny eyes glanced from Helga to Neil. She shook her head. Yeah, Helga scared him too.

"Aw, stop your fussing, Helga." Arne waved her out of the room.

"Let's go see what's on TV," Maren suggested.

"Soap operas," the roommate said. "Boring compared to you folks."

Not even the promise of television would soothe an enraged Helga. "I'm taking care of him and don't you forget it. Any more of your interference and I'll... I'll cut off his oxygen!"

"Enough." Neil turned to Rhiannon. "Run down to the nurse's station and ask them to call security. Helga's threatening your grandpa."

She returned in a moment. "They already called."

"Let's get out of the way." Neil ushered Rhi and Maren to the hall, where they could still see Arne and Dixie, but were out of reach of Helga. Unless she grew tentacles or spit toxic waste.

One officer burst from the stairwell and another emerged from the elevator. They hurried into Arne's room. "Ma'am, you need to keep your voice down and step into the hall. Now."

"I know my rights." She tried to cross her arms, but they were too short. "You can't make me leave."

"You're disturbing the other patients, keeping the nurses from doing their job."

Helga went into lecture mode. "You're under control of the one percent. You are part of the problem." When she raised her arm to point, one guard seized her wrist and yanked her out. The skinnier guard scooted behind her and grabbed her other arm. They marched her down the hall as she invoked "The People's Court," "L.A. Law," and "Matlock."

"I prefer 'Night Court' myself," one of the guards said as the elevator doors closed.

Maren hurried to Dixie and gave her a hug. She and Rhiannon took her to the restroom.

"C'mon in, Neil. Take a load off." Arne jabbed a thumb at the green vinyl chair. "Quite the love life for an old guy, eh?" He

117

laughed, making Neil wonder about his new medications, then coughed. Neil passed him a cup of ice water.

"Thanks." The liquid restored his voice. "I want you to know, about Maren, I'm not the bad guy here. No, let me say this. The girls'll be back any second. I love my daughter. She was always a good girl, except for getting pregnant. I didn't throw her out. She left on her own. Stubborn girl. I never blamed her for her mother's death. Elsa smoked like a B-52."

The change of heart was so complete, Neil wondered if he'd had a transplant. "Maren should hear that from you."

Jaw rigid, Arne stared at the ceiling. "Wouldn't have minded having Rhiannon around. She's a good kid, better than her snot-nosed cousins. Maren's too hard on herself. Maybe you—"

The women returned. Neil kept Dixie company in the hall so Arne could make his peace. He heard soft murmurs from all three Tollefsons, then a coughing fit.

Dixie's eyes were dry and her smile had returned. She studied a photo of a windmill surrounded by tulips. "So pretty. Mama would take us to see the flowers every year. It's only an hour away. You should go."

An hour? Oh, she's talking about Holland, Michigan. "Thanks. Sounds like a great idea." If spring ever returned to Michigan.

Neil peeked in to see how Arne was doing.

"Chill." Maren pressed on her daughter's head. "We've worn Grandpa out."

Rhiannon held the old man's hand. "Any requests?"

Arne blinked in slow motion, struggling to stay awake. "'Edelweiss,'" he whispered.

"Uncle Neil, do you know the song? C'mon in, then. Mom?"

Towing Dixie, Neil stepped to the end of the bed.

Maren hummed middle C and started them off with a bob of her index finger. Rhiannon's flute-like soprano hit every note with perfect pitch and compassion. Maren sang alto, weaving the harmony, and conducting with nods and tight movements of her wrist. She'd been in madrigals or a choir, Neil guessed, adding his baritone. Arne drifted to sleep during the last chorus, a smile on his face. Dixie kissed his forehead, then they all left.

A nurse caught them on their way out. "Will you sing again tomorrow? For the other patients? Music groups come before Christmas and there's nobody afterwards."

"We'll be here tomorrow," Maren assured her.

TOMORROW ARRIVED at 4:23 the next morning.

"Neil? Sorry to bother you this early." Over the phone, Maren sounded all business, her words evenly spaced, her tone matter-of-fact.

"It's ok." Flying on Reserve status had taught him to wake quickly. Juggling the phone's receiver, he rolled out of the motel bed and into his jeans. "Your dad?"

"Yes. The car won't start, buses don't run until six, and the cab companies aren't answering."

"I'll be right there." Eleven minutes later, during which the radio informed him the temperature was zero, he pulled up to the house.

Maren jogged out from the garage and climbed into the front seat. "Dr. Gibson took Rhi home with her last night."

"She's sick?" Neil whipped the rental car around in a spray of snow.

"No. The Gibsons have a daughter Rhi's age. Her husband's a pastor; he'll be home today to watch the girls."

"Any relation to the Gibson who made guitars?"

"Probably not. He didn't have any children."

He glanced at Maren, impressed with her knowledge of an obscure bit of history. "Ever think of going on 'Jeopardy?'"

She managed a quick smile. "May as well do something with my collection of useless information."

He slowed and checked the empty cross streets, then ran a red light.

"Don't get a ticket on my account."

At the next light, he stopped. Maren stared at the dark city and

119

shivered. Neil turned up the heater fan. "What did the hospital say when they called?"

"He's taken a turn for the worse."

"Maybe..." What if Helga had managed to sneak back in and turn off his oxygen? Neil did a rolling stop at the next three intersections. His passenger stayed quiet.

The big advantage of oh-dark-hundred at the hospital was finding a parking spot near the door and the elevator waiting for them.

Fists shoved in her pockets, Maren studied the scuffed toes of her boots. "I can take the bus home."

Neil punched the button for the third floor. When the doors opened, he put his hand under her elbow, not sure if he wanted to offer support or hang on. She slipped out of his grasp, rushed down the hall, turned the corner, and froze. A young man in scrubs pushed a gurney with a sheet-covered man out of room 342 and left it in the hallway.

"Dad?" Maren grabbed the limp hand hanging below the sheet and whispered, "Dad."

Arne, no. Neil clenched his fists, willing color and life back into the slack face. *Wake up and joke about your women troubles, tell me an airport story, tell me about your daughter.*

"Excuse me." An older man in surgical scrubs pushed a large blue machine down the hall, tires squeaking and metal panels clunking against the cabinet.

Neil stomped to the nurses' station. "Why is Mr. Tollefson out here? Just left out in the hall like yesterday's news?"

The clerk squeaked and scooted back from the desk. "Transport—"

"This is disrespectful to him and to his family. Who's in charge here?"

"Shh." A young nurse, barely older than Rhiannon, popped out of the back room. "Sir, please keep your voice down. Patients are trying to sleep."

"Mr. Tollefson was okay when we left," Neil glanced at his

watch, "eight hours ago. What happened? Has Helga Hoofer been here?"

"No, she hasn't." Her ponytail trembled with indignation. "We moved Mr. Tollefson because his roommate was upset about the death."

"So just leave him in the hallway?"

"We don't have any empty rooms at the moment."

"This is no way to treat—"

Maren joined him at the desk. "He's dead. It doesn't matter." Neil put an arm around her shoulder, but she didn't seem to feel it. "I'm Mr. Tollefson's daughter."

The nurse's frown softened. "I'm so very sorry."

"Is there paperwork?" She took a pen off the desk.

"Your dad completed most of it with the hospice coordinator."

Maren signed the form for the funeral parlor, then turned to leave.

"Do you want..." Neil chased her to the elevator. "I could pull him into the waiting room, give you time alone with him."

"No, thank you."

"I don't mind. Take as much time as you need."

She shook her head, entered the elevator, and pushed "Ground."

He jumped on as the doors closed. "Give yourself a chance to say goodbye."

The car stopped for a lab-coated woman. Her tote of glass tubes tinkled the rest of the ride. When the doors opened, Maren bolted out and Neil followed, watching her braid sway down her back. He opened the car door and she slid inside. This was wrong, hurrying through this time. She'd regret it later. He joined her, appreciating the few degrees of warmth the car retained. "Maren, I've been through this—"

"No, you haven't." She spoke to the glove box. "Your brother was in the prime of his life, healthy. His death was an accident, totally unexpected, a shock. This," she pointed to the hospital, "is a relief, a release from suffering."

"But it's—"

"Sorry to have bothered you this morning. If they'd been honest with me, I'd have waited for the bus. Obviously, there was no reason to rush." The trace of anger firming her voice seemed genuine.

He started the car. There had to be something he could do to help. "Would you like some breakfast?"

"No, thank you. I have a lot of calls to make."

On the route, he found a fast food joint with an open drive-through. Maren said she wasn't hungry, so he ordered all the odd numbered items on the breakfast menu, hoping to hit something she liked. When they returned to the apartment, he carried the food in, then went to the bathroom.

Neil frowned at the scruffy good-for-nothing in the mirror. No wonder the nurse tried to give him the bum's rush. Bible verses were stuck to wall. Patti had given him a plaque for graduation of Isaiah 40:31: "Those who wait on the Lord shall renew their strength, they shall mount up on wings like eagles." What did Maren have?

"'Put to death, therefore, whatever belongs to your earthly nature: sexual immorality, impurity, lust, evil desires, and greed, which is idolatry,'" Neil read. "Grim. 'Blessed are the pure in heart, for they will see God.' Okay. 'How can a young person stay on the path of purity? By living according to your word.' Oh, Maren..." He needed to talk to her about this. But not today.

He washed his hands. The bathroom doubled as a closet. Most of the rack held a brightly colored selection of girls' clothes. At the end hung the navy suit Maren had worn to Chicago, and a half dozen pairs of dark slacks and white shirts, Maren's work clothes. *Maren, Maren, your strength hides your pain.* He dried his hands on a threadbare towel and returned to the living room. The phone cord snaked out the door. What was she doing out in the cold? Neil opened the door.

"Helga." Maren curled up on the steps. She sounded even more composed than when she'd woken him this morning. "Helga. You'll be back in time for *The Price is Right.* Yes, you will. Plenty. No, it's all taken care of. I've got to call Karl. No, I'll take care of it. I'll talk to you later, after *Geraldo.*"

"Come in and have some breakfast."

Maren's breath blew white clouds in the stairwell. Shaking fingers entered the next number on her list. "This is Maren."

From the high-pitched screaming coming from the other end, Neil figured the call could take a while. He scooped up Maren, phone and all. Shivers vibrated through her coat. He set her on the couch and plugged the space heater into the nearest outlet.

"Yes, we're in the same time zone. I need to talk to Karl. I know. He's *always* been a bear in the morning. Okay, when he wakes up, tell him his father died." The other end went quiet.

Neil pressed a Styrofoam cup of hot chocolate into her hand.

"I'll spill it," she whispered.

His hand over her icy fingers, he guided the cup to her lips.

The yelling on the other end resumed, this time a couple octaves lower.

"I thought you'd want to know," Maren said into the receiver. "Can you be here Wednesday? I don't think Saturday— No, he did not want to be cremated. I'll ask the funeral home and— Fine. You plan it. Here's their number." She finished the call and hung up.

Neil followed her gaze to where his hand wrapped around hers and the cup. He let go.

Her voice shook. "Go to your hotel, finish your sleep."

"Maren, you shouldn't be alone right now."

"Rhi will be back later this morning"

Her autopilot had engaged. Instead of crying, she focused on completing the checklist. How many times in the past ten years had she done this? "You need to take care of yourself."

"I'll have her call you."

"C'mon, eat, before the food gets cold." He pulled her to stand. "Where's your car key? I'll jump it and take it to Sears for a battery… as soon as you eat."

She stared at the floor for three breaths, then nibbled on a hash brown patty as he snarfed down an egg sandwich. She set the car key on the table without making eye contact. "Jumper cables are in the trunk."

Heart heavy, he climbed up the steps and left the house. Sunrise shone a feeble light over the tundra. He popped the hood of the rental and the Olds.

A black minivan parked in front of the house. A woman emerged wearing a sable coat that would have done Aretha Franklin proud. "Neil."

How did she know Maren needed her? Neil gave himself a kick. He should have called Mr. Coffey. He should have prayed. He held out his hand. "Thanks for coming."

Instead of a handshake, Mrs. Coffey held his face in her gloved hands and stared into his eyes, down into his soul. Then she embraced him. It was like being hugged by a good-smelling, kind bear.

"Thank you," he said.

"Lay your burdens down, son." She glided into the house.

Chapter Thirteen

On the morning of the funeral, Neil picked up Maren and Rhiannon at the Upjohn hangar on the southwest side of Kalamazoo's airport. They'd spent the morning making food, then setting up the luncheon. Grief, fatigue, or the low stratus layer, neither had much to say.

Neil broke the silence. "Is Dixie coming to the funeral?"

"No," Maren said. "She was pretty shook up, so her daughter took her to Texas."

He maneuvered this week's rental car, another dark sedan, through the drifts at the cemetery's entrance and, at Maren's direction, parked in front of the hearse. Do they ever cancel funerals for bad weather? This would be a good day to start. He slogged through the bumper-deep powder to open the doors for Rhiannon and Maren, attired in the Michigan uniform—coats, snow pants, stocking caps, mittens, and insulated boots. Neil's rubber overshoes scooped up the snow and held it next to his socks until it melted and dripped ice water into his shoes.

"Glad we left the Leopard at the hangar," Rhiannon murmured, referring to the Oldsmobile. "I don't want to hear what Uncle Karl would say about it."

Neil and Maren each took a mittened little-girl hand, and with a swish-swish of snowsuit legs, headed to the gravesite. Small, dry flakes swirled, blurring the green tent. Three-dozen mourners seemed a small number for someone who'd lived and worked in this area all his life, but Neil guessed Arne hadn't had much of a social life since he retired. Or maybe the single-digit temperatures kept people away.

Maren's brother, cozy in his melton overcoat, had seated his family in the first row of folding chairs. His oldest popped bubble gum and played a Game Boy. His youngest picked up the Astroturf covering the casket's base and peered into the hole until his father noticed and swatted him. Poor kid. Neil also wondered how they dug a grave through the frozen ground.

Helga Hoofer, wrapped in a cape borrowed from Count Dracula, planted herself in a chair by the head of the casket. How had they scheduled the funeral around her television addiction?

Arne Tollefson's contemporaries filled in the second row and stood behind the chairs.

Maren guided Rhiannon to the edge of the standees. Didn't she want to move closer, into the shelter of the tent? The Coffeys and Dr. Gibson huddled around them.

The minister, a man her father's age, glanced over the group and did a double take. "Maren? I haven't seen you since..." He hurried to her, hand extended, as the mourners stared. "Arne said you'd left town."

"Reverend Johnson. Good to see you again." Maren shook his hand. "No, I've been here all along."

"We visited Grandpa every week," Rhiannon announced, earning a scowl from her other uncle.

"This is my daughter, Rhiannon, and her uncle, Neil."

The minister studied them, his forehead creased with mental calculations. "Would you like to sit up front?"

"No, thank you."

Huddled deep in her furs, Karl's wife whined loud enough to be heard over the crowd. Karl raised a leather-gloved finger and motioned for the rite to begin.

The minister returned to his place. "Brothers and sisters, we are gathered today to commemorate Arne Tollefson, husband of Elsa, father of Maren and Karl, grandfather of Rhiannon, Edward, and Herman."

Karl's wife snorted at each mention of Maren and Rhiannon.

The minister continued without reacting. "Arne was a member of Portage Christian Church, and had a long career as a mechanic in Upjohn's aviation department." He read a few Bible verses, then urged those who grieved to support each other.

A tear paused at the corner of Maren's eye. She swiped it, her index finger poking through a hole in her knit glove. This had to be hard on her, losing her father and Karl refusing to let her participate in planning the service. A wisp of hair escaped from her knit cap and vibrated by her ear. Her bottom lip trembled and her body fluttered like a windsock. Neil pushed Rhiannon in front of her mother, and stepped behind, sandwiching Maren to shelter her from the wind.

Out of mercy, or perhaps fear of Karl's wife, the minister kept the graveside service short. He announced lunch would be served at the Upjohn hangar, then pronounced the benediction.

"Hurry." Maren set a brisk pace back to the car.

They returned to the hangar and Maren raced inside. The large open space with a row of windows at the top of the walls held a turbo-prop and a bizjet, but didn't hold heat. Neil kept his overcoat on. Maren shed her winter gear and set out a tray of smoked salmon sandwiches.

"Why'd you make food?" asked a young mechanic. "Catering brought over boxed lunches."

"Dad had requests." She cut a sponge cake. "Where's the other Citation?" She nodded at the empty space beside the turbo-prop.

"D.C. Gave us enough room to set up tables."

"Anything I can help with?" Neil asked.

"Make hot chocolate for Rhi. Careful, those dispensers spit boiling water."

"Will do." Neil mixed a generous glug of cream into the water and hot cocoa mix and gave it to his niece. He considered making one for Maren, but she'd become a perpetual motion machine, greeting her dad's coworkers and managing the serving line. He and Rhiannon went through the line and sat at the nearest table.

Karl and family arrived. The boys bad-mouthed the buffet and demanding fast food. In a firm voice, Maren told them, "This is not a playground. No running. No touching the equipment."

"You're not the boss of me!" they yelled in unison.

Rhiannon slipped off her chair and disappeared. Neil scanned the room, but couldn't see where she'd gone. The hangar didn't offer many places to hide. The tugs and toolboxes were lined up against the back wall. No drops of oil marred the floors, or the aircraft. The planes were painted a businesslike scheme—white on top and gray on the belly with a dark maroon stripe down the fuselage. This had to be the cleanest, most orderly hangar he'd ever been in. Was it always this way or just for Arne's funeral?

Karl's boys ran past. The younger pushed the older so he tripped over a tow bar and smacked his hands and knees on the cement floor. He screamed bloody-murder. Both parents ignored him. Whining, the older stood, stomped to the hot water dispenser, and sprayed the younger. He shrieked. Still the parents didn't respond. No wonder Rhiannon avoided them.

"Join you?" asked a deep voice behind him.

"Sure. Glad to see familiar faces." Neil stood and shook hands with the Coffeys and Dr. Gibson, then he moved Rhiannon's plate out of the way. "Rhiannon was here, but Maren's racing around."

The grocery manager shook his head. "You won't get her to sit, no sir."

Neil frowned at the somberly-dressed people shuffling through the buffet line. "Funeral customs must be different here."

"I prefer church basements, myself." Dr. Gibson nodded and spread horseradish on her roast beef.

"No, it's not the venue," Neil's gesture took in the cavernous building and the corporate planes. "Arne worked here. Having the reception in the Upjohn hangar makes sense."

Mr. Coffey mumbled to his wife, "If you have my doings in the A&P, I'll come back to haunt you."

Mrs. Coffey raised an eyebrow. "Your ghost does not scare me."

"I thought the funeral home would pick up Maren and Rhiannon." Neil couldn't stop himself. "And then at the grave, isn't family supposed to sit together in the front row? It's like Karl was the only child."

Mrs. Coffey said. "Treating her second class makes him no class."

"We're glad you gave them a ride," the doctor said. "None of us could get away from work earlier."

Neil nodded at Helga, sitting with the remains of several fried chickens. "And the agent of death lurking around. So far, six people have told Maren to get a lawyer."

"Nine." Mr. Coffey's finger circled. "We did too."

Neil jabbed a thumb at the buffet table where Maren set out another tray of lefse. "You'd think she was the catering staff."

"Karl paid for the food, but expected Maren to make it in her tiny kitchen and serve it." Mr. Coffey shook his head as Karl yelled for coffee and Maren gave him a refill. "Don't know why she puts up with it."

Reverend Johnson approached Maren at the buffet line and they had a whispered conversation. Maren went back to work. The minister put a sandwich on his plate, scanned the room, then headed for their table.

"This is the moment I've been waiting for." Mrs. Coffey rubbed her hands together, then patted the place next to her. "Reverend Johnson, you have questions and I have answers."

"Lord have mercy." Mr. Coffey winked at Neil.

Rhiannon and a trim older man approached Maren. "This young lady wants to see her grandpa's planes."

Maren surveyed the buffet. "Well..."

"Everyone has food. Mom, please.." The girl dragged her toward the largest, a Gulfstream turboprop.

"I'd like to see it myself." Neil stood.

"Don't you fly one of those things?" Mr. Coffey asked.

"Mine's a bus. This is a limo."

The man introduced himself as one of Upjohn's pilots. He unfolded the stairs and they all climbed in. The cockpit was crowded, so Neil turned right and followed the carpeted aisle to the first recliner.

"Walt Disney has a plane just like this," the pilot told Rhiannon as he settled into the copilot's seat. "But his has Mickey Mouse on the tail."

"This poor plane doesn't even have a vitamin bottle on its tail, but, you do have a TV." Rhiannon exclaimed from the cockpit.

Maren said from the captain's seat, "It's a radar screen, so the pilots can see thunderstorms."

"Why don't they look out the window?"

"Radar helps at night or in clouds—"

"Whoa. What are all these buttons on the ceiling?"

"Circuit breakers. They pop out if there's an electrical overload." Maren explained the instruments to her daughter, but the panel didn't hold a ten-year-old's attention for long. Rhiannon wandered back, peeking into compartments, exploring the galley. She sat across from Neil, pulled out the teak fold-down table between their seats, and dealt an imaginary hand of cards.

"I see your five and raise your seven."

"Does your mom know you play poker?" Neil whispered.

She shrugged. "I learned at her work, on snow days. You going to raise or fold?"

Neil contemplated his invisible hand. "Got any eights?"

"Go fish is a baby game." Rhiannon threw her imaginary cards on the table and, with a swish of gold curls, stomped off, continuing her exploration of the rear of the plane.

"We sure miss you around here." The pilot's voice carried from the cockpit. "You were going to be our first female pilot in the flight department. The wives won't have anyone else."

"Thanks," Maren said. "I miss flying."

"Ran into Pat Schiffer a while back," he continued. "He asked about you. 'Course he remembered the best check ride he ever gave. We'd take you back—"

Rhiannon hurried toward Neil and hid under the table, as Karl's kids thundered into the plane. One of the boys spotted her. "Hey, it's the bastard."

Without thinking, Neil stood and swung, his hand catching the kid on his neck. "You will never, ever say that word again."

The second kid backed toward the door, "But Dad—"

Neil grabbed him with his left hand. "Your dad is wrong. Real men never say that word."

Maren climbed out of the cockpit, hands fisted, face red. "Apologize to your cousin. Both of you."

"Sorry," they said in a singsong tone, then scrambled down the steps.

Neil crouched and looked under the table. "It's safe to come out." When she did, he hugged her. "Oh Rhiannon, I'm sorry."

She shrugged. "I should be used to it by now."

"After today, we'll never see them again." Maren rubbed her daughter's back.

Rhiannon thanked the pilot for the tour, peeked out the door to see if the coast was clear, then left. Neil followed, ready to dump the boys and their useless parents in the nearest lav truck. But first, he turned to check on Maren.

She hesitated in the doorway. Her hand fumbled for the railing, then clutched it in a white-knuckle grip. Her eyes blinked large and dark in her pale face as she started down.

"Maren, are you all right?" Neil asked, alarm raising his voice.

Halfway down the eight steps, she crumpled. Neil stopped her fall before she hit the concrete. Her skin felt clammy. "Rhiannon, go get Dr. Gibson."

But the doctor was right there, one hand on Maren's wrist, the other on her forehead, lifting her eyelids.

"I'm fine." Maren tried to sit up.

"Don't move," the doctor instructed. "What did you have for breakfast?"

"Half a cup of coffee," Rhiannon volunteered. "I made toast, but she wouldn't eat it. She was up all night cooking."

"No food and no sleep."

"Do you want the first aid kit?" the pilot asked.

"No thank you, but juice would be helpful." The doctor consulted wth Mrs. Coffey. "My house is full of little girls and yours is full of babies." She turned to Neil. "Drive Maren home and get fluids in her—juice, soup. No coffee. She needs a decent night's sleep. I'll take Rhi to my house and check on Maren later." She turned to her patient. "Your doctor's telling your boss that you're off tomorrow."

"Agreed. She's got plenty of sick days saved up." Mr. Coffey pushed through the mourners and handed Maren's coat to his wife. "Give me your keys, Neil. I'll bring your car around."

Mrs. Coffey took Maren's car keys, then helped Maren into her winter gear.

Helga stage-whispered to Maren's sister-in-law, "I bet she's pregnant again."

Neil scowled. If he had a pitcher of water, he'd dissolve the witch.

Dr. Gibson rose to her full height, close to six feet. She stared down at the murmuring crowd. "The diagnosis is exhaustion with dehydration."

Karl loomed over Maren. "Always making a spectacle of herself."

"You want a spectacle?" Helga unfurled a sheaf of papers, her bulging eyes glittering with triumph. "Here you go—I donated your dad's estate to the Green Party, to implement their redistribution of wealth plank."

The mourners gasped.

"You can't!" Karl sputtered out a jumble of legal terms. "You're the executor, not the beneficiary. You have a fiduciary duty! I'll sue until you can't see straight."

"I saw it on Perry Mason." Helga gave a wicked witch laugh.

Time to boogie, before she unleashed the flying monkeys. Neil lifted Maren, light and boneless. The crowd parted to let them through as he carried her to the waiting sedan. Neil set her down, tilted the seat back, and buckled her in. The pilot handed him a six-pack of apple juice.

As they left the airport, Maren moaned. "I can't leave. I have to clean up."

"Yeah, you'd make a good mop about now." He stopped at the light, popped open the juice, and helped her take a sip.

"I'm fine."

"And I'm Amelia Earhart."

"I thought you looked familiar." Her voice trailed off. She closed her eyes and dozed the rest of the way to Mrs. V's.

He parked in the driveway and ran around to help her out.

"Thanks for the ride."

"You're not getting rid of me. Doctor's orders." He couldn't navigate the steep steps to the basement while carrying Maren, so he pulled her arm across his shoulder and held onto her waist.

Her teeth chattered. "I dr-ank the... ju-juice."

"Next item on the checklist is soup." He rescued the keys from her shaking fingers and unlocked the door to the apartment. It wasn't much warmer than outside. "I should have brought Rhiannon home and had Dr. Gibson take you."

"Stuck with the...co-consolation prize." Maren shivered so hard she could barely speak. "I'll gi-give you directions and you can go-go get her."

"No, I mean, how'm I going to get you into your pjs?"

She squinted in the bright overhead light of the bathroom. "I can do it."

"Sure. I'll be back in three minutes." Leaving the door open an inch, he went to heat soup. As the microwave beeped, a thud shook the wall.

"Maren, are you okay? I'm coming in."

She sat on the toilet lid, slumped against the wall. She'd changed into grey sweats.

He took the socks from her lap and pulled them onto her ice-cold feet. "One sip of juice doesn't restore you to superwoman status. Soup's ready. It's beef barley."

"No thanks."

"Doctor's orders."

He carried her to the living room. The squeaky kitchen chairs didn't have arms to keep her upright, so he propped her in the corner of the sofa, moved her Bible out of the way, then set the space heater close to her feet. Tucking a dish towel into the neck of her sweatshirt like a bib, his fingertips brushed the soft indentation at the base of her neck. *Brakes! Don't need both of us shaking.*

He sat beside her, holding the soup-filled WMU mug. She didn't move, so he took her cold hand, guiding the spoon from mug to mouth. "What did you tell Rhiannon when she was a baby? Open the hangar and let the airplane in." The spoon slipped out of her grasp and splashed into the mug. "Come on, Maren. Five more bites."

Off to dreamland she went. What could he say to keep her awake? Any other day he pushed her hot buttons with no effort at all. What subject would get her steamed? Not politics, not religion, but... "Why's Karl treating you like a slave instead of family?"

Her eyelids fluttered open. "I used to be the favorite. Now he is." Her words came out smoother, but slow.

"No excuse for being a jerk." Neil gave her another spoonful of soup. What else could they talk about? "Death is tough. At least you don't have survivor guilt."

Sleep-heavy eyes blinked at him. "You?"

"Yeah." He used the towel to catch a drip from her bottom lip... her soft bottom lip. He shook himself and lined up his thoughts. "My brother had a wife, three kids and one on the way, twenty-eight employees, several million fans. Whereas me, no one would have noticed if I'd died."

She opened her mouth and he slid the loaded spoon in.

Neil continued, "Vincent, our cello-playing philosopher, told me death has no quota system, no draft board. For whatever reason my brother died, random chance or toxic motocross riding, I couldn't have changed places with him." No matter how much he'd wanted to. Anything to stop the floods of tears from family, the band, himself. "Whenever the sads got me, I'd hold one of the kids and we'd have a good cry together."

"No crying." Her breathing quickened. "No upsetting Rhiannon."

"But she knows her grandpa died. She knows you're sad." His left arm reached around Maren, snugging her in close, pulling her upright, trying to share his body heat. He leaned his cheek on the crown of her head. "Go ahead, cry on me."

"Tired."

"Don't tell me you're worried about your makeup running." She didn't wear makeup. "Get it all out, all the hurt in your heart. You'll sleep better." He went on, mumbling more cliched stuff about grief and the cleansing power of tears, sounding like Phil Donahue reading sympathy cards.

He tipped his head to the side. Maren's eyelashes curled dry over her cheek. She breathed evenly, deeply. Yeah, he remembered this fatigue. Some days he'd felt limp as Harmony's sock monkey. Other days he'd been encased in concrete. Changing TV channels rivaled climbing Mt. Everest. Chewing applesauce, even digesting water, hurt too much.

His lips rested on her hairline, steadying her head, and she wasn't objecting. She must be asleep. His tongue snuck out and his whole body tingled with the salt of her skin.

Brakes! Reverse!

He put the soup down, scooted to the edge of the couch, and lifted Maren, lukewarm and limp. He headed down the hall. The first door was the bathroom, the end one was Rhiannon's bedroom, so this must be... He leaned back, balancing her slight weight as he caught the knob. It opened to the dark, musty gloom of the furnace. Cradling Maren, he turned in a circle. So where... Not the awful sofa. He couldn't hold her all night. Well, he *could*, but he shouldn't. Rhiannon's bed would work for tonight. He flipped back the covers with his foot and rolled her in. She whimpered and curled into a ball. He tucked the comforter around her.

Still cold in here. It wasn't safe to run the space heater in Rhi's room, with all the flammables, so he heated bath towels in the drier and covered her with them. She sighed and stretched out.

Patti never let the girls go to sleep with rubber bands in their hair. He worked the elastic off the end of her braid, then slipped his fingers between the strands. The plait unraveled at his touch. He moved higher, loosening, combing, to her nape. Warm silk rippled through his hands and spread over her shoulders. *Sleep well, Rapunzel.* Breathing hard, Neil backed out of the room.

A BED? *What happened? Not again, no!* "You're crushing me! Get off!"

"Maren?" A man stood in the doorway.

She shot up, kicking to push back into the corner, holding the pillow like a shield. "No—" The room spun and blackened.

"Maren, it's Neil." He sat on Rhi's practice chair, drawling in his easy Virginia accent, his tone soothing. "You're safe. Rhi's over at the Gibson's. You got light-headed at the reception so I drove you home." He paused and leaned forward. "Did you have...a flashback?"

"No. I don't remember anything." It's Neil. Not Alan. She took inventory of her body. Still dressed. Okay. Nothing happened. Heart slowing, she sank back under the covers, then realized he'd said something. "What did you say?"

"I couldn't figure out where you sleep." He still wore the white shirt and dark dress slacks from the funeral. Whiskers in shades of brown sprinkled his jaw. "The sofa's too short. All I could find was a sleeping bag. Had me singing 'Gentle on my Mind.' So, whose sleeping bag is stashed behind your couch?"

"Mine, of course." Why was he asking?

"You sleep on the floor every night? You don't have a bed?" He leaned forward, propping elbows on knees. "Cement is cold and hard."

Ah, that's it. "Forget it. I haven't paid you for the snowblower or winter coat or car. I don't have room for a bed and anyway plenty of people sleep on the floor..." She paused, out of energy.

"I'll bid a Tokyo overnight next month, bring you back a futon."

"Don't you dare."

"I'm joking—we don't go to Tokyo." He flashed his teasing smile on his way out the door. "I'll get you some juice."

She flopped her legs over the edge of the bed and pushed upright, fighting dizziness. "The snowblower. I've got to get the driveway cleared. What time is it?" What was wrong with her? She never slept past five. Pewter light filtered through the snow-drifted window well. No doubt Mrs. V's laundry had reached crisis proportions, and she really should go in to work for a few hours or Sandra would fall behind. "I'm getting up," Her leaden body wouldn't move, but it did notice a change in the temperature. "It's warmer in here."

"I adjusted the heat registers and thermostat." Neil returned with a glass of red juice. His wide, warm hands covered hers, steadying her.

The cranberry-apple's tartness jump-started her brain. "Have you been here all night?" she asked between swallows.

"Mrs. V let me stay on the daybed at the top of the stairs, in case you needed anything at night. She called right after you fell asleep. She'd taken a flower delivery for you, from work. You were unsteady, so I checked on you every few hours, dozed. Sorry I'm so scruffy."

Not scruffy, but comfortable. Like the broken-in pair of jeans he wore so well. "You're paying for a motel room you didn't use."

"I'll stop by and clean up on my way to work." He took the empty glass from her. "Dr. Gibson dropped by twice last evening to see how you were doing. She'll bring Rhiannon back this morning. While I was doing dishes, I heard four messages, nothing urgent. My favorite was your brother's rant about your dad naming Helga his executor."

"There is some justice in this world." She chuckled, imagining those two hard-heads bashing together. The mention of Karl raised another worry, something that had been on her mind for months. "Neil... if something happened to me...I don't want Karl...it would be complicated with your flight schedule...would you be Rhiannon's guardian? Give it some thought." A few months ago this idea seemed crazy, but now it seemed like her best option.

"Dr. Gibson says you'll be okay." He sat and covered her chilly hands. His heat ignited her defroster. "I'd be honored. I'm guardian for the other kids. My plan would be to switch to the training department, so I'd be in town."

"I'd hate for you to give up flying." Another worry surfaced. "It might involve lawyers and courts, no estate to pay for it."

"I've met Karl." Neil shook his head. "Don't have to convince me."

"The form is on the bookcase, next to the record player. Reverend Gibson can notarize it. And...could you get your brother's medical records, anything that might affect Rhi?" Maren inched away, before she became addicted to Neil's heat. "Why is the kitchen timer going off?"

"Stay awake, now. Breakfast's ready." Neil hurried from the room.

"Later." She slumped against the wall.

He returned with a tray. "A short lady with a big smile dropped this off."

"You described half the women in church."

"Sorry. I should have asked her name, so you can thank her."

Maren examined the square of egg casserole on her plate. "Tomatoes and green peppers. Sister Lucille. Sister Dorothy doesn't believe in vegetables."

Neil settled into the chair with his plate and dug in. "Good cook, whoever she is."

"They're all good cooks." Her stomach was willing, but her arms were not. "When am I going to feel better?"

"Grief is tough. Takes time, good food, sleep." He set down his plate and helped her get a few bites in. "Vincent had some advice on getting through the hard part, those first few days and weeks after the funeral. He asked me for three good times from the past year." He fed her another bite. "Finding you and Rhiannon would be my big one for this year."

"Three good things..."

A smile flickered over his face. "With a daughter like Rhiannon, you'll come up with more."

She forced herself to look him in the eye. "Rhi's progress on the cello, flying to Chicago, Rhi's concert. They're all connected to you. Thank you." She turned away from the half-empty plate and rolled down into the pillow. Then another thought hit. "Neil, are the Consequences gone?"

He sat on Rhi's chair and wrapped his hands around hers. "You weren't able to finish college, so you've had to work a low-paying job, drive junkers that leave you stranded, mow lawns to pay for cello lessons and rent...because your dad felt he'd lost respect at work, so he withdrew his love and support. Do I have that right?"

She nodded. "It never was about Consequences."

"Not the way I see it." He shook his head. "Whatever you'd like to do—change jobs, go back to school, move—I'll support you, help you provide for Rhi. Make a plan. But first, get some sleep."

"No. I have to take down Mrs. V's Christmas decorations and shampoo her carpets. And the lady across the street asked me to reupholster her..."

REUPHOLSTERING? Carpet shampooing? Maren worked harder than anyone he knew. Neil cleaned up from breakfast, then returned to Maren. She lay on her side, eyes half-open.

"You wore white in my dream," she murmured.

"I figured you'd be too tired to dream last night."

"No. A long time ago. A daydream. A white hat..." She took a deeper breath. Her tongue touched her upper lip. "At the Student Health Center. They gave me the results of my pregnancy test and a map to an abortion clinic in Grand Rapids." She flinched. "I thought, now Neil will come through the door and tell them..."

High G-forces pushed him into the chair.

"Then the hospital kept asking me about money. How was I going to pay for this baby? And you carried in a briefcase full of cash."

"Oh, Maren..." He put his hand over hers. Still cold. He'd warm the towels in the dryer again.

"You'd take us somewhere quiet, clean. No roaches, no lead paint, no drug dealers..."

"If only I'd known." His fingers picked up the tension in hers, the twitches, poised for action. "No more worries. I'm here now. Ten years late, but I'm here for you now, doing what I can to help you get your life back. I promise. And I'll tell you again when you're awake." He wanted to sing her a lullaby, but couldn't think of one. Maybe something about being a friend through turbulent times. He'd mastered Simon and Garfunkel's "Bridge over Troubled Waters" on the piano, but it was impossible to play quietly. And there wasn't a piano here. So, quiet as a whisper, he sung it. And she drifted off.

Chapter Fourteen

"Let's go get the mail," Neil called to Tango as he arrived home from his trip. He pulled on a sweatshirt and whistled John Denver's "Back Home Again" as he enjoyed Virginia's balmy weather. The low winter sun sent stripes of light through the bare tree branches. The creek, full from last week's rain, gurgled against its banks. His imaginary dog dashed through the leaves past unimpressed squirrels and oblivious rabbits.

Close to Wolfe's Den, the woods echoed with the sound of someone abusing a trap set. Neil turned toward the practice studio. "Sounds like Andy," he told Tango. "You're welcome to come... although it'll be loud."

Neil prayed for help, entered their childhood golden retriever's birthdate in the keypad, and stepped inside. Andy sat at the drum set, exercising more fury than control. He flipped his sweaty hair out of his eyes long enough to identify Neil, then went back to it. This past year, the boy had shot up, going from chubby to lean. The emerging bones, especially his brow and cheeks, were Alan's.

Neil sat on the piano bench and listened for music. There wasn't any. His eyes skimmed the wall display of album covers, and gold and platinum awards. How would Alan deal with this teenage anger? Probably shrug and leave on another tour. Although if his brother were here, Neil wouldn't have found Rhiannon's birth certificate and Andy would be chill.

Finally, the kid paused to dry the sweat off his palms and wet his whistle. Neil played the first nine notes of "Dueling Banjos" on the piano.

With another toss of his head, Andy switched to mallets, hit the eight notes on the bells, then ended with a whack on the cymbal. Neil grabbed a harmonica and picked out the next phrase.

"You're no Bob Dylan," Andy razzed. He picked up a bass and nailed it.

Neil answered with lame trumpet squawks. Andy bested him on the sax, but Neil's clarinet squeaks gave the kid a grin. They raced around the studio, snatching up whatever instrument was out and faking their best, working their way through mandolin, ukulele, accordion (awful), oboe (even worse), French horn, and synth. When Andy picked up his trombone, Neil went back to the baby grand, and the duel became a duet. They raced to a grand, noisy finish.

Neil raised his palm for a high-five.

Andy slapped him hard enough to sting. "Hey, long-lost. I thought we were going to hang out last week."

"Rhiannon's grandpa died. Didn't you get my message?"

"Oh. Yeah. I guess." He slouched, not holding eye contract. His radar wasn't picking up activity in others' lives.

"Still mad?"

"Naw." He took another slurp from his sports bottle. Neil made a mental note to check its contents. Andy focused on cleaning the slides of his trombone and took a shaky breath. "The cast list came out."

"For *Fiddler on the Roof?*" Best to check—changes happened quickly here.

"Duh." Andy gave a noisy exhale. "Melody got third daughter, Harmony's in pit. I'm stuck in the chorus with Cody."

Neil closed his eyes for a second, relieved to learn Andy's mood wasn't his fault. The auditions had been competitive. Patti had recommended extra dance and vocal coaching, but Andy had blown her off.

"At least you didn't get the third groom part and have to marry your sister every night."

"Gag me with a spoon," he said in a tone more discouraged than angry.

"The bottle dance scene could use a mandolin." Patti stood in the doorway, dressed in dark purple. Since Alan's death, her shoulders had been tense, as if trying to protect herself from the next blow. Today they'd relaxed into her normal regal posture.

"Mom. You're back." Andy straightened. "I wanted to go. Why didn't you wake me?"

"Next year. Help you decide on a vocational path other than crime boss," she said with a smile. She'd been to the Federal Penitentiary in West Virginia, on her annual visit to Alan's chief roadie.

Neil cleaned the French horn. "How is old Scorch?"

"Loquacious. He'd been in solitary for a week."

"Lo-what?" Andy plopped onto the couch. "What's that mean?"

"It's on the SAT's." Patti sauntered across the room, uncapped her son's sports bottle and took a sip. "Spend more time on vocab and reading lists, and less with TV and Game Boy."

"Wheel of Fortune has words!"

Patti gave her son a "not-impressed" raised eyebrow, then turned to Neil and tipped her head toward the house. *"Babo."* She used her Korean name for him, so he knew he was in her good graces this time. "It's about Maren."

What about Maren? Scorch had been there. What did he know?

Andy patted the cushion next to him. "Have a seat, Mom. Take a load off. Rest your weary legs."

She shook her head, her gaze firm.

"Oh, man. How'm I ever gonna learn anything?" He slumped deep into the cushions and closed his eyes.

"Like your mom said, read." Neil knuckled the boy's head, then followed Patti out.

"Scorch confirmed your guess." She climbed the steps to the porch and sat on the shadowed end of the swing, where he couldn't see her expression. Her voice carried anger. "He cooked GHB in the equipment truck and drugged...Maren."

"He almost killed her."

"Much as I want to blame Scorch, Alan *was* complicit. What he did to her was immoral and illegal. It would have destroyed our marriage, if I'd known. Alan would have been implicated in her murder and in prison." She exhaled slowly, reaching for self-control. "Mad doesn't begin to cover it, but becoming a raging maniac would destroy our family. So I'm working through it, going to counseling, giving it to God."

She turned to Neil, flicking her fingers with a give-it-to-me gesture. "Maren, before and after."

"Aviation student at the university, intern in Upjohn's flight department. Now working at A&P."

Patti winced. "All this time I've been sitting on my butt, living off royalties and publishing rights." She didn't give herself enough credit; managing Alan's business took a lot of expertise. "While Maren's trying to raise a kid on three bucks an hour."

"She mows lawns for a discount on rent and cello lessons."

Patti opened her fist and reached for Neil's hand. "Scorch is doing life, Alan is dead. No amount of money can make this right, but is there any way to make it better? What's fair? They've had ten years of hardship and shouldn't have to wait. Take what I've set aside and give it to her. Please."

"Maren won't accept help, unless it's for Rhiannon."

"Maybe I can endow a scholarship at Interlochen." Patti released his hand and stood. "If you think of anything else I can do, let me know."

Neil followed her inside. "Maren asked if there's any family medical history that might affect Rhiannon."

"I'll look into it."

"And..." He took a fortifying breath. "...she wants to name me Rhiannon's guardian."

Patti faced him, her expression worried as the implications hit. "Effective immediately? Is she ill?"

"No. She had a scare at the funeral reception, exhaustion, but she's otherwise healthy. Guardianship as part of her will. Next of kin is her brother, who's taking revenge on Maren for his childhood, when she was the favorite child. His kids are monsters."

She shuddered. "Call Parton. Get the name of a Michigan lawyer, so it's incontestable."

"Good idea." Neil's muscles unwound, relieved Patti wouldn't fight him on this.

"Your mail is in the Sealtest metal box on the porch. Figured if it came in the house, it'd be lost."

"Thanks. For keeping it all together." He hugged her, grabbed his mail, then called Tango. His steps were lighter on the way home —Patti had called Maren by her name.

NEIL DROPPED his suitcase on the hotel's luggage rack, flopped on the double bed, and reached for the phone. "Maren?"

"Rhi's asleep."

He glanced at his watch and winced. "I shouldn't have called so late."

"Where are you?"

"Los Angeles. Patti's working on family medical history for you." The rest of their conversation could wait. "How are you feeling?"

"I've gotten lots of mail this week. First, a will with guardianship. You didn't have to. Lawyers are expensive. The handwritten one was fine."

"Now it's official—no one can question it. Sign it with two witnesses and you're good."

"It's a load off my mind. Thank you." Maren paused, then said, "And thank you for the sleeping pad. Self-inflating, comfortable, and warmer."

"Saw it in a camping store near our hotel in Seattle and thought of you." He imagined Maren wearing sweats, climbing into her sleeping bag, floating on the pad, and drifting off to sleep.

"So, what's wrong?"

Was she tuned in to his voice? "Rough day at work."

"No reports of plane crashes on the radio. How bad could it be?"

"Yeah, got a point there. This captain…" He started over. "We took off from Phoenix for Mexico City. No discussion, doesn't say a word. He sets the altitude alert for the airport elevation."

"Aren't there mountains?"

Exactly what he'd been worried about. "I mentioned it for the benefit of the cockpit voice recorder. Fortunately the smog wasn't too bad. We land and he dashes out before the passengers. Five minutes before push back, he shows up with all these duty-free bags."

"Delayed Christmas shopping?"

"Almost delayed airplane. So we blast off, and about halfway back, he suddenly starts fussing about weather. Phoenix is right off the nose. The visibility's so good we can almost see Vegas."

"Is this guy new? He's never flown to Mexico City before?"

"He's one of our most senior captains. Good thing he's going on vacation, so I don't have to fly with him the rest of the month. I'll put him on my no-fly list."

"And the other unsuspecting copilots?"

They'd been on the back burner of his mind—a new-hire might get stuck with this captain when weather was dicey. "I'll give Flight Standards and Training a heads-up." He took a deep breath for the first time in hours. "Sorry. Talking too much about my problems. Maren, how are you doing?"

"The bad news is the car needed a tire, but good news is the high school music director let Rhi join the chorus of *Bye, Bye, Birdie*." Her voice carried a smile.

"A silly show, but gets a lot of kids on the stage. Our school put it on the year my voice changed, so…"

"You were cast as the kid who couldn't get a date."

"I got laughs, but no kisses. When is the show? I'd like to come."

Maren gave him the dates, but he had recurrent training that weekend. He promised to call Rhi in a few days, then they hung up.

Neil fell asleep in two minutes.

· · ·

146

"Hey girl, take a break." Royetta stuck her head into the freezer.

Maren checked off the last item on the inventory sheet and returned to the deli. "What brings you to your favorite place of employment?"

Her friend made a gagging noise, then lowered her voice. "Here to pick up an order, but first, my good news. Old Beelzebub's heart gave out. Surprised me, since I didn't think he had one. Next family dinner will be chill."

"Such a relief." Maren gave her a hug.

Royetta looked around. "You running this joint by yourself?"

"My trainee went on break."

"Without you? Probably'll get lost on the way back." She leaned against the worktable. "What's new with the uncle?"

"He came to Rhi's concert. Got me a car. And a snowblower—I do the driveway and sidewalks in exchange for a discount on rent. Helped with Christmas shopping. And took care of me when I got worn out with my dad's funeral. He's done a lot...more than I expected."

"I'm starting to like this guy."

Maren was starting to like him too. "I'm training him to call before he visits."

"Trainable. Any chance this could turn into something more than friendship?"

Maren winced. "He's Lucifer's brother. Anyway, he's all about Rhi and her music."

The Troll at the Desk marched past. "Back to work!"

"I better pick up that order for the paper mill, before I get you in trouble."

Maren handed Royetta the large box of sandwiches. "Stop by any time."

"Whenever the Troll takes a day off." Which was never. "And keep working on getting rid of those pest thoughts."

. . .

NEIL FIDDLED with a tortilla chip at the Dancing Jalapeño along the River Walk. Three boats packed with a wedding party slid by, drunk-singing Alan's "Mating Call" and howling. A boatload of tourists was next, enjoying San Antonio in their T-shirts and shorts. Maren and Rhiannon could thaw out here, visit the Alamo. Except this overnight didn't get in until after it closed. Let's see, he was off next Friday. They could leave after her cello lesson. No, he worked Saturdays this month. There's President's Day, but pass-riding on a holiday weekend was a sure way to get bumped. How about a midweek trip? Rhiannon could afford to miss school. She could bring back postcards for her class. And Mr. Coffey had said Maren had plenty of time off. If they took the six o'clock and changed planes in Kansas City—

His captain reached across the checkerboard-sized table and handed him a photo. Neil squinted in the lantern light. It looked like a poorly made Xerox copy of an old radar screen. But what kind of storm was it painting?

Captain Mike grinned at the rest of the crew. "He don't have a clue."

Neil rotated the photo. No lights went on, not even a dim bulb. "Okay, I give up. What is this?"

"Don't even have the picture right side up." The female flight attendant rotated it. "It's Mike's first."

"Your first thunderstorm?" Neil ventured.

The other members of the crew burst into laughter.

"Bachelors!" the captain hooted, almost falling into the river.

"Earth to Neil," the male flight attendant said into his hand.

Neil squinted at the picture again. It must be some obscure Russian technology, maybe something from their space program.

The waitress delivered their quesadillas. "Aw, whose baby?" she nodded at the picture.

"Mine." Mike straightened his shoulders.

"This is a baby?"

"Sure." A red fingernail tapped the picture. "Head, arm, legs. Being a little shy, here. Can't tell if it's a boy or girl."

"Boy. We could tell from the video."

"You took a video of your kid before he's born?" Something about this made Neil a little queasy, so he handed the picture back to Mike.

"Ultrasound. He sucked his thumb through most of it."

"Sign up for orthodontic benefits," the flight attendant cautioned.

The waitress flashed her nails in dismissal. "Thumb sucking is good. Shows they can calm themselves."

"Try to switch him to a pacifier." The female flight attendant pulled out her wallet and showed off a family photo. "Look at the teeth on these kids."

"And keep a pacifier in the car," the waitress added. "Nothing worse than being stuck in traffic with a screaming baby."

"My wife won't be doing much running around. She's planning to breastfeed."

When Patti breastfed, Neil knew to bring her a glass of water and a burp rag. And make sure the older kids didn't burn the house down. So he had nothing to contribute to *this* conversation. He focused on maneuvering the loaded chip into his mouth without dripping on his uniform shirt.

The waitress cleared their empty chip baskets. "Breast-fed kids are easy to tote. Grab a diaper and go. Are you doing cloth or disposable?"

Maybe he should get up, bus some tables, give his seat to San Antonio's *What to Expect When You're Expecting* guru.

"What's your holdup?" the captain asked Neil after another party flagged down their waitress. "All the single flight attendants go into heat whenever they look at you. This time next year, you could be showing up for work with baby spit on your tie."

The holdup? Maren. No one else made his heart play the trumpet *soli* from Chase's "Get It On." Yes, Patti could say Maren's name, but that didn't mean they were ready to be neighbors. "I've got nieces and nephews." Neil reached for the photos in his wallet.

Shaking his head, the older man bit into his taco. "Ain't nothing like the real thing."

. . .

A HAND too warm and large to be Rhi's slid into Maren's. The palm wasn't hard or callused, but there was a strength and firmness in the touch. She woke, disappointed to find her hand empty. Had she dreamed of...of Neil?

Lord, restrain my dreams.

Maren tried to get Rhi going, but last night's practice had her sleeping hard. "I'm leaving for my gig. The number's by the phone. We'll go clothes shopping when I get back." Thanks to the car, they could hit most of Kalamazoo's thrift stores in one day.

Rhi mumbled and rolled over, exactly what Maren wanted to do. Arne's death had more tired and weepy than usual.

Maren locked the door behind her, got in the car, and turned the key. It screeched. The battery was new, so it must be the alternator.

Unlike last week's gigs, a funeral and an evening wedding, brunch at the country club paid well and could turn into regular work...if she got there on time. Maren glanced at her watch and ran for it.

Two minutes late, sweaty, face raw from the cold wind, legs aching from the deep snow, she stepped into the country club's dining room, all coffered ceiling and white tablecloths.

The manager, Mrs. Westhuizen, frowned at her watch. Maren's first impression had been blown to bits; she wouldn't be invited back.

"I'm sorry. Car trouble." Maren hung up her coat, hurried to the piano, and played her best.

Midway through the second hour, a young guy pushed an elder in a wheelchair past the piano. The older man gave her an impish smile and muttered, "I've got a gal in Kalamazoo."

"Bet you do, as handsome as you are." Maren smiled back. "Or are you putting in a request?" The manager had said the job didn't require singing or taking requests. Since she wouldn't be invited back, she'd at least make this gent's day.

"I'll sing, you play," he told her.

Maren segued into the Glen Miller favorite and nodded for him to start. The man took a deep breath and let loose, hitting every note and remembering all the words. Maren accompanied him and provided harmony. He finished to enthusiastic applause from people whose usual was a golf clap.

"Thank you, my dear." The man extended a shaky hand. Maren clasped it, then kissed his cheek, wishing her father had been as kind as this fellow. The young man pushed him a few steps, then turned and whispered to Maren, "Thank you. He hasn't said two words all winter."

"Music is healing." Maren blinked away tears and played her entire Glen Miller repertoire, then went back to cheerful pop standards.

At the end of the session, Mrs. Westhuizen called her into the office. "Lots of compliments and tips." She handed Maren a thick envelope. "We'd like to have you back next Saturday, if you have dependable transportation."

"I live nearby, so even if it's not the alternator, I'll be here."

The manager reached for the phone. "My brother has a shop." She spoke into the phone for a moment then handed it to Maren, who answered questions about make, model, and year. After some back and forth, the man agreed to deliver a refurbished alternator for a decent price. Maren thanked him and the manager, then bundled up for the walk home.

"I'll give you a ride." Mrs. Westhuizen pulled on her coat.

Considering the single-digit temperatures, blowing snow, and her flagging energy. Maren gladly accepted.

Take that, Consequences.

Chapter Fifteen

As Neil drove, Maren closed her eyes against the bright sun heating the car. If she were a cat, she'd curl up in the window and nap.

Rhi turned on the radio. A harsh voice screamed to pounding music. Rhi changed the station. "That makes Mom spit on police officers and write bad words on the street."

"*Your* mom?" Neil sputtered.

Maren shook her head.

On the classic rock station, Barry Manilow crooned "Could it Be Magic". Rhi said, "Hey! Chopin's *Prelude in C Minor!*"

"You recognize it?" Neil asked. "It's not a cello piece."

"People can sing to classical music and get it on the radio? Cool!"

"Several Beatles' songs are inspired by classical music," Neil told her. "But, as far as I know, this is the only one that uses the exact piece."

"And there's *Hooked on Classics,* but it's all instrumental."

They bumped through a series of potholes, rattling the skis wedged between the dashboard and the rear window. Foolish waste of money, renting all this. It had been ten years since Maren had taken cross-country; she wouldn't remember enough to teach anyone. Besides, Mrs. V wanted her to take down the Christmas lights. And... what else? If her brain hadn't been turned into potato salad, she'd think of the other jobs on her list. Neil must have something better to do, preferably with his nieces and nephews in Virginia where the weather wasn't clear, eighteen degrees, winds ten knots out of 230. Ack! An aviation report. That's what comes from hanging out with a pilot. Think snow: inch and a half of new powder on a three foot base, light winds. Perfect skiing weather.

"This is it." Neil grinned as he pulled into the lot. "You didn't think I'd ever learn my way around Kalamazoo."

"Don't pat yourself on the back too hard, Uncle Neil." Rhi held up the rental agency map. "If you can find A&P, you can find Asylum Lake."

"Odd name for a park."

But a good place to learn to ski with trails through woods, open fields, and gently rolling hills.

Rhi climbed out. "The State Hospital ran a farm here. Then Frank Lloyd Wright built four houses. And now Western students use it for skiing and geophysical research and stuff."

"Geophysical research? Do their seismographs pick up cellists in snow boots?"

"Uncle Neil!" Rhi huffed. "I may not be light on my feet, but I don't register on the Richter Scale."

Smiling in spite of her languor, Maren extricated the skis from the car and stabbed them into the snowbank, then had them change into ski boots.

"Okay, so how do we do this?" Neil clapped his gloved hands.

"I know!" Rhiannon twirled the pole like a baton. "I checked out a book from the library. Skiing was invented five thousand years ago by Norwegians. They used to wrap fur around their feet and tie them on with leather strips. They went hunting and shot elk with bow and arrows. Why do people say 'bow and arrows'? Only the arrow does the shooting. It hardly seems necessary to mention the bow. Do you ever go hunting, Uncle Neil? It's disgusting, killing animals. Maybe I'll become a vegetarian, except beans are gross."

Maren set the shortest pair down and motioned for Rhi to step into the binding.

"Skis used to be made of wood," Rhiannon continued as her mother fit her mittened hands through the pole's straps and onto the grips, "but I don't think they had bamboo in Norway."

Eyebrows raised, Neil waited for help. Maren bent over his feet. He'd dragged them into this, getting Rhi all fired up, making a local outing seem like an adventure. Maren slid his foot into the binding, then positioned his pole on the latch. He pressed, locking his boot into place, then reached to lift her up.

"How long was this library book?" he whispered before letting her go.

Maren's face muscles ached from two smiles in one day. She secured her own skis.

"Now all you have to do is kick forward with one leg, and the opposite arm, and then the other leg and other arm." Rhi flung herself onto the trail. At the first curve, her skis crossed and she fell.

"One way to stop." Neil shuffled over and pulled her upright. "Let's have our teacher go first and we'll see how it's done."

Hoping she remembered, Maren kicked forward. They wouldn't have any trouble keeping up with her in this slow mode. A subdued Rhi followed, then Neil. The trail entered the woods, dropped down a gentle slope, and made a ninety degree turn to the left. Maren crouched, pushing her right ski forward, digging with the inside edge. The trail leveled and she stretched back into the diagonal pattern.

"Uh-oh! Hill! Hey, how do you stop these things? Stop, I said! Mom!"

"Whoa, baby! Watch out, Rhiannon!"

A flock of sparrows took flight and cheeped in alarm as Rhi and Neil crashed into a sumac bush.

Maren raised her right ski, pivoting it on its heel, and set it down, ending up with her feet in ballet's fifth position. She brought the left ski around to parallel, then skied back, singing "Dead Man's Curve." Rhi and Neil lay in a tangle of bushes, poles, and skis.

"Mom! Too slippery. They need wax or something!"

"Maybe we do need lessons. Like how did you do that one-eighty maneuver?" Neil reached for his bindings. "Let me get these skis off, and—"

"No. You'll sink." Maren dusted off her daughter's face, then grabbed the nearest boot, Neil's. "Hope you have another pair of slacks." She shook the snow out of the hem of his jeans and pulled his sock out and over. Somehow, even though she wore mittens, touching Neil's ankle seemed incredibly...intimate.

"Looks dorky."

He tossed a handful of powder at Rhi. "If I had cool ski bibs like you—"

She grabbed the nearest branch and shook, showering them all with snow.

Maren backed up. "I'll leave you two to your snowball fight."

"No, Mom! Get us out!" Rhi flopped like an upside down turtle, digging herself in deeper.

"Roll to your side and push with both poles."

Neil followed instructions and pried himself out of the drift. He reached for Rhi.

Maren shook her head. "She can do it."

Rhi glared. "I don't know why people think this is fun. We tried it. Let's go home."

"Does she always give up so easily?"

"High ability learners don't get much experience with failure." Maren glanced at Neil. "Sorry. Another library book."

"We should go home. My hands hurt. What would Maestro would say if they got frostbite?"

"Maestro would keep your hands in a padded box whenever they weren't on the cello." Maren slid her finger into Rhi's mittens. Warm and dry. "There's a meadow up ahead where we can work on technique." She executed another pivot turn.

Neil whistled. "Pretty as a snap roll."

Maren led them through the woods. Several yards into the rolling field, she turned to see how Neil and Rhi were moving. A fresh breeze washed through her. How long had it been since she'd done anything just for fun?

A Newfoundland and a German shepherd bounded out of the woods, tails wagging, and headed straight for them. A skier emerged from the woods, calling, "Athena! Juno! They're friendly. And excited."

Maren skied in front of Rhi. "Aren't you pups having the perfect day?"

"Can I pet your dog?" Rhi asked.

"Sure!" Black curls peeked from the woman's beanie. Her face and voice seemed familiar. Maybe she shopped at A&P.

Maren took off her mittens and sank her fingers into the dogs' soft fur. A little sweet talk had them rolling on their backs for tummy rubs.

Rhi managed to pet them without begging for her own dog. She'd heard "no" too many times.

Neil caught up to them and the dogs pounced, flopping him onto his back and licking his face. Neil laughed, and Rhi and Maren giggled so hard, they couldn't help him stand.

"Sorry, they're a sucker for Robert Redford lookalikes." The woman called the dogs and they left their plaything behind.

Maren had been avoiding looking at Neil, but she watched him wipe off his face and struggle back to his feet. Yes, he was handsome. But, more importantly, he was easygoing. He stayed upbeat and saw the good in others, except Helga who didn't have a good side. And, most of all, he cared about Rhi.

"So sorry. Say, do I know you?"

Maren braced for the woman to recognize Neil, then realized the lady had spoken to her. She tried to place her. "Maybe..."

She clapped her mittens. "Western Civ with Dr. Maier. You sat in front of me. And Thursday night worship."

They made introductions all around and caught up. After majoring in history, Leann had ended up working at the post office. Maybe Maren's underachievement at the grocery wasn't so unusual after all. What did that say about Consequences?

The dogs romped off and the woman followed.

"Have you applied at the post office?" Neil asked.

"Not yet." Maybe she should.

Rhi continued her book report. "Norway always gets the most medals in Olympics cross-country races. More than any other country."

Neil pulled his knit cap lower over his cold-reddened face. "How many sumac bushes gave their lives for those medals?" His brown eyes sought Maren's, and he grinned and winked.

Whomp went her heart. Maren turned away, facing the hill, and pressed her mittened fist over her heart. *Absolutely not. No possible way. Never. Especially not with Neil Wolfe.* She cleared her throat. "Okay, class, I'll demonstrate climbing, descending, and stopping." *Especially stopping.*

WKZO ENTHUSIASTICALLY ANNOUNCED Kalamazoo's four-thirty a.m. temperature of thirteen degrees, windchill of minus five, and blowing snow. Neil parked the rental car, still cold after the drive from the motel, and slogged across the tundra to the terminal. Alaska Airlines crews must have suitcases with snow tires, he decided as he hefted his bags over a drift. Wind sliced through his overcoat and its zipped-in lining. The automatic door whooshed open with a blood-thawing blast of warm air. He stepped inside and shook off.

"Hello, Neil. How's it going?" A bright face greeted him at the rental car counter. Louise, Lauren, Lydia? She'd given him her home number when he'd arrived. He'd dropped it in the trash at the hotel.

"Fine." He turned in his keys and trundled down the corridor.

The gate agent looked up from her monitor, then handed him a jumpseat request. "Good morning, Neil."

"Morning, Tina." He frowned at the empty ramp beyond the plate glass window. "Please tell me you're keeping my plane nice and warm in a hangar."

"I wish." She shook her Shirley Temple curls. "Stuck in Chicago last night. On your way to work?"

"Two p.m. show at National."

She winced. "It's en route. If the pilots can find us..."

Please, Lord, make it above minimums. Clear the skies, pierce the darkness, keep them safe. If he missed his flight, best case scenario, the Chief Pilot would call him on the carpet and put a letter in his file. Worst case, he'd be fired. His oh-so-sensible plan had been to take last night's flight, but he was having too much fun skiing, then eating Bilbo's scrumptious pizza. To top the evening off, he and Rhiannon had managed to beat Maren in Scrabble.

Neil grabbed a cup of coffee and found a seat facing the window. A plow growled by, stirring up a cloud of snow, shutting off his view of the field. That's the way it was with Maren: sky obscured, visibility zero. He'd wanted to talk to her alone, but Rhiannon had been around all weekend.

Together time was great. Commuting? Not so much. Neil couldn't move here. And he couldn't see Maren and Rhiannon moving to Virginia.

He glanced at the clock. 5:17. Maren would be rushing off to work, like he should be. He dug a USAir timetable out of his bag. If he connected through Detroit—

The gate agent hung up the phone, then flashed him a grin and a thumbs up. The distinctive turboprop whine broke through the howl of the wind, then the landing lights and strobes pierced the falling snow. *Thank you, Jesus.*

A ramper dressed like an Alaskan sled dog musher jogged across the apron and lit his batons. The turboprop appeared just beyond the windows. Neil crumpled his coffee cup into the trash. Whew.

I found Rhiannon in September, but I'm still looking for Maren.

THE PHONE RANG and a cheerful young voice asked for Rhiannon. Maren shut off the washer, then hurried to summon her daughter. No noisy appliance would spoil this call.

"Hello? Oh, I'm so glad you called!"

Maren retreated into the furnace room, giving her daughter the apartment's version of privacy. Please, let this be a friend. Not a classmate asking for homework help.

As Maren fit strings of Christmas lights back into their holders, Rhi chirped away, sharing the cross-country skiing adventure. She should have suggested Rhi bring her friend, but no, she couldn't ask Neil to pay for another child's ski rental.

"And then he wiped out at the bottom of the hill!" Rhi giggled.

The more giggling, the better. Growing up, Maren had been full of giggles—making taffy and cookies after school, no-sleep slumber parties, and hours on the phone—a normal childhood. Maren had missed the first step—getting married—and nothing had gone right since.

"He did what?" Rhi gasped, then burst into laughter.

Maybe now. Maybe this girl, whoever she was, would invite Rhi over. Maybe Rhi would bring her home. Maren glanced down at the speckled-brown tile which led into the living room where a Mexican blanket didn't hide the sag in the couch and an Indian scarf failed to disguise the cinder block. They would meet someplace else, take the bus, no, walk, no... Maren jammed the lights into the box, hearing one crunch and break. She closed the lid. Somehow she would find a way for her daughter to have this friend.

"Second chair viola! Awesome! You get to see the play every night! Is the music hard?"

A friend from orchestra. Even better.

"Wouldn't it be fun to be the fiddler?" Rhi whistled the theme from *Fiddler on the Roof.* "I could dance with my cello, get 'em rolling in the aisles."

Who was putting on the play? Pit would be a great experience. If this girl passed the audition, then Rhi wouldn't have trouble. And if her mom drove...

"What part did Melody get?"

Maren froze. Rhiannon was talking to one of the Wolfe children. *No!* She couldn't make friends with them. They've had all the advantages, the family name, the money. Rhiannon would find no welcome with them, only heartbreak.

Maren staggered into the living room. Her daughter lounged on the sofa. She had unbraided her hair. Gold curls spiraled around her face like a lion's mane. Like her father on his last album cover.

"Please," Maren choked out over Rhi's giggles. "Please don't run up their phone bill."

. . .

Dizzy from the smell of sugar, Maren bent over the table and squeezed the piping bag to form red hearts on the pink frosting of this week's zillionth sugar cookie. Her hand cramped and her neck muscles spasmed. She groaned, pulled the piping bag from her clawed hand, and tried to straighten her fingers. The muscles screamed. How would she finish the day? And snow removal, driving, and playing for rehearsal? She couldn't lose piano...not after she'd lost so much. Usually Neil showed up when she had a bad day. Neck muscles screaming, Maren straightened and scanned the store.

"You're heading for carpal tunnel syndrome," a young woman in a Western beanie said from the other side of the display case. "I'm an occupational therapy student."

"Sorry, I didn't see you. How may I help you?"

"I'm here to pick up an order for my study group." She gave her name, then dug in her backpack and pulled out a poster. "This is to prevent carpal tunnel. Take breaks, stay hydrated, vary your tasks, do these exercises. Could you sit to work?"

"Sitting isn't an option," said Mr. Coffey behind the student. "But I'll figure out how to raise the table. And Maren, you're on break when you finish helping this young lady."

The OT student handed the poster to the store manager. "Thank you."

"Thank *you*. I want to keep my employees healthy."

Maren handed the box of pink and red frosted doughnuts to the student and she hurried off. "Mr. Coffey, I can't leave. Sandra hasn't come in yet."

The manager taped the poster above the hand-washing sink. "She's on her way. But first," he nodded at her fist, "run your hand under warm water while you read those instructions. Lord have mercy, you cannot lose use of your hands."

*Please Lord...*her fist loosened.

"This place eats people and spits them out. One of the cashiers will hold down the fort while you take a lunch. And I'll check the schedule and get you back to deli as soon as I can." Mr. Coffey reached for the phone as she left for the break room.

When Maren returned, pain subsiding, Sandra pointed to the worktable where boxes of different heights had been stacked. "Mr. Coffey says try these out, see which works best. But no more piping today and follow the poster."

One of the timers rang.

"And we have to do the exercises every fifteen minutes." Sandra put her palms together, then grinned. "We should have had an OT visit a long time ago."

Maren made it through the day with only minor soreness. *Shower,* her body said as she returned home. *Later,* she shot back. If she had any energy left. She slogged up the driveway.

"Maren, yoo-hoo!" Mrs. V called. "You've never gotten mail before, so I didn't even look to see who it was for. Sorry!" She handed her an open red envelope.

Having her mail opened seemed like the least of her worries. The Snoopy sticker on the back indicated it must be for Rhi, so Maren clomped downstairs and dropped the card on the table. She powered through clearing the driveway, feeding Rhi, and practicing for the play, then let the shower's hot water pound her shoulders. Shuffling from the bathroom, her eye caught on the card. The front had Snoopy flying his dog house. Inside, bold, masculine script read "Happy Valentine's Day to Maren and Rhiannon! I'm so happy to have you in my life! Love, Uncle Neil."

Points for no hearts and no smell of sugar. Deduction for using the word "love." He meant it for Rhi, since he'd signed it "uncle." Maren returned the card to the table, climbed into the sleeping bag, and conked out.

She floated into a brightly lit room and found an open chair. The girls were well-dressed in earth tones, plaids, floral prints, and bell-bottoms. They looked familiar, like they might be from her church. But there weren't any boys. Mrs. Dijkstra, the high school Sunday school teacher, stood at the podium.

Why was she in a high school Sunday school class?

"... looking at a boy in a lustful manner gets you into trouble."

Catherine Richmond

Mrs. Dijkstra tapped her Bible with a manicured fingernail. "A cute boy in class? Turn your seat so you can't see him. Those guys in swimsuits at the lake? Stop ogling. A heartthrob on TV? Change the channel. Because looking leads to impure thoughts. And impure thoughts lead to impurity."

Someone behind Maren whispered, "What were you wearing?" She turned, but couldn't figure out who'd spoken.

The teacher continued, "The pure in heart shall see God. When you keep your heart pure, your body stays pure. And when you bring your pure body to your husband on your wedding night, oh what a gift!"

"You didn't fight back," another whispered.

"I was drugged," Maren said.

"The Bible tells us to flee from sexual immorality, flee youthful passions," Mrs. Dijkstra warned, "You might want to look, might be tempted, might want to please your boyfriend, but don't. Don't throw away your virginity. Save it for your husband, so you'll have a blessed sex life."

"You asked for it," a different voice muttered.

"No. I did not." Who was spreading these lies?

"Unclean," said a louder voice. "Impure."

The girl in front of Maren turned and pointed at her. "No one will want you."

"You're trash." Now they all stared at her, chanting in unison. "Filthy. Indecent. Defiled."

Maren jumped out of her seat and raced for the door, but couldn't find it.

"Sinner. Fallen. Dirty girl."

She tried another wall. No way out.

"Pervert. Slut.. Untouchable."

Trying to escape, Maren rolled and slammed into the couch, waking up. Another nightmare. She untangled the sleeping bag, rolled upright, and wiped cold sweat off her face.

Lord, I'm trying to keep my thoughts pure. Could you find another hobby for Neil, so he wouldn't come around so often?

Chapter Sixteen

Neil raced through recurrent training, wrangled a jumpseat on the late afternoon plane to Kalamazoo, and drove like a Navy pilot to downtown. The theater had been built in the grand old era, complete with chandeliers, balconies swagged in gold, and red velvet upholstery and curtains. Should he have dressed up? No, the audience wore sweatshirts and jeans.

Maren had saved his seat, second row left. He slid in, fighting the impulse to give her a kiss. She wore all black—because she was mourning or because it's all she had? He'd love to see her in other colors. She pressed her lips together as if holding in a secret, then the house lights dimmed.

The stage manager welcomed the audience, then announced the part of Randolph would be played by Rhiannon Tollefson.

Neil turned to Maren and whispered, "What?"

The overture started, so Neil had to save his questions. Had Rhiannon been an understudy? Had the director recognized her talent and given her a speaking part? How much rehearsal time did she have?

The Performing Arts School had spoiled him for other theaters. This school's sets were basic. The girls' costumes were an odd mix of poodle skirts and prairie dresses. The spotlights lagged. The microphones cut in and out, and the orchestra played over the singers. This play called for triple-threats, actors who could sing and dance. These kids could sing, but barely managed the other two skills. It went about as well as his own high school's performance.

Then Rhiannon took the stage, her hair in Cindy Brady pigtails, dressed in a striped t-shirt and jeans. She hammed it up, delivering her lines with confidence, precise articulation, and a bit of sass. She shed a golden light over the show. Neil grinned.

The boy playing Conrad tripped off the train, then fell onto the stage. When he knocked a prop over, Rhiannon ad-libbed, "Does the army know you're a klutz?" to thunderous applause. When her stage family sang about Ed Sullivan, Rhiannon belted it out, finishing an octave high.

The house lights came on for intermission.

"She's doing great." Neil couldn't stop grinning.

Maren held in her smile. "You rushed here. Are you hungry?"

"I could eat." In the crowded aisle, Neil ended up behind Maren, admiring her loose hair. His fingers twitched, wanting to run through its softness again.

Two women complimented Maren on Rhiannon's acting and gave Neil the eye. The bold one said, "I didn't know you were seeing someone."

"This is Rhiannon's uncle. Your sons are doing well." Over her shoulder, she told Neil, "They're playing Conrad and the Mayor." She slid through a gap in the crowd and hotfooted it to the end of the food line.

When Neil caught up to her, Maren handed him a paper plate with a hot dog.

"What a relief! I was afraid a fancy place like this would only have truffles and bluefin tuna."

The parent manning the hot dog cooker chuckled. "I wanted to serve smelt, but for some reason the theater said no."

"Smelt?" Neil grabbed mustard packets and napkins.

He laughed harder. "You're not from around here."

"No, he's not." Maren smiled and pointed down the line of tables. "We have other local delicacies. I recommend a Dutch apple

164

tart, if there's any left. *Stroopwafels* are good if you're drinking coffee."

"I'll pick up the tab, since you got the tickets."

"They're comped." She chose a brownie and cup of water as other parents raved about Rhiannon's performance. Neil paid for their food and followed her to an empty high table.

"How did Rhiannon get a speaking part?" The hotdog hit the spot.

"The boy playing Randolph got laryngitis yesterday. While the drama teacher was trying to figure out a workaround, Rhi started saying his lines and belting out his songs." Tears clung to her eyelashes.

"So you didn't have to run lines with her?"

"No time." She shook her head. "We'd done the songs at home with the album from the library. When we shared a house with a coworker who had a TV and VCR, we watched a lot of musicals."

"You made set design models." He remembered the cardboard boxes in Rhiannon's room. "Maren, you're remarkable."

"The church encourages her to honor God with her gift. They've shared recordings of everyone from Mahalia Jackson to the Staples Singers. When we got our own record player, we tapped into the library's collection. Music teachers gave us concert tickets."

"Resourceful, creative, amazing." And evasive.

She focused on wadding her napkin. Neil guessed she hadn't received many compliments these past ten years.

A bell chimed and the lights flashed. They returned to their seats for the second act. Rhiannon continued to shine.

The cast came out to take their bows. Rhiannon got a standing ovation, an unusual feat for such a small part. She blew kisses to the audience, the pit, and her fellow cast members, then spun and bowed. Brilliant! The audience would think Michael Jackson, not Alan Wolfe.

Neil wrapped an arm around Maren. This time she didn't stiffen or flinch. "That's our girl," he said, his lips an inch from her ear. "Stealing the show."

Maren wiped her eyes.

"Those look like Christmas concert tears. Skipping a grade won't help."

Her forehead creased and her eyes widened. "What will?"

"Call me crazy—won't be the first time—but Rhiannon needs a school where she'll be challenged and develop her skills with peers. The Performing Arts School the others go to."

Maren looked up at the ceiling. "You're Don Quixote, singing 'The Impossible Dream.'"

"The first step in the thousand mile journey is done—Patti's no longer mad at you. And we serve a God who does impossible things."

Her face showed only skepticism. "You're tilting at windmills."

She didn't say no.

EVERY ENERGY-SAVING light bulb in the house glowed. Neil jogged Tango through the cool evening to Wolfe's Den.

"Anyone home?" He muscled the door, sliding Harmony's backpack out of the way. Jim and Sun-hwa had gone to Baltimore for her sister's baby shower, but everyone else should be home.

Tinny music of a video game echoed from the basement. He navigated the debris of nieces and nephews, and pulled the calendar off the heavily papered bulletin board. Shoveling out a spot between pork chop bones and cornbread crusts, he sat at the table.

"Uncle Neil!" Melody thundered into the room. Twelve years of ballet and she still ran like a bull moose... like her father. She awarded him with a quick hug, then a canary-swallowed smile. "Have you seen Mom's office? A bouquet of red and white lilies."

Neil glanced at the closed door. "No kidding? From anyone we know?"

"A secret admirer." Patti swept into the room, shimmering in a Pan Am-blue silk dress, heels, and the full complement of jewelry.

"Wow!" Neil gaped. He hadn't seen Patti this dressed up since Alan took her to the Grammy awards for *Predator*. "You look familiar. Imelda Marcos? Elizabeth Taylor?"

"Way off on the age, *babo*."

"She's meeting *him* at the Kennedy Center," Melody whispered. "*He's* a baritone with the Washington Choral Arts Society."

"So we won't be able to give him the third degree? Ask if his intentions are honorable?"

"Yeah, Mom, where are you going afterwards? Who else will be there? Do you have your mad money? When can we expect you home?"

"Anyone see my car keys?" Patti rummaged through the junk drawer. "So, Neil, to what do we owe your delightful visit?"

"Checking your calendar. April bids are due Tuesday. Any days I need off?"

Melody pointed to the first week of the month. "Opening night, closing night, and every night in between."

He made a note. "Ah, yes. The lead in *Fiddler on the Roof*."

"I'm not the lead, I'm the third daughter."

"No small part. Lots of dancing, big emotional scene." With her stage father. Neil opened his pocket calendar. "It's Rhiannon's spring break. I hoped to get her out of Siberia."

"Bring her here."

Neil's jaw dropped again. He pivoted to stare at his sister-in-law.

"She can meet the kids, see the play, enjoy springtime in Virginia." Her finger, its nail polished maroon, tapped his jaw closed. Sparkling dark eyes met his. "She called today to thank Harmony for the hand-me-downs. We talked about the folly of Easter eggs and jack-o'-lanterns when so many people in this world go hungry. I'm thoroughly charmed. She sounds like a brilliant girl and I'd love to meet her. Bring her here."

Neil gulped. "But Maren—" —would hit the roof about the long-distance call and go ballistic from there.

"Bring her, too." Patti resumed her hunt for the keys in the silverware drawer. "Rhiannon's too young to travel by herself. We've got room."

"Who are you and what did you do with my sister-in-law?"

Melody's ballet arms outlined a giant heart in the air. "She's in love."

Patti found the keys on the microwave and stowed them in the shiny envelope he'd been told was a 'clutch.' Neil helped Patti into her white cashmere coat. "Aren't you supposed to wear mink?"

"And lose all my friends at PETA?" She sailed out. "Goodbye, y'all. Have a good time! I know I will."

Chapter Seventeen

Yesterday's rain had washed away some of the snow, allowing sunlight through the basement window, heralding Sunday morning. Maren slipped into her daughter's room and knelt by the bed. She was no angel, this wild girl, but she looked the part when she was asleep. Gold curls rippled around her face like a halo. Heavily lashed eyelids hid her usual mischievousness, giving her an air of serenity. The baby roundness of her hands grew into the long elegance of a woman's as Maren watched. Sunbeams traced the bunny appliqués covering holes in her comforter and danced on the pillow case where embroidered notes from Brahms's "Lullaby" hid ancient stains.

Lord, I'm so grateful... Cold seeped from the tile floor through Maren's sweatpants. "Time to wake up, dear one."

"Okay, Mommy." Her sleep-rough voice sounded like a toddler's. She rolled and stretched, her feet hanging off the end of the bed like a teenager's. Maren turned away, her heart to full too watch.

Rhi sang Cat Stevens's "Morning has Broken" as she dressed.

Maren unrolled the rags from her hair and frowned at her reflection as she combed out the snarls. Homelier than a vegetable garden.

One of those hot house orchids Neil flew with, all polished nails and wedge-cut hair, would catch his eye.

Ack! Think about oatmeal, compost, vacuum bags—

The door rattled with knocking. It was too early for their ride, and who unlocked the service entrance?

Rhiannon skipped into the living room and threw open the door. "Surprise!"

Neil stepped inside, shaved, polished, and perfect. "Good morning!"

Maren froze in the hallway, still wearing the sweatshirt and sweatpants she slept in. Part of her wanted to run and hide, but the angry part won. How dare he show up on unannounced on Sunday morning? Church was her refuge. She stomped to him, waving the comb. "What did I tell you about calling first?"

"I called at eighteen-hundred hours, when the last leg of my trip cancelled."

At six last night Maren had been unclogging Mrs. V's toilet.

Neil turned to her daughter. "You didn't give your mom the message."

Rhi went into an Oscar-worthy performance, complete with puppy dog eyes and downturned lips. "I hadn't seen you in so long..."

"We will talk about this later," Maren glared at her daughter, then Neil. "We agreed you'd wait at the airport."

"Uh, I heard the car had alternator trouble."

"Last month." Maren crossed her arms. "This month it was the transmission. Mr. and Mrs. Coffey are picking us up."

"I called them and said Uncle Neil was coming." Her daughter hid behind Neil. Tears made their reappearance. "I want to see my uncle. It's not fair."

Neil set two bags and a drink carrier on the table. He took Rhi's hands and sank onto the chair, eye level with her. "You didn't ask your mom. That's manipulative and disrespectful. Never play us against each other. Got it?"

Rhi glanced from Neil to her mom and back, then nodded.

Maren sighed. As if being Hollywood-handsome and impeccably groomed weren't enough, he had good parenting skills.

Neil turned to Maren. "I hope you'll accept breakfast and coffee as my apology."

"Thanks for breakfast." Now could she get him to drop them off at church, then leave? Could they skip church? Try a different one? She spun on her heel and headed for the bathroom.

Neil followed, trapping her in the small room. "Let me help. You've got a snarl."

"I don't need help." She yanked the comb through her hair.

"Maren." He caught her hands. "Stop hurting yourself."

She pulled away and closed her eyes, but she couldn't block the clean smell of him. "Out of my bathroom," she said in a fierce whisper. "Please."

After a long moment, his footsteps retreated into the kitchen. Maren locked the door and finished untangling her hair. Does he lack all boundaries? Charging into her life, her apartment, her bathroom, and now church, her last refuge. Making her want more, lust more.

Get a grip.

It's only one Sunday. Next week, church would go back to being her peaceful place. Maren changed into her suit, then, knotting the frayed cords of her self-control, stepped out.

"Uncle Neil bought a chocolate-frosted chocolate doughnut for you, Mom."

The aroma of ham and egg sandwiches awakened her appetite. "We should go."

"We have plenty of time," Rhi said. "Dr. Gibson says breakfast is important."

Neil chimed in, "You don't want to faint again."

Resulting in missing more work and more Neil hanging around. Maren ate. Her taste buds did a happy dance over the fresh ham, sweet chocolate, and strong coffee.

Wearing identical grins, Rhi and Neil gave each other a high five.

Maren narrowed her gaze, but her anger had subsided. "No fair ganging up on me."

With the two of them grinning like Cheshire cats, Maren's plan had no chance of success.

NEIL GLANCED in the rearview mirror. Maren sat with her arms crossed. She'd asked him to call ahead, and he had. Was it his fault Rhiannon hadn't given her the message?

"Your hair looks pretty with curls, Maren."

She stared out the window and didn't blink.

Rhi directed him to a neighborhood on the north side of town. "The man in that house played records on his porch, John Coltrane to Stevie Wonder. We lived in the yellow house for a while, until the downstairs neighbors took up pot smoking. Then we moved to the grey one until Yvette's boyfriend moved in."

Again, Neil marveled at how well Rhiannon turned out, considering their circumstances..

Piles of dirty snow, two-story clapboard homes needing paint, and bare trees would have been dreary, except the sun shone in clear skies. A church of tan brick with stained-glass windows, maybe early twentieth century, stood on the corner.

Maren cleared her throat. "Drop us off. We'll find a ride home."

"No, Mom. I want Uncle Neil to go with us."

Neil parked between a vintage Cadillac and a new Jeep, saying, "I'd like to stay."

Muttering about being outvoted, Maren hurried inside. Most people like to bring visitors to their church. Why didn't Maren want him here?

"C'mon." Rhi tugged him through the wooden doors.

Two dozen Black people turned to stare at him. The men wore suits and ties. The women wore suits and elaborate hats. A chilly silence swept the narthex. Maren and Rhiannon attended an African-American church. Since the Coffeys had saved her life, it made sense.

"Welcome, Brother Neil." Mr. Coffey stepped forward and

pumped his hand. The rest of the congregation lined up to make his acquaintance.

"Sister Maren!" Mrs. Coffey grabbed Maren with both hands, pulling her away from the coat rack. "Bless you! Brother Addison's out with his gall bladder. Sister Cole's in Three Rivers, tending her daughter, new baby on the way."

"I'll pray for them." Maren tried to step around her.

"We need you this morning."

Maren's voice dropped. "Hasn't Janae been taking lessons?"

"For three whole weeks. She can play 'Twinkle, Twinkle,' right hand only." Charcoal grey curls trembled under her hat. "Music will bring God's healing."

"Mrs. Coffey." Rhiannon tugged the sleeve of the woman's light-purple suit.

"Yes, child."

"My uncle Neil plays piano."

"He does?" Skepticism overrode the hope in her voice. The woman scrutinized him head to toe, giving him the uncomfortable feeling she knew not only when he'd last practiced, but the last time he'd changed his underwear. He wished he'd worn a suit and tie instead of his v-neck sweater, button-down shirt, and khakis.

"I'd be glad to help."

"He used to play in a band," Rhiannon hopped on one foot. "With my dad."

"A professional?" Mrs. Coffey raised an eyebrow. The rest of the congregation exchanged questioning looks. "All right, then, come with me." She led him into the sanctuary, past oak pews to the Yamaha upright. The choir, eight adults in black robes, took their place behind a central pulpit.

The woman handed him a five by eight card with a handwritten list of songs, starting with "Soon and Very Soon." "Are you familiar with these?"

He shook his head. "If you have the music, I can sight-read."

Her hum told him he had flunked the first test. She grabbed a spiral-bound hymnal from the organ. "'Take Time to Be Holy.' Ever heard this?"

"Yes, ma'am."

Neil propped the hymnbook open on the music stand and adjusted the bench. More folks arrived, double-taking at the sight of him. The congregation slipped into the pews. Maren sat in the third row, far left, head bowed. Next to her, Rhi gave him a thumbs up. Neil had played arenas, auditoriums, coliseums, in front of twenty thousand people. Three dozen Kalamazoo churchgoers shouldn't make him nervous. Start with the last line, right? He dried his palms on his slacks and nodded at the choir director in what he hoped was a confident manner. The director snapped out the beat and Neil began. By the second measure, he and the singers were off. He struggled to match their rhythm. At the end of the first verse, the director brought them to a halt.

"Sorry, ma'am, I didn't know you were syncopating." Neil's antiperspirant gave up and left for home.

Maren stood and walked toward him.

With a firm grip on his elbow, Mrs. Coffey propelled him back to the pews. "Thank you kindly, Uncle Neil. You did your best." She patted his hand. "Now Sister Tollefson will show you how it's done."

Neil had failed his audition. His face heated like when he bombed out of swing choir in high school, especially humiliating since his brother had been the star of every show.

"Don't you have somewhere to go?" Maren asked as they passed in the aisle.

"Oh, no." A wave of Mrs. Coffey's light-purple fingernails sent him into the pew. "He is staying. For educational as well as spiritual purposes."

"You didn't tell me your mom can play," Neil whispered.

Rhiannon made a "you dummy" face. "You didn't ask."

His memory kicked into gear. They had talked about piano playing at the after-party, but she'd given no indication of her skill.

Maren perched on the bench, exchanged the hymnbook for the index card. With a deep breath and a nod to the choir director, she rested her hands on the keys. Her right hand picked out the vocalist's chorus line from Chicago's "Does Anyone Know What Time It is?" Her left answered with a phrase from Jim Croce's "Time in a Bottle," then a few notes from The Guess Who's "No Time." She pivoted to the adjacent Hammond organ and played a vaguely familiar tune. The congregation knew it well enough to dance in their seats. He glanced at Rhiannon.

"Booker T. and the M.G.'s 'Time is Tight,'" she whispered.

What was Maren up to? Those songs weren't on the list.

Pivoting back to the piano, Maren dashed off rumbling arpeggios ascending to a crescendo, cuing the choir and bringing the congregation to their feet with an electric charge. They belted out, "Soon and Very Soon."

Neil gasped. Maren's skill went beyond capable. She mastered the instrument, dominating the keys with power.

And, like a fool, he'd suggested she apply for the *post office*.

"Uncle Neil." Rhiannon motioned for him to stand.

Neil hugged her and gulped in a breath. Maren was a pianist. A virtuoso.

He stood, swaying and adding his voice on the choruses. The congregation clapped and danced in the aisles. They worshipped without hymnbooks or song sheets—everyone knew the words and Maren knew the music. Man, did she know the music. The hands that had pulled weeds and made doughnuts raced up and down the keyboard. She added runs, glissandos, trills, all the schmaltz. Then she changed keys, picked up the pace, wound it all up, and spun it into "Woke up this Morning with My Mind Staying on Jesus."

Maren performed with passion and authority. Sometimes her eyes closed, her chin lifted, and her hair swung across her back. Her spine flexed and stretched, her hips rolled, and Neil fought off thoughts no one should think in church. Then she bent over the keyboard, tickling an intricate passage into another song, adding complex accompaniment to simple tunes, weaving in classical, boogie-woogie, and popular music. The congregation responded with so much enthusiasm, it was a wonder the stained glass didn't crack.

He should have seen it. Harmonizing on "Edelweiss" for her father, Rhi identifying a classical music piece on the radio, the stack of albums in their apartment. He should have seen it, but he'd been too busy giving his brother all the credit for Rhiannon's talent. It was Maren, her nature and her nurture.

He'd been an idiot.

The series of fast choruses melted into "Take Time to Be Holy" on the organ. At the "amen," the congregation sat.

Rhiannon passed him a Kleenex. Neil wiped his face; hadn't realized he'd been crying. Maren had blown him away. She stepped down from the piano. As she passed the first row, Mrs. Coffey said, "That's what I'm talking about!" The man in the second row gave her a fist-bump and a "Yes and amen." Neil stood and stepped into the aisle. One hand behind his back, the other on his heart, he bowed. Several people chuckled. Maren, eyebrows raised and lips quirked, took her seat on the other side of Rhiannon, and Neil joined them.

"Time." Reverend Gibson said from the pulpit. "We all want to know what time it is. What time is the game on? When's the birthday party? And most important, what time will this sermon wrap up?"

He got a few laughs and one loud "amen."

"And we all wish to save time in a bottle—the day you passed the driver's test, when the baby's born, Grandma's last hug. But Brother Booker T. said it—'Time is Tight.' And Brother Andre Crouch tells us, soon and very soon, you will meet your King. And He will want to know what you did with all His gifts. Psalm 90 asks God to teach us to number our days."

The minister referenced the parable of the talents, the potter and the clay, salt and light. He touched on the transformational power of God, and being fearfully and wonderfully made. He warned against prosperity theology. Then he leaned on his pulpit and lowered his voice. "Brothers and sisters, let go of your past. Throw off everything that hinders. Lay your burden down. Anyone insult you, abuse you, condemn you? Yeah, they treated our Lord Jesus bad too." His voice raised to a shout. "But He showed them, busting out of the grave! You are His child, filled with the power of the Holy Spirit. Blessed to be a blessing, to give glory to Him! So let your light shine!" He concluded with, "Now to God, who is able to do more than we ask or imagine, be the glory! Amen!"

Was the pastor talking to Maren? Encouraging her to leave behind her father's "consequences," quit the grocery and lawn mowing, and let her light shine. Neil wanted to look at her, to see if she received the message, but she hurried back to the piano.

With the musical eruption of "Oh Happy Day," the service ended. Neil squeezed Rhi's shoulder. "Amazing! Let's take your mom out to lunch."

Before he could reach the front, he ran the gauntlet of greeters, wanting him to feel welcome in spite of his rhythm impairment. Mr. Coffey pumped his hand, and Neil asked, "Was the sermon directed toward Maren?"

The man's sly smile grew into a big grin. "And for you, Brother Neil."

For him? But he worked as a pilot. Wasn't that what he was supposed to do?

A larger crowd gathered around the Maren. She greeted each with a hug. Finally the last one left. Neil stepped forward, arms open.

"I'm sorry." She turned away, busy covering the piano. "I embarrassed you in front of the church."

"I'm the one who has to apologize. All those comments about Rhi inheriting Alan's talent—" Oops, he'd said his brother's name.

With a swirl of light brown curls, she left the sanctuary, snagged her coat on the way out the door, and marched across the parking lot.

Neil followed. "Why didn't you tell me you're a musician?"

"It doesn't make any difference at all."

"Yes it does. I need to give credit where it's due. With you." Neil glanced back. Rhiannon chatted with a group of girls about her age. He had a moment. "Was the sermon for you?"

Maren crossed her arms and tipped her head toward the church. "I've heard it all before. From all of them. As if I *want* to work at the A&P and live in a basement the rest of my life."

"But you can play piano."

"So can you, but you chose a better-paying career." She rotated her wrist while fisting her hand, the same motion a conductor uses to end a song. Again, how could he have missed it? "Yes, I've picked up a few gigs since you gave us the car, but accompanists can't make a living wage and don't get health insurance. The few full time jobs go to people with degrees. I don't have one."

"Neither do Billy Joel or Elton John." A memory tickled his brain, of *Bye, Bye, Birdie's* cast members greeting Maren by name. "You were the rehearsal accompanist for the play, which is how Rhi got involved. What else?"

"Funerals, weddings, Saturday brunch at the country club." She crossed her arms and stared at the pavement between her feet. "I *have* tried. I've met with recruiters and entrepreneurs, gone on interviews. But since I have no family, I need a stable business, regular hours, no travel. Everyone needs groceries all year long, so it's dependable. It just doesn't pay...enough to support a cellist."

Was she sabotaging herself, afraid to take the leap into a better paying job? Could he be her safety net? "If you do any kind of work, anywhere in the world, what would be your dream job?"

Maren fixed her gaze on her daughter. "My dreams aren't important. It's doing what's best for Rhi, a job that will pay enough to support her, without taking me away from her."

"Okay, I'll pray for that." And a chance for Maren to use her piano skills.

Rhiannon continued to chat with her friends. Still safe to talk. "I'm hoping to take you two someplace warm for spring break. The other kids also have that week off, and they're doing *Fiddler on the Roof*. Patti suggested you both visit. Great time of year to check out DC. And the kids have been wanting to get together."

"You are out of your mind." She took a step back.

"Rhiannon could visit the school." His pager went off.

"There's a phone in the church office." Maren pointed to the door. "I'll get Rhi."

Crew scheduling wanted him to pick up a Chicago leg. Neil hurried back to the parking lot. "I've got to run."

Rhiannon gave him a hug.

"Mrs. Coffey will give us a ride home. Safe trip." Maren extended her hand.

He couldn't get a hug, so he settled for a touch of her fingers. "We'll talk."

RHI AND NICOLE raced off across the street to the Gibsons' house.

Strolling behind with Maren, Mrs. Coffey belted out, "This Guy's in Love with You."

"I didn't know you sang Herb Alpert, Mrs. Coffey."

"And that guy did not know you played piano." She chuckled. "Oh, the look on his face. As Gomer Pyle says, 'Surprise, surprise, surprise.' Could have knocked him over with a feather. Big old tears rolling down his face. Oh, Maren, he's got it bad."

"Like the stomach bug, he'll get over it."

Mrs. Coffey sang, "He needs your love."

"Seriously? How could this possibly be God's plan?"

"Oh Maren. Think of the young mothers I've worked with, those you've met. Who's the biggest danger to the child of a single mother?"

"The boyfriend." *Which is why I don't have one.*

"Got that right." She shook her head. "But Neil knows Rhiannon is his blood. He feels protective of her. And you."

"There's no guarantee."

"True. We trust in God and keep our eyes out for red flags. Haven't seen any yet. And you haven't either or you wouldn't have a signed a will naming Neil as Rhiannon's guardian." She paused, then asked, "What are you afraid of?"

Myself and the feelings I can't admit to anyone. Rejection when Neil finally realizes I'm impure.

They entered the parsonage's large kitchen. The girls sang in the basement.

Maren set the table. "How's this for crazy—Neil wants us to meet his family."

Dr. Gibson brought out the iced tea. "Understandable that you wouldn't want to have anything to do with them."

Mr. Coffey carried in a casserole dish. "Reminds me of when that truck driver died and his two wives moved in together to raise the children."

Mrs. Coffey glared. "Two wives? Did they shoot him or stab him?"

"Diabetes." Dr. Gibson filled Maren's glass. "Might be easier for Rhiannon to meet the other children now, before she hits the rocky road of adolescence."

"How about never?"

"As much as Rhiannon's wanting to meet them?" Mr. Coffey snorted. "When's he want to go?"

"Spring break. Diego just started training in deli. I can't leave."

He shook his head. "We'll be fine. Use your time off."

"By spending it with the family of the man who raped me?"

Mrs. Coffey wrapped an arm around her shoulders. "Is that how you see Neil? Because he sure isn't thinking of his brother when he looks at you."

But he should be.

"What happened to you was awful in so many ways." Reverend Gibson reached for her hand. "You're in the tough spot between what your daughter wants and what you're comfortable with."

Comfortable? When had she last been comfortable? She spilled her biggest argument. "He thinks the school the others go to is right for Rhi. As if she could go there."

Mrs. Coffey kissed her cheek. "Like I said when you moved out of Northside, you need to stretch your wings, get a fresh start. It's been a privilege to be your family, but I've always known it was for a season. This might be your way forward."

"A fresh start...with them?" Maren shook her head.

The girls pounded up the steps.

"Please, not a word," Maren said. The adults nodded.

Rhi and Nicole harmonized the chorus of "Count Your Blessings," then they all sat for dinner.

Instead of counting Consequences, could she count her blessings?

Chapter Eighteen

It took three tries for Maren to catch Royetta at home.

"Hey girl. What's up?"

"Rhi's uncle—"

"—the prince of presents—"

"—wants us to visit his sister-in-law and the kids. In their home."

"Lucifer's wife okayed the visit?"

"Yes. The house is probably covered with giant posters of him."

"Wouldn't his wife get rid of those when she found out about Rhiannon? I would if my man done me dirty."

"Maybe." Maren couldn't imagine Patti's emotions. "Rhi wants to meet them. Dr. Gibson thinks now might be better than later, when she's a teenager."

"You're calling *me* when you're getting advice from Dr. Gibson?"

"This is a weird situation, visiting the house where Lucifer lived. Who else would know?"

"So what pests are running through your brain?"

"What if these people are like that TV show, *Lifestyles of the Rich and Famous?*"

"Are they rich and famous? Well, you jet on out of here and into their mansion, hold your head up high, and enjoy whatever nonsense they got going on. Try out their Rolls-Royce, swim in their pool, boogie in their ballroom."

"What if Rhi doesn't want to come home? She's already talked to the kids on the phone and likes them."

"Their mama's not going to want another kid around the chateau. Rhi's gonna come home with you. I know it. But I also know, from watching your girl grow, that when she decides to visit those people, nothing and nobody gonna stop her."

"Now I'm really worried."

"Yeah, I shouldn't have put that pest-thought in your head." Royetta cleared her throat. "Girl you've done good—show up for work, never use, supermom to supergirl. You never get mad."

"I've been mad plenty of times."

"At God?"

"No, at my father. I'm still working on forgiving him."

"No rush on that, long as you've been shoveling out from your dad's bad juju. Now he's gone and this uncle's singing 'We Are Family.' So here's what I know from support group—it's your life, your deal. You decide if and when you're ready to meet Lucifer's family. Only you. And nobody dis you. Nobody steal your joy."

In the background, her son sang, "I got the joy, joy, joy, down in my heart."

"Darius, get yourself in bed and now," Royetta yelled, then said to Maren. "I don't make it to church much, but you're in my prayers."

They ended the call. Maren leaned her head on the cinderblock wall. *Dear God, please help me get out of...*out of this trip to Virginia, out of this dead-end life, out of these feelings for Neil.

God answered, *I'll go with you.*

NEIL STOPPED by Wolfe's Den to pick up his mail and found Melody helping Patti get ready for another date.

"She's going to the Birchmere with a bass player," Melody informed him as her mother, wearing her emerald green tunic and slacks, hunted for her car keys.

Neil joined the search. "Quick question before you leave.... If you took Liberace, Jerry Lee Lewis, and Arthur Rubinstein and put them together, who would you come up with?" The memory gave him the chills. "Oh, and add Scott Joplin, Dave Brubeck, Elton John, Murray Perahia, Jelly Roll Morton, and Billy Joel."

"Who are the twentieth century's best pianists?" Melody answered in Jeopardy style.

"It's Maren. She's a musician. She's the reason for Rhiannon's talent."

Patti paused, her head tilted as if listening to distant music. "Interesting."

"Tell." His niece flexed her fingers. "Instrument, genre, venue."

"Piano and Hammond organ, all of them, church."

"Everybody can play in church."

"Not me. I bombed." The memory had him breaking out in a sweat. "They syncopated."

"During worship?" Their church stuck to conventional rhythms. "And what do you mean 'all of them?'"

"Rock, jazz, classical, pop, boogie-woogie, soul, blues. Everything."

"In church, during a regular service?"

Neil nodded. "Took my breath away."

Patti murmured, "I expect there's a lot about Maren we don't know."

"This whole time, I've been giving all the credit for Rhiannon's talent to Alan. Makes me wonder how many other times I've put my foot in my mouth."

"*Babo.*" His sister-in-law's eyes twinkled.

"It's not funny. I can't fix this."

"True." She found her keys in the fruit bowl, then pulled on her denim duster. "But you can support Maren as she fulfills her own calling. Are they coming for spring break?"

"She's...reluctant."

Melody tapped her watch. "Mom. Traffic. Get a move on."

"I'm off like a pack of poodles."

. . .

As MAREN UNROLLED her sleeping bag onto the camping pad Neil had sent, the phone rang. She didn't recognize the voice —no surprise—people who knew her wouldn't call after nine.

"Hi Maren. This is Patti. Patti Wolfe."

Maren froze. Her throat closed as if stuffed with a bath towel. After a long moment, she croaked out, "I'm sorry."

"You have nothing to apologize for."

Was Rhi still awake? Maren took the phone into the stairwell. "I'm not a groupie. I never meant for this to happen, any of this. I didn't know about you and your family when I sent the birth certificate."

"You did it to help your daughter."

"I told Neil to go away. I told him not to tell you." The cold seeped through her sweats and she shivered.

"If he'd asked me, I'd have said to leave you alone." Patti's voice sounded kind, sympathetic. "Now I get it, why he tracked you down. He took the tiger by the tail and we cope. I was furious at first, but none of my anger was ever directed at you."

Maren pressed her fingers to her forehead. "You don't want to kill me?"

"You've already been poisoned. It's a wonder Scorch didn't do any permanent damage." Her voice softened. "Maren, in different ways and to a different degree, we're both victims. But together we can be victors. *Cheesy.* Now you see why I never took up songwriting."

How can she be so upbeat?

"Anyway, I'm calling about spring break." Patti continued, full speed ahead. "It's the perfect opportunity to get the kids together. Mine are in *Fiddler.* Melody's playing the third daughter, Andy and Cody are in the chorus, Harmony's in the pit. We've got plenty of room. The cherry blossoms will be a little past peak, and it might be early for azaleas, but the daffodils will be out. Neil will get you passes."

"What..." Did they speak a different language in Virginia or was the shock of Patti's call affecting her brain?

"We can do the tourist thing: Smithsonian, Mount Vernon."

"You're inviting Rhi to your house?"

"And you too. She's too young to be gallivanting around the country by herself. And you can escape from winter."

"I appreciate the invitation, but this is..."

"Way-out, freaky, kooky? My counselor tweaked my perspective. This is like when people marry and get in-laws. Your daughter is related to my kids."

"The counselor thinks this is okay?"

"She thinks meeting each other will normalize the situation. Then, when Rhiannon is outed, our 'no big deal' will keep it from being a scandal."

"It's inevitable?"

"From everything Neil has told me about Rhiannon and from talking to her on the phone, I can't see her or any of these kids becoming hermits." Patti's voice softened. "You probably have more reasons to say no than I can imagine. This spring or any other time, you're welcome here."

"Thank you, but..."

"Your daughter, your call. Absolutely. Well, I'd better let you get some sleep. Neil says you work early. Goodbye." The line went dead.

Maren hurried inside to her sleeping bag, trying to warm up. In the morning Patti will realize what she'd done and retract her invitation. Or Maren would wake up and find it was all a nightmare. She flopped onto her side and contemplated the stain-blurred plaid of the sofa.

"God, if this is your will, and not Neil's," Maren prayed. "Show me one way this will be good for Rhi."

Be strong and brave, for the Lord your God is with you wherever you go.

MAREN CLOCKED OUT, then headed to the front end. Giant wet flakes plopped and slid down the store's windows. They'd be pretty if she hadn't seen far too many of them this winter.

At the service desk, next to Mr. Coffey, stood the last person she wanted to see. "Neil. What are you doing here?"

"Giving you a ride home." He reached across her shoulders to give her a squeeze. His unbuttoned overcoat showed the uniform beneath. "Mr. Coffey's got good news."

The store manager flipped through a green and white striped computer printout. "You can have the week off, spring break."

Wasn't anyone on her side? Maren rubbed her forehead. "Even Muzak agrees."

"Can't hear it over the customers." The manager raised questioning eyebrows at Neil.

"Patsy Cline's 'Crazy.'" He leaned on the service desk. "Patti sees it like a family reunion."

"Not by any stretch of the imagination are we family." Maren put on her gloves and hat, then turned to her boss. "What if these people are addicts?"

"Whoa." Neil raised his hands. "We don't do drugs. I'm clean. You know the FAA regulations."

"Against the rules!" The Troll at the Desk proclaimed from the adding machine.

"We're regular, normal folks," Neil said. "Like *The Partridge Family*, with more talent and a minivan instead of a bus."

Mr. Coffey frowned at the registers where cashiers and customers gaped at the drama at the service desk. He pointed both hands toward the parking lot. "Speaking of TV shows, this is a grocery store, not *Family Feud*. Take it outside, you two."

Neil led her to the rental. He opened the passenger-side door. "Sit up here, look me in the eye, and tell me why you're so upset."

She plopped onto the seat and focused on the tracks the wet snow made through the grime on the Jeep in front of them. No way could she look at Neil and talk at the same time. When he got behind the wheel, she asked, "How will this benefit Rhi? What if my child sees everything those kids have, and becomes resentful or loses her confidence? You've seen how we live, how we dress. We've never gone anywhere or done anything. We'll look like country bumpkins next to your family. What if the kids are rude to Rhi?"

"They're kind-hearted. They understand Rhiannon hasn't had the advantages they've had. That's why Harmony sent clothes. If there's anything left in your emergency fund, you're welcome to buy whatever you need. For both of you."

"It's all there."

Neil leaned into her field of vision. "You didn't spend any of it? But how'd you pay for car repairs?"

"Those weren't emergencies. Piano gigs bought the alternator. I installed it. Then the mechanic took it and the battery in payment for towing."

"Sounds like the car was more hinderance than help."

"It got us through the worst of the winter."

Maren's father would have told her to stop fussing already, but Neil asked, "What else?"

"What if someone recognizes Rhi, because she's with the other kids?"

"You may be right that my brother's old news. And if the kids are together, it's not the headline-grabbing scandal a gossip rag wants."

Maren pressed her fingers into her forehead. "This is why I didn't go back to the support group. No one else gets invited to their rapist's house."

Neil winced. "Sometimes I wished we could all move. But old memories are being covered by new. Maybe someday, Wolfe's Den will just be where your daughter's kin live."

"Why is Patti inviting us?"

"One of the roadies confirmed what happened, and it's like she's been released from widowhood. She's dating, more relaxed, actually cheerful." Neil leaned into Maren's space, his breath warm and smelling of toothpaste. "She's in love. With a baritone. Remember the last time you were in love?"

Maren scooted to the car door. Her first, last, and only love was the man sitting next to her. She checked her watch. "Rhi has a lesson. Last time, I asked Maestro about her options for school. He said he'd think about it."

Neil started the car and headed toward Mrs. V's. "What else?"

"Where would we stay?"

"Patti suggested her house. She has space. But I can get a motel for you. "

And add that expense to the list of what she owed Neil. "Rhi will probably want to spend every minute with the others. Tell me about the house. The butler, the maids, how many forks you use when you dine."

"The way we heat our caviar over burning hundred-dollar bills."

"Caviar isn't heated, you—"

"It's an old house, big, but not fancy. Lots of kids, lots of clutter. Smoke detectors and fire extinguishers on every level. Upstairs, the girls have their own bedrooms, with a bathroom between. Harmony has a trundle bed for Rhiannon. Boys on the other side of the hall. Patti's room is at the end. The guest room and bath is in the basement, but it has sunlight and it's comfortable. It used to be my room. My house is a short walk though the woods." He stopped to take a breath. "I thought about having you two stay at my house and I'd take the guest room, but you're right—the kids will want to spend time together and you'll want to be close."

"True." And staying in Neil's house would fuel her lust.

"There's a Korean couple living above the garage who cook and do yard work while they polish their English and await immigration paperwork. Meals are a mix of basic Korean dishes and American standards like pizza and tacos. Chopsticks, fingers, and occasionally forks. The kids wear jeans and sweatshirts when they're not in pajamas or costume. Patti's self-conscious about her baby weight, so she wears tunics with slacks. What else can I tell you?"

"We don't have a suitcase."

"I'll take care of that—airline discount.. It'll be fun. If it's not, you can leave. With passes, you can go any time. Pass riders, non-revs, are supposed to dress business casual. Skirt or slacks with a shirt or sweater. Loafers or flats instead of sneakers. Can I take you shopping?"

"No, thank you." She looked away. "I'm not at peace with this and I don't think Rhi should go either."

"Will you ever be ready? Will there ever be a better time?" Neil parked in Mrs. V's driveway. He turned to face her, which further unnerved her. "Back to your question—how this will benefit Rhiannon. She'll be with kids who are wired like she is. They're all hams, driven to perform. And, Rhiannon's knowledge of music and her emotional intelligence is on par with theirs, in spite of the difference in their parents' income. If she doesn't see that, I'll point it out to her. She needs to give her mom credit for extraordinary parenting in difficult circumstances."

"Thank you."

"Rhi's bus hasn't come yet. Let's pray."

Before she could move away, Neil clasped her hands.

God, you see the problem here? I can't keep my thoughts on You when Neil's around. Please provide a way out of temptation.

"Amen," Neil said. Uh-oh. What had he prayed for?

Maestro met them at the door, sent Rhiannon to tune, and said to Neil, "I have some thoughts about school."

Much as he wanted to be in on this discussion...Respect. Maren was Rhiannon's mother and a musician. She knew what was best for her daughter. He gestured to Maren. "It's up to Ms. Tollefson."

"Keep Rhi busy," she told him with a nod. To the Maestro, "Let's talk in the kitchen."

The music stands held a piano-cello duet. Neil carried a chair to the baby grand and sat. "Is this what you're working on?"

"No." Rhiannon tossed her curls. "That won't stop me, but three flats might. Who writes in C minor?"

They plunged in, taking it slow, repeating difficult passages, stumbling through the first page. What was taking so long in the kitchen?

Finally Maestro rolled out and removed the music from the stands. "Not for you. Not yet."

Maren followed, asking Neil without eye contact, "What's on the schedule for Wednesday of spring break?"

Maestro raised his arms, a conductor commanding attention.

"National Symphony cellist Lloyd Gerson-Zeitz master class Performing Arts School."

Rhiannon eyes widened and she stopped breathing for two seconds. Then she leaped off the chair. "Can I go, Mom? Can I meet my brothers and sisters? And see their school?" She danced with her cello. "Pretty please with sugar on top. I'll be good."

"Yes, we can go." Maren's jaw was tense and her eyebrows low, but she managed a smile.

"Wednesday's good." Neil would make it work.

"We're going to Virginia for spring break!" The girl hugged her mom, who took the cello, so she could hug Neil and Maestro. "We're really going?" Here came the tears.

"Yes, we're going. I know you're excited and have a hundred questions." Maren handed her a tissue. "Deep breath. Focus on your lesson now."

Rhiannon wiped her face, took back the cello, and resumed her seat with a grin. "Major key please, Maestro. I'm too happy for minors."

Neil followed Maren into the garage. "So what changed your mind?"

"I asked God to show me if the trip would help Rhi. He told me it would help me too." She plugged in a vacuum and carried it to the wheelchair van. "This has to be done before the end of the lesson." She tackled the grime with a vengeance, her motions stiff as she gave fierce attention to every crevice. In spite of her fear, Maren would go.

Neil would do everything possible to give Maren the best vacation ever.

Chapter Nineteen

Sunlight through the airliner's window lit the food on Maren's tray table. She couldn't choke down any of it.

"What a cute little cream cheese! Can I keep it?" Rhi pawed through the blue lunch box, finding a sandwich wrap, bag of pretzels, and a handful of grapes.

"So, y'all are with Neil Wolfe." The flight attendant, resplendent with the glamour of a Texas beauty queen, poured a 7-Up for Maren. She tipped her head toward the cockpit where Neil rode on the jump seat. "Mr. Bodacious has left a trail of broken hearts all over this airline. Not to mention unreturned phone calls. You must be magic."

Rhi leaned across Maren, curls popping from her French braid. "It's a family secret."

"Family?" Miss Texas repeated. She studied the girl as she delivered her cranberry juice. "Well, I'll be."

"You'll be what?" Rhi, a pro at humoring adults, asked, but Miss Congeniality had moved on to the next row.

Watch out, Wolfes. Queen Rhiannon is on her way.

. . .

Neil led Rhiannon and Maren out of the employee shuttle and across the parking lot to his car. The old Toyota station wagon wasn't stylish, but it had gotten him through flight school, and could haul four kids and their instruments. He opened the doors for Maren and Rhiannon, but nobody moved. They stared at the vehicle's interior. Uh-oh. Should have gone over it with an extra-large trash bag.

After a moment, his niece spoke. "Wow, Uncle Neil. You're messy."

"It gets good mileage," he offered, not earning a reprieve. "All those rental cars have spoiled you."

He rearranged enough debris to stow their bags, set his uniform jacket on top, and got everyone buckled in. They headed to Wolfe's Den. Rhi began an archeological dig in the front seat. "Taco Bell. Burger King. P-U! Petrified fries. How long has this— Oh, here's a receipt. February 10. And this one says September 12."

"Think how it will smell when it gets warm here." Neil turned on the vent and cracked open the front window, letting in flower-sweet spring air. DCA's weather had cooperated for their visit— sunny and sixty-two with light winds from the south. "Too much wind, Maren?"

She found a brown plastic Safeway bag. "Pass the trash back, Rhi."

"Dunkin' Donuts. Can we go there? Please?" Rhi handed the bag to her mom and resumed excavating. "*Flying, Professional Pilot, Airline Pilot.* Is this all you get, airplane magazines?"

"Don't throw away my mail." Maybe sorting his recycling could keep Maren's mind off their destination. "Your mom's got all the good stuff. What did you find, Maren?"

She held a rusty cube of metal. "A Volkswagen Beetle wiper motor."

She knew what it was? "Don't pitch it. Andy and I are restoring a '68 Bug. Or rather I'm doing the work and he's dreaming about looking cool behind the wheel." Neil glanced in the rearview mirror. "How'd you get to be an expert in VW parts?"

"How'd you, the most safety-conscious person I know, buy a VW Bug?"

Neil smiled. He'd gotten a compliment from Maren. "So Andy can learn about engines. Patti will probably get him an American-made tank when he hits sixteen."

Maren dug under the seat. "Here's your May bid sheets, a dirty uniform shirt—"

"Had to change a flat."

"Soak it in dish soap. Flashlight with dead batteries, a letter from Oklahoma City about your last physical."

"What?" He swerved, almost going off the road, as his career flashed before his eyes. The FAA's office in Oklahoma City handled medical certification for pilot licenses. One glitch could ground him.

"Never mind—it's an ad from a landscaping service." She stuffed it in the trash. "Just sharing the joy."

"That bad?" He hadn't seen any sign of jitters—no picking her fingernails. But then again, Maren hid a lot.

The view on the right caught her attention. "Look Rhi. The Washington Monument." Maren sneezed.

"Mom, did you take your allergy pill?"

Dogwoods and daffodils—spring at its best—brought on a lot of pollen. Neil rolled up his window and switched on the air conditioner. The rearview mirror showed black slacks draped over well-shaped empennage as Maren reached over the back seat for her medicine.

The right front tire bumped on the shoulder's rumble strips, telling Neil to stop gawking and focus on driving. Rhiannon hadn't noticed as she was checking out Lady Bird Park and the Lincoln Memorial. Maren resumed her seat. Neil said, "There's probably some bottled water rolling around back there—Evian, LaCroix."

"Too late."

"You dry-swallowed your medicine? Talented in every way." He changed lanes, scooting around an oil-belching Ford Maverick.

"Virtuosa of pill taking." The corner of her mouth pulled into a wry smile.

The feminine of virtuoso. So smart. What could he say to reassure her? "Think of this like stall-spin training. Afterwards you'll be relieved and wonder why you ever worried."

"You better believe it." Rhi nodded. "She's my mom."

The GW Parkway followed the Potomac upriver past Roosevelt Island and under Key Bridge. Maren rode in silence, but Rhi commented on everything from the navigation buoys' resemblance to basketballs, to the incongruity of a sign for the CIA. After a mile on the Beltway, they exited onto a two-lane road through the woods, past old stone colonials and new mansions. Neil glanced at Maren, catching her worrying her bottom lip. The lip he'd like to kiss.

Focus.

A few more turns put them on an unmarked drive, parallel to a small river full of spring runoff.

"Is that Great Falls?" Rhiannon asked.

"The boatmen of the Potomac Company named it Difficult Run."

"Appropriate name," Maren muttered. "What do you do when it snows?"

"Wait for it to melt." The drive opened to the Neil's favorite view of Wolfe's Den, the white house backed by green trees.

Rhi bounced on the copilot's seat as they crested the hill. "It's so pretty. And big."

"Room for lots of kids." Neil parked by the kitchen door and the family burst out, Harmony first.

Rhi disappeared into a whirling mass of children. She hugged everyone, even reluctant Cody.

Neil found Maren behind the car. "Hiding?"

"No. Waiting for you to open the hatch, so I can get the suitcases."

He jingled his keys. "You ok?"

She looked away from him, scanning the woods. Under her tension, he saw longing, like the day six months ago when he'd watched her study the Tudor house on the corner in Kalamazoo.

"Hey, Uncle Neil. Need some help?" Andy slouched around the vehicle, his chin and shoulders doing a jerky-dip like he was auditioning to be a gang member in *West Side Story*. The teen straightened when he saw Maren, his a head-to-toe inspection going bug-eyed. "*Hello.* I'm Andy." He gulped, then stuck out his left hand.

"Nice to meet you." Without missing a beat, Maren returned the left handshake.

"Here." Neil opened the hatch, then shoved a suitcase into the kid's chest, breaking his grip on Maren. Andy backed up, nearly crashing into his mother.

"Maren." Patti glanced, then looked away. "Welcome. Come on in. Your daughter is lovely. The photos don't do her justice. How was your flight?"

Neil had heard Patti give enough prepared speeches to recognize this as one.

"The flight was fine. What a beautiful place you have here."

And there's another prepared speech.

"Thanks." Patti straightened her shoulders, managed a second of eye contact, then focused on the nearest empty flower bed. "I'm glad you decided to visit. I admire your courage." That speech had been cued by her counselor.

Maren nodded at kids. "Anything for the children."

"Totally." Patti went into air traffic controller mode, directing suitcases, guests, and brother-in-law inside.

MAREN HAD EXPECTED the Wolfes to have a mansion like the South Fork ranch from the TV series *Dallas*, and she'd seen a few of those on the drive in. But their place was more like *The Waltons'* house. The white paint and dark green shutters shone with a recent touch-up. The way it nestled in the shelter of the trees said safe and secure. But the wrap-around porch with its swing, seen in the family photo Neil shared, said Alan Wolfe had been here.

She crossed her arms, chilled, but not ready to go inside. "You grew up here? Any wildlife we should watch out for?"

"Supposedly there's copperheads, but I've never seen one. I think the kids' noise keeps them away. There's mosquitos and ticks. We keep bug repellent by the back door." Neil pointed.

Catherine Richmond

The garage, large enough to be a bungalow, held a Volvo and a minivan. A BMW and a Honda Civic were parked in the circular drive. A small barn sat further back in the trees, a flagstone path leading from it to the kitchen door. "Did George Washington sleep here?"

"Maybe. Washington used to own this land and planned a canal around Great Falls. The house started as a log cabin inn for river travelers, a place to stay while they recovered from portaging cargo around the falls." Neil pointed north. "Over the years, innkeepers doubled the size and added clapboard siding. Business dropped when the C & O Canal opened on the other side of the river. In this century, Patti added on again, updating and making it energy-efficient."

Maren followed him inside.

Neil introduced Jim and Sun-hwa, the couple who helped around the house and grounds.

"Dinner in ten minutes," she said.

"You have an early call. Get changed." Patti shooed the kids up the stairs.

"You change for dinner?" Like Buckingham Palace? Maren gulped.

"Clean jeans and t-shirts." Patti told her. "They've been playing outside all day."

Neil picked up her suitcase and led her downstairs. "Let me show you the guest room. It's quieter down here. I hope you don't mind."

Hide the pariah in the basement. "I'm used to subterranean living."

He opened a door at the bottom of the stairs and turned on the lights. "You have your own bathroom. And baseboard heaters if it gets chilly."

The walls and furniture were painted a warm shade of cream. A cushiony armchair sat in the corner by a bookcase. In the adjoining bathroom, thick white towels were stacked on the rim of a whirlpool tub with a shower.

"Lots of daylight." Maren crossed the oatmeal-colored carpet to the sliding glass door with a view of Difficult Run and the woods. She braced a shaking hand on the frame. "I suppose Thomas Jefferson installed this?"

"As far as we know, Jefferson never visited." Neil stood behind her. "This has always been a wide opening, covered by a heavy wooden door. They'd float supplies up the creek on rafts and store them here. The walls used to be stone, which looks good, but feels cold and you can't put up posters. Out in the yard, I've found metal rings from casks, Minié balls, glass bottles... Sorry, not everyone's into history."

"I am."

A voice from upstairs called, "Dinner in five!"

"I'll change out of my uniform and be right back." Neil touched her shoulder. "It's not so bad."

"Sure." Maren faked a confident smile.

Neil left by the sliding glass door.

A business envelope on the nightstand caught Maren's eye. Her name was printed on the outside in blue ink. Inside was a sheet of copier paper. "Medical history for Rhiannon. First degree relative —" *Thank you for not using his name.* "—the usual childhood illnesses. Height as adult: 6 ft. Healthy. Grandparents: healthy, tall. Paternal great-grandmother: diabetes, breast cancer, colon-cancer, lived to age 85. Paternal great-grandfather: stroke, lived to age 82. Siblings: the usual childhood illnesses. Both Melody and Harmony started their periods at age twelve." Maren returned the paper to the envelope and stored it in her suitcase.

Dress for dinner? Patti had on a maroon silk tunic and slacks. *Jeans and t-shirts, indeed.* The black polo with a scarf, cardigan, and slacks that Maren wore on the plane would have to do.

She returned to the main floor. Maren had expected professional interior decorating, furniture suites straight out of a magazine ad, Alan's music piped over the intercom. Instead, the decorating theme seemed to be clutter, furnishings were well-worn family pieces, and stereos engaged in a sound fight. The kitchen's high-end appliances weren't a surprise, but the mess was. The floor was an obstacle course of kid debris. Newspapers, catalogs, and schoolwork drifted across the counters. Sun-hwa declined her offer of help, so Maren followed the sound of her daughter's giggles up the oriental rug-covered stairs to the second floor.

The younger children, including Rhi and her suitcase, had gathered in Harmony's room—pink, purple, and packed with stuffed animals, art supplies, and piles of clothes. Harmony wore her concert blacks and the rest of the kids wore clean school clothes. Maren dropped the dirty ones into an empty hamper.

"Aren't you glad Dad didn't name you?" Cody asked Rhi. "You could have been Sonata or Treble Clef, or Downbeat."

"A girl in orchestra has a shirt that says 'I'm a Fermata; hold me,'" Rhi said, earning more giggles. Her voice sounded a fifth higher than usual. Maren chalked it up to excitement more than nervousness. "Her name really isn't Fermata. It's Kelsey."

"Could be worse." Harmony pulled Rhi's curls into a high ponytail and secured it with a shiny scrunchie, styling it like her own. "Frank Zappa named his kids Moon Unit, Dweezil, Ahmet, and Motorhead."

"Motorhead was his sax player," Melody yelled from the girls' bathroom. She'd swapped her jeans and sweatshirt for a maroon minidress. "His youngest is Diva."

"Whoa. Are they boys or girls?" Rhi asked. "Who's Frank Zappa?"

"Rock musician, Mothers of Invention. Is your mom, like, really strict? How do you not know Frank Zappa?" Melody looked up and realized Maren was listening. "No offense," she said with a toss of her curls, implying Maren must be a Neanderthal.

"None taken." Offense was a luxury she couldn't afford.

"Hey." Cody threw a wadded sock at his oldest sister. "I never heard of Frank Zappa either."

"An old rock and roller," Maren told the boy.

Cody smiled. "Zappa is cool name."

From the kitchen, a bell rang and Sun-hwa called, "Dinner."

Andy emerged from his room, shirt tucked in and hair combed. With the gesture of a royal courtier, he motioned to Maren. "After you."

Patti directed the two youngest to sit on either side of her at the end of a long farm table in the kitchen. Maren sat beside Rhi, to supervise her manners. Neil took the chair on Maren's other side. Sun-hwa set out pots of fragrant beef stew, rice, and kimchi, then she and Jim sat at the far end of the table. The kids filled in the rest of the chairs.

The family sang grace in four-part harmony, then dug in.

They all seemed curious about Rhi, but her mother was another story. Patti's narrow glances indicated suspicion, even though she tried to be a good hostess. Melody employed hostility like a weapon. Maren wasn't sure what to make of Andy's fancy manners and staring. Harmony focused on Rhi. Cody might be her sole ally. Well, it didn't matter how Neil's mash-up came off for her, as long as they were kind to Rhi.

The food tempted her taste buds, but the turbulence in her stomach limited her to plain rice. When the others had their mouths full, Maren thanked Patti for the medical history.

"You're welcome. I should have thought of that...earlier."

Yeah, that probably wasn't her first impulse when she realized what her husband had done.

Maren ran her hand down her water glass, then rubbed the condensation on her neck. "At the school... how will you handle introductions... if anyone asks?"

Patti caught the attention of her children, then gave Rhi a warm smile. "This is Rhiannon and her mother."

Okay. They had a plan. Maren managed to swallow a bite of the spicy stew.

As they ate and shared their excitement about the play, Maren glanced around the table, finding bits of resemblance. Alan Wolfe's success made it impossible not to know what he looked like. His face with large blue eyes, strong brows, wide mouth, and shoulder-length platinum blond waves smiled from posters all over the dorm and in every store. Andy, with his prominent brow and cheek bones, looked like him the most. Harmony had his mouth and curls, but otherwise looked more like her mother. The wave of Melody's long hair seemed her only connection to her father; her features were a delicate version of Patti's. Cody's round cheeks could be his mother's or baby fat. Maren steeled herself and glanced at Rhi. No wonder Neil had declared "spitting image" when he saw her.

Patti turned to Rhi. "So, what would you like to do while you're here? Smithsonian, the White House, Manassas, Harper's Ferry? Harmony wants to teach you to ride. Of course *Fiddler* is tonight, that's why we're eating so early. Thursday's *Post* lists all the events, special exhibits, and performances."

Rhi sipped her milk, wiped her mustache, and leaned toward Patti. "What I'd really like, what I *really* want to do the *very* most of all..." The kids stopped talking, stopped wiggling, stopped breathing. "...is learn about my father."

Chapter Twenty

The cast sang their farewell to their home town of Anatevka, then the violinist sounded the final notes of *Fiddler on the Roof*. Pounding out applause, the audience jumped to their feet.

Maren wiped her eyes and joined the standing ovation. Kalamazoo is Rhiannon's little village. She'll never want to return, not after touring the Wolfe's fancy house, meeting her siblings, and seeing their school's professional-quality acting, music, and dancing.

The cast finished their bows and the audience headed for the exits. Rhiannon scrambled to the aisle, swimming against the flow, and jumped into the orchestra pit. Harmony stood to greet her. They hugged, then pulled back, nose to nose over a music stand to share some secret. The stage lights backlit identical profiles: tall foreheads, blade straight noses, round chins.

Maren gasped.

"What?" Neil turned to see where she was looking. "Wow."

"We've got to separate them. What if someone notices?"

Bracelets jingling, Patti reached across Neil and stilled Maren's waving hand. Her dark eyes held Maren's gaze for a moment, then she nodded. "You and I have nothing to be ashamed of. *Not a thing.*"

"And everything to be proud of." Neil ushered the women into the shuffling crowd.

The cast mixed with the audience around the commons area. Parents focused on taking pictures of their kids in costume against a *Fiddler* backdrop, paying no heed to the golden-haired girl bobbing through the crowd. Maren leaned against the stone wall, beside a case filled with music trophies.

Patti joined her. "Neil's rounding up the younger duo, I mean trio. Melody and Andy have a cast party."

Maren tried to hide a yawn.

"I imagine this little jaunt of Neil's has kept you up a few nights." The older woman smiled. "Don't worry. We'll sleep well tonight."

NEIL WOKE as headlights swept his ground-level bedroom and locked on the closet door. Now what? Why didn't he buy curtains, the room darkening, sleep-all-day kind? He rolled upright, squinting first at the clock, 2:58, then through the window. His oldest niece staggered out of her BMW, leaving the door open and engine running, and lurched into the woods.

"C'mon, Tango." Dogs, even imaginary ones, are always ready for adventures. Neil threw on sweats and shoved his feet into sneakers. Grabbing a flashlight, he jogged into the cool night. He turned off the car and its headlights, pocketed the keys, closed the door. His niece crashed through the underbrush, heading for home. The three-quarter moon showed her slipping through the basement sliding glass door. Uh-oh.

Two female voices screamed, "Ow!"

"Get off me!"

"What the heck are you doing on the floor?"

"What are *you* doing?"

Neil raced to the house. He reached inside the door, hit the light switch, and pushed through the curtain. Melody sprawled over Maren on the carpet. Neil dragged his niece off, inhaling the sour odor of beer sweat. He had a glimpse of Maren's perfectly-proportioned legs stretching from an old t-shirt before she sat up and covered herself. Her hair spilled in glorious waves over her shoul-

202

ders. What fun they could have if— Neil wrenched his attention back to his niece.

"You scared the—" Melody flipped her hair out of her face, trying to recover her usual bored sophisticate act. "Why are you sleeping on the floor?"

"Why are you barging in at this hour?" Maren clutched her bent knees, giving Neil a glare. "Both of you."

"I'm chasing the party girl." Hands on hips, he frowned at his niece. He thought he and Patti had guided her well, but Melody had gone way off course tonight. "I don't have to ask what you've been doing."

Melody followed her uncle's gaze to her inside-out dress. "Oh," she groaned, then narrowed mascara-smeared eyes at Maren. "Well, it's not like you never had sex."

"Melody!" Neil growled.

"And look where it got me." Maren spoke in a quiet, but firm voice. "Do you want all your plans for the future, all your most-likely-to-succeed dreams, to fizzle out like a box of bargain-basement fireworks?"

"You know better." Neil glared at the girl.

"Melody," Maren leaned forward, "you have two brothers, and now two sisters who look up to you. Like it or not, you're an example to them."

Neil added, "VD, AIDS—"

"Stop ganging up on me. You two—you're worse than parents!" The teen staggered out. "I'm sorry and I'll never do it again!" She clomped up the stairs.

Maren slid her fingers back from her forehead, letting free a ripple of golden-brown hair. It fell like a ribbon over her shoulder, ending in a curl at her waist. "Neil?"

Oops, he'd been enchanted. "Uh, sorry. Sleep-fog." He swallowed and focused on retying his sneakers. Here he was, intruding like *Predator* personified. "What did you ask?"

"Wasn't Andy with her?"

"He got a ride with the guy who played Tevye. He made curfew, unlike his sister." Neil hunted under the curtain. "Here's the dowel we use for a security bar. In case you see Patti first, I'll leave Melody's car keys with you." His hand brushed against hers. "You're cold."

"No, I'm fine, but—" She swatted her arm. "You're letting in mosquitos."

"The downside of living on a creek." Neil hesitated, fighting off the urge to... to what? Hold her until she warmed up? Kiss her good night? See if her hair is still silky? He'd better get some sleep before he did something irrational. "Do you think God still loves Melody?"

"Yes. Of course."

"Then certainly God loves you." He slipped out through the curtain. "See you in the morning."

MAREN UNTANGLED herself from the sheet, locked the door, and put the dowel in place. No chance she'd fall back to sleep with her heart pounding. She grabbed her Bible and sat in the armchair.

Do you think God still loves Melody? Then certainly God loves you.

Neil would have a whole different opinion if he knew how often she thought about jumping his bones.

Please forgive me for lusting. And help me get back to sleep.

Needing a calming read, she turned to the Psalms. The last verse of the fourth Psalm echoed through her heart: *In peace you will lie down and sleep...*

Maren looked at the bed with its pillow-top mattress, sateen sheets, puffy comforter, and supportive pillows.

In peace you will lie down and sleep...

In bed? Moving slowly and listening for a course correction, Maren closed the Bible, put the sheet back on the bed, climbed in, and pulled up the comforter. Ah...

In peace you will lie down and sleep...for you are loved.

WHAT A NIGHT. Worrying about his niece alternated with images of sleep-rumpled Maren, keeping Neil awake for hours. He shuffled upstairs, said good morning to Tango, then fired up the coffee maker. Only the occasional sighting of deer coming to drink at the creek compensated for waking up this early. He wandered to the windows and searched the morning mist. Sure enough, a graceful silhouette slipped through the trees and paused at the edge of the clearing. She blinked at the house, cautious, watchful. He would have to move with the utmost stealth or she would startle and bound off into the woods.

PERFECT, Maren thought. Whoever turned this barn into a house knew exactly what to do. Sunlight wove through the budding trees and glinted off the wall of windows. No basement darkness here. The view from the lookout tower must be spectacular—woods up close, hills in the distance. The pine-topped slope and the ripple of Difficult Run muted traffic noise—this house could be deep in the country instead of minutes from the nation's capital. The reddish browns of the cedar siding set off the cool gray of the fieldstone chimney. Leaves had been left as they fell to keep down weeds. If it were hers, she'd add azaleas and drifts of daffodils, maybe mountain laurels. The patio around the outdoor fireplace got enough sun for flowers. Wildflowers would be perfect. Maren imagined the family gathered around the fireplace, popping popcorn, making s'mores. And later, after the children went to bed—

The sliding glass banged open and Neil Wolfe, wearing the sweats he'd slept in, lurched onto the porch. One arm stiff in front of him, he staggered down the steps and across the yard.

Drugs! I knew it!

"Whoa! Bad dog! Heel! Slow down! Easy, boy!"

The imaginary dog?

Neil's outstretched arm jerked right and he followed, plowing through the leaf mulch straight to Maren. "Down, boy! Now see what you've done, bad dog? He slobbered all over you. Sorry, Maren." A warm palm wiped her cheek.

"What—"

"What kind of dog is he? Irish wolfhound. Figured it'd be a good

205

fit with my last name." Neil circled her, reaching around her waist. His hair curled in all directions and a haze of whiskers darkened his jaw. "Silly dog, tangling Maren in your leash."

"How—"

"How long have I had him? Not long enough to do any training." He brushed her shoulder. "Muddy footprints."

In spite of herself, Maren watched his waving fist as he made another pass around her. Working at the closest grocery to the State Hospital had taught her how to handle hallucinations. Taking a deep breath, she commanded, "Sit!"

Neil's arm dropped to his side. He gaped at the empty space by his feet. "Well, look! He obeys you! Not only are you a genius at raising a daughter, but you have a gift with dogs, too."

Maren spotted the gleam in his eye. She crossed her arms. "Does your dog have a name?"

Neil shook his head. "I've been calling him Tango, but if you have a better suggestion..."

"Tango suits him, the way he runs and pauses, then takes off again."

Neil grinned. "Look at his ears perk up. He listens to you. What's he— Oh, no! Hang on!"

A squirrel, a real one, scampered across the brick patio and up a poplar tree. Neil's warm hand grabbed hers and pulled her through the underbrush toward the house. "Call him inside!" He swung her toward the door.

Maren stepped inside. "Here, Tango. Come here, boy." She clapped her hands and whistled. *Are hallucinations contagious?*

Neil tumbled in and she closed the door behind him. He unlatched the invisible leash, then went to the corner kitchen "All this dog drama is exhausting. How about some coffee?"

"Is it *really* coffee?"

"From my last Seattle overnight." He held up a package with a Starbucks logo. "Cream or sugar?"

"No, thanks." He'd poked around her apartment; Maren could satisfy her curiosity. She circled the open space, stepping around the thick hearth rug, the leather sofa, and coffee table piled with aviation magazines. The spiral staircase had a brass DC-3 finial. A stained-glass ornament hung in the kitchen window. "A Piper Colt! My dad—" Tears closed her throat.

"Not many people can tell a Colt from a Tri-Pacer. Hey." A warm arm wrapped her shoulders, bringing the clean scent of Dial soap. He leaned his head against hers and lowered his voice. "Hits like clear air turbulence, doesn't it. Maren, this is your vacation. I've got plenty of space here, if you want privacy for a good cry."

If she started crying, she'd flood the state. And if his arm stayed around her a moment longer, she'd throw herself at him. Maren scooted away. "I should get back. "

"After all the trouble I went through to imagine a dog?" Neil handed her an EAA mug. "You won't get any coffee over there for hours, not until Sun-hwa starts work. And with Melody's shenanigans, we need it.."

The aroma of fresh-ground arabica beans tingled her nose. Taking the opposite end of the sofa, she studied the interior fireplace to keep from staring at the space where his T-shirt had come loose from his sweatpants, or to stop thinking about the dark brown swirl of chest hair she'd seen last night. "Did you ever have unwanted traffic when you lived in the house?"

"No, but I snuck in and out that door a time or two. Never drunk with inside-out clothes though." He rubbed his face. "Wonder what happened to all my posters? The airplane ones probably aren't worth anything, but Andy Warhol and Peter Max might be valuable."

"So, will this dog of yours ever become real?"

"Like *The Velveteen Rabbit?*" Neil shook his head. "Real dogs don't fit with flight schedules."

"Wouldn't one of the kids take care of him while you're gone?"

"You've seen how busy they are. Jim wouldn't mind. He likes dogs. But..."

"The dog would end up being Jim's."

"Exactly."

Maren studied the soaring ceiling while wiggling to scratch her back. "Who designed this house?"

"When I left for flight school, Patti sent my high school drafting project to a builder. He made it work in spite of my amateur input." He set his mug on the coffee table. "What's all this squirming for? Got an itch?"

She pushed back into the corner of the sofa. "A mosquito came in with you last night."

"I've got aloe vera." He loped to the kitchen, returning with a green bottle. "Works good on bug bites, poison ivy, burns. Where'd the bloodsucker get you?" He flipped her braid over her shoulder and snagged the back collar of her t-shirt.

"I'll have Rhi—"

His breath tickled the hair at the back of her neck. "Whoa, got you good. Hold still."

Icy goo dripped down her spine. "Ooh!" She inched away, as far as she could with his hold on her shirt.

"Sorry. Should have warned you. Have to keep it in the fridge since it doesn't have preservatives."

The hem of her shirt pulled out of her jeans. Warm fingers spiraled up her backbone.

"Neil!" She broke out in goosebumps.

"Done." He returned to aloe to the fridge.

Maren grabbed her mug, trying to stop shivering.

He came back to the couch. "I've been thinking, you could have been in my first officer class."

"My plan was to fly for Upjohn."

"So what would you like to do? I'll help you make new plans." He propped his elbow on the back of the couch. His T-shirt pulled away from his sweats, showing his trim waist. What was wrong with her, that a glimpse of skin set off impure thoughts?

"I'm working on it." Planning would be easier if her thoughts wouldn't stray to him. She carried the coffee to the sink and dumped it down the drain. "Rhi will be awake."

"Those girls were up all night giggling. We won't see them before noon. Let me get dressed and I'll walk you to the house."

"No, thank you." She hurried to the door. As she left, she called, "Bye, Tango."

Chapter Twenty-One

Neil dropped the carton of video tapes on the floor of the TV room. "The Alan Wolfe film festival is ready to begin."

Rhiannon, wearing an outfit from the Melody and Harmony collection of fine hand-me-downs, opened the box flaps. "Wow. His whole life must be in here."

"Yep. Where do you want to start?"

"Chronological, please."

Patti raised her eyebrows at Neil and mouthed *"Chronological?"* She turned to Rhiannon. "You could help Andy with vocab prep for his SATs."

"Be glad to." She flipped the tapes so the titles faced the same way. "Do you have any from when he was my age?"

Patti searched the bookshelves. "His drummer did a photomontage for the funeral. Lots of baby and kid pictures. Should have brought your photo albums."

"There aren't any. You'll have to ask Mom."

Ask Mom? Good idea. Neil found Maren in the kitchen, washing pots and pans. "You're supposed to be on vacation."

"Sun-hwa said I could help."

Reality kicked him in the gut—Maren would rather scrub a fry pan than see a photo of Alan. "There's no baby photos of Rhiannon?"

"You can't buy film with food stamps," she whispered.

"Oh Maren," he murmured. "Want to get out of here? We could hike Great Falls."

"Keep an eye on Rhi." Her glance showed a lot of pain. "Please."

"Will do."

"I found it!" Patti called from the other room.

"Wait for me!" Cody, still in pajamas, vaulted over the back of the sofa.

The children studied each other with too-wise eyes, united by a father they didn't know.

Patti settled on the wing chair and pulled Cody onto her lap.

Rhiannon plopped on the couch next to Neil. "Riding the Updraft," Alan's last hit single, played from the speakers.

Neil pointed to the drooling infant on the projection television. "There he is." Still pictures formed and melted: the baby banging on a Fisher-Price drum, the toddler reaching on tiptoe for the keyboard of a piano. Clips from old movies showed Alan racing through Christmases and birthdays, curls springing from his head.

Rhiannon ran her fingers through her hair.

"His parents had it cut short for school," Patti said.

"And the heel of his hand rubbing his forehead." Neil pointed at the screen. "You do that."

Preschool faded into elementary years, and another baby appeared in the background of a picture—himself. The focus never wavered from his older brother, whether the occasion was a family party or the neighborhood kids playing in the sprinkler. "Little brother arrives and is ignored," he murmured.

Rhiannon leaned on him.

"That one." Patti hit the remote's pause button. On the screen, Alan bent over his first guitar, a six-string Yamaha he'd named "El Kabong" after some cartoon. "When I saw Rhiannon, I thought of this picture. Her face, her hands."

Rhi held her arms up, comparing them with the images on the screen.

The tape started again with the background sounds of a guitar being laboriously tuned. More stills of junior high days flashed across the screen, accompanied by the uneven plinking of "The House of the Rising Sun."

"Ack!" Rhiannon covered her ears. "Totally flat! He can't be—"

"The one and only Alan Wolfe." Neil patted his niece's back. "Good thing you got perfect pitch from your mom."

Video clips of musical productions and choral numbers followed. Alan played the oldest son in *The Sound of Music,* and the lead in *Pirates of Penzance, Grease,* and *The Music Man.*

"Alan was in everything," Patti said. "The fool graduated a year early, then found out he couldn't perform anywhere because of liquor laws. Here's some of his bands."

The film showed Alan with an ever-changing mix of musicians.

"Cello?" The couch shook with his niece's energy.

"Vincent had a hard time convincing him to try it," Patti said. "Some country bands had fiddles, but cello was unusual."

The music changed to "The Wedding Song."

"Now who's singing?" Rhi asked.

"Peter, Paul, and Mary. The required song at all nonconformist weddings." Patti continued narrating. "That's me when I was skinny, wearing a traditional red Korean wedding dress to keep my grandmother from flipping out. Your uncle. Your dad, his first, last, and only time in a suit."

"His hair was almost as long as mine," Rhi noted. Would she ever call him "dad?"

"My grandmother and your grandparents."

"What? I have more grandparents?" Rhiannon bounced off the couch and turned to Neil. "Why didn't you tell me? Where are they? Are they...kind? Do they know about me?"

Patti stopped the video and backed up to the shot of their parents dancing like Fred and Ginger. They glowed with energy and love for each other.

"I wrote to them in September, after I met you," Neil told Rhiannon. "They're in Nepal, working on earthquake-proof clean-energy projects, so we don't hear from them often."

"They'll be so happy to meet you and your mom," Patti assured her. "They're crazy about grandchildren."

Rhiannon perched on the couch until she recognized another face on the video. "John Denver?"

"And Willie Nelson behind him," Neil pointed out. "Alan made friends fast. This was before he goosed Minnie Pearl and got kicked out of the Grand Ole Opry. Or was it Loretta Lynn?"

Patti sighed. "No. His publicist started those rumors. His lyrics got him thrown out of Nashville." Alan, minus the suit jacket, had joined the band at his own reception. Neil sat behind him at the electric keyboard. Patti motioned toward the screen. "Here's a lesson for you, Rhiannon, if you marry a musician, you won't dance at your own wedding."

"Don't feel sorry for her—she danced all night." Neil's fingers moved to the music. "I wish we'd recorded the jam session. No lawyers worrying about who's signed with what label, just music and lots of it."

"Advice number two—don't marry someone better looking than you." Patti sighed. "I'd forgotten what a hunk he was."

Neil nodded. "He had some sort of otherworldly glow, like a permanent spotlight. When he came into a room, everyone noticed him and the rest of us faded into the backdrop."

"Tchaikovsky!" Rhi bounced. "Uncle Neil, you're playing 'Romeo and Juliet'!"

"Trying to give the wedding a little class. And show off."

The video rolled to a finale of Alan leading the wedding party in a wild rendition of his first hit single, "Howling Down the Moon." Rhi and Cody joined the dance.

His nephew asked, "Where's your mom?"

"Making breakfast."

"I love breakfast. C'mon, Rhi, we'll watch more after we eat."

The kids galloped down the hall.

Neil shut off the VCR. "I offered to take Maren out of here while we do this. She asked me to keep an eye on Rhiannon. She's in the kitchen helping Sun-hwa."

"Burning off nervous energy, maybe. I don't know how to

convince her I'm on her side," Patti said softly. "What's up with Rhiannon asking if her grandparents are *kind?*"

No children in earshot. "Her grandpa was mean. Wish I could blame it on cancer, but he'd treated Maren like the family whipping boy since she told him about her pregnancy. He barely tolerated Rhiannon. Her uncle and his family are obnoxious too."

"We'll be her family." Patti squeezed his hand. They headed into the kitchen, where the conversation was in Spanish.

"How did you learn Spanish?" Patti asked.

"Jim and I learned when we worked on a cruise ship." Sun-hwa set out rice, bibimbap, and a platter of fried eggs. "I couldn't think of English words so I said *galleta y salsa.*"

"Biscuits and gravy." Maren attacked the cutting board with a scrubby. "Our friend Josefina lived with us when Rhi was little. She was from Guatemala."

Patti refilled her tea cup with coffee. "None of us have made any progress learning Korean, so let's switch to Spanish, get a head start on summer school."

"*Buena idea,*" Sun-hwa said. "I'll tell Jim."

"Maren, please sit." Patti enthroned herself at the head of the table. "If you don't have plans for tonight, the National Symphony's playing at the Kennedy Center."

"Can we go, Uncle Neil?" Rhi pounced on him, almost knocking over the sauce. "Are they sold out?"

"We have season tickets."

"Do I have to?" Cody slouched under the table.

"We have to take down the set, goof." Andy rumpled his brother's hair. "Good morning, Maren," the boy said with an affected accent. He'd tucked his shirt into his jeans and wet-combed his hair. "I trust you slept well?"

"No, she didn't." Melody slithered into the seat next to Maren. Lank hair hung around her puffy face. "I am so sorry. I acted like a total jerk."

"It's all right—"

"No, it's not anywhere near all right," Patti interrupted, then faced Maren. "Your words of wisdom last night seem to have made an impact on my wayward daughter. Thank you."

Neil stretched. "If we're going out tonight, we'd better take naps after lunch."

"I'm fine," Maren said.

The matriarch leaned back in her chair. "I'll bet you take naps as often as you take vacations. Just stretch out and read for a while."

"After your nap," Melody brightened. "I'll help you get ready for tonight, as my apology. *Chez Melody* is ready to serve!"

"Only if I get to do Rhiannon." Harmony stumbled in, still wearing her University of Virginia sleep shirt. "Hey, Mel, bet your homecoming dress would look good on Rhi's mom. She's a Summer with a dash of Autumn. Or maybe an Autumn with a dash of Summer."

"No poofy sleeves," Patti said.

"And no stage makeup." Neil filled his bowl with rice, vegetables, beef, and spicy bibimbap sauce. "You look fine just the way you are."

"Mighty fine," Andy seconded in his best imitation of a seductive voice.

"If you dress up," Neil said between bites, "I'll have to wear something other than jeans."

"Your light grey suit, French blue shirt, and grey silk tie," Melody decreed.

"I have a French blue shirt?"

"We gave it to you for your birthday." Harmony sniffed. "I'm totally offended you don't wear it."

"Mom, please." Rhiannon hugged Maren and she started to soften. "We'll have so much fun!"

Maren cleared her throat. "As long as it not an inconvenience..."

Patti reached for the younger woman. "C'mon, hon. When's the last time you played dress-up?" With a wink to her daughters, she added, "Find out all her beauty secrets, will you?"

. . .

214

MELODY AND HARMONY went into full-on makeover mode, complete with hair, makeup, and wardrobe. And Rhi was right, it was fun.

A lot of fuss later, Maren stared at her reflection in alarm. She tugged at the neckline of the navy dress, low even with safety pins pulling it together. It plunged in back, left her arms bare, and clung to the rest of her. "Too little."

The makeup erased her freckles and brought out her eyes. "Too much."

"Foxy mama," Rhi declared.

"Totally glam," Harmony agreed. "And Uncle Neil is totally fly."

Neil called from the kitchen, "Time to go."

Stomach whirling, Maren took the stairs slowly in the unfamiliar high-heeled sandals and long dress.

"Uncle Neil! Get your tongue back in your head. You're worse than Andy." Melody tapped under his chin. The grey, European-cut suit with a blue shirt showed off his wide shoulders. Handsome enough to outshine Robert Redford. Maren put her hand over her heart, trying to hide its thumping. Throwing herself at him would confirm their suspicions about her.

"Miss Maren," he reached for her hand, and sang the first lines from Chris de Burgh's "Lady in Red."

Maren's face heated. Neil probably sang love songs to all his women. It meant nothing to him, but way too much to her. "Does the FAA know you're color-blind?"

"Mom went to a party with one of her baritones, but left this for you." Melody draped a white alpaca shawl over Maren's shoulders and handed her a white clutch.

Maren moved her tissues, driver's license, and mad money from her black shoulder bag.

"Look what Harmony's letting me wear!" Rhiannon bounded into the room in a swirl of purple lace. Gold ringlets framed her face.

"My shining stars." Neil hugged Rhi, then ushered them out.

Rhi opened the Toyota's door. "Wow, what happened? Where's all the trash?"

"I paid Cody big bucks to clean it out."

"He vacuumed all the dog hair," Maren said from the back seat. "Tango doesn't shed much."

"Who's Tango? You have a dog?"

His sparkling brown eyes met Maren's in the rearview mirror. "Private joke."

Neil... handsome, fresh-smelling, with a smooth singing voice. He had a gentle way with Rhi and the other children, understood musicians, had a great sense of humor, and liked dogs. She'd prayed against temptation, prayed for restraint. And here everything she wanted dangled in front of her. She fixed her gaze on the lush Virginia countryside. *Self-control.*

Help me, Lord.

"Wow..." Maren gaped at the lofty ceiling hung with flags in the Kennedy Center's Hall of Nations. Her head tipped back, showing the long column of her throat. Waves of curls rippled to her waist, giving a glimpse of her back beneath. Her skin glowed against the dark blue dress. And his hand tingled with the wish to stroke her arms, her shoulders, her back.

Rhiannon twisted between them, straining to see everything. "I have the urge to yodel."

Maren startled from her trance. "You will not."

"Kidding." She skipped across the red carpeted Grand Foyer to the floor-to-ceiling windows. Evening sunlight colored the Virginia landscape gold and purple, echoing his niece's colors.

"Wish I'd brought a camera." Neil finger-framed the image.

Maren's eyes misted. "This is like a fairy tale come true for her."

Rhiannon pushed open a glass door and raced across the marble terrace. Murmuring mother-cautions, Maren followed. Some pretty boy, hair slicked back like a Nordstrom's model, held open the door. Neil followed the guy's gaze, noticing the way the dress clung to

Maren's dancer's figure and the slit in the hem highlighted her shapely calves.

Neil hurried after his ladies, giving the guy a don't-touch glare. "Didn't know the Kennedy Center had doormen. Thank you, sir."

Rhiannon leaned on the wide rim of the terrace. "Uncle Neil! You can see the river from here!"

He pointed out landmarks. "Roosevelt Island, straight ahead, good place to hike. Roosevelt Bridge to the left. Rosslyn, on the Virginia side. We wave to all the people in those office buildings on final for one-five." He slipped an arm around Maren's waist, fitting his hand to the slim curve of her waist. "Next door is Watergate. Upriver is Key Bridge,"

Maren pivoted away, reminding him— again—he hadn't asked permission. "We should go in, find our seats."

"Let's dance!" Rhiannon grabbed Neil's hand and swung him into a waltz, complete with a whistled "Blue Danube." He forgave her tendency to lead, since she provided the music.

"You took ballroom lessons?"

"Mom taught me," she sang to Strauss.

"Then she should have a turn. Keep singing. Can you whistle Clapton's 'Wonderful Tonight?'" Neil caught Maren's hand and bowed. "May I have this dance, milady?"

"C'mon, Mom. Show him how it's done!"

"You two."

Neil counted Maren's wry smile as agreement. He sang as he twirled her in a great arc around the terrace. Ahh, perfect fit, perfect grace, lips within perfect kissing distance. He could dance all night, but at the end of the second verse, she stiffened and stepped away.

"The concert."

Not the concert, but the upcoming mention of *love* in the bridge had stopped her. A glimmer of love had shone in her eyes, but she wasn't ready for any declarations. "Rhiannon will want to see them tune up."

Neil escorted his ladies through the crowds and up the stairs of the Concert Hall. Even blasé Washingtonians paused for a second look as they passed. He couldn't tell if Rhiannon or Maren attracted more attention. They arrived at the First Tier and found their door. The usher handed them *Stagebills*.

Rhiannon flipped through the forty-eight-page publication. "This is the program?"

"It's mostly ads."

They stepped into the chandelier-lit auditorium, gleaming in deep red, white, and bronze. Rhiannon gushed, "An organ! I hope they're playing Saint-Saëns."

"Four thousand pipes."

Maren caught her daughter by the bow of her dress. "How many people have fallen off this balcony?"

"None." Neil was used to the low railing, steep steps, and seats soaring above the orchestra seats and box tier. "I'll go first." He went down, turned, held his hand out to Rhiannon, then saw her safely seated in the first row.

Maren towered over him on high heels. Her cold fingers slipped into his hand. As she stepped into the Concert Hall's light, the low rumble of murmurs increased in pitch.

"You are so beautiful," he whispered. "Can't take my eyes off you."

"I'm quite sure *Name that Tune* is not allowed in the Kennedy Center." Moving gracefully, she lowered herself onto the velvet seat. "Oh. You wanted to sit next to Rhi."

"This is..."

The older man on the other side of Rhiannon opened a yellowed book.

"The *score*?" She asked, breathless. "You have *the score* for *tonight*?"

"Yes, it is." He smiled. "I hope it doesn't bother you."

"Would you..." Rhiannon switched into charm mode, tilting her head and giving the man a smile he couldn't refuse. "Would you mind if I looked over your shoulder, followed along..."

The man caved. "Not at all. You're a musician?"

"Cellist."

"Ah, you must be here for Dvořák."

"They're playing his Cello Concerto? All right! Say, do you know which one is Lloyd Gerson-Zeitz?"

"Sorry, I don't."

The two bent over the music.

Neil smiled. "No need to switch seats."

Maren swung her hair to her front, then scanned the Concert Hall. Neil leaned back to check on Rhiannon and the aficionado, his view crossing Maren's bare shoulders. "How's your mosquito bites?"

She scooted back in her seat so he couldn't touch her and anchored her hands to the far armrest. "Fine. Melody put something on them."

"Glad to hear it." But not really. "Are you warm enough?" He tugged the shawl over her shoulders. "You could wear my jacket."

"I'm fine. My hands are always cold."

Sounds like an invitation. He closed his hand around hers.

Her breathing picked up tempo, and heat rose in her cheeks. "Neil..."

The orchestra drifted onto the stage. Rhiannon leaned on the rail. Maren grabbed her daughter with both hands. "I want seat belts. You're used to the height. You probably come here all the time."

He couldn't remember the last date he'd brought here. "In August I brought the kids to hear Bobby McFerrin, the jazz vocalist." Oops. Now he'd done it, dropping the name of someone she'd never heard of.

Maren eased her grip off Rhiannon, but didn't bring her hands within Neil's reach. "He came to Western. Excellent musician and entertainer."

The conductor took the stage and the National Symphony treated the audience to a premier of a new symphony, a ballet from Ravel, and the Dvořák.

Neil faced the stage, but focused on Maren—the long line of her thigh as she leaned away from him, the tiny movements of her fingers in time to the music, the tear catching in her lashes at the swelling of a brilliant passage.

Catherine Richmond

He didn't hear Ravel or Dvořák. Not a note of it.

Instead Neil's heart sang Queen's "Crazy Little Thing Called Love."

Chapter Twenty-Two

M aren stepped into the empty kitchen at Wolfe's Den on Sunday morning. No one stirred upstairs. She'd learned her lesson about wandering the woods and crossing paths with Neil. She made coffee, took it to the porch and sat in a rocking chair, listening to bird song and the gurgle of the creek as the sun lifted the mist from the land. A fox stepped from the trees, stared at her for a moment, then trotted across the clearing. So relaxing...but shouldn't she be doing something?

Sun-hwa and Jim emerged from the carriage house, all dressed up.

"You're going to church?" Maren asked. "I wish I'd known, so I could go with you."

"The service is in Korean. I'm sorry." Jim bowed, then nodded at the big house. "They will awake later, church later. In English."

"Can I help with breakfast?"

"Usually cereal on Sundays," Sun-hwa said. "Patti says 'make yourself at home,' so you may cook what you like. If we are out of a food, grocery list on the refrigerator. There is a second refrigerator in the pantry."

"I don't know any Korean recipes."

"The family eats everything."

As they drove away, Maren returned to the kitchen and took inventory. In the hour before anyone woke, she made a pastry with ham and Gruyere, eggs Benedict with smoked salmon, and a fruit salad.

Cody padded down the steps, still in his pajamas with his hair on end. "Smells great."

The boy hugged her. Surprised, Maren stiffened for a second, then she wrapped her arms around him. He cuddled, warm and loose from sleep, like Rhi. "Is anyone else awake?"

"They will be. I opened their doors and curtains." He poured himself a glass of milk and sat in the closest chair. The family didn't seem to have assigned seating.

Patti arrived next, in spring green tunic and slacks. "Ah, breakfast."

"I hope it's all right." Maren wiped the counter.

"It's grand. I adore being spoiled." She poured coffee into a teacup. "Must be different, cooking for such a crowd."

The difference was in having high quality food, in such variety, and the freedom to make whatever she wanted. "Instead of the hundreds I usually cook for? I work in the deli and bakery."

"Oh? I thought you were a cashier." The older woman brightened. "That's creative, requires skill. Perhaps a stepping-stone to your own catering business?"

"Variations on the theme of grocery store." Maren shook her head. Time to change the subject. "Thank you for the loan of your shawl and clutch last night. I left them on the shelf outside your office. The girls said I was 'glam.'"

"No doubt you outshone the Kennedy Center. How was the concert?"

Maren gave her the highlights as the rest of the children and Neil straggled to the table.

The family sang "Be Present at Our Table, Lord," then attacked their food like wolves.

"Eating like our namesakes," Neil said.

Maren lowered her face, hoping her expression hadn't given away her thoughts.

"Tastes. So. Good." Andy raved between bites and the rest added their appreciation.

Rhi rubbed her forehead with the heel of her hand, eyelids at half-mast. Harmony looked equally groggy. They both wore pajamas and had serious cases of bedhead.

Maren asked, "How late did you two stay up?"

"Dunno," they echoed in unison.

"I issued a cease and desist order on giggling when I got home," Patti said. No one asked what time it was, but Maren guessed it was past midnight.

"What time do you leave for church?" Maren asked.

Neil looked at Patti, who glanced at the clock. "We missed it, so we'll have home church after breakfast."

Was it really too late? Or did they want to avoid questions about who their guests were?

"Andy and I've got it," Melody said.

Patti raised a sculptured eyebrow. "You had time?"

Her daughter smiled. "It came together easily, Holy Spirit powered."

They finished breakfast, then assembled in the large room on the west side of the house. Pillows, afghans, and rugs in bold colors and geometric patterns livened up the dark brown leather chairs and couches. On three sides, windows gave a view of the woods. The fourth wall held a fieldstone fireplace.

Maren looked up. The beams showed ax marks. "Wow."

"Recycled from old outbuildings, probably warehouses," Neil explained.

Rhi plopped into a wing chair and slouched, palm holding up her head, one heel propped on the edge.

"Feet off the furniture," Maren hissed as she sat in the next chair, as far as possible from Neil.

"Stay right there. Don't move." Patti left, returning in moments with a Nikon. She took Rhi's photo. "She looks like..."

Maren braced for another mention of Alan.

"...a Botticelli angel." Patti handed her the camera. "This is for you. Please, take lots of photos."

"There's plenty of film." Neil passed her the case. "Peoples Drug can develop them."

They were giving her a camera? To keep or just to use while she was here?

Melody sang Dolly Parton's "Coat of Many Colors," accompanying herself on the guitar. Then she set the instrument down and stood. "Well, Jane," she said to Andy in an officious tone, "tell me about our applicants."

"We've got some real winners, Mr. Drysdale," Andy said with a hoity-toity accent as he pulled a paper from his file folder. "This man worked in animal husbandry until his brothers sold him into slavery."

Melody gasped. "Dreadful family dynamics!"

"He had a successful stint in a management position, but lost it when his boss's wife came onto him."

Rhi straightened and whispered, "Joseph!"

Melody shook her head. "We can't hire anyone with a hint of scandal."

"While in prison—"

She thrust out her palm. "No. No one with a record!"

"—he rose to become superintendent. Through his skill as a dream interpreter—"

"Not a Department of Labor recognized occupation."

Patti chuckled.

"—he came to the attention of the administration. He managed agricultural production for the entire country, preventing a famine throughout the region."

"So he made something of himself after that tough beginning." Melody waved her hand. "Who else?"

Andy pulled out another piece of paper. "This one is a citizen. He was highly educated with a big-name professor. Skills include tent making and writing. He became a fanatic, persecuted heretics, then joined the fringe religion."

"Switching sides. Sounds indecisive."

"Paul," Rhi murmured.

"While on a speaking tour, he was arrested, thrown in prison, lashed, beaten, and stoned. And shipwrecked three times."

"One disaster after another. Was he born under an unlucky star, cursed, jinxed?" She rolled her wrist in a "move on" gesture. "Who else? Any female applicants?"

Andy pulled out another page. "Here we go. Pregnant before she married."

Melody slapped her forehead. "Doesn't anyone have any morals?"

That's me. Maren shifted in her seat, but Rhi whispered, "Mary, mother of Jesus."

"She and her husband snuck her son across the border twice. When the son grew up, she encouraged him to kick off his speaking tour by turning water into wine—"

"Wine? Not around Methodists and Baptists!"

Patti and Neil laughed.

"She supported her son's itinerant teaching career—"

"He couldn't hold a job, so *she* had to support him? Sounds like an enabler."

"She witnessed his execution and resurrection—"

"Execution and...what? Where are you getting these sketchy characters?" Melody grabbed her head. "What about good credentials? What about *normal*?"

"Normal?" Andy made a crashing cymbal sound.

The siblings moved out of character and sat. Maren's worries were for nothing. This family was anchored in the faith.

Melody held up the Bible. "Normal? Not in this book. Joseph, Paul, Mary the mother of Jesus, and everyone in here has a messy story. Same with all of us today." She reminded them everyone's broken; no one's in a place to bad-mouth another. There's no bad luck. No one's jinxed. No condemnation. "If you're going through trouble, keep your focus on Jesus and watch how He uses hard times for His glory."

Picking up the guitar, Andy led them in singing Ephesians 4:32.

Melody and Andy accepted her. Maren glanced across the room. Patti gave her a genuine smile and a nod.

Catherine Richmond

Bad stuff happens, but isn't always Consequences. *No condemnation...*

AFTER A LATE LUNCH prepared by Sun-hwa, Rhiannon asked to see Neil's house. They followed the path through the tunnel of trees.

Maren whispered, "Are you going to tell her about Tango?"

"He's our secret," Neil murmured. "Are you going to tell me why you're limping?"

"It's nothing." She tugged away from him.

He opened the door. "Leave your shoes on the patio, ladies. Sun-hwa doesn't clean here."

Rhiannon kicked off her Reeboks and dashed into the kitchen. Maren eased her feet out of her sneakers, wincing and closing her eyes for a second.

He held her arm and frowned at her sore heels. "Melody's sandals got you."

"You can let go of me now."

He stepped back and stuffed his wayward hands into his jeans pockets.

"Uncle Neil, can we have a fire in the fireplace?"

"Inside or outside?" Neil started to show her the layout, but the phone rang. His long-winded union rep grumbled about a problem with the training department.

As Neil listened with half an ear, Maren spoke to Rhiannon and made arcing gestures. She pointed to the windows, then overhead. She understood how the energy efficient windows and the passive ventilation system worked to keep the house comfortable. Impressive.

The union rep said, "Send the rough draft by the first of the month. Do you have the address?"

"Uh, sure." Ack! He'd been so lost in watching Maren, he'd agreed to write a newsletter article on...on what? "Did you, uh, have a title in mind?"

"How about 'Land and Hold Short Operations: A Critical Juncture'?"

LAHSO, he wrote. Due the first.

The union rep started in on strike preparedness, but before he could get too wound up, Neil interrupted. "I've got company—"

"Hot date in the hot tub?"

"Family." Although the hot tub's a great idea. He signed off.

"You're finally off the phone," Rhiannon said. "On with the tour."

"We'll start at the top." They climbed a spiral staircase to a small room walled with windows. "Architects call this a belvedere, meaning 'beautiful view,' but I call it a treehouse."

Rhiannon jumped into the pile of floor pillows. "I've always wanted a treehouse!"

"Some people build around a tree..."

"Which can damage it." Maren's mouth curved with the hint of a smile. "This is perfect. With the windows open, you can get a good airflow going, save on air conditioning."

Neil nodded. She got it. "And in the winter, a fan circulates the sun's warmth down."

Rhiannon flopped back into the pillows. "If I had a room like this, I'd bring up a stack of books and read all day."

And Neil would fill the room with candles, bring Maren up at twilight, and—*Hey, not in front of the kid!*

Rhiannon peeked under an old quilt. "An electric piano."

"I figured this would be a good place to write songs." For Maren.

A pair of squirrels dashed down a branch, scurried across the roof over their heads, and leaped onto another tree.

"You'd better hide, Uncle Neil. They're looking for nuts."

Maren's smile broadened into a grin.

Rhiannon hurried down to the living room. "How's the acoustics? Pretty good with these high ceilings, huh? Any requests?"

"Let your Mom choose." *I'm getting the hang of this respect thing.*

As she reached the main level, Maren let loose with an old

gospel tune, "Woke Up This Morning with My Mind Stayed on Jesus."

Rhiannon sang descant and clapped. Neil came in on bass and motioned them to the room's sweet spot. The tones swirled to the post-and-beam ceiling. Maren closed her eyes, singing and worshipping. Long hair, slender neck, smooth skin, dark lashes, and rich contralto voice...God's beautiful work.

His niece lost interest before he did. She picked up the only decoration on the mantel. "Who made these flowers? You really need to dust them."

"From Melody's career in Brownies."

"We made a vase like this in Sunday school. Masking tape and shoe polish. What's downstairs?"

He hesitated. The last girl he'd dated was horrified. She'd thought he needed another level above, which would ruin it. And Maren wasn't a fan of basement living. "Bedrooms, but they're not finished. I close off the registers in the unused rooms," he assured them.

Maren followed her daughter down the steps.

"The windows keep it from being a cave. And it's cooler for sleeping." Maren peeked into an empty bedroom, then a bathroom. "Glass block. Energy efficient. Burglar proof. No need for curtains."

Rhiannon found his room. "You're almost as messy as Harmony."

"Hey, you can see the floor." He'd left the comforter wadded in the middle of the bed, socks spilling off the top of the dresser, and piles of aviation magazines by his bed. Not much to commend himself for. He hurried them past his dirty laundry. "Here's the best part."

The sliding glass door opened onto what could be a garden if he was home long enough to tend it. A six-foot-tall privacy fence protected the area from weather and varmints. Neil folded back the cover of the hot tub and reeled in the string-held thermometer. "The water's fine. Ladies, roll up your cuffs and try it out." He cranked the timer and the water bubbled to life.

"I should have brought my swimsuit." Rhiannon scrunched up her jeans and stepped in. "Come on, Mom."

Neil tugged on her wrist. "Your feet need this after Melody's shoes."

She eased in, one foot at a time. "Aah."

"Is this a Jacuzzi? Lauren, the first violinist, has one. Her slumber party got to try it. I wasn't invited. She's a fifth grader. Isn't this great, Mom?"

Maren leaned back on her hands and lifted her face to the sun. Neil settled in next to her, but he really wanted to sit behind her, be her back rest, and send Rhiannon into the house.

Brakes! He shot a look at his niece, making sure he hadn't betrayed his thoughts. But no, she seemed as happy as ever, still his perky princess. He glanced back at Maren, stretched out on the deck, her feet bobbing in the jets. If he could keep her this relaxed... the rest of her life...

Wishing for more time with Maren, he whistled "Precious and Few." He saw the exact moment she recognized the song—her eyes opened, she swung her feet out of the water, and she hummed the Guess Who's "No Time."

"I prefer harmony over dissonance." Rhiannon splashed her feet. "You two need to sing the same song."

I agree.

Harmony yelled from the path, "Hey, what's taking so long? Let's go riding!"

Rhi jumped out of the hot tub, swiped her feet on the towel Neil provided, then dashed inside. Maren hurried after her, fighting the impulse to grab Neil and find out if his lips tasted as good as they looked.

"Maren—" Neil tried to catch her.

She raced upstairs. "Are these horses used to inexperienced riders? Do they ever buck? Are there helmets? Does Rhi need riding boots?"

"They're the most chill horses on the planet," Neil said as they reached the main floor.

Harmony carried two helmets decorated with Bedazzled ponies. "They never buck."

Neil rooted in the back of his coat closet and emerged with a pair of flip-flops and handed them to Maren. "These won't rub your heels. Patti gave them to me when I lived in Florida. They were too small, so I never wore them."

Maren slid her feet into them. A little large, but comfortable. "Better. Thanks."

"Done much riding?" he asked her as they followed the girls.

"Occasional trail rides. Then I started flying..." She couldn't afford two big expenses.

"It does take over your life."

The path opened to a paddock with a small stable. Despite their full hay rack, the horses stretched through the fence to eat grass.

Harmony held up a carrot and the horses sauntered over. "Quick, Rhiannon, give Ed your carrot."

"Hi, Ed." Rhi let go as soon as Ed lipped it. "He's big."

Harmony reviewed the basics—no squealing, hold on with legs, relax arms—and showed her how to mount. She maneuvered BB in a figure-eight, giving instructions on reining.

"Next." Neil motioned for Rhi.

"Maybe I should watch this time."

"I'll walk with you."

"Isn't there a smaller horse?"

Neil made an exaggerated scan of the paddock. "Nope. Ed's been waiting for you." He guided Rhi into position, then talked her through mounting.

"Whoa, it's high up here."

"Heels down." He adjusted her stirrups and showed her how to hold the reins, then sang Mr. Ed's theme song as they started around the paddock.

"Cliché!" Harmony passed them. "Sing something else!"

Motioning for Maren to join in, he sang America's "Horse with No Name." After the last la-la-la-la, he let Rhi go on her own.

She followed Harmony as Neil segued into "Ghost Riders in the Sky."

"C'mon girls, sing along and pick up the pace." He belted out "Tennessee Stud."

The girls giggled at the trot-induced vibrato in their voices. Maren took photos. Here was the life she wanted for Rhi—relaxing, trying new things, enjoying each day without worrying about money.

Dear Lord, she's going to want a horse.

Beloved, you can't always get what you want, but you get what you need.

God? Is that You?

Neil put his hand, warm and gentle, on her back. "Are you okay?"

"Does God listen to rock? I think He just quoted the Rolling Stones."

To her relief, Neil took her question seriously. "He hears our prayers. He's omniscient. And He'll do anything to get our attention, even make a donkey talk." He leaned closer. "Which song?"

"I was worrying, praying about Rhi wanting a horse. The cello and lessons are hard enough."

"Two high-cost interests." Neil sang, "Did you ever have to make up your mind? No, that's the Lovin' Spoonful, not the Stones. Which song did God quote?"

"'You Can't Always Get What you Want.'"

"Close to 'God will meet your needs,' in Philippians."

"He comes through for us every time, but I still worry."

"You and the Israelites after escaping Egypt." His hand rested on her shoulder. "Any worries you've got, I'll pray with you."

"Hah. You'll open your checkbook."

"There's not enough for a horse, so we'll see what God decides Rhiannon needs."

"Thanks." Maren stepped away from him as an older man built like a jockey walked into the clearing.

Neil sang James Taylor's "Sweet Baby James" to slow their ride to a walk. The girls dismounted and gave their horses another carrot.

Catherine Richmond

"This was so much fun," Rhi hugged Neil. "Let's go again! On the paths!"

"You need more experience before you do a trail ride. The bridle paths around here have as much traffic as the roads." Neil glanced at his watch. "Run back to the house and find out when dinner is."

The girls took off their helmets and raced away.

Leaving Maren alone with Neil and at the ragged end of her the self-control.

"I TOLD Sun-hwa I'd help with dinner." Maren bolted down the trail, sticking Neil with the job of helping Jerry remove the saddles. He walked to the house singing the chorus to Eric Carmen's "All By Myself."

Why did Maren run away? They'd had no opportunity to talk... or do anything else. Yet, while the girls were riding, she shared a conversation with God. So...she didn't like to be touched? Didn't like *his* touch? Didn't like how much he thought about touching her?

Neil entered the kitchen to Maren to stirring veggies, and Sun-Hwa pulling galbi, Korean grilled short-ribs, from the oven.

"Smells great." His stomach growled, a distraction from the rest of his body's focus on Maren.

Neil rang the bell and the family—minus Melody who'd gone out with friends—arrived. Maren ate well and joined the conversation. How could he get her alone?

As the meal finished, Neil asked, "What's everyone up to tonight? More videos to watch?"

"You're taking us to Great Falls," Cody said. The rest chorused, "Hooray!"

Rhiannon grinned. "How *great* are they?"

"Epic!" Cody yelled.

Patti put her hand over her youngest's mouth. "Good idea. Less crowded this time of day. You'll need the minivan, if you can find the keys."

Maren pointed to the wall by the back porch. "On the holder."

"An unexpected delight." Patti gave her a wink.

"Bug spray," Neil reminded everyone, then to Maren. "Are your feet ready for sneakers?"

She nodded.

They loaded up and took the short drive into the park. Neil started to explain the geology and history, but Cody interrupted.

"We learned this in school." For a nine-year-old, he had a good radio voice. "Great Falls is located on the fall line which runs from New Jersey to Alabama. It's where rock on the west meets sandy soil along the ocean. It was a trading center for the Powhatans," he emphasized the first syllable, "Piscataways, and Iroquois. People who were enslaved built the first canal. Some other people tried to build a power plant."

"There's a ghost town called Matildaville," Harmony said, "but no ghosts."

"There used to be a carousel," Andy said. "Dad always got the brass ring."

Neil didn't need a reminder of his humiliation. As he parked, he told them, "Stay together. Don't touch poison ivy, get near the edge, or climb on the rocks."

Rhiannon opened the van door. "Oh! I can hear the falls!"

They took the path past the closed visitor's center, between large rocks, to the first overlook, the sound growing louder. Spring runoff had the river flowing high and brown. Water surged through the gorge and spilled over cliffs, foaming and splashing.

"Be careful!" Maren called to the kids, then she spotted the waterfalls. "Wow!"

Neil stood close to speak over the roar. "When I was Cody's age, the river smelled like chemicals. Factories emptied waste in streams and it ended up here. It's cleaner now."

"Beautiful." She took photos, making Neil regret finding a camera for her. "No wonder they had to portage around it."

Dodging tourists and dogs, the kids raced to the next overlook and they followed. At the third, two kayakers, wearing helmets and floatation devices, launched into the river.

This early in spring, the river was visible as they hiked through the woods to the ruins of Matildaville and the canal. Cirrus clouds streaked the sky as the sun set.

"Time for s'mores!" Cody yelled.

"S'mores!" The rest chorused, then they raced for the van.

"Cody knows his role in the family," Maren said.

"I'm a sucker for the youngest."

"Understandable." Maren gave him a smile. "Need supplies?"

"What kind of uncle would I be if I wasn't stocked up? Got skewers too. Patti says no more than two s'mores a night."

"Avoid stomach aches."

"Exactly." The children had gone around the curve in the trail, so he reached for her hand. "Thanks for a wonderful day."

"It was." She squeezed, let go, then sped to the van.

It was? As in *it was until you made your move?* Or, *yes it was a marvelous day?*

They left the van at Wolfe's Den, grabbed flashlights, and took the path. Maren continued evasive maneuvers.

At Neil's, Andy took charge, lighting the kindling in the outdoor fireplace and sending the younger kids to find sticks. Neil brought out the ingredients, but paused over the ukulele. They usually sang around the campfire. He didn't want to embarrass Rhiannon if she didn't know how to play.

"I'll take it." Andy grabbed the instrument. He sat in the pool of light from the fire and launched into Johnny Nash's "I Can See Clearly Now." The family sang backup and tapped their legs for rhythm. Neil played John Denver's "Country Roads." Cody hammed it up on "Grey Squirrel," making up for missing a few chords with his acting. Harmony demonstrated her picking skill on "Puff the Magic Dragon," then turned to her half-sister. "Have you played ukulele before?"

Maren twisted her braid around her fingers, as if she too might be worried about her daughter.

"No, but I'll give it a try." Rhiannon took the instrument and easily sang, "He's Got the Whole World in His Hands."

Maren's shoulders relaxed. Andy and Harmony exchanged glances.

Cody crossed his arms, faking anger. "How'd you get so good?"

"It's only two chords." Which she'd figured out by watching the others. She shrugged and passed the instrument to her mom.

With a relaxed smile, Maren taught the kids the echo to "You Can't Get to Heaven on Roller Skates." Anyone who knew piano as well as Maren did could manage ukulele, so her skill wasn't a surprise, but her voice and performance were. Her sultry contralto captivated and her blues vibe kept the song from being too sweet. The firelight brought out the red in her hair. On-the-fly compositions of verses about Andy's VW and Uncle Neil's Toyota had the kids laughing. And let the kids know where Rhiannon got her musical background.

Maren fit in here too. If the kids would go home, they could try duets...and see how she fit in his arms.

"Where'd you learn that song?" Neil asked. Had she made peace with God?

"I was a church camp worship leader."

"Fun job." Only given to teens with good reputations and solid walks with Jesus. Another way Alan had trashed her life.

The fire turned to coals, perfect for s'mores.

"Roll up your sleeves," Neil cautioned as Maren reminded the kids, "Hot marshmallow burns, so don't fling it around."

"Already had one trip to the emergency room." Harmony lifted Andy's bangs and showed his scar.

He swatted her hand. "Hair covers it."

"Hope you don't go bald."

"Perish the thought!"

For some reason the phrase, or the end of their quota of s'mores, had the kids fencing with their skewers, raising the possibility of another ER visit.

Neil declared bedtime. The kids protested, but Maren rounded them up and found their flashlights. Rhiannon hugged Neil, the kids chorused their thanks, then they headed back to Wolfe's Den. Their voices faded, leaving him in silence.

Days full of family were the best...except... Neil looked down at the empty space by his left leg. "Thanks for staying, Tango."

. . .

MAREN STEPPED into the tub for a soak, then showered with the expensive-smelling shampoo and body wash. She dried with plush towels, then slathered on exotic lotion. Life at the Wolfes' was like staying in a luxury hotel. No... a luxury resort. With theater—*Fiddler on the Roof*, music—the Kennedy Center, and recreation—horses.

But the highlight of the day had been home church, where she'd learned Melody and Andy accepted her and faith mattered to this family.

No condemnation. The sun rises on the evil and the good. Flat tires, interrupted schooling, tough job markets happened to all sorts of people. So... was she free?

With a deep breath, Maren slid between the soft sheets. She could get used to this. Rhiannon certainly had. Except for...Neil.

If only Neil wasn't such a *good* uncle... Such a *good* friend... With a voice as deep and rich as dark chocolate, and a sense of humor and humility. His face crinkled when he laughed, he made a great cup of coffee, his warm and gentle hands—Stop!

In her head, Elvis sang, "Can't Help Falling in Love."

Was falling in love a sin? It might not be on the Bible's list, but lust definitely was. The Wolfes didn't condemn her for her past, but if she acted on her feelings for Neil, they might change their opinion. Rhi would be hurt. That couldn't happen.

Chapter Twenty-Three

Neil followed the sound of voices into the kitchen Monday morning. The place smelled like a foreign country. Maren giggled with Sun-hwa over the cutting board. Smiling and relaxed, padding around the kitchen in bare feet, she looked even prettier than Saturday night.

"What are we having?" He lifted the stockpot lid. "Kor-wegian? Lutefisk kimchi?"

They laughed harder.

Maren spooned a chunk for him. "What do you think of this?"

He frowned at the strip of meat swimming in dark brown sauce. "Better not be octopus."

"If you won't try it, maybe Tango will."

"Speaking of Tango, he missed you this morning. Had the coffee ready and everything."

The ladle inched closer. "Are you going to try this or shall we round up another taste tester?"

Responding to the dare in her eyes, he popped the chunk into his mouth and chewed. Hmm. "Chicken in soy sauce?" he guessed.

The two women collapsed into each others' arms, laughing.

"The kids won't eat mystery meat."

Maren started to respond, then tilted her head. From upstairs the three younger ones sang, "Good morning to you, good morning to you. You look rather drowsy, in fact you look lousy. Is that any way to start a new day?"

She started for the stairs. "They'll wake Patti."

"I'm already awake." His sister-in-law emerged from her office. "They're annoying Andy and Melody."

The growl echoed through the house.

"Our bass is awake!" Rhiannon cheered. "Barber shop quartet!"

They repeated the song in four-part harmony, then in a round. Rhiannon held her own.

A door banged open and Melody took it up an octave, *Oklahoma* style. "Oh what a horrible morning, oh what an awful day, I've got hideous siblings, if only they'd go away."

"No belting it out without warmups," Patti called up the stairs. "Breakfast in five."

"Cinnamon rolls and quiche." Sun-hwa whisked pie plates and sheet pans out of the oven. "Maren made them before I got here."

The phone rang. Sun-hwa answered, then turned to Patti. "Sol?"

"I'll take it." She listened for a moment, then covered the mouth-piece and whispered, "newspaper." Neil passed her the morning's *Washington Post*. She flipped through the sections, stopping in the middle. "I really couldn't say. They do. Quite photogenic. I'll tell Neil you called. Give my best to Leah." She hung up.

"That was Sol Rosen, Predator's publicist, asking about Neil's date." Patti pulled out the Metro Section with a flourish. "As Bonnie Raitt would say, you gave him 'Something to Talk About.'"

Maren gasped. The spatula and a chunk of baked egg hit the floor. She hurried to clean it up.

Neil read the story over his sister-in-law's shoulder. "The president of Czechoslovakia. I wondered why the photographers were there."

"Rhi?"

"You can only see the top of her head. The Secretary of State stepped in front of her."

Maren sank onto the nearest chair. "The whole world reads the *Post*."

"Have you eaten, hon'? You look pale." Patti motioned for Sun-hwa to serve their guest, then turned back to the paper. "Sol thinks you're the Eileen Ford model who went to the Grammys with what's-his-name, the guitar player who rolled his Jeep."

"The only Ford he's seeing is Betty." Neil studied the picture. The photographer had caught Maren at her best. She shimmered down the red staircase, curls rippling over one shoulder, her smile radiant. She did look like a model. "Great shot. We were laughing over the viola jokes Rhiannon learned from the guy with the scores."

"Don't people have to get permission?" Maren clenched her coffee mug.

Neil shook his head. "We were in a public place, behind a VIP."

"Sooner or later, Sol will find out about Rhiannon. His ears will perk up, and his whiskers twitch, and he'll race around in circles. But he won't do a thing. No promoting without a signed contract." Patti nodded as Sun-hwa served the quiche. "Nothing to worry about, might as well eat."

The last airport quiche Neil had tried required a steak knife to saw the crust. Maren's had a flaky crust and a smooth filling. He took another bite and closed his eyes. Ah, heaven.

Cody grabbed a cinnamon roll and made for the family room.

"Table," Neil said.

The boy did a one-eighty and took the seat next to him.

Rhiannon marched in. "Uncle Neil. I have some questions about this music."

"Good morning, Rhi," Maren said.

"Good morning, Mom." She set Alan's albums on the table. "Now, this first one, why only four chords: G, E minor, C, D7?"

"He didn't know any others." Neil served quiche to her and Cody. then watched Maren pop a slice of bread in the toaster. "You have a good ear."

"It's obvious to even the most casual listener." She held up *Night Hunter*. "This one is better. But on the fourth song, it sounds like you and the cello player are riffing on the 'Third Brandenburg Concerto' in the background."

"We were. Vincent's classically trained."

Maren took the toast, dry, and went out.

"And this one." Rhi set *Banned in Nashville* on top. "This was the best. The percussionist stopped acting like he was conducting."

"The record company made us use a studio drummer for the recording session."

Rhiannon turned the album over. "And the guitar player—"

Guitar player? Not "Dad"? Maybe she felt less claim on him around the other children.

"—picked instead of strummed. He's more confident in his solos, not afraid of key changes, chord changes on the mark."

"You're kinder than any of our critics."

"They must have hated this." She pulled *Alpha* from the stack. "The good stuff from the first one disappeared."

"Have you heard of sophomore slump?"

"Tell her the truth." Patti glided to the coffee pot for a refill. "*Alpha* is a testimony to the greed of the record company, trying to ride the coattails of 'Howling at the Moon,' the single. And proof illegal substances do not enhance musical skills. Remember it well."

Rhiannon hid it at the bottom of the pile. "Ugh. A more powerful warning than any 'this is your brain on drugs' ad. Did he ever... get better?"

"He came clean," Patti said. "And did some of his best work. Not enough for an album, but we've got them on tape out in the studio."

"His studio! Can we—"

"I thought we were going riding." Harmony plopped onto the seat next to Rhiannon.

"Breakfast first." Neil reminded them. How could these two look so much alike? Except for their coloring, they could be twins. Rhi had gotten almond-shaped eyes, straight brows, and smooth cheeks from her mom.

Rhiannon spotted the newspaper. "Hey, Mom and Uncle Neil."

"It's a good photo. You're welcome to keep it, if you'd like." Neil would run by the 7-Eleven and pick up his own copy.

"Thanks!" Rhiannon dashed upstairs with the paper, then returned to the table.

The phone rang again. Sun-hwa stretched the phone cord into the hallway and spoke in Korean.

Andy and Melody grumbled down the stairs.

Sun-hwa hung up. She hurried to the driveway where her husband and Maren—there she was—unloaded a truck from the garden center, then the couple rushed inside to Patti's office. Maren came in and loaded the dishwasher.

Moments later Patti emerged. "Sun-hwa's sister went into labor and the baby came early. Sun-hwa and Jim are going to Baltimore, to help with baby Stephanie and their business. We'll eat take out."

"Pizza!" Cody cheered.

"I'd be glad to fix meals," Maren said. "Sun-hwa stocked the freezer, so no trouble."

"Neil, tell the garden center to take the plants back. We'll reorder later."

Maren held up a pencil drawing with notes. "Jim gave me his layout, so I can put them in."

"But you're on vacation," Neil said.

"I accept your generous offer. There's sunscreen, gloves, and insect repellant in the garage." Patti nodded at Neil and Andy. "You two do mulch."

"We've been volun-told." Andy fist-bumped his uncle.

"I'll help with lunch." Melody said, leaving unanswered the question of her dinner plans.

"What do you want us to do?" Harmony motioned to Rhiannon and Cody.

"Dishes, then studio."

"Let's pray," Neil said. The family joined hands. He grabbed Maren's before she could scoot away, hoping God listened to his prayers in spite of his ulterior motives. "Dear Jesus, please help baby Stephanie grow and be healthy."

Maren spoke next, "Help her mother heal and be strong."

Then Patti, "Bless the family with the peace of your presence."

Melody, their new driver, prayed for safe travels. Jim asked for wisdom in managing the business. Harmony requested the best from the doctors and nurses. Andy said "Amen."

"Thank you." Sun-hwa and Jim bowed, packed up, then drove off into the morning traffic.

Neil put in a couple hours of digging holes, hauling compost, and mulching trees with Andy and Maren, then went inside for water.

"I got three calls asking about your date at the Kennedy Center," Patti said.

"I had two on my answering machine, from coworkers wanting Maren's phone number. What did you say?"

"I can't keep track of your social life." She shrugged, then looked out the window. "Making progress."

"Trying to keep up with Maren." He searched the cupboards for sports bottles. "This was supposed to be her vacation."

"Work may de-stress her, make her feel less like a charity case, that she has a purpose here. " Patti emptied the coffee grounds into a can under the sink. "Add this to the compost bin when you go out."

He found the water bottles and filled them. "She's sleeping on the floor here, like she does in her apartment."

"Koreans sleep on the floor." Patti watched Maren work. "Maybe she's doing penance."

"Isn't that a Catholic thing?"

She shrugged. "Maybe I'm taking advantage of her. Maybe she works to escape the prison of her father's condemnation."

"He's dead, but she's still slaving away."

"Or maybe she's enjoying herself. She seems more relaxed, content even." Patti pushed him toward the door. "*Babo*, it's still not your job to fix her, but you can take her water."

MAREN PLANTED the formal bed in front of the house, finding a healthy mix of topsoil and compost over a layer of red clay. Blue scilla and yellow narcissus had naturalized into the surrounding woods. Eastern red cedars and a variety of oaks formed the backdrop for azaleas and dogwoods. The new flowers would be a beautiful addition.

Andy sauntered, John Wayne-style, towards her. Had Neil ever been this awkward? "How may I help you?" he asked.

"This section is ready for mulch and water." Maren finished the last plant, collected the empty pots, and headed to the garage. "Your uncle has a windshield wiper motor for the VW. And you may as well replace the push rods while you have the engine out."

Andy bounced beside her like a puppy, tongue out and eyes wide. "Are you going to help me?"

"You'll figure it out." Maren pointed Andy to the wheelbarrow and mulch pile. She consulted Jim's list and took the next flowers to the adjacent barn. As she dug, snippets of guitar mixed with birdsong. Someone was practicing... even though school was out. Rhi shared that passion.

"You must be ready for a break." Patti, elegant in a denim tunic and slacks, brought out a pitcher and refilled Maren's sports bottle. "Looking good out here."

They weren't ready for eye contact, maybe never would be. Maren smiled at the plants. "This is so satisfying. You've chosen great perennials—native to the area, low-water-use, sequenced bloomers, and attractive to pollinators, but not deer and rabbits."

"All credit to Jim. He spent the winter researching and put in the order."

The barn doors creaked open, revealing a music studio stocked with instruments, mixing board, recording equipment, and three budding musicians holding acoustic guitars.

Maren gasped. "I didn't know this was a studio. The soundproofing is amazing."

"Kept the band from waking the children. And now, keeps the children from waking me."

"The thermostat says it's seventy degrees, fifty percent humidity." Harmony motioned to Cody and Rhiannon. "Any requests?"

"A song about flowers," Patti said. "Pete Seeger's 'Where Have All the Flowers Gone.'"

"All right! We can use the four chords you know," Harmony told the younger kids. They tackled the song, their playing growing stronger with every verse.

When they finished, Patti picked up a saxophone. "'Build Me Up Buttercup.' Grab your euphonium, Cody. Maren on keyboards. We need percussion. Hey, Andy!"

The boy burst out the kitchen door, chewing on something, and sat at the drum step.

"There's an F chord in this song." Harmony showed Rhi. "Fake the key change."

"I'll sing lead." Neil ran from the garage to join them.

Maren played the intro and Neil belted out the tune... straight at her. She focused on singing the backup "ooh, ooh, hey-hey-hey," but ended up echoing his "I need you." Her irrational heart took the thought and ran with it, heating her face. Maybe they'd think it was sunburn.

Patti's solo at the end gave Maren a lifeline. "You play sax!"

"High school marching band and jazz band," Patti was a musician. "You're a piano wiz."

"We know another song about flowers—Edelweiss." Rhi plucked out the tune.

"Okay with you?" Neil asked and Maren nodded. He joined her on the bench. She slid off as he explained, "It's slow enough we'll do it 'Dueling Banjos' style. Each of us plays a line, then switches instruments. While you're switching, someone else is playing. Try something new."

Rhi stowed the guitar, then grimaced. "I want to try euphonium, but..."

Cody sprayed the mouthpiece, wiped it, and passed it to her. "Ready for you!"

"Okay, Mom, start us off!" Rhi handed her a violin. "I took Suzuki when I was little."

"So you and your mom have been playing ever since?" Patti asked.

"The car died and Suzuki was too far off the bus route, so we had to stop. I started cello last June."

"I should..." Maren glanced at her watch. "...help Melody make lunch."

"We have time." Patti said. "Go for it, Maren."

Maren played the violin, Patti jazzed the clarinet, Rhi mangled the euphonium, Neil squawked the French horn, Harmony's mandolin sent it in a bluegrass direction, and Cody picked out the tune on guitar. Second time around, they upped the tempo and added vibraphone, ukulele, clarinet, piano, and the bass. The third rendition had them laughing with the harmonica, accordion, tambourine, castanets, and a plastic pantyhose egg containing cat litter. Rhi grinned, her face glowing as she exchanged high fives with her siblings.

"All together now!" Neil led them in a grand finale, with everyone playing their favorite instrument. Rhi managed on the full-sized cello. Maren went back to the violin, so she wouldn't have to share the piano bench with Neil.

"Let's do this all day!" Rhi tinkered with the vibraphone.

"Great ear training." Maren hung up the violin.

"Maren said smart kids need to learn to fail." Neil cleaned the French horn.

"So true." Patti nodded. "This gives them a chance to laugh at mistakes and explore without needing to be perfect."

Before Neil could sing another love song, Maren escaped to the kitchen.

Rhi enjoyed playing by herself or with Maren, but making music with her siblings in a studio full of instruments launched her joy into the stratosphere. Hands down, Wolfe's Den was the best environment for her daughter.

They couldn't afford to move to northern Virginia, but maybe Patti would let them visit again.... if... if she could keep from throwing herself at Neil like some sex-starved groupie.

Chapter Twenty-Four

"Tourist time." Neil poured milk for breakfast, then asked Maren, "Smithsonian, White House, Capitol? What interests you?"

Patti added, "Washington Monument, National Zoo, Mt. Vernon?"

Maren set the platter of croque-madame breakfast sandwiches on the table. "I should finish planting."

Not on his watch. She needed a vacation and he was the guy to give it to her.

Rhiannon said, "I want to hear the recording sessions."

Neil turned to Maren. "There's cuss words, trash talking."

"Can't be any worse than what I hear on the school bus." Rhiannon huffed. "I'm interested in the creative process."

"There's one," Patti broke in, "right after Harmony was born that's mostly music. And another, after he had his come-to-Jesus. I could supervise...no, I have a date tonight."

"Another date?" The kids asked. "Same guy? Where are you going? What time will you be home?

Her smile said she had no intentions of sharing details. "Different guy. Library of Congress concert. Before midnight."

Neil cut through the kids' demands for information with, "I'll stay with Rhi while she listens."

Maren nodded. "Appreciate it."

"So where are we going this morning?" Cody was ready for anything.

"Count me in." Harmony said.

"Schedule conflict," Melody said, too cool to hang out with the younger kids.

"I'm in," Andy said between bites. "Can't Take My Eyes Off You" was his theme song since Maren arrived.

Four voices debated what to visit.

Neil locked eyes with Maren. "Air and Space?" he mouthed. Her face softened and she gave him a thumbs up. He raised his voice. "Take off for the Air and Space Museum in half an hour."

"You'll need the minivan." Patti headed for her office. "Maren hung up the keys. I could get used to being organized."

They drove in on the tail end of rush hour. Neil found a parking spot within sight of the museum, prompting the kids to sing *Fiddler's* "Miracles of Miracles."

Maren smiled, then she went into mom-mode. "Stay together. Don't wander off."

Neil added his bit of parental wisdom. "If you get lost, go to..."

"The Bell X-1!" Rhiannon said. "The orange jet that broke the sound barrier."

Once inside, when Rhiannon spotted the Wright Brothers' plane, she burst out with "Those Magnificent Men and Their Flying Machine." Game on! They sang "Danger Zone" for the Bell X-1, "Rocket Man" for the Mercury capsules, "Leaving on a Jet Plane" for the early jets, and "Wind Beneath My Wings" for the golden age biplanes. In the hubbub of students on field trips and children on spring break, the Wolfe kids were the least of the noise.

Neil paused a beat. Was he thinking of Rhiannon as a Wolfe? Of course! As far as he was concerned, she became part of the family the day he met her. Convincing Maren however...

In the space race exhibit, Andy did a Frank Sinatra impression on "Fly Me to the Moon" and "Come Fly With Me." Maren scatted the piano part, which made him more googly-eyed than ever. No doubt, Neil's expression was just as love-struck.

"Can't lose them if they keep singing," Maren said.

"Better than tying balloons to them."

"Your usual technique?" Was she worried about his parenting skills or could she tell he was kidding?

"Only for the zoo."

Her mouth quirked. "Don't want them mistaken for an inhabitant."

They ate lunch and picked out souvenirs from the gift shop, then, in the late afternoon, left the museum. Halfway to the mini-van, Rhiannon yelled, "Bagpipe!" and took off down the sidewalk, the rest in hot pursuit. The piper and a guy drumming on paint buckets performed Bob Marley's "One Love." When they finished, Rhiannon requested Michael Jackson. All the kids could dance, but Rhiannon's spins, kicks, and gestures were spot on. A crowd gathered and cheered.

"You wanted to leave before rush hour," Maren said.

Neil put his arm around her shoulders. She didn't move away. "Where else can we see kids channeling the Jackson Five to a bagpipe and paint bucket duo. How did she learn this?"

"When we lived in Northside, neighbors took great pride in polishing her moves. Uh-oh." Maren tensed, then marched up to a guy with camera bigger than the usual tourist's. She raised her voice. "Sir? Sir? Don't take pictures. Let them be kids."

The man went down on his knee to angle his shot. Uh-oh, indeed.

"You're done." Neil fake-stumbled into him, but the photographer kept his balance. He reached for the lens. "Enough."

Maren stepped in front of the photographer, trying to block his shot. Instead he adjusted focus, snapped a few of Maren, then stood. "Hey, blonde girl. Who's your dad?"

Rhiannon and the others yelled, "Michael Jackson!" They moonwalked. The spectators cheered and moved to block the photographer. Finally he left.

Maren turned to Neil, her face pale. "Paparazzo?"

"Probably."

The musicians finished to hearty applause. Neil dropped money in their tam-o'-shanter.

"Uncle Neil, I want a bagpipe!" Cody hugged his uncle.

"Ask your mom." No chance. Neil pointed to the minivan. "Ready for takeoff!" The kids ran for it. Neil held out his hand to Maren. "You okay?"

She shrugged. "Lunch, gift shop, entertainment. This is expensive."

"The Bible asks why we spend money on things that don't satisfy." He motioned at the kids. "What's more satisfying than family?"

"Thank you." Her cold hand slid into his, gave a quick squeeze, then she hurried after the children.

Deep in his heart, Carole King sang, "So Far Away."

AFTER DINNER, Neil found the tapes Patti recommended. He loaded them as Rhiannon flitted around the studio. Yesterday she'd explored with intention, trying each instrument. But today she wandered.

"You asked about the creative process." Neil opened a file drawer and sorted through the papers, looking for the scrap sheet that matched the tape. "Alan started with lyrics, melody, chords. The band expanded it. The engineer combined the tracks and sent a copy off to the record company. In Nashville, he'd redo it with session musicians." He handed her the lined notebook page covered with Alan's notes.

Rhiannon studied the scribbled pages. "Messy writing."

"His hand couldn't keep up with his ideas." Neil started the player.

A voice on the tape said, "'Riding the Updraft.'"

Neil whispered, "That's the engineer."

Alan sang and accompanied himself on guitar, then the drummer and bass player did their parts. His instructions to them were muffled, but, with a few corrections, they managed to lay down their tracks.

When they finished, the drummer asked, "What you pointing at me for?"

"You the man," Alan said. "Good job." This must have been after Patti's talking-to about perfectionism and valuing his band.

"Hey, keyboards, switch to the organ." After a few measures, Alan yelled, "No, no, no. When I howl, you need to do that descending notes thing."

"Like this?" The keyboard player riffed descending arpeggios.

"No, meathead!" Alan picked out the melody of "House of the Rising Sun." "Less old fogey. More sexy, mysterious, exotic. This is a make-out song. Not that you know anything about making out."

"Why didn't you say so?" He dashed off a few bars of "The Stripper."

Alan snorted. "Keep your clothes on."

Rhiannon motioned "stop."

Neil pushed pause.

"Uncle Neil, that's you. He's calling you names. He calls people in his band by their instrument."

"He could be a jerk."

"He's rude. And he doesn't know musical terminology."

"Music theory is a senior level class. He skipped senior year. Eventually the label got him some tutoring." Neil restarted the tape.

Alan howled and Neil tried to come up with the notes his brother heard in his head.

The bass player interrupted Alan's rant. "What about recording some real wolves?"

"Where are we going to get wolves?" asked the rhythm guitar player.

"Sears has everything." The drummer hit his crash cymbal.

"Let's all howl." The rhythm guitarist's howl ended in a cough.

"Why are we howling?" Neil's younger self asked. "Isn't this song about eagles?"

"Yeah. Eagles are quiet. I saw one at Great Falls." Alan whistled. "John Denver did a song about eagles. I'd call him, but he'd razz me about being a city boy."

"He used strings," said the engineer. "Call him after we finish."

"Patti could do that thing with her saxophone, like Bob Seger's 'Turn the Page,'" said the drummer.

"Sure," Alan said. "Go take care of the kids."

The bass drum thumped. "You take care of them. They're your kids."

The engineer reminded them, "The clock is ticking."

"How about a wind sound?" The guitar player blew into the mic.

"With vibraphone." The drummer played arpeggios. "I know! We need a didgeridoo."

"Not even Sears has a didgeridoo," said the guitarist. "Or someone who knows how to play it."

"Let's go to Australia." The drummer tapped his cymbal.

"Do that again and you're fired," Alan said.

The drummer whacked it harder.

Suddenly the tape filled with the squealing and shrieking of young kids.

Neil whispered to Rhiannon, "Alan hit the intercom button to the house. That's Melody and Andy, age four and three."

Alan yelled over the racket, "Hey babe! Run down to the Australian embassy and get us a didgeridoo player."

"Soon as you come get your kids. Babe." The noise of the children stopped.

Neil pressed pause on the recorder as the door opened and the real children, all four of them, entered.

"We thought you might need backup." Melody took the arm chair. "Actually we thought you might need Dal-Rae, our counselor, but she doesn't make studio calls. So you got us."

"Learning your dad is a blockhead can be yucky." Harmony joined Neil and Rhiannon on the couch and Cody squeezed in with them. Snuggling with the kids was the best; he hoped Rhiannon felt the love.

Andy brought over the drummer's stool, then glanced from the tape to Rhiannon. "You okay, kid?"

She shook her head. "He's mean to Uncle Neil. And your mom."

"Mom had her ways of dealing with Dad, but she couldn't stop him from picking on Uncle Neil." Melody motioned for Neil to go on. "Hang in there."

Neil started the tape again. The band ran through the song, with the organ and guitar underscoring the verses, then the vibraphone playing arpeggios as Alan blew wind sounds into the mic. The next run-through was *a tempo*. "Play it back." It sounded good, but Alan proclaimed, "it needs a bridge and another verse."

"Are you out of your mind?" The engineer groaned.

"Somewhere else you got to be?" Alan blew a raspberry. "A hot date? Do I need to get another engineer?"

"I have instructions from the boss to keep it tight, no messing around, don't run up the bill."

"I'll handle Patti. Everyone take five."

Rhiannon held up Alan's notes. "He wrote this bridge and last verse in five minutes?"

The recording caught shuffling footsteps, a slamming door, then Alan picking and muttering "soar, roar, before. Fly, black eye, dark eye, sky." He had it all written by the time the door opened again.

The guitar player said, "Look who we found outside. This is David."

"G'day, mate, you call for a didgeridoo player?"

"Yes I did." Alan introduced himself and the rest of the band, proving he did know their names. He offered a chair and a music stand, which David declined.

"Your wife worked a miracle. Got us a didgeridoo player in an hour," the engineer said. "You'd better thank her."

"Every time I do, she gets pregnant." Alan laughed, but no one else did.

They played their most recent version. David tried out a variety of sounds and the drummer reworked his part. They finally got a run-through clean enough to send to the label. Neil remembered his relief and pride when Alan said, "Nailed it."

The recording ended. Neil returned the tape to the cabinet.

"Can we get a didgeridoo? Please?" Cody asked.

"School might have one you can try."

Rhiannon frowned. "There's no didgeridoo on the album."

"Good ear," Neil said. "The label made the wind sound with a synth, otherwise we'd have to bring David on tour."

Cody leaned forward and looked him over, as if gauging his strength. "Uncle Neil, did you ever fight with Dad?"

"Yeah, but fighting made it worse." Cody was too young to hear about Neil beating up Alan after he'd raped Maren, except…Neil gulped. Dropping in on Maren six months ago had forced her to tell Rhiannon about the rape. He hadn't apologized enough.

Andy nodded at the tape Neil loaded. "Dad's last recording."

Alan's voice had lost its angry edge. "I don't usually do covers, but this is where I'm at." He sang, accompanying himself on the guitar, "What A Difference You've Made in My Life." Amy Grant's version was reverent, Ronnie Milsap's was country, and B.J. Thomas's was pop. Alan's came out rough, from his heart.

When Alan finished singing, he paused and sniffed, as if he might be crying. "In AA, I had to make a moral inventory. It was grim. I say my wife and family are important, but I don't make time for them. I say 'couldn't do it without you' to my band, then treat them like crap. I preach taking care of the planet, then trash it."

He sang a country-rock version of "For the Beauty of the Earth."

"I've done a lot of wrong things in my thirty years on this earth," Alan continued. "With God's help, I hope to do better in the rest of my life. I don't know why Jesus forgives me, but I know he does and I'm thankful. I've wronged a lot of people. I hope they'll forgive me too." He cleared his throat. "More later as I learn to praise Him, but for now…I should talk to Kris about this. He gets it." Voice cracking, Alan launched into Kristofferson's "Why Me Lord?" After the last chorus, he segued into the doxology, then the recording ended.

The kids were quiet as Neil put away the tape.

Melody passed the Kleenex box around.

"The last tape…sounds like someone I'd want to know." Rhiannon wiped her tears.

Melody leaned forward, chin propped on her fist in imitation of Dal-Rae. "Some people journal their feelings, but we turn them into music."

"Yeah, Mom pounds out Prokofiev, but cellos don't like to be hammered."

"The drum set works for me." Andy said. "Have at it."

Harmony put an arm around Rhiannon. "My favorite metaphor is the backpack. You can't take everything with you—"

"Especially if you're carrying a cello."

"—so pack the essentials and leave the rest behind. What's your takeaway?"

"Be polite to your band members."

"Dad wasn't a good example, but he could be a warning." Andy's fingers tapped his knees, playing a composition only he could hear.

"And our moms are epic!" Cody said and the rest gave Maren rave reviews. "Radical!"

"They're keeping it together for us," Melody said.

"Thanks for finding me," Rhiannon said to Neil. Then to the other kids, "Now that I've seen how close you are, I'm sorry about taking up so much of Uncle Neil's time, leaving less of him for you."

"We can share Uncle Neil."

"Thanks, baby bro." Rhiannon squeezed his hand.

Melody quirked a smile. "He is our *favorite* uncle."

Harmony patted his knee, making him tear up, "Highly rated in every survey of great uncles."

"So we'd better show you how to take care of him." Andy grabbed Neil's ankles and yanked him onto the floor. They piled on, tickling him.

A sharp whistle split the air. Patti said, "Maren made dessert."

The kids raced to the house.

Neil groaned. "They're getting too big and I'm getting too old..."

Patti gave him a hand up. "But you're not going to stop them."

"Got that right." He put an arm around his sister-in-law. "You're raising some mighty fine kids."

"Thanks for your help, *babo*."

"Always. So what did Maren make?"

"Cherry ice cream to help them sleep, since Rhiannon has

master class tomorrow. If it works, I'm feeding it to these Energizer Bunnies every night." Patti headed to the house.

"Hope it works." Neil put the tape and scrap sheet away, then followed.

Maren stood on the porch, drumming her fingers on the railing, as a whippoorwill called from the creek. "How did it go?"

"It could have been rough, but the kids shared their counseling insights, shed a few tears, praised their moms. Rhiannon's handling it." Neil climbed the stairs and rested his hand on hers. "You're the one who did the heavy lifting six months ago. I'm sorry I put you in that position."

She stared at the woods. "Thanks for being there tonight. I couldn't..."

"You're here, and that's above and beyond the call of motherhood." He stroked her palm with his thumb. "Anything I can do to help?"

She gave him a second of eye contact, then hurried inside. "See you in the morning."

Neil slumping against the porch post. *Please heal her, Lord. I can't.*

Chapter Twenty-Five

In the morning, Neil drove Maren and Rhi to the Performing Arts School to give them a tour before the master class. He showed them auditorium walls that could be adjusted to reflect or absorb sound, acoustic clouds on ceilings, cutting-edge recording studios, sprung floors in dance studios, wellness labs with exercise equipment, and well-stocked libraries of books and music. Each classroom had at least one window, fitted with acoustic glass and providing natural light. The walls and HVAC systems were sound shielded to keep music from intruding into other rooms.

"Your restraint is impressive—you've only said 'state of the art' once on this tour," Maren said as Rhi practiced dance moves in front of the mirrors. "What's the school's take on competition?"

"Let's see if I can remember the tour guide script." Neil shifted into "radio voice." "Consultants in mental health, physical health, and child development helped shape the curriculum. Some students are fixated, internally or by parents and teachers, on winning a contest or playing Carnegie Hall. Staff redirects their energy whenever possible, since meteoric careers lead to burnout and repetitive stress injuries." He lowered his voice. "If it weren't for this place, the Wolfe kids would be juvenile delinquents. Too much energy and creativity for a regular school."

Rhi moved on to a percussion ensemble room and Neil resumed his "radio" voice. "Talent is valued and practice is a normal part of every day. Students perform with others of their caliber instead of being confined by grade level. We hope every student, even those who don't have a career in the arts, will enjoy their time here, avoid overwork, and become a well-rounded adult with good social skills, a wide range of interests, and emotional resilience."

"You give tours?"

"No, but I helped Patti write the script. I'm forgetting something." Neil gave an embarrassed smile. "Oh, yes, there's career and legal guidance—understanding royalties, licensing, rights."

"So they don't get taken advantage of by their manager or recording label." Tuition must be in the "if you had to ask, you can't afford it" stratosphere.

"And it's next door to the Wolf Trap, the only National Park for performing arts."

"Appropriate name."

"No connection. The wolves were gone when my ancestors arrived." He walked beside her, hands in his pockets and a bounce to his step. "The students get a chance to meet performers, be a part of professional productions. The park gets an enthusiastic labor force who work for music."

Rhi's dream school. Maren's nightmare. Here she would lose her daughter.

Light from the clerestory windows gilding her hair, Rhi hurried past lockers large enough for a double bass, then found a door with a photo of Pablo Casals. "Cellos!"

"You found them." Neil opened the door to a practice space with a wall of cellos. "Pick out a three-quarter cello and bow." Neil motioned toward the rack of instruments arranged by size.

"Wait, Rhi isn't going to play in this master class, is she?" Maren whispered to Neil. "This school must have a bumper crop of advanced cellists. She isn't ready for high level critique."

"Best to be prepared, in case she has the opportunity." Neil glanced at his watch. "I'll find out out where they're holding the class. Please help with tuning and play something fun for a warmup. I'll be back for you."

Rhi picked up a cello and tried it. Maren sat at the piano. Whoa, this school has a Baldwin upright in a *practice* room. How much are kidneys selling for these days?

A man wearing a khaki shirt and brown slacks hauled a toolbox into the room.

"Oh, I'm sorry." Maren stood. "We were told it was okay to warmup here."

He motioned for her to sit. "Go ahead. Please. I'm doing an acoustic check. Whatever sounds you make will help." The man went to the back of the room and unscrewed a speaker grille.

When would she have another opportunity like this? Maren returned to the piano bench. Three sheets of staff paper with penciled musical notation sat on the music stand. Maren tried it, finding a fun mix of baroque and bossa nova. No doubt the students here were all gifted composers.

Maren finished the piece, then cut loose with a little Chopin. Oh, wow... what a sound! And what a feel! This piano liked being played. Next up, ragtime, then, since they were so close to the nation's capital, a little Sousa.

"Mom, Mom! Sorry to interrupt—you sound great—but I'm ready."

Tuning took only a moment for the high-quality cello.

"Uncle Neil said fun." Rhi launched into "All for the Best," a duet from *Godspell,* complete with its accompanying soft-shoe routine: shuffle, stamp, shuffle, stamp, ball-change.

"Hey, you're supposed to be warming up the cello, not your singing and dancing."

"C'mon in, Mom, the acoustics are fine!" Rhi laughed and kept going.

They sang counterpoint, combining different melodies simultaneously. Rhi gave her own rendition of the percussion parts while singing the slow part. Maren accompanied her with the melody while singing the fast part. They picked up speed and wrapped it up with laughter.

"How about something less silly?"

"How about the Dvoràk?" Rhi played the first two phrases, mimicking the National Symphony first chair's regal expression.

"You have an orchestra in your pocket? Let's hear the etude you were working on with Maestro."

She bobbled her head, ending with a loud sigh. "If you insist." She played the étude, then segued into Sousa's "Washington Post March." Maren added the rhythm on the piano.

Neil returned. He slid onto the bench next to Maren and took over the bass clef. She moved right, playing an octave higher than Rhi.

Maren couldn't keep from gushing, "What a piano!"

Rhi accompanied herself while singing a few lines from Arrow's "Hot, Hot, Hot."

Neil laughed. "Calypso? Do you play every genre of music?"

"Let's not keep Mr. Gerson-Zeitz waiting." Maren motioned her out the door. She turned to thank the maintenance man, but he'd slipped out, leaving behind his tool box.

Neil led them down the hall. The syncopated bounce in Rhi's step indicated her internal sound system was still tuned to the West Indies.

Dear Jesus, don't let this teacher crush her spirit.

Nine cellists, all older than Rhi, straggled in, chatting with each other. Parents hovered along the acoustic-panel-covered walls. This strings ensemble room bore no resemblance to a Kalamazoo public school cafeteria. And Lloyd Gerson-Zeitz looked less like Maestro and more like Bobby McFerrin. He danced around the students, rapping,

"Get your cello,
Out of its case.
Put a smile,
On your face.
And get it, get it, get it,
In tune!"

Rhiannon stumbled into a music stand trying to watch the six and a half foot tall cello master. "You didn't wear beads in concert."

He paused in his moonwalk and shook his red, yellow, and green hair ornaments.

"Dreads can stay,
but beads go.
Can't have percussion,
from the cello."

He pointed Rhi to an empty seat, then waved out the adults, "Now we're gonna get down and dirty.
So see you back at eleven-thirty."

One of the bolder parents stepped in front of Maren. "I thought this ran until noon."

"You'll sit on your duff,
we'll show you our stuff."

He shut the door in their faces.

Maren raised an eyebrow at Neil. "Has the Maestro ever met Mr. Gerson-Zeitz? And are you sure this is the cellist we saw with the National Symphony?"

"Well..." He wiped a bead of sweat from his forehead. A flawless cello cadenza sounded from the other side of the door. The parents breathed a collective sigh of relief and left.

Leaving her alone with Neil.

"LET me to introduce you to my favorite piano." Neil led Maren through the concert hall's backstage entrance and clicked a switch for one spotlight. There, in the middle of the stage, shone the majestic, incomparable Steinway concert grand.

Maren raced to the instrument and dashed off a bit of Chopin. "Wow." She sat and pounded out Rachmaninoff *fortissimo*, filling the hall with sound. "Wow."

Neil had stopped by the music library during Rhiannon's warmup. He put a stack of duets on the rack. "Four hands one piano?"

"Oh, yes, please!" She slid to the right.

He took the *secondo* seat and they launched into the Schubert.

Neil stumbled on the four flats. "Sorry. I'm rusty."

"Let's take it slow." She counted the rhythm. "We can do it."

With coaching from Maren, they got through the piece. Brahm's Hungarian Dance No. 1 went better; it had only two flats. His arm brushed Maren's and he grinned. He'd found a way to keep her close.

"How about this one?" Neil opened the next duet. "It's in C major. Supposedly Mozart composed it when he was nine."

The sonata started all prim and proper, then Maren's hand rubbed against his, shooting tingles up his arm. Her breath quickened. The notes had him sliding beneath her wrist, then over. He heated up, every part of him wanting more. She scooted to the edge of the bench, but the music brought her back, reaching, stroking, her shoulder against his. Seeking more of her, he pressed his leg to hers and her muscles tightened. More touching, his body said. Closer. Together. On the edge of bursting into flame, they rushed through the last page to the final chords.

"Wow," she breathed.

"Yes wow." Neil rested his hand on Maren's. Would she make eye contact? He turned. Her lips met his, soft, pulling him in, finding the perfect fit.

Yes!

Then with a gasp, she shot off the bench.

"I'm sorry." She ran to the exit. "I shouldn't have...forget I did that...What would Patti say? The children... If anyone saw us... No making out in school, on stage..."

"My house? In the hot tub?" He followed, but the hallway was empty. He knew the school well, but didn't know where Maren would hide...or why. He did know where she'd be at the end of the master class.

Neil waited outside the strings ensemble room. As the time neared, other parents drifted in. When Gerson-Zeitz opened the classroom door, Maren emerged from the restroom, her eyes puffy, avoiding looking at him. She sat at the end of the row and Neil pulled a chair next to her.

Rhiannon, curls stuck to her hairline, gave them her usual self-confident smile. Together, the students played one of Bach's cello pieces. It must have been one of Johann Sebastian's more difficult works; the kids alternately grimaced at the music and sent worried glances at the instructor. Rhi focused, her expression placid. They performed well. The piece ended with a flourish and Gerson-Zeitz's enthusiastic motions.

"I promised a drink,
If you didn't stink."

With a grin, he passed out quarters. The students hurried to the vending machine.

The teacher stood, surveying the adults from his great height. "They're gone, so I can talk like a normal person again. Who's here for Raj?"

A short lady in a suit stood.

"Where's he applying for college? Good. I'll write him a letter of recommendation. Summer music camp? Good plan."

"Brooke's parents." He passed a business card to the next couple. "I understand she broke her ring finger playing football. Here's the name of my hand therapist downtown. Fixed me up after I jammed mine in volleyball. A little joint manipulation, ultrasound, get her vibrato back."

Down the line he came. Maren pressed her hands together. Neil laid his arm across the back of her chair and she leaned forward.

You kissed me. So, why are you keeping me at arm's length?

When the other parents left, Maren stood. Neil touched her back. She inched away.

"Rhiannon's folks." Gerson-Zeitz greeted both of them. "When Maestro called, I turned him down flat. I don't do ankle biters. But your daughter..." He grinned. "Incredible artistic maturity and quick. Man, wish I learned so fast. Although I think Maestro is rushing her into vibrato before she's mastered intonation. I'd like to mentor her in the Young Artists Program with the Kennedy Center. Once the rest of the section hears her, I'll have to beat them off with a bassoon. Please tell me she's not spoken for."

Maren gulped. "We live in Michigan."

"Interlochen. Excellent program, beautiful campus." He nodded. "Whatever you decide, keep in touch." He passed Neil his business card, then hip-hopped out, saying goodbye to the juice-guzzling students blowing off steam in the hall.

Dr. Wolman, the director of the school, stood from the piano bench and walked toward them. "This school's advantages include opportunities for exploring, performing, and transitioning into the international arts community."

Neil introduced him.

Maren's voice squeaked. "I thought you were the sound tech. Was this an audition? Rhi wasn't prepared."

"I've worked as a sound tech." He motioned for them to sit. "As much as possible, we like to avoid the yips, stage-fright, especially at this age. Although I have a feeling Rhiannon could handle anything." He slapped his knees. "Academics?"

With Maren at a loss for words, Neil answered, "Straight A's. Ninety-ninth percentile on standardized tests."

"When can she start?"

He said, "Her school's out June 5. She can attend the summer session."

Maren gasped. "Are you saying... she's accepted? But... the tuition..."

"Neil didn't tell you? Alan left an endowment for the kids, which would be nepotism at its worst if they weren't all so incredibly talented." The older man's eyes misted. "He'd be thrilled."

Her hand covered her mouth. "But...we need a place to stay here, my job..."

"What line of work are you in, Ms. Tollefson?"

She said, "Grocery store deli," as Neil said, "Rehearsal accompanist, church pianist, background music."

"But I heard you play." The director raised his eyebrows and stroked his beard. "You sight-read. Your technical and expressive skills are excellent and you've memorized some challenging pieces. Who arranged 'All for the Best' for you?"

"Rhi and I did."

Dr. Wolman's smile grew. "Would you be interested in an accompanist position?" He named a tremendous starting salary, with benefits, then handed over two Performing Arts School folders, one labeled "Prospective Student," the other "Prospective Employee."

Her whole body shivered. "I didn't finish my degree."

"The Performing Arts School values ability and experience over credentials, but we do offer a continuing education benefit, if you'd like to complete your degree." He looked down, thinking a moment, then tipped his head up. "Based on Rhiannon's knowledge and skills, I'm guessing you're a gifted teacher."

Maren blinked back tears. "I accept. For both of us. Thank you."

Dr. Wolman shook it. "I look forward to working with you."

Neil touched her shoulder. "We'll figure out the details."

"Make it happen, Neil. Sending Rhiannon to fifth grade strings for another round of 'Jingle Bells' won't cut it." Dr. Wolman chuckled. "Her impression of the National Symphony's first cellist...she's a hoot! Can't wait to see what she does here!" He shook their hands, then left.

"God did more than we could ask or think. Congratulations!" Neil pulled her close and spun her in a circle. "Let's go tell the kids!"

"No! Where is Aretha when I need her? Respect!" Maren pushed away. "Before you say a word to anyone, run this by Patti first. She can't possibly want me around."

"Sure she does. She invited you here."

"Is this real? Why didn't you warn me—"

"Yes, it's real! What did you play for Dr. Wolman?"

"Mom! Uncle Neil! It was the most fun ever!"

Maren forced her face into a smile, turned, and wiped her daughter's forehead. "Are you all right? You're all sweaty."

"LGZ didn't let me get away with anything." The girl lowered her voice, then leaped up, arms stretched overhead. "It was great!"

Chapter Twenty-Six

The one master class Neil had taken had wrung him out, but Rhiannon had more energy than ever. She chattered a mile a minute on the short ride from school. Maren stared out the window without talking, the school folders clutched to her chest. Was she thinking about Rhiannon's acceptance? Her job offer? Their kiss?

Back at Wolfe's Den, Maren set out sandwiches and cut-up veggies she must have prepared before dawn, and they ate lunch. After a change of clothes, Harmony took Rhiannon and Maren to the stables.

Whistling "Oh Happy Day," Neil went in search of Patti. He followed the sound of voices to the girls' bathroom.

"...freaked out about being respectable and modest. She pinned the neckline so it barely showed any..." Melody spotted him coming down the hall. "She uses Vaseline to remove makeup. Coconut oil as moisturizer. Lemon juice as hair rinse. Baking soda as facial scrub."

"Grocery list?" Neil bounced on his toes.

Patti said, "Maren's beauty secrets."

No need for makeup; she's naturally beautiful inside and out. "You mean, instead of making a pilgrimage to M Street, paying for parking, and shelling out big bucks for tiny bottles with French labels, I can shop for you at Safeway, where parking is free?"

Melody patted his cheek. "What else would you do with your big paycheck, Uncle Neil?"

Patti studied him a moment, then snapped her notepad closed and headed out. "Show me how the landscape is coming." She set a brisk pace down the driveway, barely glancing at the plantings, then turned her radar gaze to his. "What's up?"

"Rhiannon was accepted to school with a scholarship and Maren has job as an accompanist." Neil felt like laughing, crying, and clicking his heels. "She wanted me to tell you first, in case you have any objections."

"Absolutely none at all." Patti's smile bloomed and she gave him a quick hug. "It's a delightful surprise, but it feels so right to have them here. *Babo*, this is justice. Better than compensation, although we should do that too, this restoration. Maren getting her life back."

"Making it right." Neil kissed the top of her head. "Maren asked if it was a setup, if you pulled strings."

"I told Dr. Wolman to keep an ear out for Rhiannon. Wonder what Maren played that impressed him."

"Ask her to play for you." Neil shrugged. "He recognized the family resemblance."

"Who cares?" She hightailed it back to the house. "They're more than welcome to stay here until they find a place. I'll call the neighbors, see if any might have space or a car for sale."

"Let's go out to dinner to celebrate!"

"Cody asked for pizza, so Maren prepped a half-dozen this morning." Her voice softened with awe and her open hands emphasized each word. "Homemade pizza from scratch. Wish I had another carriage house."

"Sorry you have to make your own celebration dinner." Patti set the table, an island of calm in her emerald green tunic and slacks.

"It's my way to thank you for hosting us this week." Maren prepared salad and dressing.

"Homemade dressing too?" She tore off a strip of lettuce, dipped it, then tasted. "My taste buds say *delizioso!*"

Sibling warfare erupted upstairs. Maren started for the stairway. Patti stopped her. "I don't interfere unless there's blood or radioactive fallout."

Rhi's voice echoed. "...trees *died* because you use paper cups."

"Want me to wash them?" Andy shouted back. "That'd use up water and soap."

"I suspect every great debater, from Socrates to Abraham Lincoln, must have had a sister." Patti raised her arm. "Can you see Patrick Henry—Give me paper cups or give me death!"

Rhi upped the volume. "...your towels instead of leaving them on the floor to grow mold."

Andy countered, "Oh, yeah? Penicillin is mold. Bet you didn't know that."

"Bread mold, vacuole-brain, not towel mold!"

"I'm sorry," Maren said. She'd told Rhi to be on her best behavior and here she was spewing insults.

"Rhiannon's blowing off steam after her master class. She fits in with this bunch like a long-lost puzzle piece. Listen." Upstairs, the harsh voices had moderated into laughter.

Patti opened the refrigerator and held up a shallow glass with a long stem. "What's this?"

"Chocolate mousse. It comes together faster than cannoli, so I could finish planting." It didn't use ricotta, the one ingredient missing from their giant refrigerators, and Maren got to try out the fancy professional-grade stand mixer. "I hope it's okay to put it in the coupe glasses."

"It's perfect. I'd gotten out of the habit of using them since Melody was born. Hey, what do you know, my kids are old enough to use actual glass." She sang the line about children getting older from Fleetwood Mac's "Landslide" and Maren harmonized the next line. Patti raised her hand for a high five and, when Maren gave it to her, she wove their fingers together and smiled into her eyes. "Let's grow old together, show them how it's done."

In Maren's heart, a string loosened, coming back into tune. "Lead on." Tears filled her eyes and Patti pulled her into a hug.

Cody rushed downstairs, did a U-turn, and yelled up the stairwell. "Hey, Rhiannon, our moms are hugging!"

"Whoa. I know what that means." Rhiannon thundered down to the kitchen and grabbed a tissue box.

Patti motioned the children over. "C'mon in. There's love enough for everyone."

After a few seconds of hugging and sniffling, Cody asked, "Is it pizza yet?"

"Round up Uncle Neil and the rest of the kids and it will be."

In minutes the kitchen filled with family.

"Smells great." Neil's smile set a different string vibrating in Maren. He sat next to her at the table and bowed his head. "Lord, our hearts are overflowing with gratitude and excitement."

"And our stomachs are growling. Amen," Cody said, earning a thump on the head from his nearest sibling.

Maren brought out the pizza.

Neil took a bite. "Wow. Better than Bilbo's."

"You have a pizzeria named Bilbo's in Kalamazoo?" Melody asked. "Cool!"

"We even have books and libraries," Rhi smart-mouthed.

"Rhi," Maren hissed, then turned to the Melody. "It's a college town."

"Speaking of school, any questions?" Patti asked Maren and Rhi.

Maren took advantage of Rhi having a mouth full of pizza to ask, "Is there a dress code for staff?"

"What you wore to the Kennedy Center!" Andy suggested.

"You wish." Patti shook her head. "Some wear business casual, like khakis and polos, others wear their blacks every day."

Harmony waved jazz hands overhead. "Ready to take the stage at a moment's notice."

While she figured out a budget, Maren would get by with her current stash of concert blacks. "And for students?"

"Harmony and I have that covered. We went through our closets and found everything except leotards and ballet shoes. I have some calls out to girls who might have outgrown theirs."

"That's a lot of work." Maren passed Melody the salad. "Thank you."

"Score one for procrastinating on closet clean-out." Harmony drew a notch in the air.

Rhi said, "I want to Bedazzle them all, but Melody and Harmony recommend against it—might scratch the cello. Stick to backpacks, shoes, headbands."

Maren mouthed "Thank you" to the older girls.

"While you're networking," Patti said to Melody, "ask if anyone knows of a place to rent and a good used car."

"Is there an apartment over the stables?" Maren asked.

Everyone spoke at once. "There's no air conditioning." "It's stinky." "The only shower is the hose for the horses." "There's no kitchen." "The flies would drive you crazy." "And the mice." "Not with your allergies, Mom."

No sense mentioning they'd lived in worse places.

"Wyeths have a guest house." Andy started on another piece of pizza.

"They use it as a pool house all summer," Neil said. "Too noisy."

"The Dandridges added on last year," Melody filled her plate with salad.

"A first-floor bedroom with a bath for Mr. Dandridge. He has Parkinson's and can't do stairs anymore." Patti refilled the children's glasses. "Maybe they'd rent their upstairs."

Andy raised his arms. "I'll finish the VW, so you can drive it."

The family razzed the boy about his lack of progress. Andy scowled at his plate. The problem wasn't his lack of skill, but that Neil had been spending his spare time in Michigan.

"I can drive a stick." Maren gave the boy her vote of confidence.

"You need a safer car than that," Neil said.

Melody belted out, "Oh Lord won't you buy me a Mercedes Benz."

"No singing at the table, especially Janis." Patti turned to Maren with an upraised index finger. "Take the minivan. You might notice a few children with musical instruments in the back, but they'll be perfect angels." She gave the children her fierce stare, which had them all giggling.

Maren tapped her chin. "I'm taking the angels to school, so who's driving these kids?"

They toasted each other to more laughter.

Next question: "Do students brown-bag lunch?"

"No way," Andy grabbed another slice of buffalo chicken pizza. "The food is almost as good as yours. Almost."

"Healthy and free, for students and staff," Neil murmured.

Free she could afford.

"I hope you can come for summer session," Cody told Rhi.

Patti chose veggie pizza. "Every summer the students study a different country—language, food, music, dance, songs, history. We have guests from the embassy and touring performers. This year it's Spain."

"Rhi already knows Spanish," Harmony told her brother. "She won't be in the beginners' group with you."

"Wait, I thought I'd be in Cody's grade." Rhi bit her lower lip, nervousness showing for the first time since they arrived. "Maybe Guatemalan Spanish is different."

"The teachers sort us out. Hey, let's practice." Cody pointed across the table. "*Passe la pizza au pepperoni.*"

"Impressed you remembered your French from last summer." Patti handed him a slice.

"Close," Rhi told him. "*Pasa la pizza de peperoni.*"

"*Très bien. Muy bien.*" Patti asked the family, "Anything else?"

"The usual school supplies. Water bottle for voice and dance," Andy said.

"Can I use a school cello?" Rhi asked.

Maren's breath caught. Her pay had improved, it wouldn't cover a cello on top of everything else. She should have asked this right away.

"Sure," Patti said. "Until you grow enough for the one in the studio."

"I can use Vincent's?" Rhi grinned. "Oh wow, thank you. It has such a big beefy tone."

Maren wondered about nearby thrift stores. Asking might embarrass Rhi. Who might know? "Any word from Sun-hwa and Jim?"

"Baby Stephanie came home this morning." Patti doused her salad with dressing. "As long as she continues to do well, they'll be back soon."

"Another reason to celebrate! Thank you, Jesus!" Neil turned to her. "Maren, are you crying?"

"Happy tears." She wiped her eyes, but the tears kept coming. Rhi hugged her and she buried her face in her golden curls. Neil's warm, strong arm came around her shoulders. The lump in her throat eased and she looked into the faces of the family. "It means so much, such a blessing, to have your support and your advice."

Andy jumped up, singing and dancing to Kool and the Gang's "Celebration." The rest of the family joined in, hooting when Rhi showed off her dance moves. Neil pulled Maren to her feet and they added their voices and moves.

Thank you, Lord, for bringing us into this family!

At the end of the song, Patti clapped. "Dr. Wolman raved about your duet. Would you be willing to reprise it for us?"

"Would we ever!" Rhi raced for the door.

THE FAMILY SETTLED on the upholstered furniture in the corner, but Neil took a seat behind Maren's right shoulder, where he could see her hands.

Maren played the arpeggiated dominant seventh chord, then the honky-tonk tune as Rhiannon sang the first part of *Godspell's* "All for the Best." Turning into a percussionist, the girl tapped her sneakers on the floor, ran a finger up the highest cello string, rapped her knuckles on the body of the instrument, patted her hands on the strings.

Maren sang the second part as Rhiannon accompanied pizzi-
cato, then they sang counterpoint while playing. The family joined
in the chorus for the ending, then applauded.

"The musical equivalent of rubbing your head while patting
your tummy," Melody said.

"You think that's impressive, you should have heard Mom on the
school piano."

"Well, ours isn't a Steinway, but it is in tune," Patti said. "Go
for it."

"The complete pieces could run to fifteen minutes. You want
the sampler, so you don't have to wait for dessert?" Maren looked at
Andy, the kid with the unwavering appetite.

"Let's hear it all!" He raised both arms.

Patti gestured. "Dessert's safe in the fridge. Take it away,
Maren."

Rhiannon whispered to her mom and got a nod in return.

Maren began with Horowitz's version of Sousa's "Stars and
Stripes Forever." Her shoulders held tension at first, but by the
second line, she relaxed. She aced the separate rhythms with ease,
playing with strength and authority. The family clapped and
complimented.

Before the noise died down, Maren launched into a complex
ragtime piece.

Neil leaned forward. He'd heard a recording of this, but never
had seen it played. His ears said it was impossible, but his eyes saw
her hitting every note at breakneck speed. The family sat up straight
and applauded. Andy yelled, "Bravo." Patti said, "Holy moly." And
Harmony declared, "Awesome."

Maren dove right into Chopin's "Heroic Polonaise," a piece Neil
had attempted once and determined it was beyond his skills. Maren
sailed through all the technical challenges without breaking a sweat.
She let the notes carry the emotion. The music became a metaphor
for her life, a celebration of rising from adversity to victory. She
landed the final majestic chords. In the silence, she turned to him.
"You're crying?"

Neil blinked back tears and choked out, "Magnificent."

"We're all crying." Melody passed out Kleenex. "Great music does that to us."

The family gave her a standing ovation.

Patti wiped her eyes, then pulled Maren into a hug. "Neil told me, but I couldn't wrap my mind around it. I'm sorry I mentioned catering and let you risk your fingers in our kitchen. They should be insured by Lloyd's. And I'm sorry for the last ten years. How did you practice?"

"We lived near church. They gave me a key so I could practice for Sundays."

Andy got his hug in. "Your second piece was totally cool."

"Jelly Roll Morton's 'Finger Breaker,'" Maren said. "A neighbor had a recording of it."

She figured out that complicated piece by *listening* to it?

Cody grabbed Maren's waist. "Teach me!"

"I'd be honored." Maren hugged the boy.

Harmony pried her brothers off for her hug. "Have you thought about entering the Chopin?"

"Trying to get rid of me already?" Maren smiled. The contest was in Warsaw.

She shook her head. "You are competitive."

"Thanks, but I'm not a competitor."

Melody took her turn. "You're a great addition to the school."

"Way to bring down the house, Mom." Rhiannon gave her a cuddle.

My turn. Neil wrapped Maren in a hug before she could escape, and wished the family would make themselves scarce so he could reprise the kiss. "By far, the best music this studio has ever witnessed. Your dad would be proud of you."

She leaned her face on his shoulder, her lips out of range. "He said I couldn't support myself in music."

"Wonder what else he might have been wrong about?" Neil whispered into her ear, then let her squirm back a half-step. "Hey, you did it. You got your dream job all on your own merit. No white knight needed."

"Don't sell yourself short. I wouldn't be here without you."

Maren hurried out of his arms and out of the studio. "I don't know about the rest of you, but I've worked up an appetite."

Patti, Rhiannon, and the kids had shown Maren she's worthy of working at the Performing Arts School. How could he convince her she's worthy of love?

Chapter Twenty-Seven

N eil woke up wondering if Patti had come up with a place for Maren and Rhiannon to live. Having them close, getting to spend time with them, knowing they were safe was the best. He dressed, then jogged over to Wolfe's Den.

He found Maren making pancakes for the kids. She glowed, even giving him a big smile and a warm, "Good morning, Neil!"

Patti refilled her coffee, then tipped her head toward her office. "Maren, Neil."

Uh-oh. Maren handed the flipper to Melody.

The kids sang the first four notes of Beethoven's *Fifth*.

"What did you do now, Uncle Neil?" Andy asked.

What *had* he done? He followed Maren into the office and they sat.

"Is this about the Steinway?" Maren asked.

"Uh, no." Patti gave them a puzzled look, then pulled a bank envelope from her desk drawer. "I started a prodigy fund. There's not much in it, but it's yours to help you settle in."

"I can't accept this." Maren tried to pass it back. "We'll be fine."

"It's in your name." Patti shook her head. "Next, our publicist called."

"About the Smithsonian?" Maren groaned. "I should have stopped Rhi—"

"Hey, a bagpiper playing Michael Jackson is a can't-miss opportunity. Our therapist says these kids are like plants that will burst out of their pots if confined."

"A friend of Stevie Wonder's told me something similar." Maren nodded. "We tried to stop the paparazzo."

Neil's hands fisted. He'd wanted to punch the scumbag and break his camera, but being arrested would make the news.

"Like trying to stop the plague." Patti tapped her pen on her notes. "The photographer recognized my three and Neil, asked all sorts of questions about the blonde girl, and has you as a *Sports Illustrated* swimsuit model."

"So he hasn't figured out I'm the mom."

Patti returned her mocking smile. "Not the sharpest pencil in the box."

Neil asked, "What did you tell Sol?"

"I'm still the queen of *Nothing*." Patti took a sip of coffee. "Sol asked the Post's photographer to fax his other Kennedy Center shots showing you two. We're lucky none of those ended up in the paper —Rhiannon was recognizable." She drummed her fingernails on her cup. "Last winter, Sol had gotten a call from someone who works for Oprah, with a heartwarming story about a little girl who sang to cheer people up in a waiting room. The photo was grainy, but the resemblance was clear. He didn't say anything to me, in case I didn't know."

"That was my fault," Neil said.

"Stop blaming yourselves." Patti waved her hand, then faced Maren. "Rhiannon bubbles with joy. You should be proud of her for using her gift to comfort others."

"Yes, but...now what?"

"Sol wants us to spill the beans to *People* or on Oprah's show."

Maren stood. She navigated the stacks of files to the stare out the window, holding her arms close. "Please, no. Rhi had enough trouble making friends in public school. I want her to fit in, find her tribe.

Out of the public eye. And me, probably the least qualified person to work at her school...if the staff decides I'm a charity hire..."

Neil started to object, but Patti cut him off. "A few bars of Chopin will clear that up." She rubbed her temples. "I've been trying to keep the lid on since the kids were born, so they can develop as individuals instead of understudies for their dad. That's even more crucial for Rhiannon, as winner of the look-alike prize. Let's table it for now. We can't stop rumors, but they won't spread from school. And you're safe in this neighborhood." Patti glanced at her desk clock, then stood. "At the airport, assume you're being photographed."

Maren followed her to the kitchen.

"No one ever mistakes me for a swimsuit model," Patti said. "Best I ever got was Yoko Ono."

Yoko? Because they're both Asian and had married musicians?

Maren rolled her eyes. "Yoko doesn't play saxophone."

Patti smiled and hugged her. "We got this."

Okay, so Patti and Maren were getting along, joking even. *What am I? Chopped liver.*

They finished breakfast, said their see-you-soons, then Neil drove Maren and Rhiannon to the airport. He had an early flight the next day, so he couldn't accompany them.

Maren worked on a moving list. "Should I bring your snowblower?"

"It's your snowblower, so do what you think is best. Honestly, we don't need it here."

As they approached the terminal, a group of men raised their cameras. Neil stepped between them and his family. The automatic doors opened and an actress emerged, drawing the photographers' attention.

"Hey, dancing girl, what's your name?" The paparazzo from the Smithsonian came after them.

Neil rushed them into the terminal, badged into a secure hallway, then led them down a back hall. They returned to the concourse by a different door.

"This is like 'The Fox and the Hound' movie," Rhi said.

Maren scanned the crowd. "Maybe we should wear disguises."

"I'll be Batman," Neil said.

"You'd be more inconspicuous in a Dolly Parton wig and a red leather miniskirt." Maren grinned.

Their laughter shook off their stress. His girls were adaptable. Neil was doing it again...thinking of Maren and Rhiannon as his family. And—why didn't he think of this earlier?—he could make that happen.

"We'll be moving back here soon!" Rhiannon squeezed Neil's hand as he escorted them to their gate. He found seats for them in a semi-enclosed area behind the gate agent's station, where it would be difficult to be photographed without their knowledge and they could watch the planes. His niece was more interested in the nearby food kiosk. "Can I have a snack?"

"I have an apple and mozzarella sticks in my bag for you," Maren pinned Neil with a hard look as he handed the girl a five-dollar bill. "Really?"

"I want to talk to you, privately, about a solution for your housing dilemma. I've enjoyed our week together." Scanning between Maren and Rhiannon, he sat and lowered his voice. "So why not move in with me? I've got plenty of space. It's close to school. I'll paint one of the bedrooms for Rhiannon. We'll get a dog. It will be great."

Maren gasped and turned pale. Was she going to faint again? He reached for her and she pulled back, with a look of horror usually reserved for nuclear spiders. She whispered, "After one kiss, you lose all respect for me and want to shack up? You think I'm a groupie, a degenerate without any morals? I will not live in sin with you."

"No, Maren, no. I meant..."

Her face reddened and her fists clenched. "You will *not* tell anyone, especially Rhi, about this conversation. Tell her you have to leave early and go. Now. Go." She rubbed her forehead. "Oh dear Lord, what am I going to do?"

"But, I mean—"

"Get out of here."

Since arguing would cause a scene, he left. He hugged his niece, told her he'd call, then hid behind a magazine rack at the news kiosk. He watched, making sure no one bothered them, until they boarded.

Where did he go wrong? He'd thought he and Maren were getting along, becoming a family, making everything right . She'd kissed him. But... *shack up*...? Where did that come from?

His heart spiraled into his gut where it crashed and burned.

Breathe, Maren told herself, choking with unshed tears. Dad was wrong about supporting herself with music, but he was right that no one would marry her. She'd accepted the single life...until Neil made her want more...his companionship, his touch, his love.

"What's happening?" Rhi slid into the seat next to her and put her hand over Maren's. "You're picking your cuticles."

She looked out the window, watching a 737 taxi to the next gate. "Lots to think about. What snack did you get?"

"They're pretty good. Want some?" Rhi held out a bag of sweet potato chips. "What are you and Uncle Neil fighting about?"

"We're not fighting," Maren said, then realized she'd lied. *Forgive me, Lord.*

"Yeah, right." Her teenage siblings had honed her sarcasm skill.

"Adult stuff. Nothing to worry about." Maybe a potato chip would settle the nerves doing the electric slide in her stomach. She took the bag and read on the nutrition label. Fairly healthy. Tasted okay. "Hmm. Not bad."

"You're shaking. If you don't tell me what's going on, I'll ask Harmony."

"It will be easier to work things out without everyone weighing in." Would they have a family if this got out? "Please don't say anything to anyone."

"Patti and the kids have a counselor. Maybe she could find a counselor for you."

Maren nodded, then grabbed the nearest change of topic. "You had a good time this week?"

"Great!" Rhi stood and executed a Michael Jackson-style circle slide, in spite of wearing sneakers and dancing on carpet. "I love having a big family. They're all awesome, even stinky Andy. And I've never ever been so excited about school. It's going to the best year ever." She wrapped her arms around Maren for a second. "And you have an awesome job! This is going to be epic!"

With a new job and new school, it should be epic...if she could avoid Neil.

NEIL DROVE HOME ON AUTOPILOT, to the big empty house where Maren tested the acoustics with her head tipped back, explained its energy efficiency to Rhiannon, and disciplined his imaginary dog... who wouldn't even wag his tail at his homecoming.

In his half-baked efforts to be helpful, to be her white knight, he'd fallen in love...and started imagining a future together. A future full of music, becoming a family, adventures in the hot tub.

He called her, even though he knew they wouldn't be back yet. "Please forget my foot-in-mouth moment. I've never..." How could he keep Rhiannon from figuring out what he'd done? "This is new for me. Please call when you get home. I miss you more than I can say."

Neil trudged to Wolfe's Den. His steps echoed through the empty house. "Anyone home?"

"Up here," Patti called.

Neil followed her voice upstairs.

"I don't know how early Maren got up, but she did laundry and cleaned before she—" Patti looked up from studying Harmony's closet. "*Babo*, what happened?"

He sank onto the end of the bed, one part of his brain noting he'd never seen it made before. "I floated the idea that Maren and Rhiannon could move in with me, but Maren thought I wanted..."

Her eyes widened. "You offered an arrangement for her to pay for housing with her body?"

"That's not what I meant." *Maren loves me. Maren hates me.* Swamped with defeat, Neil propped his head with his hands.

"Oh no." With a groan, Patti sat beside him. "*Babo.* Were you trying to propose? Without mentioning love, wedding, marriage?"

"The middle of DCA's terminal seemed like the wrong place to talk about love." He scrubbed his fingers through his hair. "Of course I love Maren. Since I met her ten years ago. I wouldn't have proposed if I didn't love her."

"Yet you didn't think to mention that fact." Her head wobbled back and forth: no, no, no. "Good thing she loves you."

"Maybe she doesn't. She wouldn't even let me hold her hand." He swallowed. "Although she kissed me after we played a duet on the Steinway. She got upset, asked what you would say, then ran and hid."

Patti made a humming sound. "Maren works hard to hide her feelings. I'm guessing her father dumped some serious shame on her, so she tries hard to be respectable."

"She keeps saying 'respect,' but I thought that was about how she raises Rhiannon."

"Respect is about everything." Patti emphasized each word. "I hope Rhiannon didn't hear you."

"She didn't." Although she seemed concerned, almost suspicious, when he left. Neil looked up and tried to swallow the lump in his throat. "How am I going to fix this? I mean, not that Maren needs fixing. But me...this proposal..."

Dark eyes studied him. "*Babo,* in high school, girls went out with you in hopes of crossing paths with Alan."

Neil groaned. "Thanks for telling it like it is."

"Always." Compassion softened her face. "In college, you were so focused on your career, your only dates had propellers and wings. Now you've grown into a good-looking guy with a job and pass privileges, attracting the attention of women who want to help you spend your paycheck. But you are over-the-moon, starry-eyed, goofy over Maren. With one flutter of her eyelashes, she could wrap you around her pinky and drain your bank account dry."

"She wouldn't."

"A lot of women would... for their child, but Maren wouldn't. That's integrity." Patti ran her foot across the carpet. It was purple and surprisingly clean. "I'd forgotten what color this was."

"Me too." The laundry hamper was empty. The shelves were organized, books separated from craft supplies. Clothes hung in the closet, shoes on the rack, sweaters on the shelf above. "Did Maren do all this?"

"Yes, The guest room and bath are ready for the next visitor." She motioned toward the adjoining room. "Be sure to take a look at the girls' bathroom. And your honey-do list in the pantry?"

"The one I haven't looked at since I found Maren."

"Your brain on love." Her mouth tilted in a half-smile. "Maren ran through the list like a hot knife through butter. She tightened the kitchen door knob, got the third junk drawer back in its track, replaced the doorbell... everything."

"Sorry."

"You're a pilot. When the car breaks down, when something goes wrong in the house, you could be anywhere from Portland to Puerto Rico. You need a wife who can hold down the fort and won't get the vapors."

The laundry room door closed and footsteps echoed in the hall.

Neil looked up. "Who's home?"

"Appliance repairman. The washer gave up the ghost. Glad it waited until after our guests left."

"Maren broke it?"

"No, she used the downstairs washer."

"Good afternoon. I am Abdul." A bearded man in neatly-pressed blue work clothes bowed from the doorway, then faced Neil. "No, your girlfriend did not break the washing machine. The motor seized. It is very old and worn out. I cannot repair it." He handed Patti a bill.

"I'll write you a check." Patti stood and headed for the stairs. "And Neil, bottom line—you have low time in your romance logbook. I'll get some educational reading material for you."

Abdul put his toolbox on the floor and sat in Harmony's desk chair. "My friend, I'm sorry to hear you are ill-fated in love. Perhaps your sister-in-law might negotiate with the bride's father."

"Her father died." Was this guy working on the washer or eavesdropping?

"Perhaps another older relative?"

Neil shrugged. Mr. Coffey?

"You are correct—the terminal is too noisy for a proposal. I recommend a candlelit dinner. Or a walk by the river. You live near Great Falls. It is romantic." Abdul picked up his toolbox and headed out. "And prayer. Much prayer."

"Thank you. I'm praying." Would Maren ever speak to him again? Would she refuse to see him? She wouldn't turn down the accompanist position, would she? And... what education material did his sister-in-law have for him?

Patti returned with the first three books of *Anne of Green Gables*.

"Aren't these children's books?" Neil flipped through them. Lots of words, no pictures.

"*Babo.* Swap the cover with a Tom Clancy, if you're embarrassed." Patti gave him a hug, then tapped the *Anne* books. "The hero got a second chance to propose. I'm praying you do too."

His sister-in-law wasn't usually a rabid optimist, but Neil was pretty sure no amount of romance reading would pull him out of this stall. He trudged home, found Tango wasn't talking to him, and dove into the books. Anne and Gilbert fought a lot. Anne turned down his first proposal.

Neil read every spare moment on his trip. Late on the night he returned, he finally got to the part where Anne accepted Gilbert's proposal. So the next morning, when Patti called, he was still in bed.

"*Babo,* the new washer is coming this morning. I have to go into D.C. Sun-hwa and Jim won't be back until this afternoon."

"I'll be right over."

"I cleared a path and started the coffee...and left you a few more romance novels."

At Wolfe's Den, Neil went into the pantry and studied the

honey-do list. Planting a truck-load of flowers hadn't kept Maren busy. So much for giving her a vacation.

Neil had finished breakfast and a couple chapters before the appliance truck arrived. He directed them to park by the front door —it had a wider opening and a straight shot up the stairs.

"Morning, I'm Billy Bob and this here is Bubba." The stocky men wore overalls with plaid shirts. They grabbed a hand truck and a toolbox. "We'll take out the bad one first."

Neil led them upstairs.

Billy Bob unhooked the water supply lines. "Hear tell your girl kicked your butt to the curb."

Bubba connected the siphon and drained the water. "Proposal went over like a lead balloon."

Did Abdul put Neil's failure on the front page of *The Post*? "She turned me down."

"We know a few girls might marry you. Want us to set you up?" Billy Bob rolled the washer out.

"No thanks. Right woman, wrong proposal. I'll try again."

"Some mighty pretty places in this state," Bubba hooked up new supply lines while Neil swept the lint from the floor. "I'm partial to mountains, get her breathing hard, make sure she's sturdy."

Billy Bob returned with the new washer. "Take her fishing. Make sure she can bait a hook and not scare the fish away."

Bubba squinted at Neil. "You livin' in Great Falls, I gotta wonder why you didn't take her there."

"It was an impulse." Neil rubbed the back of his neck.

"Can't jump the gun." Bubba hooked up the new supply lines. "Gotta make you a plan."

Billy Bob handed over the operating manual, showed him the basics, and had him sign for the delivery, then Neil walked them back to their truck.

"Thank you."

"Don't forget to pray," they yelled out the truck window.

Neil grabbed Patti's recommended reading, locked the house, then plodded home. Pretty sure Mr. Coffey would also recommend prayer. So... "Hello, Jesus? I'm listening."

. . .

AFTER A ROUGH DAY back to work at A&P—the deli workers had made a mess then quit—Maren found Mrs. Coffey out front, parked in the fire lane. She motioned toward her minivan. "Hop in, child."

Maren climbed in and buckled up, bracing for a review of their talks about reputation, virtue, and setting boundaries. "Mr. Coffey called you."

"Yes, he did."

Tears and words spilled. "It was all going so well. The accompanist job is a gift from God. Neil said it was more than we ask or think. I can do work I enjoy, be near Rhi, with good pay and benefits. The children were friendly. Patti and I were getting along. I thought I was finally free of Consequences. Then Neil suggested we live together. Of course I said no, but how can I see him, how can he be in Rhiannon's life, knowing he thinks I have loose morals? Then when I got home, he'd left a message on the machine, withdrawing the proposal I didn't realize he was making."

"Take a breath. Slow and easy." Mrs. Coffey turned into Waldenbrook and pulled over in a spot where they could see the school bus stop, but Mrs. V couldn't see them. She clasped Maren's hand and said a prayer. "Lord, you've said where two are gathered, You are with us. Lead us in your way. Amen." She let go. "Now, what have you been thinking about Neil?"

Maren groaned. "All these years, I've focused on God, taken captive every thought, set my mind on things above." She covered her face, hating to admit her failure to the woman she respected most. "But now all I think about now is making out and making love." She peeked at Mrs. Coffey. "I even kissed him."

"Good for you. Desire is normal. It's how God made us, and you are wonderfully made," she said calmly, not at all shocked. "You're in love with him and he's in love with you."

Maren peeled her fingers off her face and turned to Mrs. Coffey. "Neil said nothing about love."

"Did you mention it?"

"Well, no. I could barely breathe. But he can't marry me, after his brother..."

"It's going to be a difficult conversation, one you shouldn't have on the phone and shouldn't have around Rhiannon. Drop her off with us or the Gibsons." Mrs. Coffey gave her a good long hug. "Call anytime. Ongoing prayers for you, dear one."

The school bus roared around the corner and screeched to a halt. Maren thanked her, heart heavy, and hurried to meet her daughter.

Chapter Twenty-Eight

Neil straightened the sheets of staff paper on the music stand and pulled a half-dozen sharpened pencils out of his jeans' pocket. Since Maren left eight weeks ago, it had been radio silence; his calls had been answered by the machine or Rhiannon. Every day he'd tried to write a love song for Maren. Inspiration hadn't come at home, so he'd moved to the studio.

He stared at the ceiling. Dust motes circled like planes over Chicago center. Okay, where's the song? He pulled the bench closer and played a C chord. How did Alan do this? Neil closed his eyes. His brother had started with an idea, maybe a chorus. They'd worked on it in the studio or on the tour bus. He'd throw out a few licks on the guitar and they'd all shout out suggestions, lyrics, key changes for the bridge. And it would all fall together: platinum, Grammy, CMA award.

Could Neil ask the band for help? Considering how crude those guys could be, no.

Neil tried E minor. How was he going to write a love song for Maren? Not here, with all these memories of Alan intruding. He gathered his pencils and staff paper, and trudged back home.

A white flower bloomed beside the path, then another further along. Neil followed them to his house. He hadn't noticed them in daylight; did they only bloom at night? Maren must have planted them. Oh, Maren...

When he walked in the door, the answering machine was blinking. Yesterday Rhiannon had left a message that her mom had sold her hair. Hoping Maren had finally returned his calls, Neil pushed the button. "Neil, this is Mr. Coffey. Rhiannon is going up north with the Gibsons for the long weekend. They'll be back Monday. Maren stayed in town, picking up night shifts. If you have the time off...I can't tell you what to do, but I'm praying God will."

Neil listened to the message a second time and checked his calendar. Days off? Yes. *Hello, God?*

This late, he wouldn't get a flight out of DCA. Listening for divine guidance, Neil drove to Dulles, talked his way onto a freighter heading to Willow Run, and spent two hours being slammed around on a DC-8 jumpseat. Two more hours bumping along I-94 in a Yugo, spilling gas-station coffee in his lap, brought him no closer to figuring out Maren. He had no idea what to say to her, how to convince her. Her love song hovered at the edge of his brain, just out of reach.

His watch read 4:15 when he joined the half-dozen vehicles in the A&P parking lot. He spotted Maren on the other side of the plate glass window. Her hair was piled on top of her head, so he couldn't tell how much was gone. She emptied a dustpan in the garbage, then went back to swaying and sidestepping. She should be doing that on the terrace of the Kennedy Center, wearing a designer gown instead of an A&P smock, holding him instead of a broom.

As he walked in, the Muzak changed from "Moon River" to "Strangers in the Night." Maren put away the cleaning supplies and carried a cardboard box to the cigarette carousel. She glanced up. The carton hit the floor.

"Neil?" She shook her head. Splotches covered her face. Red rimmed her eyes.

"You've been crying."

"Allergies." She picked up the box and restocked the carousel. "Why are you here?"

"That's my question. Why are *you* here?"

"The night checker quit, so I'm picking up some extra hours. U-hauls aren't cheap."

"How much do you need?"

Two young drunks in WMU Broncos T-shirts lugged six packs to the open checkout lane. Maren explained that it was illegal to sell beer after two a.m. They told a convoluted story about one of them becoming a new father a few hours ago. "Congratulations. Sounds like a good reason to stop drinking." Maren moved the beer off the belt. The drunks left, then a woman in a silver vinyl minidress bought a package of rolling papers.

"Beam her up, Scotty," Neil muttered, drawing out a smile from Maren.

The background music changed to "A Whiter Shade of Pale." He motioned toward the ceiling speaker. "Can you turn that down?"

"Mr. Coffey says it's always that loud. You just don't notice during the day."

The register beeped. She counted out four hundred dollars in twenties, banded it with brown paper, added her signature, and stuffed the wad into a safe behind the front-end desk.

No more customers appeared. She resumed stocking cigarettes. Somewhere in the back, a machine whined and boxes thudded, but Maren was alone in the front of the store.

"How often does this store get robbed?"

"Thinking about another career? Loitering too slow for you? Don't you have an airshow this weekend?"

"Doug will find someone else to go with." Arg. He should say something romantic, about missing her, about how he couldn't be apart from her another day. Where was that love song?

A tall man with dreadlocks entered with a fellow sporting a Day-Glo orange crew cut.

"If colorful characters is what you want, DC has a few," Neil said.

She raised her voice. "What I want is for you to get out of here."

A clean-cut man in a windbreaker strolled to the register with a bag of M&Ms. He faced Maren, but kept his gaze on Neil.

"Mike, this is my daughter's uncle, professional pest. Neil, this is Officer Culver."

"Pest, huh? Kinda on the large side for Raid. Better call Orkin." Mike reached into his hip pocket, giving Neil a glimpse of a shoulder holster. "Sir, I'll have to ask you to leave."

"Okay." Neil backed up, open palms toward the law. "Maren, I'll give you a ride home. What time do you get off?"

The cop took another step toward him. "A&P frowns on anyone harassing their employees."

"I'm trying to save the lady some bus fare."

"I'm sure you are," he said in heard-it-all-before tone.

Maren busied herself waiting on the odd couple and wouldn't make eye contact with him. Neil turned on his heel and marched out. He started the Yugo, but instead of heading for a king-sized bed at the nearest motel, he pulled around beside the building and parked in a dark corner of the parking lot.

What's the matter with you? Are you nuts? You're going to get arrested.

He slid the driver's seat as far back as it would go, two inches, tried and failed to get the seat to recline, tried and failed to adjust the headrest, and crossed his arms. *Fine.*

BANG, bang, bang. "Neil. Wake up, man."

Sleep-stuck eyes pried open to see Mr. Coffey, backlit by dawn, tapping Yugo's door with his knuckles. Neil straightened and ran through the checklist: Head? Aching. Neck? Cramped. Back? Burning.

"Brought you coffee." The store manager held up two paper cups. He walked around to the passenger side. Neil pushed the door open, and he climbed in. "Almost didn't recognize you—you look terrible."

"Thanks." Neil inspected himself in the rearview mirror. Mr. Coffey was too kind. Eyes? Baggy. Face? Scruffy.

The store manager passed him a cup. "Now what are you doing camping out in my parking lot?"

"Officer Culver disapproved of my loitering."

"Just doing his job." Mr. Coffey inched his seat back, but his knees hit where the glove box should be. "You got my message."

He nodded. "Thanks. When does Maren get off work?"

"At one. She'll need a ride to church to practice piano." The big guy shifted, his knee against the gearshift, so he could pin Neil with a stare. "First time around you gave Maren the impression you wanted to shack up."

Neil grimaced. "I'd never—"

"Second time around you retracted the proposal you didn't make. So, far as I can tell, you've got two strikes."

"If I don't hit a home run, I'm out."

He gave one slow nod. "So what're you going to say to Miss Maren? You got a plan?"

Neil shook his head. "How did you propose to Mrs. Coffey?"

"Holding hands on the back porch of her parents' house. Her mother was in the kitchen, ready to bean me with her cast iron skillet if I didn't get my courage up." He squirmed in seat again. "Doesn't matter what pretty speeches others give. Find the words Maren needs to hear."

Neil blinked. "What words?"

Mr. Coffey's frown, one eyebrow up and the other down, indicated his skepticism. He handed Neil directions and an address printed on the back of a receipt. "Disposable razors, aisle 13B. Sleeping in this car is not doing you any favors and you need your wits about you, so drive over to my house. Shower and nap. I'll call Mrs. Coffey, tell her you're coming. See you back here at 12:45 in the Floral Department." He pried himself out. "We are praying for you both."

"Do I have your blessing?"

His face softened in a slow smile. "Not my blessing you need to worry about—it's God's."

NEIL ARRIVED at the deli counter on time, freshly shaved, and carrying a dozen dark-pink roses mixed with a dozen white carnations. He bowed and held out the flowers. "Congratulations on your last day of work."

Maren stiffened, looked behind him, then sighed. "I suppose I have to ride with you." She didn't take the flowers or the arm he offered, so he had to trail her through the store as her coworkers hooted and wished her good luck. The Troll at the Desk pointed and opened her mouth to reprimand him, but he flashed his receipt and got a surly nod instead.

Neil led Maren through the muggy parking lot. Humidity had loosened a halo of curls, spiraling along her temple, down her cheek, along her neck. Ooh—he'd never seen her neck before. It was beautiful, a perfect place to kiss. If she'd ever let him.

He stopped at the Yugo. Afternoon sun showed the faded paint highlighted with rust. He should have gotten a decent rental instead of taking a nap.

Maren frowned. "Looks like an airport car."

"From Willow Run."

"Your airline doesn't go to Willow Run."

"I took a freighter."

She peeked inside. "There's no air conditioning."

"Drove at night and used the two-sixty method—roll down both windows and drive sixty. Takes a lot of pedaling to get up to highway speed."

"I can't believe you took this pop can on the highway. You're usually so safety conscious."

He sang a few lines from the musical *Oliver's* "I'd Do Anything."

She recognized the song and modified the lyrics to, "'Drive to Kalamazoo?'"

"'Just for you.'"

She stared at him for a long moment, head tipped, eyebrows creased. "Why?"

"We need to talk before Rhiannon gets back."

She shook her head. "I need to pick up the U-Haul, load the boxes from Mrs. V's, practice, then take pizza to Coffey's."

"I'll help." Neil ran a mental inventory of the apartment. "Patti said you'd shipped Rhiannon's clothes. How much is left?"

"The church took the furniture and kitchen stuff for those in need, so I'm down to two cartons and our suitcases."

"That U-haul? Next to the car rental place?" Neil pointed across the highway. "How about you get your deposit back and I'll rent something safe? Tomorrow, when Rhiannon gets back, we'll fly to DCA."

"The airline takes cardboard boxes? I wouldn't have to drive? We have a plan."

The passenger door wouldn't open so Neil ran around to the driver's side, hopped in, pulled the lever, and pushed the door. Maren climbed in, figured out the seat belts, then took the flowers. The Yugo started on the first try and they headed out. The car hit a seam in the parking lot, jolting them on the thin seats. He took advantage of a traffic light to exit the parking lot; no break in traffic was long enough for a Yugo. The light turned green and Neil stomped on the gas. Would it reach the speed limit or implode? They sputtered across the highway to the U-Haul. A half-hour later, Maren had her deposit back, and Neil drove a rental with all its parts working.

"Sorry I can't get your hair back."

"It was causing headaches. Short is more professional for my new job."

He parked in Mrs. V's drive. "How short is it?"

She popped the clip and her hair curled around her shoulders, Farrah Fawcett style.

Neil broke out into Joe Cocker's "You Are So Beautiful."

"You won't think so after hauling my boxes." Maren twisted her hair up.

Neil loaded the boxes and Maren gave the apartment one last inspection. Empty, it looked even more forlorn. Next stop, church.

Neil followed Maren inside. "Why practice? You're leaving tomorrow."

She locked the door behind him. "For my new job. To honor Dr. Wolman's faith in me and not embarrass Rhi."

"You've got the chops."

Sunlight through the stained glass gave the sanctuary a yellow glow. Maren turned on a few lights and the air conditioner. He followed her down to the kitchen, where she found a vase for the flowers. She set them on the altar. "Please go, so I can get some work done."

"Leave you alone in this neighborhood? No way." He pulled the cover off the piano.

"Rhi and I lived here for nine years," she said, leaving open the question of how safe it was. "You obsess more about safety than anyone I know."

"When it comes to you..." Sitting on the bench, he played the last chorus from the R&B hit "Stand By Me." He took a deep breath. Heavy-duty floral hinting hadn't accomplished anything. Time for a direct approach. "Let me start with what I should have said in DCA." He softened his voice. "Maren, I love you. I want to marry you and spend the rest of my life with you. I'd like to hear your thoughts about marrying me."

Without looking at him, she blew out an exasperated sigh and perched next to him. "Your only interest here, has always been—" She pounded out the opening measures of Fleetwood Mac's "Rhiannon".

"She's wonderful, but—" He rolled a chord and sang, "I Only have Eyes for You."

"Once Rhi's off to college, it'll be..." She played "Hit the Road, Jack."

He tried the first line of "Looking for Love."

She stared straight ahead. "You have not spent a lifetime looking for me."

"I didn't know where to look or your last name until I found your letters." He segued into the Turtles' "Happy Together".

"That's another thing. We're not happy together. Most relationships start out here." She played an octave-high version of the classical piece cartoons use to accompany dancing butterflies. Then she hammered out the "1812 Overture" crescendo, leaning across him to slap her fist on the bass notes for the cannon fire and cymbal crashes. "We started there."

"Makes it more interesting, plenty of room for improvement, nowhere to go but up." He sounded out the tune for "Cherish."

Maren countered with an angry "What's Love Got to Do With It?"

The dissonance made him stop. "You love me? Great! No problem!"

"Of course I love you. You're everything I want in a husband— you have a strong faith, adore my daughter, family is important to you. We have common interests in music and aviation. You're smart, funny, handsome. With you, I'm safe. But..." Head down, breathing hard, she transitioned into Mary Magdalene's song from *Jesus Christ, Superstar*.

She loves me! But..."You don't know how to love me?"

Her fists hit the music stand. "It means I had sex with your brother!"

Neil's mouth went dry. "I should have stopped him—"

"No! It's not you!" She sobbed.

"We're both mad at Alan. We agree on that. You can't be mad at yourself. It wasn't your fault." Moving slowly, Neil put an arm around her trembling shoulders.

"No!" she gasped and pulled away. "You shouldn't touch me."

"You don't like to be touched?" He wanted touch her all the time.

"I like it too much, but..." She struggled to get the words out "... I'm damaged. I don't deserve..."

Neil's heart ached. Patti was right; Maren was punishing herself. Neil shifted her toward the cross glowing in the stained-glass window over the altar. "We fall short of God's glory, but Jesus fixes us." *Jesus fixes, not me.*

She pulled out of his arms. "Church said...I'm no longer pure."

Maren had heard enough sermons, read the Bible. She needed his heart. He closed his eyes, afraid to see her reaction. "When I got my driver's license, I took a condom from my brother's drawer, and went all the way in the back of my car with a girl who, according to locker room gossip, was willing. It was...awful. Even then, not knowing much about God, I could tell I'd messed up, ruined something beautiful. I apologized to the girl, who laughed at me. And I decided to wait until I fell in love and married. God erased that bad mark off my record."

He opened his eyes. To his surprise, Maren met his gaze. A tear slid down her cheek. Neil wiped it away. She turned her head and brushed her lips across his palm. He pulled her close. "Maren, when I look at you, I see the wonderful person God made...and made whole with His sacrifice. If you need...more counseling, spiritual guidance... we'll get that. Anything you need to help you heal. I love you."

"Yes."

One word, like the flash from a rotating beacon on a dark night, lined him up for a short final. He lowered his head, his mouth finding hers, her lips soft and welcoming. He settled in for a perfect landing. This was where he was meant to be. Her hand slid from his ear to his neck, her other circled his back, pulling him closer. He breathed in her salty smell. His pulse whooshed. *Oh, Maren, I've been waiting so long...*

With a gasp, she squirmed off the bench. "I'm sorry. Being around you turns me into a...sex fiend, as bad as a groupie. When you're around, I think about your Jacuzzi, your tree house, your bed...I lose control, I lust."

"Oh Maren. God made us for intimacy, to desire each other." He reached for her and, with a gentle tug, brought her back. "I want you too. Together, wearing only our wedding rings. In the hot tub. In the treehouse by candlelight. And on a pile of blankets in front of the fireplace."

"The fireplace..." she whispered, having a hard time getting her words out. "But isn't that lust?"

"Like those verses on your wall?" Neil thanked God for the Christian counselor who'd helped him sort this out. "Lust is about a body, body parts, pleasing self. Desire is about the whole person, wanting to share pleasure. Like our love, it grows the more we know each other, deepening our relationship toward marriage."

"So Mrs. Coffey's right—this isn't bad, it's *normal.*"

"Yes. It's a gift from God for us to share. It's part of love."

She sounded out the chorus to June Carter Cash's "Ring of Fire."

"There's a Bible verse about that." It had been rolling through Neil's head for the last month. "It's better to marry than burn."

"Really?" Skepticism gave way to humor, and she laughed and fanned herself with an old bulletin.

Neil grinned. "Really."

NEIL CARESSED HER HANDS, studying her with his warm brown eyes. "Maren, please know, I love you, I'll always love you, and I want to marry you and make a life together."

Instead of being repulsed at her desire, rejecting her for wanting, he seemed more *interested* than ever. He validated her feelings, saying they were normal. He loved her.

So...could she escape the Consequences *and* marry Neil? Could she have it all?

He pulled a rectangular box from his pants pocket and gave it to her. "Patti sent this."

Maren's heart sped to *vivace.* "Patti's okay with...us? She doesn't think I'm a groupie?"

"More than okay. Thrilled. This is a gift to congratulate you on your new job."

The box held a gold necklace with a pendant shaped like a rounded pentagon.

Neil said. "It's a pianist's necklace, to hold your rings when you play. I brought one of Mom's to show you how it works." He pulled a smaller box out. It contained a ring with a blue stone. He looped it onto the pendant and it held.

"I've never seen anything like it. So thoughtful." Maren tried it. Easy and simple. Like the ring, a round violet-blue stone in a plain setting. "This is beautiful."

"A tanzanite. From Mom and Dad's trip to Tanzania, their first trip working on international water projects. She said the stone is a symbol of new life."

"New life? Yes, I'm ready to sweep the bad vibes out of my head, no more blame and shame, and make a fresh start. If she wouldn't mind sharing, I'd be honored to wear it."

"Or, we could shop together and you can pick out one of your own, maybe with a circle of diamonds." Neil slid it on her ring finger, then fastened the necklace on, his gentle touch setting off more wanting.

Maren reached up and brushed her fingertips over his face. Muscles rippled with his smile. Eye contact had been frightening for so long, to hide her wanting, but now she looked directly into his golden-brown eyes, letting him see her heart's contentment, joy, and yes, desire. "Yes, I love you. Let's get married."

Neil's smile widened and he inhaled as if preparing for a big speech. But Maren didn't want to talk, didn't want to think, didn't want to do anything but...kiss. She leaned in, slid one arm around his neck, the other over his wide shoulders, and drew him close. His breathing quickened and his arms circled her waist. Their lips touched, a duet of warmth and texture, exploring and enjoying. It was like flying together, like making music together, like...better than anything. *Oh yes!*

Chapter Twenty-Nine

Neil turned onto his driveway and glanced at Maren. She glowed. It wasn't only her new clothes—ivory slacks and a sweater set in a green she called sage. Or her haircut, the waves brushing her shoulders. Or the ring and the necklace. She stood taller, held her head up. The tension in her face had been replaced by a relaxed smile. Joy filled her.

"I'll let Tango out." Maren gave him a kiss as he parked. She got out of the front seat—the front seat!—took his keys and hurried inside his house. *Our house.*

Rhiannon climbed out of the back and watched her mom with a contented grin. "Uncle Neil, when you marry Mom, we should get a real dog. This imaginary dog isn't cutting it. My friends will think you're weird."

Neil smiled, glad Rhiannon anticipated making friends. "Your mom knows a lot about dogs."

"And also you should adopt me. Then people will think I'm yours and Mom won't have so many questions to deal with."

Neil stopped unloading the car and pulled his niece into a hug. "I'd be honored to be your dad, but we'll have to talk it over with your mom."

"Of course. I'll run over and tell the kids we're back. We'll get this wedding figured out." Rhiannon hauled her suitcase down the path to Wolfe's Den.

"Ask your mom for her thoughts," Neil called after her. No wonder Maren wanted him to consult her on decisions—her daughter could bulldoze with the best of them.

"Thoughts on what?" Maren held the door open for him.

"Everything." He paused to kiss her on his way in.

"Tango made a mess." Maren pointed to the wadded sheets of staff paper under the spiral staircase.

"Can't blame Tango. I'm trying to write a love song for you, but it's not going well. Let me change and we can figure it out together." He ran downstairs.

In two minutes, he returned wearing T-shirt and jeans, finding his songwriting flotsam and jetsam gone. Maren's cardigan hung on the DC-3 finial at the bottom of the staircase. He climbed into the treehouse and sat next to her on the piano bench. Sunlight through the leaves painted her skin with golden light.

Maren looked through a stack of duets for four hands. She gave him a quick kiss, then returned to the pile. "Classical, contemporary, jazz. Where did you find all these?"

"Music stores on my overnights."

"We'll try them all." Maren grinned and set the pile on the shelf, then turned to the crumpled staff paper. "And your songwriting."

"I wanted to write something original for you, but..."

"You're writing an overture."

"Like the beginning of a play?"

She nodded. "The beginning of *us*." Then, using his scribbled notes, she played the outro of Elton John's "Your Song," then a bit of John Denver's "Annie's Song", and finished with Randy Travis's "Forever and Ever Amen." Maren had transformed his pencil scratches into an overture for them, a preview of their life together.

"Can you add one more?" Neil put his hands on the keyboard. "I keep coming back to...." He played and sang Graham Nash's "Our House."

Maren harmonized and descanted. They changed "two cats" to "one girl." Her thigh pressed his. On the la-las, she embellished. Her arm slid over his for a phrase, then beneath his to catch a low chord, and came to a rest atop his hand for the final chord.

She wiped away tears. "That's the song my heart sang just before you came into our lives. I'd asked God for a safe home for Rhi, where she could practice and have friends over." She fanned herself with a sheet of staff paper. "Who knew piano duets could be an aphrodisiac?"

Neil kissed her earlobe. "Let's keep that our secret."

"It's never happened with anyone else." Maren smiled and leaned into him. "Only with you."

"We've talked about our wedding and honeymoon." Neil swallowed, hoping it wasn't too soon to ask. He turned to see her face. "We haven't talked about...your thoughts on having another child?"

Maren met his gaze with a smile. "My new job has maternity leave." She pulled him close, her kiss deep and slow. Her fingers ran through his hair, then down his neck. Joy chorused through them.

Children's voices echoed through the woods.

"Grandma and Grandpa are here!" Rhiannon yelled. "And they like me!"

"Here come our wedding planners now," Neil helped Maren off the bench and pulled her into his arms. "Welcome home."

Acknowledgments

Writing is an opportunity to ask questions. Music teachers Kitty Reip, and Karen and Jeff Crylen told me about their experiences with prodigies. Author Tosca Lee gave me the right Korean word. Mental health practitioner Lorinda Riley confirmed the challenges and pathways of healing. And worship leader Megan Elford shared her expertise in music.

On the writing end, Victoria Goessling, Jeanne Reames, and Caryl Brown critiqued, Katherine Barnett proofread, and A.C. Williams edited. All mistakes are my own.

An extra special thank you to those who shared stories of trauma. You are survivors; I'm in awe of your strength.

And last but never least, thank you to my readers, especially those who've read every story, posted reviews, and recommended my books to friends - you can't imagine how much I appreciate your support! You are the best!

Also by Catherine Richmond

Spring for Susannah

Through Rushing Water

Third Strand of the Cord

Gilding the Waters

Off the Ground

The Shelter of Each Other

I love to hear from readers! Please write to me through my website CatherineRichmond.com or Facebook.com/CatherineRichmondFans.

If you enjoyed *Two Hearts One Piano,* a review would help other readers find my book. Thank you so much!